CW01111802

Empire of the Void

Double Feature

By Andrew Valenza

Valenza Publishing

More from Valenza Publishing

Andrew Valenza

Three Short Horror Stories

J.T. McGee

Thrall

Praise for
Empire of the Void

"I loved this book. I couldn't wait for it to be published and I read through it quickly the first time. The second time I slowed down and it was even better. Can't recommend highly enough."
— AMAZON REVIEW

"It is truly an incredible story from start to finish. It has been a while since I have actually finished a book from beginning to end, but with your book, I was able to find my love for reading again."
— AMAZON REVIEW

"A great sci-if story with just the right touch of inter-personal relationships and interactions. The plot is fast paced, with several twists and turns. Looking forward to the sequel."
— GOODREADS REVIEW

"Truly never read anything like this... Andrew Valenza clearly has an incredibly creative mind and incredible world building skills as he kept me hooked from The Void and back!"
— GOODREADS REVIEW

Valenza Publishing
Hadley, NY 12835

"Empire of the Void" first published in 2023
Aboard the Brighter Day first published in 2023 in the "Three Short Horror Stoies" collection
"Lost Worlds of the Void" first published in 2024
This hardcover published in 2024

Empire of the Void:
Copyright Andrew Valenza, 2023
Cover art copyright Matthew Gunther 2023

Lost Worlds of the Void:
Copyright Andrew Valenza, 2024
Cover art copyright Matthew Gunther 2024

"Aboard the Brighter Day" and "Lost World of the Void" edited by Dr. Stephen Hull

All rights reserved. No part of this publication may be reproduced or transmitted in any form or by any means, electronic or mechanical, including photocopying, recording, or any information storage or retreival system, without prior permission in writing form from the publishers.

ISBN: 9798989136872

Copyright for this book has been registered with the Library of Congress

Dedication

To my Dad. For all your favories you sat us down to watch when we were way too young. For the times we could watch our favorites together and make constant jokes but still love them. And for all the times you stood next to the TV to watch a movie with me instead of on the couch, because that's what Dads do.

Table of Contents

Preface..9

Book 1 - Empire of the Void..15
Prologue..17
1. Happy Anniversary..20
2. Prullen - 1..34
3. Royal Void Outpost - 19..46
4. Prisoner..63
5. Ships That Don't Exist..69
6. Transport...79
7. Creatures of the Nebula..86
8. New Friends..100
9. Reechi..110
10. Tools from the Empire..122
11. Trouble on Reechi...131
12. An Audience with the Emperor..149
13. Dex Arrives...159
14. One Heart to the Next..174
Epilogue...204

Interlude - Aboard the Brighter Day..207
1...208
2...212
3...226

Book 2 - Lost World of the Void..229
15. Flight of the Silent Horizon..230
16. The Spaceport..238
17. Voyage to Taranok...249
18. The Lost World..266

Preface

If you've been to any of my signing events you'll have heard this schpeal before, but to those of you who haven't been, or haven't read these books before, thank you for giving me a chance.

I always wanted to be a director. My dad used to joke with people about me that I was the kind of kid to watch even the credits of movies to know every single person involved in the making of it. I was raised on film by him and his brothers, and I loved it.

My dad introduced me to the classics of his childhood, as well as plenty that no one else has ever heard of, like "The Idolmaker," which is a great movie by the way if you can ever find it. His oldest brother taught me that all you need in life is Clint Eastwood and Martin Scorcesse movies. Seeing the bridge scene from "The Good, The Bad, and the Ugly" irrivocably changed me. The middle brother introduced me to the stranger side of cinema. I have to apologize to him because I still haven't seen "Pandora's Box."

But the ones I watched more than any, though, were "Star Wars." Sci-fi and fantasy were, and still is in many instances, the greatest movies. I believe that the further from reality a story is, the stronger potential for greatness it has. It's easy to connect with something somebody can immediately relate to; a war movie about a conflict the viewer might have taken part in; a historical event we all saw on the news; a story about a tragic break-up. But a movie like "Star Wars" where on the surface the only thing we can connect with is the fact that a few of the characters are human? The fact that it's one of the most widely beloved movies of all time and connects with people on a deep emotional level is nothing short of a miracle.

That's what I wanted to do, create something that had that effect on people. And even when I applied for college, it was all about film. But the only thing I was doing to prepare myself for that kind of career was write. And that was thanks to my grandma.

She sat me down at the kitchen table one night when I couldn't sleep. I was maybe eight. She handed me a pencil and a five-page essay booklet and told me to wright something creative. I churned out a short medieval fantasy story and thought it was the greatest thing ever. In hindsight it wasn't that great, but it showed me something else I enjoyed, writing.

In the years following, I tried again and again to re-write the short fantasy story into a novel and every time it was terrible. I had a story idea, but no idea how to actually write, or how proper storytelling worked. I was also thirteen and way to edgy so one draft of the book was just... a little much.

I think though that most importantly, my writing didn't go anywhere because I didn't have anything to say. And I don't mean I was trying to write the next "Dune" or "1984", but the stories I was writing didn't have heart. They didn't come from anywhere meaningful. That was until August of '22.

I was in a hotel room on Fort George G. Meade, Maryland, for Army training. The idea just popped in, what would characters like Flash Gordon or Ellen Ripley be like if you swapped their respective sub-genres of sci-fi? What would Ripley be like in a space opera, or Gordon in a horror film?

This idea morphed quickly into taking the reader on a tour through the eras of sci-fi film history through serialized adventures, and Gordon & Ripley are now a couple. As the idea developed, the personas of the characters were by and large dropped so I could create original ones, and my fiance offered the name Prullen.

At that point, Dex and Lacy became real people.

I wrote the prologue that day and thought I'd finally found a story I believed in.

As "Empire of the Void" developed, I had to constantly remind myself not to lose focus with it. "Empire" was through and through a fun adventure story. I love with all my heart "Lord of the Rings" and "Dune," but I know I'm no Tolkien or Herbert. I would keep "Empire" simple as my first outing, just give the reader a good time.

There were a few scenes where I feel I let my personal beliefs bleed into the work. The most blatant example of this was the use of "Rhapsody in Blue," a.k.a., the greatest piece of music ever written.

It wasn't until I got to the last page of "Empire" that I realized these wouldn't be serialized adventures. I'd had the rest of the story mapped out before I finished the first three chapters of "Empire," and have had the last sentance of the series written down since the very beginning. There was going to be some re-working, but as long as I keep it to the spirit of taking the audience through the eras. I just had to get through the first book first.

I don't think I even knew I was going to do anything with the book until I was close to the end. I'd never published a book before and I had no idea what I was doing. Thankfully, I had an incredibly supportive co-worker at the time who mentored me through the self-publishing process. I wish I used him then as my editor as well, but, what are you gonna do?

What surprised me the most about that book's release was the (and I don't mean to brag) incredible success it had. Family and friends could have bought it and given me a pat on the back, but no. Everyone was buying it. People I'd never met were messaging me and asking for signed copies, leaving incredible reviews, and even a handful of people I met in passing have done a double take saying things like, "Hey wait, I read your book!" Those have been the coolest interactions.

It was all the more motivation to get going on the next book, "Lost World of the Void."

With this one, I was going to really put all I had into it. Esecially because I'd already realized that "Lost World" would be the objectivly best one, while the fourth book, "Visitors from the Void," was going to be my personal favorite for sentimental reasons.

One thing I think is fair to say about "Empire," is Dex and Lacy are not the deepest characters, and Dex is no hero. He's a good guy, sure, but for Lacy.

"Lost World" is inspired by two movies I didn't love as much as a kid as I do now, but were still highly influential to me, "King Kong" (1933) and "Indiana Jones and the Temple of Doom."

"Temple of Doom" is hands down my favorite of the series.

"Raiders" is perfect, there's no denying, but Indy doesn't go anywhere in that movie as a character. The "fortune and glory" scene in "Temple of Doom" is so incredibly under-appreciated by fans of the series, but sets up one of the greatest character arcs I've ever seen on screen. That, I realized, was what Dex needed. But this is a sci-fi series and there had to be roots in that genre as well.

One genre I never really got into but do have the utmost respect for are the creature-features and Lost World type movies. Although "King Kong" isn't exactly sci-fi, it still has the characteristics of what made the genre so great. I personally grew up on the 2005 version of the movie and it's still my favorite, but I remember seeing the original when I was a kid and being absolutely blown away by the special effects. Honestly, I still am.

With those two works as the foundation, the rest of the story slowly fell into place. There were plenty of dropped ideas from the original outline, such as the use of a dual narrative, where half the book would be from the antagonist Romek Amari's perspective, and his hunt for the Earth fugitives. I dropped this entirely because it felt like a cheat. The reader *is* Dex or Lacy, whoever you want to step into, and therefor, should only know as much as them.

But one thing I knew for certain I absolutely *had* to incorporate in this one was Dex's religous journey. As a person who has been on a long and winding journey of faith, I wanted to communicate through his journey an understanding of those who may have lost their faith, or might not have really understood it, but also reassurance that there is hope and light. As a Christian I believe in good and evil. While stories of moral ambiguity can have their place in the world of storytelling, in Chrsitian teaching we do face true evil that masquarades as good. I believe Satan is real and is always at work to lead people away from God to worship himself, but I don't think the people that fall for this falshood are inherently evil people. Confusion is one of the things he does best. C.S. Lewis talked about this perfectly in his final Narnia book, "The Last Battle," a series that has had a major impact on me, as well as "The Screwtape Letters."

In my books, the Emperor (to be honest I regret the name I gave him) is truly evil, but I don't condemn his people. Lacy shows unwavering faith in them because I do. This isn't a spoiler for later books, don't worry. Even as the author, as I've said, these characters have taken on a life of their own, and as much as I would love to give everyone a happy ending, that isn't how free will works.

Going forward in this series, what I can promise is there will be beautiful moments, there will be tragic moments, funny and terrifying. If any of it makes you cry, I apologize, but I hope its for the right reason.

These are the first two books, and I hope you stick with me until the end of Dex and Lacy's journey.

This collection doesn't have an afterward or any acknowledgements, but I would like to give one shoutout. My sister-in-law did the borders for the books in here and aren't they just so cool? Thank you so much Anna!

And to the rest of you, I hope you enjoy the read!

-Andrew Valenza
March 31, 2024

Book 1

Empire of the Void

Prologue

"It is day 400 of our journey aboard the *Silent Horizon*. I'll bet our compatriots back on Earth reckon we've gone crazy by now. Up here where nothing ever changes, a year feels like a decade. I guess that makes my upcoming anniversary with Lacy feel that much more meaningful. It's almost like we've spent a lifetime together already." Dex turned to look at his wife asleep in the bunk against the port-side wall. The starboard-side bed hadn't been touched since their "unofficial" wedding night, and had accumulated a fair amount of dust.

"Yes sir…who would have thought it would only take us seven weeks to give in to each other like that. To be fair, after that one date before launch, we agreed to wait until our return to Earth to carry on our romance. I bet the boys back on the ground had money on us succumbing to passion like that sooner. That's why we were picked for the mission right? If anything is to happen, worst case is we restart the human race on a new planet. Well congrats boys, hope you're sending another ship out with our anniversary gifts. Never got the Christmas one, must have been lost in transit." He paused the recorder and laughed to himself. Would he ever celebrate Christmas again back on Earth? Would there ever be a Christmas gift again for that matter? He resumed the recorder. "I'm hoping that by day 500 we'll have at least some sign of another planet. We've passed beyond the scope of what our friends on Earth can see, and thankfully, the terror of flying blind like this hasn't quite set in yet. I'm not the only one getting antsy either. Lacy's spending half her time at the computer watching the radar rather than piloting this craft. I'm beginning to think she's had enough of me-"

Dex was cut off by a hand touching his shoulder. He looked back and saw Lacy's blue eyes looking down lovingly into his. She then leaned into the microphone, and said with a smile, "Lacy has not had enough of you quite yet." She paused the recorder then said to Dex, "If I want to find a planet now, it's just so we can build ourselves a bigger home than this ship."

With his eyes still on her, Dex resumed the recorder one more time. "It seems as though this is my signal to close out today's log. Captain Dex…"

"And Lt. Lacy Prullen, signing off."

Lacy sat on the edge of the console, arms crossed and chin raised just a bit. Her smile was now a smirk.

Dex rotated his chair in her direction. "Something on your mind LT?" As a tease, he added, "These logs aren't important to you anymore?"

"These logs are between you and everyone back on Earth. And with so little to report, I think you can ease up with the daily ritual."

"Have something else in mind we can be doing?"

Her smile turned coy, and she arced her eyes across the ceiling as if to say, I had a few ideas. Dex took the bait.

He gave a small chuckle, and he asked, "What is it this time?"

She looked back down at him, then took a seat on his lap and placed her arm around him. "I've been thinking. By the time we get back to Earth, how much time will have passed?"

Dex thought for a moment, exhaled deeply then answered, "I don't know. Orders say we're allowed to turn around if nothin's found in five years. But say we're back on Earth ten years after we left. Given the fact that time works different in space, who knows how much time has passed for them? We could have missed the whole rest of the century and land in…I don't know, 2021!"

Even with the miracles of science they left behind in 1958, even thinking of the possibilities of what 1980 would bring boggled their minds.

"Can you imagine?" She asked. "2021. By then maybe the colonies will be extending far past our solar system. Travel might be a hundred times faster than this beautiful ship."

"And robots enslaving all mankind, or evil aliens assimilating us! Yeah, that'll be the day." They laughed together.

Lacy got off Dex's lap and took the other seat at the console.

"More than likely there won't be an earth to go back to," Dex continued. "Either another race will overpower us, or we'll destroy ourselves."

"Very optimistic." The smile began to fade from Lacy's face.

Dex wasn't deterred. "The world we left behind was great, but even this mission just goes to show the end is near. We're racing to get off the earth. This craft is beautiful, yes, but the energy we harnessed to make this? It could wipe out half the U.S.S.R in an instant." He looked out into the void. In the distance on the port side was a nebula swirling green and purple stardust, as if he were looking from the sky down into a whirlpool. "Yeah, I'm glad I made it out when I did. And more than that..." he reached out to hold her hand. "I'm glad you made it out with me."

When the smile returned to her face, Lacy's blue eyes gleamed more beautiful than all the nebulas and all the mystical colors of the galaxies in the universe could ever dream to be.

"Call me a pessimist about the fate of Earth, but looking towards the future of this mission, and the infinity of what's out there waiting for us...all I see are infinite ways to make happy the woman I love."

"Well with all that pessimism, what if we don't go back to Earth?"

"What?" Dex was taken aback by the idea, but not completely against it.

"Just thinking. As you said, there might not be an Earth to go back to. How bad would it be if we just found a new home out here?"

"You and me?" Dex laughed.

"You and me. Just a thought." Lacy smiled and leaned in to kiss him.

Their future together truly would be far beyond what anybody they left behind on earth could possibly imagine.

1. Happy Anniversary

The *Silent Horizon* drifted through space at a rate just below the speed of light. It was a small two-person ship, with a cabin only about twenty-five feet in length, and eight feet wide. The outside of the craft glistened with a material like silver that had been discovered on one of Saturn's moons. It made the ship look like a star piloting itself through space. The bow of the ship was tipped with a long needle that housed the main antenna. About three feet behind that was the viewport, a single glass pane that wrapped 180 degrees around the command console. Moving to the rear of the ship, the passengers had a cabinet with a fold-out table, chair, and their full supply of provisions. Down further were their bunks, with drawers on the bottom for their clothes. Compartments on top were for storage of their personal effects, mostly scientific tools for when they found another planet, medical supplies, and a bottle of wine for if they ever found a habitable planet. A locker stood beside the bunks, housing their red with gold trim Planetary Exploration Suits, field packs with emergency gear, and the standard white spacewalk suits that had seen far more use than the P.E.S's. These suits had no independent oxygen tanks but were fed air through a tube that ensured they wouldn't drift too far away from the ship when doing repairs on the hull. On the port side of the back wall was the latrine, and on the starboard side was a hallway that had three doors. The first was a greenhouse in case they found any plant life to bring back, then the engine room, and along the back wall, the airlock.

To call it a small home was an understatement. Yet they had enough to stay busy. The ship's computer was equipped with a database of films, books, and music from Earth. Their fold-out tables were equipped with a vast library of board games that could be projected onto the surface.

Thanks to the artificial gravity on the ship, Dex and Lacy had been able to keep up with some moderate physical activities to keep their muscles from total atrophy. They still worried though, from time to time, about how their bodies would treat them if they did ever find a planet or return to Earth.

Conversations never went stale as their interests in media consumption differed greatly, but they were both curious about each other's thoughts on what they were currently invested in. Dex explored the library of films and was into swing music and the new wave of "rock and roll" that was gaining popularity before their mission began. Lacy was far less of a film enthusiast. She would indulge him with a movie night here and there, but otherwise had the vast majority of the book library all to herself and would keep Dex up at night talking about what she'd read and the issues all the characters were facing. Musically, she greatly preferred classical symphonies and jazz. Growing up, swing music was played too much in her home and she grew to hate it. But since Dex loved it, she would dance around with him to his favorites, and he in turn would suffer through her symphonies. The jazz he was more tolerant towards. Specifically, "Rhapsody in Blue," because how could he not love it?

The one physical book they did have was Dex's pocket Bible. It was a gift his father gave him from when he served in the Army. Abner Prullen wasn't the most religious person but carried the Bible at all times while deployed for a sense of comfort. He'd hoped it would give Dex the same comfort as they drifted into space.

All things given, this was enough for Dex and Lacy. Additionally, they had a better view than any of their old neighbors from Earth.

* * *

Day 416 began with a soft beeping coming from the ship's computer. It was almost an hour after the beeping began that Lacy woke. She heard the sound coming from the console and tried to ignore it, thinking it was some part of a dream that kept with her as she came back to consciousness. Eventually, the beeping could no longer be ignored. She navigated around Dex's body and climbed out of bed.

As her head became more clear, she realized they hadn't heard a sound like this one since they left Earth's solar system. An unidentified ship had drifted too close to them. It had turned out to be a private space-yacht that was knocked way off course, but the computer was alert for any mass not yet programmed into it. Planet or ship. Once things began to click for Lacy, she became as alert as the ship's radar.

"Dex!" She yelled over her shoulder. "Dex wake up!"

Dex lifted his head the smallest bit and let out a groan, "What is it darling?"

Lacy raced back to the bunk, and grabbing her husband by the hand, yanked him out onto the floor.

He jumped to his feet, thoroughly annoyed but instantly recognized the excitement on his wife's face. "What happened?"

All she could do was smile and jump like an excited kid with a secret they were dying to tell the world. "Happy anniversary!" She jumped into his arms and kissed him as hard as she could.

Dex kissed her back but his eyes were focused beyond her, on the console. Slowly he put her back down. "What do you mean? What's going on?"

She took his hand and led him to the console. Lacy pressed a button next to the large central computer screen and Dex slowly understood. After so much time staring into emptiness, Dex had begun wondering if the *Silent Horizon* was incapable of traveling far or fast enough to find anything in the vastness of space. It seemed, thankfully, that he was wrong.

"How far out is it?" He asked.

"About 8 hours. It's 0430…" She looked at the screen again, "37. So we have plenty of time to get all done up before we land." She turned to rush over to her dresser under the bunk but was stopped by Dex's hand on her forearm.

"Is this a planet or ship?" He asked.

"What? I-"

He turned to face her. "Lacy, this is very exciting, there's no doubt. But there are protocols for something like this."

Lacy pulled her arm away, but not in disdain. "Dex, no matter what protocol says, it has never been put into practice. This is an incredible moment for humanity. The first object found in space outside of anything we've ever been able to see!"

"Which is why protocol is so important. It won't mean anything if we're never able to report what we found. Be excited, please, I love to see it in your smile." He touched her cheek, "but we have to be smart about it too."

Lacy lowered her head in acceptance. "Ok. I'm going to shower, then let's eat and figure out a plan." She turned and walked to the head.

Dex decided to use this time to try to boost the ship's sensors in an attempt to see if he could pick up any hints about what this new object could be. He diverted power from as many of the other computer functions as he could spare. When that wasn't enough he began looking for ways to divert power from other parts of the ships, at one point forgetting about Lacy in the shower, and eased up on the artificial gravity. She gave a shout of surprise and he quickly restored power. No matter what he tried, the object was too far outside the scanner's reach to identify anything other than the fact that something was sure as hell out there.

The next best course of action he saw at the moment was to document this discovery.

He turned on the recorder and adjusted the microphone. "Day 416. Lacy and I received a nice anniversary gift today from the universe. Which is great because I did not get her anything. So hopefully she'll enjoy this one." He paused and heard the water stop. After over a year, how much of their recycled water was actually keeping them clean? "According to Lacy, we discovered the signal at around 0430 this morning, but we don't know how long it has been going for before we woke up. Maybe from now on taking shifts wouldn't be a half-bad idea. I've done all I can to boost the ship's scanners but it's still too far off to get a good reading on anything."

Lacy was back in her standard-issue underwear (guaranteed best choice for true American astronauts) when she stepped out of the head and rushed around with excitement to get dressed.

Dex continued, "We're…optimistic about what this could be. My guess is with how vast space is, our odds of finding intelligent life by chance are nigh impossible. Most likely an asteroid, but even that can hold incredible potential for us. Still, we have our blaster just in case. I'm sure it'll be ready for anything. Hasn't been touched once since it was loaded with the rest of our gear, and I hope it doesn't have to be."

Behind him, Lacy was now dressed and opened up the food cabinet and unfolded the table. The food was less than a meal, really only a massive supply of pills. One was taken for each meal to give them all the nutrients they needed. Romantic dinners had died a long time ago for this couple.

"Hopefully within another two or so hours, we'll have a better read on this thing. By hour five we should have visuals, given a constant speed, and if this thing is stationary. We'll record another log when we have more information." Dex turned off the recorder and swirled his chair around towards Lacy, who was about to swallow her breakfast pill.

"Thanks for the little thrill in the shower. Thought we came on that thing a few hours too early." She swallowed her breakfast and chased it down with a small glass of water. The only drink they'd had in over a year.

"Sorry, got a little ahead of myself with the controls."

Lacy shrugged. "I heard a good amount of the log. No need to brief me on your…findings."

He gave a small laugh.

"Just an asteroid you think?"

"Just an asteroid. Still, it'd be a good idea to prep the gear. Make sure no mice or aliens got into anything," Dex joked.

"Well, I think we may have really lucked out here. I'm betting it's a beautiful world with a bright blue sky just like back on Earth. Rolling mountains and vast oceans, and quiet. Imagine if it's just plant life. No animals except for you and me when we land!"

"No animals? After all this time I wouldn't mind a nice alien steak."

She laughed now, "Oh come on, we've got all the gourmet meals we need right here!" She tossed one of the pills towards him like candy, which he caught in his mouth.

He swallowed and almost instantly the pill sent waves through his body that told his brain he tasted bland pancakes with soulless maple syrup, then a second wave that had the simulated taste of the powdered eggs that men like his father had to eat during World War II and the Eurasian War.

"Ah. Goddamn delicious," he said with as much sarcasm as he could muster.

* * *

Three hours later, the computer was able to give a better reading of what Dex and Lacy were approaching. It was a solid mass, just under 100 kilometers in diameter.

"That's…that's smaller than, what? Long Island maybe?" Lacy asked.

Dex typed something into the console. "Yeah," he said. "Just about."

"We may be too far out," Dex said, "but not picking up any atmosphere. Won't be larger than your thumb until we're right on top of it. And with a rock that small, gravity will be real low. Gotta be careful when we land, no jumping around. Might drift too far out."

Lacy giggled at the thought. Of course she would be safe, but the idea was so silly to her.

* * *

Another hour passed and the computer was able to bring up an image of the rock.

"Looks like Earth's moon but…it's so smooth. Strange, isn't it?"

Dex studied the computer screen. "May be small, but maybe it's denser than expected. Could have a stronger gravitational pull." He looked at his wife, "Helps smooth it out."

"So jumping around is allowed again?"

He smiled at her, "We'll see how much celebrating is allowed when we get there. If nothing else though, there's still the ship."

* * *

Hour five slowly crawled toward them. Far off in the distance, they saw the smallest speck, differing from all the other stars in the vastness of space only by the intensity of the light bouncing off of it and its size, slightly larger than the stars themselves.

"There it is baby. Your moon," Dex said. "And seeing as you're the one that found it, it's only fair you name it." He smiled at her lovingly.

Lacy, sitting at the co-pilot seat staring out into space at the moon, failed to notice his expression. "Who'd've thought... Us, of all people, would one day be out among the stars naming our own celestial masses?"

Dex's smile faded to only a smirk. "Don't get too excited. It's a big rock drifting along. Not even a moon. Chances of finding anything past dust is almost null."

She looked up at him with a gleam of eagerness in her beautiful blue eyes. "Yes, but where there's one, there's another. And another."

Dex looked back down at the console. Still nothing on the radar except the rock. He wanted to bring her back to reality but now didn't seem like the right time. Not on their anniversary.

"So what about a name?" He asked.

"Darling," she giggled, "This could potentially be one of the greatest finds of human history!"

"Or a rock."

She scoffed his comment away. "There's no way for me to come up with a name for it on the spot like this. This rock, as you're so keen to remind me, whether desolate or the home of some material that could somehow save the human race, is a first step in the expansion of the human race past our own solar system! It needs a name to match its awesome importance."

They both sat in silence for a moment, thinking of a name worthy of such a major moment in human history.

After some thought, Dex reached out his right hand for the button on the console that presented the keyboard. "Prullen-1. Putting it in the log."

With a laugh, Lacy reached out to pull his hand away. "Dex!

There's no way we're calling it that!"

"With all due respect, Lieutenant, you were taking too long."

That smile could disarm anyone, she thought.

Dex held his left hand above the now-present keyboard. "Well?"

"Can we change it later at least?" Lacy pleaded.

"Only until we find Prullen-2."

Lacy let go of Dex's hand and slumped back in her chair. The minutes were beginning to slow. In their minds, the excitement told them time should be speeding up, that it would pass in the blink of an eye. But with such a focus on the coming discovery, the entertainment on the *Silent Horizon* lost all appeal. The music and film library seemed dull in comparison, and neither one of them could keep their focus on reading for more than a hundred words before their thoughts brought them back to the rock.

* * *

Hour six. Prullen-1 was only fractionally larger, and the anticipation was killing them.

* * *

Hour seven. Out of the ship's window, Prullen-1 was only half an inch large, but in the grand scheme of their exploration, it was growing quickly.

To Lacy, it was inviting, but the more Dex observed the readings he was getting from the computer, the more hesitant he was to land the ship.

"This can't be right," he started.

Lacy was sitting in the seat to his right. The anxiety in his voice did nothing to bring down her spirits. "You're worrying too much. We're so far outside the reaches of what we used to know. Why should this rock have the same laws as Earth or…hell, any of the planets of our solar system?"

Dex looked at her with hardened eyes. "Lacy, it's a rock that's half the size of Long Island but just about the gravitational reading is all...hazy. It's like I'm getting interference."

"It's just a rock, Darling." Her tone was half teasing, half reassuring. She put a hand on his shoulder.

He looked out the window at the slowly growing rock, then turned his head back towards her. Gently taking her hand, he raised it to his mouth and kissed her.

"Promise me you won't drop your guard." He commanded her, with just a touch of loving concern. Never had he really commanded her. Even with the official rank they held, at the end of the day he only ever treated her as his wife.

"Yes sir." Lacy knew when to respect the rank, but this far into the voyage, emotions held the highest rank. To break the tension she puffed up her cheeks.

Dex recognized instantly what this was and followed suit. Early in their romance, there was one night they shared the shower and Lacy being playful showed him how guppies kissed. Puffing up her cheeks and when their lips met, blew out the air(more like a pufferfish than a guppie, but that was part of the silliness).

They both had their cheeks puffed up, then raspberried out when their lips met. "Guppie kisses," they said in unison. An odd thing.

Hour eight. Dex was handling the flight controls manually now. Lacy was in the rear preparing their gear. She lay the P.E.S.'s on Dex's bed, then looked through the storage container above, planning out what to take.

"What should I pack with the P.E.Ss?" She asked. Dex rotated his head slightly to the right but kept his eyes forward. "Pack light," he said. "I don't think we're gonna have a whole hell of a lot to explore. Maybe a cave if we're lucky. But I still don't see any readings for life on the rock. Plant or animal. Just load up both the flashlights and some water. And grab the laser cutter. I wanna get some samples of whatever it is this rock is made of."

Lacy did as she was asked.

As they approached Prullen-1, Dex felt the controls get tougher. It took more and more strength with every passing moment for him to keep the ship steady.

"Baby I'm going to need you up front!" He called to her, trying to hide the strain he was feeling at the helm.

Lacy dropped what she was doing and jumped to her seat. "What can I do to assist, sir?" She asked playfully.

"Prepare the landing gear. We might be coming in a little hot." On any other planet, and at this speed, this would have been the point where Dex and Lacy would be seeing heat coming off the bow. Dex did what he could to reduce speed, but the gravitational pull got stronger now by the second. Faster than he was able to adjust.

"Landing gear is good to deploy," Lacy announced.

"Not yet, don't want to crush them on landing. Just want it ready to go."

"How about some mood music?"

Dex shrugged, "Whatever sounds best to you."

Lacy flipped through the library quickly. "How about this?"

"Pines of Rome" by Ottorino Respighi began to play.

Dex laughed awkwardly, but his lightheartedness was broken by a jolt in the ship's controls.

They were nearly on top of the rock. Sweat started to break out on Dex's forehead, but he was doing all he could to keep his cool. Partially for his own sake, but mostly because in his mind, he was still trying to impress Lacy with a calm and collected demeanor. As Prullen-1 got closer though, he couldn't help but worry more. He had decent control of the ship, but it was hurtling toward the rock far too quickly. They had to reduce speed quickly or their anniversary would be cut far too short.

"Shift all thrusters in reverse." He commanded Lacy.

"Righto, preparing to-" she began but the ship lurched violently and Dex cut her off.

"Don't prepare just DO it!"

She was taken aback, and for the first time that day, her smile dropped. Her training kicked in, and she reverted to her military training. She did as was commanded by her superior officer.

Lacy punched in the commands to shift the thrusters, but without time for them to adjust, they felt a massive CRUNCH! from somewhere in the back of the ship. The lights in the main cabin flickered for a moment. Out front, they could see fumes and the tips of the flames of the forward thrusters shooting out ahead of them.

"We're losing speed," Dex announced. "Should be on the ground in less than two minutes."

Just then an alarm went off that sounded almost loud enough to destroy both of their ears. They both looked towards the center console. A red banner flashed quickly telling them, "FIRE IN THE ENGINE ROOM."

Before Dex could say anything, Lacy was out of her chair and racing to the engine room. "I got it!" She called to him. "I'll be back for the landing gear just try to hold it steady till then."

She hadn't noticed, but as soon as he read the fire notification, the sweat started streaming more profusely. Lacy had no idea how hard he had been fighting the controls. One wrong move and he was sure to throw them off their course. They would make it to the surface most definitely at this point, but on which side of the ship would it be? And how much damage would there be to fix? And at the speed they had been going, would they even be alive to fix it? That last problem may have been solved, but now with the engine on fire, how badly had that been damaged? Would there be enough working parts to get off this rock? Would Prullen-1 be their doom?

Happy anniversary, he thought to himself.

In the engine room, Lacy was scrambling to put out a fire that was slowly crawling toward the rear wall. Between two bursts with the extinguisher, she smacked a hand on the wall intercom to send a message to Dex.

"Captain! Captain, can you hear me?"

At the controls, Dex responded but kept his focus on the descent. In another minute and a half, they'd be on the ground in any condition ranging from moderately ok to totally and completely screwed.

"I hear you," he said. The strain was more than apparent in his voice.

"We have to vent this place! The fire's too big! If we want to save anything on this ship we have to vent, now!"

A minute twenty left. If they vented, the engines would be inoperable for too long. They would surely crash with this trajectory. If they didn't vent, he knew, they'd land most likely in one piece, but they'd never get back off the rock.

A minute ten. "Dex! Dex what are your orders?!" Lacy screamed through the intercom over the sounds of the raging flames.

Dex was lost. Either choice was the wrong one but he had to make one. An idea clicked. "Lacy! Baby get out of there I'll vent!"

"I copy!" Lacy called back. She gave up on the extinguisher and dashed out of the room, locking it behind her. She ran up the hall, ensured the door to the main cabin was locked behind her, and raced back into her seat.

Fifty-five seconds until impact. Lacy strapped in but Dex couldn't afford to take his hands off the controls.

"Venting now," Lacy announced and put in the commands on the console to vent the air out of the engine room. The next window she brought up showed live feed from the room and outside the ship. The fire was diminishing with the lack of air. But it was at this point Dex truly lost control.

Dex looked over at her screen and saw exactly what he had hoped for. "We just might make it out of this one," he told her.

In the center of the console, she saw the gyroscope had recognized a gravitational pull from Prullen-1. Ever so slowly, their angle of descent was increasing, and they were listing slightly to the left. "What's happening?" She asked Dex.

"The vent is angled. The force of the flames and air ejecting is nudging the trajectory. With any luck, we'll land on our side instead of the nose, and save the engine."

Twenty-five seconds. The surface of the rock was taking up their entire window now. Lacy grabbed Dex's hand as tight as she could. So much so, that it began to hurt, and her nails were digging into his skin. But he pulled her hand to his mouth and kissed it again, and this time he prayed, oh God…please save our goddamned butts! As soon as pseudo-prayer was thought and given out unto the universe, They noticed the smallest sliver of black space creep into the window.

Fifteen seconds. The sky was coming on slowly and the horizon was angled but just maybe they would make it!

Ten seconds, what happened next came in a stroke of lightning. The computer announced the venting was complete and the fire extinguished. Lacy grabbed her hand away from Dex's and rushed to get the engine running again. It had to warm up but Dex couldn't wait. Seeing what Lacy had done, he thrust upwards as hard as he could with the controls. Their angle of descent leveled out just the littlest bit more. He screamed with determination as he tried to save them from their doom. Lacy covered her eyes, preparing to crash.

Impact. With a deafening boom, they hit the surface. Lacy screamed in terror. A rock slammed into the window and left a small crack.

As they hit the ground, the two of them were thrown forward. Lacy was saved by her seatbelt but Dex slammed with full force into the console, hitting his head on the edge of the computer screen, leaving a gash in his forehead just above his left eyebrow.

Lacy was struggling to breathe. The pressure on her chest from the straps and her racing heartbeat nearly through her into an anxiety attack. She tried to slow her breathing and gradually came back to a calm state. Lacy fought hard to stay conscious and control her breathing through the crash.

Dex, finding himself back in his seat, with blood dripping along his face and into his left eye, felt relief at least that they never put the landing gear down. It would have been torn off on impact. Now the bay doors for the landing gear would be jammed or wrecked, but at least fixable.

They slid for maybe a half mile before the *Silent Horizon* came to a full stop. Alarms were going off like crazy in the main cabin. The feed from the engine room showed that a fire had started again. Dex began to stand up to take action, but Lacy was up faster than him and told him to stay there. She would get the medical kit on her way back.

As he moved, he felt a jolt of pain in his core. Most likely a broken rib, he thought.

The fire in the engine room was much smaller this time. Lacy used the extinguisher to douse it and once the smoke had cleared, she saw the thick glass pod that covered the engine had a chunk missing. Small pieces of glass were all over the place. A terrible smell was coming from the engine itself, and though it was spinning, its motions were about to go ape, sputtering viciously here and there. She knew it was fixable, but it would take time. Right now though, she had to care for Dex.

She walked back to the cabin, this time in more of a daze. Her breathing still felt restrained, but she didn't know what condition Dex was in. She retrieved the medical kit from the locker where the space suits were kept.

Kneeling beside Dex, she unwrapped some of the gauze and applied it to his forehead.

"Hold this," she said tenderly.

"I'm sorry," he squeezed out.

She was feeling his core now for broken ribs. "For what?"

"I shouldn't have yelled like that."

At that, she laughed. "Darling, right now, I don't think your tone in that whole…mess, is our biggest issue. But you can apologize for that god-awful landing."

He laughed back at that but was cut off by the pain caused by the broken ribs. "At least we landed. This rock can't break us that easily."

She smiled but said nothing.

"Hey."

Lacy looked up to lock eyes with him.

"Happy anniversary," he said.

As Lacy applied medical aid to her husband, something below the surface was alerted to their crash.

2. Prullen - 1

Dex dictated his log into the ship's computer between painful breaths of air.

Lacy was in the engine room cleaning up from the explosion to pass the time while Dex finished his oh-so-important Captain's Tasks. The room still felt about 120 degrees due to the fire. At least five times a minute she would wipe the sweat from her face with the blouse she'd taken off and tied around her waist. She tried not to think too much about what was waiting outside for them, but there was far too much excitement in the air. But in the meantime, she could clean up and get a reading on how much repair the *Silent Horizon*'s engine would need.

The outer shell was almost entirely destroyed. Thankfully, that wouldn't hinder the ship's performance. But it did help protect harmful fumes from escaping, which were recycled into fumes that could be used to give the ship an extra boost when fuel ran out.

The engine itself, however, had been strained nearly to a breaking point in their landing attempt. It would run again, but only after plenty of work.

Covered in sweat, and hands stained and cut up by glass and grease, Lacy decided she'd waited long enough. She was now more than just itching to get outside their claustrophobic ship for the first time in over a year. She wiped her hands on her pants and then called to Dex through the intercom.

"Hey baby, I've done what I can for now. This thing won't be able to fly for at least another day or so. And since we're in no real rush…are you about ready to go for a walk?"

Dex paused the log when he heard her voice. Activating the comms on his end, he responded, "Just about. Was almost done recording, then we can get suited up." He sat back.

"Dex if you're not up to it…if you're in too much pain it's ok." She was trying to sound considerate.

"Think I'm gonna let you have all the fun, Darling? This is a moment that'll go down in the books. We'll share it together. Just let me finish this up and we'll get going."

Instead of words, he heard the sound of her blowing him a kiss over the comm. He smiled and resumed his log. "It seems we're about to leave the ship for the…harsh…desolate…awe-inspiring and soul-crushing plains of Prullen-1. Maybe by the time we get back, we'll have a better name for this rock."

The hallway door opened and Lacy walked through. Dex swiveled around in his chair. He saw her there, wearing just her skivvies on top, a blouse wrapped around her hips, and covered in sweat. Exploring out on the rock suddenly seemed much less interesting.

"Sure you don't wanna spend just a little more time on the ship?" He stood to walk towards her. "Who knows what dangers are out there," he said with a smile as he put his hands on her sides to pull her closer. "Could be the last moment like this we have together."

As he went in for a kiss, she put her hand on his chest and bit her lip just the littlest bit. With a light, airy voice she teased him, "Sounds like fun but…" She rotated her body towards the P.E.S. laid out on the bed but kept facing him. "But I'm gonna get a lot of excitement out of this." She tipped her head up slightly and gave him a playful look with her eyes as she walked away to suit up.

"Not even gonna shower first?" He asked.

"Baby, right now nothing could stop me from going out there." She unwrapped her blouse from her hips and then slid down her pants. Dex followed suit and soon they were checking each other's gear to make sure everything was squared away and in the right place on their belts.

"Water pack full?" He asked. "
Check."
"Flashlight?"
"Check."
"Laser-cutter?"
"Check. Guppie kisses?"

He gave her a guppie kiss. They laughed together for a moment then he looked over her suit. "You're all squared away. Nothing unsecured. Check me?"

He rotated slowly as she inspected his suit. "You're all set. You sure you don't want to bring this?" She handed him their one blaster. "You've got better aim than I do. Range day didn't lie."

"No sign of any life on this rock."

"Prullen-1." She corrected with a smile.

He exhaled with fake annoyance.

"There's no sign of any life on Prullen-1, Lieutenant."

She giggled and saw her breath fog up her helmet just in front of her mouth.

He continued, "Just extra weight. We'll save our storage space for the rocks we find."

She shrugged and placed the blaster back into the storage container above his bunk.

"And when we get back," He reached out to a medical scanning device in the container and held it up in front of Lacy. "Full scans. I don't want to carry anything toxic or radioactive back to Earth with us."

"Roger sir," Lacy said with a joking salute.

Dex took a deep breath, which hurt just a bit because of his broken ribs, then said, "I guess it's time to head out."

* * *

The airlock opened with a hiss. It wasn't as regal as Dex and Lacy had hoped it would be. No onlookers were watching the arrival of the aliens. No fireworks or parades to welcome them. Even without a show, their first steps onto Prullen-1 were disappointing. The ramp that ejected from the base of the airlock was designed for a level surface. With the nose of the ship stuck in the ground, the base of the ramp hovered about a foot over the surface.

Lacy was the first to leave the ship, followed closely by Dex who held her hand. The sensors on the gloves of their P.E.S.s simulated the feel of each other's hands so it felt like they weren't wearing gloves at all. As an astronaut, it was one of Dex's favorite advancements in modern technology.

Lacy was speechless from the view, now unobstructed by the ship's window. On the ship, they may as well have been watching television, or one of those virtual reality roller coasters on Coney Island. But this was like stepping into a brand new world. Though the surface was bland and wavy like grey sand dunes, she knew in her heart this rock was the beginning of something incredible. Whether it was the first in a long string of planets they were to find, or as she believed in her heart, Prullen-1 itself held all the mystery they were looking for.

Dex was as far on the opposite end of the spectrum as one could be. Lacy turned her head to look back at him. As she did, a distant star reflected on her visor. It sparkled in her blue eyes just as they locked with his. His care for the rock or what would come next disappeared. He was here, far from all other life, far from all worries. Nothing in his whole universe mattered except for the woman he loved. And oh how beautiful she looked. He fell in love all over again.

They said nothing but exchanged a small laugh, the kind that's more of an exhale than a laugh but both parties involved know, that's better communication than any combination of words.

Lacy and Dex stepped off together down the ramp. The gravity was not too far off from Earth's. They felt about ten pounds lighter, but Dex still helped her down from the edge of the ramp.

The sands of Prullen-1 felt so peculiar to them from the moment they stepped down.

"You feel that?" Dex asked.

Lacy knelt and scooped up a handful of the sand. "It's got the right consistency of Earth's sand," she said as she sifted it through her fingers into Dex's hand.

"If it's sand, why does the ground feel so…spongey?" They both looked at their feet, where they noticed clear indentations in the ground like they were stepping on the world's largest mattress.

"E-tool?" Lacy asked. Dex nodded. He did a 180 and a small hop back onto the ramp then walked towards the airlock.

Inside the ship, he rummaged through the storage above his bunk to find the E-tool, a highly convenient tool that worked as a shovel or blade and folded into itself for easy mobility.

Just a minute after leaving Lacy, Dex was back outside, but there was no sign of his wife.

"Lacy?" He asked the empty world and received no response.

He jumped off the side of the ramp and landed comfortably on the spongy surface, sand flying up to about knee height around him.

"Lacy, where are you?" He asked, concern growing steadily in his voice.

She stepped out from behind the port side of the ship. Her steps made the softest sounds in the sand.

"Dex? I'm just over here!"

He spun towards her. "Sorry, I thought-"

"Thought what?" She smiled with her hands on her hips. "Thought I'd already gotten lost?"

They walked towards each other, Dex ducking under the high end of the ramp.

"Possibly," he said. "Could've rushed off into one of this planet's many lush forests."

They laughed together.

"No," she said. "I don't think we'll be traveling very far. Especially with the ship in this condition." She pointed her hand towards the base of the ship. "We're gonna have to do a little bit of digging on top of engine repairs before we fly again. Never thought I'd find myself actually lodged into a planet."

Dex let out a deep sigh. "Thank God we got one of the smaller ships." He began to walk around the perimeter of the *Silent Horizon*, inspecting the damage to the hull, led by Lacy.

"Really the damage is only cosmetic," she told him. "Scratches here and there, but no tears. This sand isn't as coarse as it is back home. The nose is the real problem." They bounced forward, taking advantage of the slightly lower gravity. She pointed to the antenna, their biggest problem. "The metal housing on the antenna is strong enough, but it's deep in there, almost the full three meters. I don't know if it really is damaged. It's not like we can test it out and call home. So that's gotta be dug out before we even boot up the engine. If it's only being held together by a thread, I can probably fix it, but if not, no communication with Earth until we're back on it." She looked up at him for some sort of acknowledgment.

He thought for a moment, then asked, "Is there anything in such critical condition, it needs immediate attention?" Antenna's not going anywhere right?"

"No, it's nice and cozy stuck in the ground."

"Copy. Well, tonight you start working on the engine again, and I'll stay out here digging this out and pulling security."

She crossed her arms and raised an eyebrow at the idea.

"At ease Lieutenant. You're too cute to be giving me that look when we're supposed to be professionals."

She smiled, "Roger, Sir. So does that mean it's time to go out?"

He placed his hands on the sides of her helmet as if to touch her cheeks. The sensors picked up the texture and coldness (automatically adjusted to be a more comfortable temperature by his gloves), and he wished it could sense through that and simulate the feel of her skin. He then leaned in as if kissing her forehead. "Time to explore."

An hour and twenty-seven minutes after "landing" on Prullen-1, Dex & Lacy began their journey across the grey sand of their own private rock. Nighttime didn't exist here. The planet was cold but illuminated by the vast sea of stars that surrounded them, and some small suns far and away. No matter how long they walked, they never got over the strangeness of the ground under the sand.

They had dug about three feet deep around the antenna before leaving but found nothing except more sand. If there were something just below the surface, creating the spongy mattress effect, it wouldn't have been that far down. Dex was more and more determined with every scoop to find something, but Lacy was itching to leave. She believed with every fiber of her being, something was out there beyond the dunes.

For the first three miles or so, nothing. They had stopped once to have a drink. On the suit's right forearm was a series of buttons. One to magnetize their boots in zero gravity situations, one to activate their internal comms, one to clear their visors if they got foggy, and one to activate a straw in their helmet that ejected from the liner on the neck and came perfectly to their mouths.

In the lower gravity, it was taking less strength to walk around, but Dex couldn't get his mind off the repairs the ship needed. And with nothing else happening on Prullen-1, it was hard to think of anything else. The initial excitement had worn off a mile back. Lacy though, was still enthusiastic. After every dune they crossed over she would call to him, "Just one more dune! I know we'll find something!"

He never had the heart to tell her that he had his doubts. Maybe she was right about there being other planets close by, now that they'd found the first. There were probably better odds too that they'd find the others more interesting than this one.

Another two miles before they turn around, he told himself, realizing they'd probably circle the whole planet before actually retreating. And then once that lap was complete, she'd want to circle the perpendicular lap.

Under Lacy's optimism though, one thing nagged at her mind she wasn't quite comfortable with sharing yet. Someone's watching. She thought. Maybe that was why she was so confident in carrying on. From the moment they'd left the ship, she'd felt eyes on her. And they didn't belong to her husband. But there were no sounds, no shifts in the sands or winds from any direction telling her who or what was watching. Maybe a satellite farther off into space. An eye of a distant alien spying on them from another solar system. Whatever it was though the tiniest voice in the back of her mind told her she was in someone's line of sight. But the optimism and excitement of discovery overpowered it. The warning voice was muted down to nothing more than a dog whistle to a young adult. It was just barely a perceptible frequency.

Just before mile four, at the top of one of Prullen-1's many dunes, Lacy stopped in her tracks.

"Find something?" Dex asked, trying to hide the sass in his voice with fake optimism.

"Dex, I know you're tired of this, but I think your patience has finally paid off."

Dex took a few steps to catch up with her and when he did he was overwhelmingly…disappointed. More sand.

More…god damned…SAND. He shouted internally but kept a calm face.

"Do you see it?" Lacy asked with the widest eyes.

"No, Lacy," Dex replied sternly. "What is it I'm supposed to be seeing?"

"Oh come on! Look! Tell me you don't see it!"

Dex studied the landscape for half a minute before he began to understand what Lacy was talking about. How she was able to notice it so quickly was beyond him. His eyes began to widen all the same. Over the miles of Prullen-1's surface, they'd inspected, the dune's size, shape, and frequency had been as natural as hamburgers and beer on the Fourth of July. But here there was a clearing, perfectly rounded with what seemed to be one continuous dune. They looked into the crater of sand and were amazed by the ecological anomaly.

"It has to be man-made," Lacy said.

"Well, not man-made," Dex corrected. "But I suppose it is unlikely this formed naturally. I mean, if it's a crater, you'd expect there to be some debris in the center that pushed all the sand away. But even then, the perimeter is so perfect."

"Think it's time to dig again? Maybe something did crash."

"If something did…" He looked her dead in the eye. No romance this time. If anything, she thought she caught a glimpse of fear. "Who buried it?"

Trying to alleviate the tension of Dex's ominous question, Lacy tried to laugh it off, but for once, even she felt truly uncomfortable in their situation. The laugh came out weak and did nothing to help them feel better.

"Well," Dex started, looking back into the crater. "What are we here for if not to explore?" He took the first step into the crater.

The ground felt the same as the rest of the planet, but now it was like stepping on holy ground. A chill came over him which nearly caused him to lose his footing. The crater itself was only about three feet deep from the top of the perimeter but had a diameter of about ten meters.

As Dex neared the center. He looked back and saw Lacy waiting patiently at the top of the hill to see what would happen. He gave her a nod, signaling all was okay, then unlatched the E-tool from his belt and extended it. At full length it was only about two feet long, so he had to kneel to use it.

Dex stabbed once into the ground and lifted a small mound of grey sand. Some of the surrounding sand slid into the hole he'd made, but it was a start. He stabbed again and excavated more. Nothing. Another scoop, and another, and another. Nothing. No debris, no rocks, no nothing no how. But it was the first sign of anything remotely interesting on this planet. Though Dex was losing patience, he didn't want to let Lacy down or give up on her hopes, so he kept digging. He scooped faster and faster, channeling the growing annoyance he had into the power of his scoops until one thrust too hard into an unexpected guest.

Pain shot up through his right arm. He could have sworn it was an electric shock.

Lacy shouted behind him in shock and raised her hands to cover her mouth, forgetting her helmet was in the way.

"Dex! Are you ok?!"

Dex gritted his teeth and the pain dissolved. "Fine! I'm fine! Just stay up there. I think I found something but...just stay for a sec." It couldn't have been electric. Just too much force into a hard surface. Regardless, whatever he hit was unknown. And if it was dangerous, he didn't want Lacy around to get hurt.

Instead of digging more, he collapsed the E-tool and re-clipped it to his belt. Now he brushed away the sand to find what he'd hit. About two feet under the surface, he found he was wiping sand off of a hard metallic surface. Inspecting it, he realized the E-tool had made no dent or even a scratch on the metal. Even more amazingly, it was smooth. Unnaturally smooth and perfectly flat.

He brushed more sand away and eventually scooped some more up with his hands to reveal more of the surface area of the strange sub-surface metal until he revealed a line. A perfectly straight and deep line in the metal.

"Lacy!" Dex shouted.

"What is it? Can I come down?" Dex considered. He wanted her in on the discovery, but he knew something was wrong. Nothing this perfect came naturally. He needed to know it was safe before she came down.

"No! No, not yet, just...just toss me the laser cutter."

Lacy unlatched the laser cutter from her belt and tossed it toward Dex. For once her time on her high school's softball team paid off.

Dex caught the perfect throw and lowered the tool to the metal. Just a few inches before making contact, Dex felt another electrical tingle like a forcefield trace up his arm. He retreated a few inches and then pushed through. The electric sensation started up again but he needed to know what was causing it. Right on top of the surface, he activated the laser, and a bolt of pain shot through him again, this time knocking him on his ass, and sending the cutter flying a few feet away.

He cursed in pain, which Lacy took as a sign to help him. But as she took her first step into the crater, the ground moved. No, the planet moved. They were both knocked to the ground and heard creaking and booming underneath them.

Dex got to his feet as quickly as he could and raced towards Lacy. "Get out of here!" He shouted, but after the first few steps, he felt the ground moving underneath him. It was pulling him closer toward the center.

He could no longer run, the sand was shifting too much underneath him. Looking back at the center of the crater and saw that where that perfect line had been, there was now a bigger one, reaching the whole length of the crater into which the sand fell. The ground was opening underneath them, and Dex couldn't pick himself up.

Lacy didn't fare any better. As hard as she tried to crawl back up the perimeter, the sand kept pulling her towards the opening. She screamed in fear, and Dex could do nothing to help.

The crevice was drawing closer to him, and he could see on the opposite side as the sand on top of the metal began to diminish, poles were coming out of the metal that gave him the immediate thought of a bank vault.

It can't be! He thought, and the thought had cost him. He hadn't realized in the time it took for him to stop and think, he'd fallen back with the sand at was at the lip of the pit. He came to the realization just in time and before he fell, grabbed a hold of the empty slot the poles had come out of.

"Lacy! Get out of here! Run!"

But she couldn't hear him over the sound of the machinery working underneath them. She was still doing all she could to just keep her balance. When she was able to stand, she realized there was no longer a slope up to the perimeter anymore, but a wall left behind from all of the sand that had fallen away. She couldn't escape, and now there were only about five feet between the wall and the edge of the pit. She had to work fast. If it was a door, it only opened so far, and it was fair to assume the perimeter of the crater was that endpoint. She pushed away the sand as fast as she could until she found a raised platform. When there was enough space, she stood on it and prayed to keep her balance. With the door moving closer to her, she saw her husband hanging on for dear life and realized then just how fast a heart could beat without exploding.

The door came to a halt. There was Dex, hanging on to the inside of the door, and Lacy, on a 1x1 platform just above him. The wall of sand around her was still about four feet high, and the wrong move would send her down into the abyss from an avalanche.

"Dex! Just hold on a moment, I'll get you up!"

"I'm holding! Just be quick!" The gloves were doing nothing to help his grip. They were designed for basic protection and accessibility in unknown environments, not rock climbing.

Lacy moved quickly, first activating her magnetized boots from her forearm pad. Then she began knocking away the sand to her left, pushing it into the abyss. It was a fast process, and the 1x1 space soon became a 1x2.

"Lacy hurry!" Dex was never one to win a weightlifting competition, but in times of crisis, most people will find untapped strength in them. Dex was finding this strength but it was diminishing quickly.

Back on top, Lacy had cleared enough space to safely kneel. "Ok! Grab my hand!" She reached towards him but Dex wouldn't reach back.

"I- I can't!" He screamed. Lacy reached further down, trying to grab his hand so desperately clinging to life. As soon as she made the slightest contact with his right hand, it shot up and grabbed her forearm.

"Okay, work with me now!" She said, trying to be gentle. The adrenaline had helped, but now Dex was feeling the pain in his side. He took deep breaths, trying to ignore the pain but it was flaring up too intensely. Under the helmet, he was sweating profusely and fogging up the visor.

"Almost there!" Lacy reassured him.

Dex's heart beat rapidly. Vertigo threatened to take over him, as they struggled to pull him up to safety.

They both took a moment to breathe and clear their visors.

Dex was the first to break the silence. "I guess I should have thought of the boots sooner, huh?"

Part of her wanted to hit Dex for being so casual after almost plummeting to his death, but it was a laugh that escaped her. Lacy fell into his embrace and laughed with him, as a few small tears leaked out.

Neither one of them knew how to comprehend the situation. What do you say after such a thing? *Hey honey, want to check out this deep dark vault that someone obviously lives in? Why not, could be fun! Or if they went back to the ship, well that was fun, good mission darlin', now back to earth and tell them we bailed at the first sight of anything!*

Dex put his hand at the base of her helmet, what would've been her chin, and raised her head. "Everything's going to be all right now."

Dex knew it was a lie, for as soon as the words came out, a voice from across the pit shouted, "Identify yourselves!"

3. Royal Void Outpost-19

They couldn't believe their ears. There was no way someone was actually talking to them! Lacy shook her head nervously, her terrified expression towards Dex unbreakable. But the voice came again.

"Identify yourselves or we will fire!" It was a deep artificial-sounding voice like someone was speaking through a megaphone.

Dex pulled Lacy in closer toward him, shielding her eyes from whatever was there with them. He looked around and in the center of the now open crater, he saw a large platform hovering with three figures occupying it. They looked like robots to Dex, wearing all-black suits of armor. The only color was a thin purple strip across the face where he could only guess was how they saw anything. Otherwise, there were no identifying marks on their suits. They were so polished and clean. There were no breaks or joints, it was like the suit was their whole being. There wasn't even a holster for the blasters they held pointed at them.

"This is your final warning!"

Without hesitation, Dex mustered all the courage in him and raised his hands in surrender. "My name is Captain Dex Prullen! Pilot of the *Silent Horizon*! With me is my wife, Lieutenant Lacy Prullen!"

There was a moment of silence from the dark figures then, "From what colony do you hail? Answer quickly or be annihilated."

Dex and Lacy exchanged a look of confusion. "No...no colony...sir!" Dex eked out.

The robotic figure that led the others looked at the two others as if in confirmation, but their blasters never fell away from Dex and Lacy. A moment of silence passed, then a bridge extended out towards where they stood.

"Step towards us. Move quickly," the lead said.

Dex and Lacy stood their ground. Lacy fell back a little behind Dex's arm. "How about you identify yourselves first!"

Instantly, Dex regretted his words. The figure to the lead's right flicked a switch on the blaster with his thumb and pulled the trigger. A surge of pain rang in Dex's head crippling him. He fell to the ground on all fours. Thank god the bridge had come out to meet them or he'd surely be falling to his doom.

The leader spoke again. "This is your final warning."

Lacy helped Dex to his feet. "Let's do as they say, darling. I'm sure we'll be all right. Let's just go."

They stepped towards the dark figures slowly. The blasters maintained their focus on their heads, not even swaying an inch. When they reached the robot-like figures, the two on the sides moved in a flash of lightning.

Their blasters were lowered to their hips and assimilated into the suits. They both placed a hand on Dex and Lacy's shoulders and shoved them onto all fours.

The leader spoke, "In the name of Visconos Armourus, Holy Emperor of the Void, you are under arrest for trespassing and laying siege to Void military territory."

The descent into the abyss was brief but pitch black. Once it had begun, the door closed above them and they could only now see the purple lines across their captors' visors.

Lacy opened her mouth to speak to Dex, but their captors sensed it coming. Before a single breath escaped her mouth she felt the butt of one of the blasters crash into her spine.

She cried out in pain.

Dex's initial instinct was to fight off his captors but he was kept restrained on the ground. Instead, he mouthed to Lacy, Don't worry, we'll be all right.

It was irrelevant anyway to mouth it. As he did, he watched their captors put a device on Lacy's helmet and assumed they did for him as well. It was a small metal cylinder, about two inches long, with a suction cup device sticking to the helmet. As soon as it was attached, he realized he was unable to make any sound. Not only that but when he looked at Lacy's mouth, it seemed to be clouded over. Like he was looking at an out-of-focus picture.

"Prisoners will refrain from speaking unless given permission."

They were terrified. Dex saw a tear stream from his wife's eye. He felt one coming too but tried to refrain. He had to stay brave for her. If he couldn't tell her, he could show her, everything would be all right.

The platform came to a halt and a door slid open in front of them. A blinding light came in, and there stood another one of the robotic figures behind a tall desk, with the same black suit and purple line across their eyes.

Dex and Lacy were lifted by their captors and shoved forward.

In the same semi-robotic voice as the rest of their captors, asked. "Identification?"

Unable to give a name or title to this new foe, the first connection Dex and Lacy had made was to military police officers stationed at the gates of army posts they had once worked on. This did nothing to comfort the two Earthlings, and if anything, made them resent the "gate guard" by association.

"Spies, or saboteurs. From a region called *Silent Horizon*. They refused to answer further."

The gate guard typed something into a panel on his desk. The captors waited patiently for a response, and Dex and Lacy's eyes darted back and forth. They stood in a tunnel that seemed to be made of pure light. He then looked back up. "Take them to cell block 1138. The next transport back to Golloch is in two days' time. Until then, I'll schedule them for interrogation. Carry on."

The leader stepped forward past Dex and Lacy to lead the way. The two others shoved them forward down the corridor.

There was no end in sight, and no markers on the wall telling them where to go or where they were. Eventually, the lead just stopped, did a right-facing movement, and placed his hand on the wall. A blue light appeared as an outline of a door, then was pulled back and slid up. He gave Dex a shove in the back, ordering him to move.

He knew he couldn't speak to Lacy so he did the first thing

that came to mind. He swirled his head quickly to lock eyes with her, then puffed up his cheeks. It told Lacy everything she wished she could hear. I'll be ok. I'll see you soon. I love you.

Dex was shoved again and followed by one of the black-suited figures through the door. It shut promptly behind them He tried to rush to escape, but his captor raised a hand and like pushing over a child, shoved him to the ground.

"Stay down," the electronic voice told him.

Dex tried to shout but the device on his helmet wouldn't allow for it. He instead tried to stand, but faster than he could stand, the guard drew its blaster from his suit.

"STAND DOWN!" The voice shouted now. It felt loud enough to shatter the room. Dex clutched the sides of his helmet in pain, trying to cover his ears, and again felt his ribs hurting him. "Now, disrobe. And don't try anything."

As if this was any crazier than anything else that had happened to them, Dex was still taken aback by the demand.

"None shall wear the Emperor's colors. Remove them now or suffer more," the robotic man ordered, gesturing his weapon at Dex's scarlet P.E.S.

Dex complied and was happy to do so when it meant the voice suppression device would come off. He twisted his helmet an inch to the left and air hissed out telling him it had come far enough. He lifted it off his head and, though he didn't want to risk trying it, he knew his voice had come back. He then continued with the rest of the suit, taking off his belt first, then zipping down from his left shoulder to his right thigh. After taking his arms out of his sleeves, he let the suit fall to the ground and kicked his feet out.

Standing there in his skivvies he realized just how cold it was. There was no cot in the cell to sleep on, and no blankets. Not even a toilet.

Without a word, the robotic man picked up Dex's P.E.S. and left the room.

There was no indication of just how long he would have to wait for…for what? *Interrogation?* He thought. *Torture? What do I have to hide? Did he really call me a spy? Who in the hell would I be spying on? And Lacy…if they hurt her I'll…I'll tear this whole place apart!*

But what could he do? He was standing in an empty room with nothing but his underwear, against enemies who most likely weren't even human, and moved with incredible speed. If only he could get his hands on one of those suits. He thought that maybe he could knock one of the robotic men out the next time they came in. If it was just a suit, he could take it and try to break Lacy out. But once they did, how would they get back to the ship? What's to say these guys didn't already get to the *Silent Horizon* and start scrapping it? So many questions were running around in his head, but most importantly he wondered, where's Lacy?

* * *

As the door to Dex's cell shut and disappeared back into the wall, Lacy was shoved forward by the two robotic men. They walked about another fifty feet before stopping and a door appeared for them. Lacy entered, followed by one of her captors, and the door shut behind them. She was given the same orders as Dex and put up less resistance.

Scooping up her clothes, the robotic man turned to leave. The door opened as he began to move like it had sensed he was coming.

Lacy wanted to say something, ask about Dex, or at least be told what was happening to them, but she held her tongue, not wanting to instigate her captors further.

* * *

Once the doors were closed, time became irrelevant. The lights in their rooms never turned off. No outside noises were creeping their way in, and though they banged on the doors and walls, no one ever answered. It was like they had been abandoned in this pristine prison. The only sign of time passing was for Dex was a five o'clock shadow. If nothing else, they would let their bodies do the work telling time for them, granted they let their sleep cycle take and release them naturally.

Lacy was the first to go. She had recognized after the first few hours (though it felt like a full day), they would be attended to on their captor's time. Dex on the other hand wanted to stay alert to whatever would happen next. It was his idea that their captors were monitoring them, and if they came back, it'd be while they were asleep. *Easier to handle once we've given up*, he thought. He only hoped Lacy was feeling the same way.

And he had been right. Dex was pushing his body too much, what with the broken ribs and the stressors of being taken prisoner by an unknown enemy. Though he tried fighting it off, his body eventually shut down. Ironically, it was one of the best sleeps he'd had in years.

A short while after he passed out, his cell door opened and one of the robotic men entered.

* * *

When he opened his eyes again, his retinas were burned by light flooding in. He flinched and immediately felt hands (*HUMAN HANDS*! He thought to himself) press down on his shoulders.

"Easy now," a stern but educated voice said. It brought back a memory for Dex, of a cocky officer he trained alongside back on Earth. That alone helped Dex not trust the man. "Just calm yourself, let me do my job."

Dex didn't know what to say. Was it a dream? Was he back on Earth? He slowly began to realize how strange his core felt. Dex began to lift his head but the voice's hand gently pushed his head back down.

"Trust me you don't want to see this quite yet," the voice told him.

Dex was regaining full consciousness quickly. "Where… what's going on? Where's Lacy?"

"Not to worry about that now. Once we've finished up here you'll have plenty of time for questions."

Dex felt a chill on his core. No, not *on* it… He lifted his head quickly this time and wanted to scream in terror.

He was in an ER. The walls were like the hallway he'd been escorted through, and in each corner was one of the robotic men. Directly past his feet, there was a window where a man, a real flesh and blood being with human features, watched the proceedings. But it was what the doctor was doing that scared him the most. Standing on four legs on his abdomen was an empty frame where Dex looked through to see his internal organs.

Dex felt a cry for help stuck in his lungs and again his head was thrown back by the surgeon's hand.

"Keep quiet now," he said. "You'll be all right I'm just about through."

Though he wanted to, the scream wouldn't come out. But he was barely able to squeeze out a rough, "What are you doing to me?"

"Helping, sir," the surgeon said. "You've suffered a serious injury, and if you'd PERMIT ME," he said sternly, "I'm trying to fix you." The surgeon turned to grab a tool that looked like a chrome pop bottle, with a trigger on the top. He pulled the trigger and a mist sprayed on Dex's now mostly repaired ribs.

Dex felt like screaming again but realized he felt nothing.

"What is this…thing?" He asked.

"Just a coating," the surgeon replied. "I've done what I can to fix the bones, this just holds everything together until the fillings dry." With this, he gave Dex a disingenuous smile, then pressed a button on the top of the framed device.

Dex looked down and saw that within the frame, his skin seemed to grow back.

"Or did you mean this?" The surgeon asked.

Dex nodded.

The surgeon laughed quickly, "Ha ha, modern science at its best, is what it is. Just because you're a spy doesn't mean we won't treat you with respect. No, you'll be in the best shape possible for your interrogation." Another smile, though more ironic than the last.

"Spy? I'm not a spy."

"Of course! Don't worry, I'm just the doctor, you can say whatever you'd like to me but it won't matter in the end. If you'd like my advice though, stop fighting the Zar-Mecks." He took a moment with a deep breath. "Well, I've done all I'm good for. Good luck out there, you're in the hands of the Emperor now." He looked over at the window and gave an "all clear" gesture to the man behind the glass. "Soon you'll be off to meet him.

"Him? The Emperor? Who is this Emperor?"

The surgeon turned off the overhead light he'd been using, and Dex was able to get a good look at his face. He had mostly human features, except for his eyes. They were overall the size and shape of his, but the irises leaked into the whites of his eyes like an egg yolk flowing into the whites. "As I said, I'm just the doctor. No need for spy games with me, won't get you anywhere."

The man behind the glass was gone, and the robotic men, Zar-Mecks as the Surgeon called them, drew in close. The Surgeon was now holding a data pad and typing something. "You'll be escorted back to your cell until we are ready for you. Good day."

Two of the Zar-Mecks grabbed Dex by his arms and lifted him off the operating table, onto his feet. H

e turned his head back to the Surgeon to speak, but as soon as his mouth opened, one of the Zar-Mecks punched him in the jaw. "YOU WILL NOT SPEAK UNLESS TOLD TO, SPY!" It wasn't a shout, but his volume was intense.

"Excuse me! Gentlemen!" The Surgeon again. "Please refrain from your brutality. I just gave all that time mending him, would you be so kind as to *not* break him again?"

The Zar-Meck that punched Dex was silent for a moment, then turned away to face the wall. An outline appeared as it had with the cell.

Just after they stepped off, a piercing alarm sounded. The Zar-Meck guards holding him showed no reaction past stopping in place, but the sound was brutal for Dex and the Surgeon.

The Zar-Meck stood in place like they were downloading information, then after ten seconds started walking again, escorting Dex through the doorway and down the hall.

Once through the doorway, a voice came over an unseen speaker system. "INTRUDER…INTRUDER IN SECTION 1-9-7-7…INTRUDER…" This repeated, every phrase separated by about three seconds, then "INTRUDERS…INTRUDERS IN SECTIONS 1-9-5-6…1-9-6-8…1-9-7-7… AND 1-9-8-0… INTRUDERS."

At 1-9-7-7, the two lead Zar-Meck raised their blasters from their thigh "holsters." Dex understood what this meant. He was either about to be saved…or killed.

They kept walking, but off somewhere, buried under the blaring alarm, Dex could swear he could hear blast sounds.

The source of the blasts was getting closer until an outline on the wall appeared. A door opened and in walked a line of clunky grey robots. These were nothing like the slick Zar-Mecks. They stood on two feet, but they looked hobbled together from scrapyard junk. Their arms were massive tangles of wires and metal, and they had tiny heads that were no bigger than Dex's fist, with one antenna sticking out the top with a green light, acting as an eye. In each hand, they held the biggest blasters Dex had ever seen. They looked like 50 caliber turrets his father manned in the Eurasian War, but they were handled by the robots as if they weighed no more than a 45 Magnum.

As soon as the first of the robots had walked through the doorway, the two Zar-Mecks in the front opened fire. Their aim was incredible, every shot hitting its target. But the blaster bolts seemed to do as much harm as a BB gun. Burn marks stained the junkyard metal but it did nothing to hinder the behemoths approaching Dex and his captors.

In sync, the Zar-Mecks adapted their aim to fire on the antennas, but as the bolts came close to their target, they ricocheted off a blue shield wrapped tightly around the head of the robots. Nothing was stopping them.

The Zar-Meck in the lead raised its arm, and a protective barrier ejected from the wall, leaving four openings for the team to shoot through.

The Zar-Mecks holding Dex's arms stepped in front of him, now acting like his bodyguards, and then they too opened fire. By now, three more of the junkyard bots had entered the hallway on the other side of the barrier. And though they couldn't fire on their enemies, they were determined to kill.

The first junkyard bot to come through ceased its firing. The guns it carried slid up its forearms, and in their place, a metal shell covered its fist. The bot raised its right arm and ran with all force into the barrier. With one punch it left a dent extending at least five inches deep. With force like that, Dex didn't know if he was really about to be saved.

Punches kept coming, and the door was beginning to show signs of breaking. In response, one of the Zar-Mecks held out its palm upwards, and an orb grew out of its hand. He tossed it through the hole in the wall, and the four of them ducked in sync. Dex put two and two together and fell to the ground with them.

A blast from the other side of the barrier shook the hallway. The pounding stopped momentarily, and all they were left with was the sound of the alarm.

At that moment, Dex didn't feel like he could carry on. There was too much going on that he didn't understand and knew he was caught in a fight between two enemies that probably both wanted him dead. And where was Lacy in all of this? In his confusion and fear, he'd forgotten all about her. Had those junkyard bots gotten to her already? Was she already on her way to this Emperor the Surgeon mentioned? What was he going to do about it?

With his mind racing, the pounding started again, and he made his choice. The Zar-meck stood up to begin firing again and dropping more grenades through the holes. By now, the other side of the barrier was clouded in smoke, but the Zar-Meck's attention was stuck on it. Dex saw the opportunity and took it. In a flash, he was up on his feet and running in the opposite direction

All four Zar-Mecks noticed this immediately. One in the rear flicked a switch on its blaster and a blue beam shot out after Dex. He dropped to the floor dodging it, but immediately after, he felt the Zar-Meck on top of him, boot in his back.

"STAY DOWN." The Zar-Meck ordered.

Adrenaline pumped too quickly. The thought of Lacy being in danger made him act. Dex rolled to the right and grabbed the Zar-Meck's leg, yanking him down. When he hit the ground, the right side of the purple visor chipped, and Dex could see an organic eye, with white pupils that leaked into the rest of the sclera. He was shocked, but couldn't let it get to him.

A few yards back the rest of the Zar-Mecks and the junkyard bots were continuing their fight.

Both Dex and the Zar-Meck raced to their feet. The Zar-Meck quickly holstered his blaster in his thigh and removed a small two-foot-long baton instead. He jabbed first into Dex's gut. Dex attempted to dodge the blow but was too slow and was locked back against the wall. Another blow was coming, this one Dex did manage to dodge. As he did, he grabbed his attacker's forearm with both hands and pulled with all his might to slam the Zar-Meck into the wall.

Back at the barrier, the others took notice of the fight. One of them flicked a switch on their blaster and fired a blue beam at Dex.

Dex, still holding the Zar-Meck's arm, pulled him close to use as a shield. The beam hit the Zar-Meck and Dex saw the pure white eye widen in shock. Its body then slumped over unconscious on top of Dex, with the baton falling to the ground.

Dex pushed the unconscious body off and saw the three remaining Zar-Mecks had traded their blasters for Batons.

At least they want me alive, for now, Dex thought to himself. The only saving grace was that the barrier looked like it was about to give in at any moment. But the Zar-Meck's priorities were clear, and this was an un-winnable fight. Dex turned to run in the opposite direction, but another barrier closed behind him.

The Zar-Mecks descended on Dex. A single blow struck him, shattering the bones in his left hand as he tried to block. The sound of it, for as painful as it was, was too loud for a baton. After the blow, the three Zar-Mecks turned around, switched out their batons again back to their blasters, and opened fire. The junkyard bots had broken through.

The sound of the blasters on top of the alarm still going was torture to Dex. He had nowhere left to run and feared the bots as much as he did the Zar-Mecks. But he wouldn't fear them for long.

The bot's aim was good and began quickly tearing through the Zar-Mecks who had locked themselves in a corner. Dex saw their armor blast off their bodies where they were hit and thought he saw pale flesh underneath it. Even as they fell to the ground defeated, they continued firing their weapons aimlessly. They were silenced when the junkyard bots crushed their heads under their heavy feet.

Dex stayed where he was, lying on the ground, holding his broken hand.

One of the bots retracted its weapon and in their place, three long fingers extended towards Dex. In a fully artificial voice that seemed to come from the core of the machine, Dex heard it say, "Prisoner, you will come with us."

Dex didn't move. Why trade one captor for another?

"You will come with us," the bot said and grabbed Dex by wrapping its hand around his chest. He felt like Fay Wray and was carried off down the hallway. His nerves had gotten the better of him at this point and he felt himself going into shock.

* * *

From her room, Lacy heard the alarm, and what sounded like explosions coming from down the hall. She sprang to her feet and put her ear to the door.

Running! She heard people running!

"Help!" She called out! "Somebody help me, please!"

The sound of the footsteps drew closer but never slowed as they approached her door. Lacy pounded and screamed for help as loud as she could, but the sounds of people or robots rushing by paid her no mind.

No one would come to save her.

All alone in her cell, Lacy was afraid.

* * *

Dex was coming to grips with the fights breaking out around him. The Junkyard Bot had let him walk on his own and when he tried to flee, one held out its massive arm in his way and asked in its electronic voice, "Please don't run, we'll transport you to a safe area."

He was surprised by the attempt at politeness but didn't want to test the extent of it. He'd been beaten too many times today to open his mouth out of place again.

The group of six bots and Dex made their way down the hallway, cutting through Zar-Mecks as they did. Dex had no sense of direction or location as every hallway looked the same. When a door appeared on the wall and they walked through, they would just be in another identical hallway. The only difference was the Zar-Mecks had begun to up their game.

The Zar-Mecks switched up their tactics. Instead of focusing on re-capturing Dex and stunning him with their batons, their weapons morphed into blades, and they attacked the junkyard bots.

The bot's armor was thick but the build was gangly and amateur that weak points were found easily. For a moment the tide of the fight seemed to be turning. Two of the bots were taken out briskly, and a third nearly joined them, when it gave a similar motion the Zar-Mecks had to shut a barrier between itself and the rest of Dex's party. The bot closest to Dex rushed to wrap itself around him as they heard what sounded like a hundred pounds of dynamite had just gone off.

The barrier had almost completely blown away, leaving just bits of sharp, hot metal along the edges, with the rest having been blown down the hall, or sticking out of the bots.

The bot wrapped around Dex let him go then told him, "This is where we start to *really* move." It wasn't much, but the three remaining bots were pushing themselves as much as their weight would let them. If a Zar-Meck got in their way they used their size to ram into them, hopefully doing enough damage to temporarily incapacitate them.

"We are almost there!" The bot told Dex.

"Where? Where's there? Did you find Lacy?"

The bots gave no answer. They only continued knocking aside the Zar-Mecks.

As they ran, one of the Zar-Mecks swiped the dull side of its blade at the back of Dex's knee. It missed but in the worst way. Instead of the blunt force hitting the knee, the tip cut across his calf. A chunk of flesh hung down, and blood began to pour out profusely.

The junkyard bots took a moment to notice this and when they did, the Zar-Mecks were already back on their feet racing to him. As one of the Zar-Mecks descended upon him, the closest bot ejected its bulky arm, propelling it through the air, over Dex, and crashing into the approaching Zar-Mecks. It held out its remaining hand to Dex, but he brushed it aside and limped along at their pace.

Instead of helping, the bot motioned its already extended arm upwards and a barrier closed between them, but it wouldn't hold for long.

Thankfully, it didn't need to. The next door they passed through led them back to the desk of the gate guard, who was now dead and lying next to its desk, and the vault door, with more of the bots waiting for them.

"Go," the one-armed junkyard bot told Dex, "You are almost safe." It gave a gentle push and Dex did as he was told, limping along much more willingly than before thanks to the choice of language.

Standing on the platform that would bring them back to the surface, one of the bots that had been waiting held out a black box. "Put this on." It told Dex.

Dex gave the box a confused look and the platform began to ascend.

More sternly, the bot told him, "PUT THIS ON. The airlock will open momentarily."

Without hesitation, Dex reached out to grab the box and instantly it began to crawl across his skin, covering every inch of him. It immediately gave him a sense of relaxation and warmth. He knew a normal reaction to a strange fluid covering his body should be striking fear in him, but he also realized this must be what the Zar-Mecks were wearing. As his face was covered, a purple visor opened in front of his eyes. Hovering in front of all the bots were numbers, he guessed IDs. There was even a full heads-up display with a heart rate monitor, and a notification telling him he had taken damage in his left hand and right calf(as if he needed a reminder).

The bot spoke to him again. "You may want a blaster for this."

Dex had no idea how to access the blaster or any weapon in the suit for that matter. Before he could find it, the door opened and Dex immediately heard the sounds of all-out warfare going on outside. They crested over the doorway and the once dull gray desert had become a battlefield.

Robot carcasses and Zar-Mecks lay scattered all around. Missiles flew across the sky and erupted on the ground with such force it felt like the whole planet was shaking. All around the surface, bunkers had popped up, occupied by Zar-Mecks providing covering fire to their fellow soldiers facing the junkyard bots head-on in melee combat.

Though outnumbered, the junkyard bots had managed to outmaneuver and overpower the Zar-Mecks. Mixed in with the tanks that had taken Dex, were smaller, more nimble bots. These bots stood no more than two feet tall and attacked in packs, racing up to a single Zar-Meck and tearing it limb from limb. The blood being sprayed by the Zar-Mecks was a deep blue and gave the planet some of the only color it would ever see.

What stuck out the most to Dex was there was no rhyme or reason to any of the forces' tactics. The junkyard bots were attacking and moving in any and every direction. The Zar-Mecks on the other hand were organized into fire teams, working as one mind to defend their positions.

The one-armed bot put a hand on Dex moments after the platform stopped moving. "Our transport is almost here."

Dex looked around and over the horizon came the largest ship Dex had ever seen. The saucer-shaped ship was at least half the size of Earth's "Grand Central" Space Station, and fifteen times bigger than the *Silent Horizon*. It moved with incredible speed. In no time it was right on top of them, taking up the whole sky as it hovered thirty feet above them.

Dex was again struck with awe over what this new world was showing him.

Overhead a bright light appeared. Dex shielded his eyes, and through his fingers, he could see a ladder descending.

It was then that a voice called out as clear as day with a real sense of urgency and care, "Climb! Climb for your life!"

Dex took only a moment to gather himself, and with some help from the bot attempted to climb. He had been so eager to reach safety he'd completely forgotten about his injuries. When he grabbed a rung of the ladder with his left hand, a bolt of pain ran through him and he nearly fell back into the bots.

The voice called to him, "All right just hold on right there! This is gonna be fast!"

The introduction of the ship had not been stealthy in any sense of the word. The Zar-Mecks on the battlefield began shifting their aim towards the ship, and the ladder especially.

The ladder was fast though, so fast he almost lost his grip, but he held on for dear life, and in no time he had shot through the porthole the ladder came through. Before he crashed into the ceiling where the ladder was stored, a hand grabbed him off and pulled him to the floor.

"Drop the decoy!" The strange voice shouted to an unknown recipient.

Though Dex couldn't see it, a corpse was dropped from the porthole he'd climbed out of.

"All right, we're good! Punch it!" The voice shouted. The ship lurched forward and Dex no longer heard the sound of the battlefield.

Dex now lay on his back, looking up at the room he was in, with a man standing next to him. A very human man, but with the same leaked-iris eyes as the surgeon.

"Surprised we made it out of that one so clean! Come on, let's get up," the man said, extending his arm.

Dex raised his right hand to meet the man's, and through the pain in his right calf, got to his feet.

"Sure you've had enough excitement for one day, so I'll wait to ask questions." He raised an eyebrow inquisitively towards Dex, "Unless…you've got any?"

As soon as it came out, Dex knew it was the wrong question. He wanted to know Lacy was safe, but the first thing that came to mind was, "What…the HELL is going on?!"

Though the pain rushed through his body, he grabbed his savior by his jacket and pushed him into the wall of the small cargo hold they stood in.

"Easy, guy, easy!" The man held his hands up in a feigned surrender. "Calm down all right! I'm just here to help!"

Dex was breathing deeply. His heads-up display in the suit told him his heart was racing too quickly and he'd been losing too much blood. It also warned that he may be about to overheat. He thanked God for the suit, hopefully making him look more intimidating than he would have been without it.

"My name is Korr," the man said gently. "Korr Montori. All right? Good place to start eh? I saw an alien vessel on my radar and decided I'd do better with it than the empire. Fair enough?"

Dex lowered his hands. "So...so you're just like them. We're your prisoners now?"

"We?" Korr asked.

4. Prisoner

The alarms and running about had ceased nearly an hour and a half after the initial attack on the outpost. Another three hours later, Lacy's isolation was interrupted by a Zar-Meck. She sat huddled in the corner with her arms wrapped around her legs. As she raised her head, the first thing she noticed about the Zar-Meck was that it was holding a folded-up olive green jumpsuit.

"PUT THIS ON," the Zar-Meck told her in a cold voice, then tossed the suit her way.

She did as she was told without question.

The suit was basic, with two breast zip-up pockets, a thick rigger belt, pant pockets, and soles built into the feet of the suit, with straps that tightened over her feet and just above the ankle. Once the suit was on she attempted to roll back the sleeves but the Zar-Meck stopped her.

"COME WITH ME." The Zar-Meck told her, and Lacy followed.

Lacy sat now, alone again, in a white room. It was not unlike the ones she and Dex took their psyche exams when being recruited for the mission. She was upright with her hands resting on the long grey table in an attempt to show resolve in case anyone had secretly been watching her. Lacy noticed earlier that when she stood up to stretch her legs, the table those with her to maintain its height relative to her, but it didn't follow her around the room.

Eventually, her patience was rewarded. No footsteps were heard building up to it, but a door opened across from her and a man walked through. A man with very human features, save for irises that leaked into the whites of his eyes.

He wore a dark grey uniform, with navy blue trim. The blouse was buttonless, instead folding over across from the right side to more of a third of his body where it was held together presumably by a magnetic strip within the lining. Over his left breast was a single horizontal while line about an inch long, and on his lapel, he wore a gold pin that looked like a crown. Under his right arm, he carried a black tablet and held onto it tightly with his left hand.

The man walked briskly towards the table and a chair rose out of the ground to meet him. As he sat down he placed the tablet on the table. Lacy saw nothing on its surface but noticed the small white dots dancing around in his eyes. A reflection of what he was seeing on the tablet.

Eventually, he looked up from the tablet and spoke to her, "I understand you go by the name First Lieutenant Lacy Carradine Prullen."

Lacy hadn't spoken a word out loud since they were taken captive on the surface, save for her brief cries for help in her cell, and was still a little bit afraid to speak.

"Don't worry," the man said. "You're granted permission to speak. Please confirm your name for me."

Lacy placed her hands on the table, fingers interlocked. "Yes. That's my name."

"Real or alias?"

"Excuse me?" Lacy leaned in slightly.

The man sighed and tapped on his tablet. "You have permission to speak, but I'd advise you not to test my patience."

"It's my name. My only name, Lacy Prullen."

The man squinted his eyes looking back at the tablet, and spoke without looking back up at her. "Explain the rest of this to me then. If 'First Lieutenant' and 'Carradine' aren't your names, what does it mean."

"'First Lieutenant' is my rank." Lacy declared with some pride in her voice.

The man's eyes opened. "Ah, so you are here on military terms!"

Lacy realized she would now be treading water with every answer. "N-...no. Not exactly. Coming here was a mistake, see-"

"Oh, I'm sure it was Ms. Prullen."

"Mrs." She corrected.

He continued tapping on the tablet like he was typing notes. Then, like he hadn't been interrupted, "I can imagine it's just luck that you happen to land in restricted sectors of the empire. Probably happens every other day is that right?"

Lacy gave him an inquisitive look. "You misunderstand. We weren't searching for this place. It came up on our radar and all signs say uninhabited."

"Do you expect us to advertise our presence?"

Lacy was silent for a moment.

"I've been reviewing your ship's log. Baffling encryptions I must say."

An analyst, Lacy thought. *Great.*

"Your cover is…interesting…but ultimately laughable."

"How do you figure that?" Lacy asked.

"Sending two life forms into unknown space in hopes of discovery. Ma'am that's a job for a cruiser or a probe. So why don't you tell me why you've landed here? I promise the pain will be much less…unbearable…if you cooperate."

"You think I'm a spy, don't you?"

The Analyst only gave her a look to say, *that much was obvious.*

"My husband and I came here as explorers. We were seeking out new worlds to expand our race."

"Your…" he reviewed notes on his tablet, "*Earth…*Empire correct?"

Lacy smiled at the misunderstanding. Even with how awful the situation was, there was no way Earth could ever fall under just one Empire. At least not in her lifetime. "No, not an empire, none for a decades. Many different nations."

"All on one planet?" The Analyst asked, now showing the smallest hint of genuine interest in his voice.

"Yes, all on one." "And you're able to refrain from war?" He was nearly glowing. Literally. His skin began to radiate a golden color. It was barely noticeable, but if he was in a pitch-black room, it would be obvious.

She continued to smile. If she kept his interest, maybe she'd have a way out. But what should she tell him? What would keep him going? *Lie,* she decided. *Tell him whatever he wants to hear.* "Yes, it took some time. Many, many wars, but we've accomplished peace."

The Analyst had all but forgotten about his tablet, he was leaning much closer now.

"We fought three wars back to back on a global scale, but we were able to come together by uh.." She had to keep the story going quickly but couldn't think of any figures or names that would make sense. *What does it matter? It's all a lie anyway and he wouldn't know the difference anyway,* she told herself. Thankfully, she didn't have to think of a name.

"Flash Gordon? It was Gordon that united them, correct?" The Analyst asked eagerly.

"Yes!" Lacy exclaimed, "Yes, it was Gordon! He overthrew the evil dictators of the world and brought us all together. Earth has lived in peace ever since!"

The Analysts' smile shifted devilishly, "and that's why they sent you out to explore the universe? No wars left on your Earth to fight?"

Lacy gave pause to think. "Y-yes. You know, don't need us fighting anymore, why not?" She tried to laugh it off playfully, but she saw his interest was shifting.

"I see," the Analyst said as he picked his tablet back up. "And, who was one of these dictators Gordon overthrew?"

Lacy was at a loss for an answer. Dex was the film buff. She knew he'd definitely mentioned the Flash Gordon serials from the ship's computer at least a dozen times but right now couldn't remember a single thing about them. She sat there thinking for too long. The Analyst was the only one in the room with her but she felt like a hundred pairs of eyes were locked on to her. A bead of sweat formed at her hairline and slowly fell down the side of her face. It was all the Analyst needed.

"Ming." He said. "Funny. Emperor…Ming."

Lacy fell back in her chair.

The Analyst sat back in his chair. "It's strange. Earth hasn't had empires for, 'decades,' as you said, but your last war, the one you say Gordon fought in and defeated Ming, ended just three years before you left on your planet." He scoffed. "The database in your ship's computer is totally incoherent. Fascinating, but incoherent.

And because of that, it's so easy to tell when you're lying. Clearly, you haven't had enough time to take in your situation, spy."

Before Lacy could stand in protest, she felt an electric shock run through her body. She screamed out in pain, but couldn't pull herself away from the seat, and her eyes felt like they were about to explode out of her head. The pain lasted a lifetime in her mind, but as suddenly as it began, it ceased. The first thing she saw when she was able to focus again was the Analyst's face. His smile was completely gone.

"Ms. Prullen I have no qualms with making your existence as painful as rákingly possible. I'll continue to go through your ship's computer but as I said, it's very difficult to decipher so if you'd please cooperate…well, I can't promise this will be over any time soon, but it will be less painful." He waited a moment for Lacy to respond.

She sat there, heart beating heavily and stared at him. She felt paralyzed in her chair.

"Hm…maybe I went a little too far with that. How about this, I'll scale back the shock level and you tell me if it fits you better." He began tapping something on his tablet, and the lights again flickered in his eyes.

Lacy was terrified of what was next to come and managed to squeeze out a "…wait…"

The Analyst stopped what he was doing and met her eye.

Lacy was trying with all her might to sit back up in her chair. "At'a girl."

"It's…it's not real."

The Analyst gave her a disappointed look. "A lot of suspense to tell me again your story was a lie." He hovered again over the tablet.

Lacy saw his hand move and shouted as loud as she could, "The TAPES!"

Now the Analyst stopped, "Tapes?"

"The files on my ship's computer." She stopped to catch her breath. The mental strength it took for her to try to put words together was starting to make her nose bleed. She felt it trailing down her nostril, but it hadn't yet made it out. "They're just movies. It's not real…"

At this, the Analyst showed real confusion.

Lacy recognized the look. "You know, stories. It's just entertainment. Fiction." The blood crept out of her nose.

"My my my," the Analyst began. "So many questions do I have for you."

Lacy wiped her nose. "They filled up the computer with movies and books so we didn't lose our minds on the journey. We had no idea how long it would take to find another planet we could land on."

"So…what you're saying is, your ship is full of…" The confusion had passed, and now he looked offended. "Lies? You are a sick, unholy breed." He stood up and his chair disappeared into the floor. "It's no wonder your instinct is to lie. Even in the face of torture!" He was shouting now in anger, "You blaspheme your own history! And you DARE to bring the Emperor's colors where they *DO NOT BELONG!* It's clear that a being of your…distinction…has only one place in this universe." The Analyst attempted to calm himself down, breathing deeply. He then picked up the tablet and placed it back under his arm. "You will be terminated."

Her eyes widened in shock.

"And dissected."

Horror.

"It's clear there is nothing I can trust you to tell me."

She again rose in protest by instinct and was caught by the shock of the chair. Again she screamed, and as she did so, she prayed that he would truly kill her.

5. Ships That Don't Exist

Dex and Korr sat at a table in a makeshift kitchen. The Zar-Meck suit was in its cube form, sitting on the table.

Korr had placed a device, similar to the one the surgeon at the outpost had except smaller, over top of Dex's broken last hand. It had first sprayed an alcoholic-smelling chemical on his hand, then opened up his skin like it was a window to reveal the broken bone. Next to his hand was a first aid kit Korr was using to operate on Dex with.

"So is this a common find in any household around here?" Dex asked.

"Miracle of modern science, jarrmin box," Korr told him. "We can't fix everything. But most things are pretty easy. And best part, no pain." He finished up the job and tapped a side of the small jarrmin box.

Dex's flesh closed over the insides of his hand. As Korr had said, he felt no pain.

"Need something to eat? Drink?" Korr asked as he stood up.

On the wall behind where Korr had been sitting was a line of floating cabinets. He opened one of them and cold air rushed out. From the cabinet, he took out two cans which made Dex think of a nice cold beer, but Korr didn't bring them back to the table. Instead, he warmed them up on the dinkiest hotplates Dex had ever seen. When Korr had served it, Dex was hesitant at first. The beverage had no scent, and it looked like bile, but Korr insisted he'd feel better.

Dex took one sip and almost vomited. He hadn't realized until too late that this was the first thing thicker than the water he'd had in over a year, and his body wasn't keen on trying new things quite yet.

Slowly, he was able to get it down. It was warm and tasted like spiked hot chocolate. Just the thought of it nearly gave him a buzz.

After a few sips, Dex pleaded with his new host. "We need to turn around, we need to get Lacy."

Korr didn't say anything for a moment. He only dropped his head slightly in discomfort.

"Did you hear what I said?" Dex asked. "We have to go back!"

"I'm sorry my friend, but we can't it's too risky," Korr told him. "A quick attack here and there? Sure. But believe me, if they weren't on high alert when I came in before, we can expect an armada this time."

Dex dropped his head and spoke gently, trying not to push too far with his host. "I just don't understand any of this. We weren't hostile. We didn't even know anyone was there for Christ's sake!"

"Who's sake?" Korr asked.

Dex waived it off and took another small sip of his drink.

"Look, I think I'll be able to clear the air a bit," Korr said with sincerity in his voice. "Just tell me your story first, and hopefully I can fill in the pieces."

Dex lifted his head again, thought a moment, and began to speak but caught himself and slowly pushed his drink away.

"What's wrong?" Korr asked and tilted his head trying to hear if something was amiss.

Dex stood up. "Why should I trust you? I don't even know who you are. You kidnapped me just like they did!"

Korr stayed seated but his face hardened at the disrespect of his guest. "Wait a minute now, I saved you!"

"Yeah and left my wife to die! What, are you just taking me to sell off to someone else? Is there a bounty for discovery of new aliens out there? Is that what I am?" There was real anger in his voice now.

"Dex, sit back down, now."

"I think I'm fine right where I am, and maybe you should start talking!" Dex's hand shot out for the Zar-Meck armor box, but Korr was faster.

Korr was leaning back in his chair, with his feet planted on the box. He'd lifted his hand in a finger gun gesture. "I wouldn't do that if I were you…friend."

To Dex, he looked like a gunslinger like Gary Cooper or John Wayne, if they'd forgotten their side iron at home. He wanted to laugh, and that did a bit to calm his nerves a bit.

"Easy now, just have a seat."

"Why, gonna shoot me?"

As the words came out, the flesh on Korr's hand morphed into a silver blaster barrel protruding from his forearm.

"Jesus Christ!" Dex shouted and jumped back nearly a full yard.

"I might," Korr said coolly before the blaster morphed back into his hand. "Dex, I'd like to help you out. Please, just sit."

Dex did as he was told but with reservation.

Korr leaned forward again, feet on the floor, and let out a deep sigh. "All right, how about I start?"

"Yeah," Dex agreed. "Start with why you felt the need to get me out of there."

Korr pursed his lips to the right side, then began. "Here's what I'll tell, and all you need to know. I grew up on Wiccar and my life was dedicated to the Emperor. As soon as I was old enough, I began studying at my planet's military academy. There are lots of paths for servitude where I'm from, I mean I could have been like my mom and gone into the priesthood. But my father was in the Army. I hadn't met him until I was nearly an adult but, I'd grown up hearing the stories of how the Emperor's Army had liberated and developed so many planets. I thought that was a true honor, bringing more souls into the Emperor's keeping." Korr laughed to himself, then locked eyes with Dex. "I don't know where you're from, or what gods they have there, but they're nothing like Emperor Armourus." He said the name with reverence.

"Well, our gods don't *usually* come down to our planet and tell us how to do things," Dex said, as he took another sip of his drink.

Korr scoffed. "Well, mine does."

"So which side is he on? Yours or those..." he gestured to the cube between them. "Those guys, the Zar-... the robot guys."

"Zar-Mecks. That's his army, his ground troops at least."

"But you still accept him?"

Korr tried to hold back frustration. Not with Dex, but with

himself. "Evil is one side of a coin, my friend. And I've seen that coin with my own two eyes." He leaned in further and pointed to his broken pupils as he said it. "It's hard to deny things like that. I accept that he's real, and maybe he is a god. But not a benevolent one. Wherever that one is, he hasn't reached our borders yet."

Dex registered the pain in Korr's voice. "Okay, so, you saw something bad and a bunch of you took off? You guys some kinda rebellion, saving guys like me that wander in?"

Korr shook his head. "No, just me."

Dex leaned back and took it in. "But, hold on, all those robots that broke me out of that prison…you couldn't have done all that yourself!"

Korr laughed politely, "Well, you'd be wrong." Stood and walked back to the cabinets. "Smoke?"

Dex thought he understood but, there was no way they were on the same page. "What, like…"

"Like smoke. Do you smoke?" Korr opened one of the cabinets and pulled out a small box with what looked like real Cuban cigars. He walked back and put the box on the table for them both to have.

Dex picked one up, smelled it, and let out a sigh of relief. "It's just like back home!" The butt was already cut, and Dex put it in his mouth.

Korr reached over and the tip of his thumb popped back revealing a small flame to light the cigar. "Glad you like it."

Dex reclined and took a deep draw of the cigar, then laughed out a hard cough. "Oh, yeah, no I love it. I remember when my dad gave me my first cigar right after I got my commission."

Korr smiled politely but clearly had no idea what that meant. He then lit a cigar of his own and puffed it.

"Okay," Dex began again. "So you saw some things you didn't like and you got out of dodge."

"I guess. I had to bide my time, which was by far the hardest part. You see, you won't find anyone under the Empire's thumb that doesn't give themselves completely to the Emperor."

"But you can't be the only one in history that's ever left."

"Maybe not. But if so, the Empire does a great job of finding you before you can make the choice. I've never known anyone who's defected. The people of this universe give themselves completely to the Emperor. It's an honor to die for him. The poorest people either become priests or officers of his army." He laughed, "There's so much demand to serve him most do it for the bare minimum. He's proved himself time and again and the people will never stop following him."

"It's just one man though. Right?"

Korr waved the remark away and tried to speak but Dex kept going.

"Back when my world was young, there was a country called Egypt. They had their gods, but they also had human rulers. The belief is when they died they became gods, but at the end of the day, they were still born, still died, and lived a normal human lifetime!"

"The Emperor is no mere man. He's not mortal. The Emperor has existed long before even the planets formed and he'll live long after they die."

Dex tried to laugh it off, "But…but that can't be. Everything dies eventually."

"Not him. His followers won't allow it."

At this Dex was able to laugh, "That's too bad! I said I wouldn't let my dog die when I was eight but he did anyway, it's nature!"

"The Emperor doesn't care about what's natural."

Dex stopped smiling.

"This is what I saw that made me doubt. The Emperor has survived for so long because he feeds on the people. Not their bodies, their energy. Their very souls. My second duty station was as a deck officer on one of Wiccar's temple's transport ships. A priest or priestess would bring their offering to the Heart of the Void, the center of the Empire. These offerings were people. Volunteers who would give their lives to extend the Emperor's. Dozens of ships go out each year, with hundreds aboard, all going to their deaths. But I saw what these feedings look like. When the color leaves their skin, and the life leaves their eyes, there's no peace. All they leave behind is pain and regret. I've seen men die in battle. When they die for something they believe in, they're at peace. But when you realize everything you believed your whole life was a lie, that your life is stolen, and fed to a… I don't know. God, I guess. All I know is their souls will never find peace again. Not in this world, or whatever comes next."

There was silence between them for a full minute. Korr rested his chin in his hands and looked down past Dex like he was no longer there.

Dex felt it was best to let Korr have his moment, but after that, he knew it was time to get back on track. "Korr, I'm sorry for what you've been through. I can't imagine what it's like to have your world turned on its head so disturbingly."

Korr didn't lift his head, but he did raise his eyes to meet Dex.

"But I do know what it's like to leave everything you've ever known behind," Dex continued. "It feels impossible to start again. But once you find something to fight for, once you have a purpose again, it's easy not looking back." At this, he stood. "Now I know this is a lot to ask, but my wife is still out there. With or without you, I will get her back." He held out his hand in kindness. "But I don't think of all the paths in the universe to cross, I came by yours just by luck."

Korr looked at Dex's outstretched hand, then back to meet Dex's eyes. He then stood. "I'm sorry, but I can't help you like that." He then turned to walk away down a hall towards the ship's stern.

Dex grabbed the Zar-Meck cube and followed after Korr. With annoyance in his voice, he asked, "What do you mean you can't? You broke me out once! Why can't you do it again?"

"I don't have the resources!" Korr exclaimed without turning back. "On paper, I don't even have this ship. The Empire believes that it, and everyone on board including me, was destroyed. All records of it say so, and no one has had any reason to argue otherwise. I made sure of it."

"Yet, here I am, courtesy of your efforts."

"You're not the first undocumented life form to land on the Emperor's doorstep. I have to pick my fights. Building up my force takes time, and when I go in, I have to go with everything I've got. So right now, I'm empty."

Dex grabbed Korr's left shoulder and forced him to stop.

Korr's reaction was quick. His right hand shot up and grabbed Dex's hand, as he spun around and threw it off. "Don't mistake my hospitality for weakness, Dex." With that, he turned and continued down a long, narrow hallway.

This hallway had a semblance of the pristine nature of the outpost's architecture but looked ten times more worn down. The walls were a dirtier brown, and anywhere there was decor it felt to Dex as incredibly out of place. Nothing seemed to flow or have any particular motivation for its design. It was like a hobo living in a boxcar made do with whatever he could find. Where Dex figured doors should have been, were just lazy paint jobs a different color from the wall and marked in writing what was behind the door. Dex thought back to the hallways of the outpost, how the outline of the doors only appeared when the Zar-Mecks approached or activated them.

As they walked, Korr continued. "If the Emperor's officers follow protocol, they'll realize she's an undocumented species and they'll bring her to an audience with the Emperor. She's probably on her way already."

They reached the end of the hallway and faced a blank wall. Korr pounded on it as if there were something past it. "Come on, damn busted door!" He lifted his hand to chest level and his fingers shifted into an array of strange small tools.

Dex watched as a port near the corner of the wall opened, and Korr's mechanical finger messed with the circuitry inside. "What does that mean? An audience."

"Well, I don't know how to put it nicely. Every species carries different levels of energy with them, right? A bug is much more insignificant than a being like you or me. So if that's the case…" A shock ran from the circuitry to his cyborg's fingers. Korr shook his hand to get rid of the pain then continued to work. "Stupid door. Anyway, the Emperor will use her to figure out how powerful your race is. How much your kind can sustain him."

"You mean, she'll be killed? Like all those others?" The fear in his voice was clear.

The door opened, but Dex didn't register what was behind it, his eyes were fixed on Korr with anticipation and doubt as to what he knew Korr would say next.

Korr turned to Dex and said the words that Dex didn't want to hear. "Yes, she'll be sacrificed."

Dex was speechless. His eyes went wide and the words he wanted to say were caught in his throat.

"I can't attack another outpost, Dex. I can't put myself out there and help wage a two-man war on the Empire. And I know that I won't be able to stop you from whatever it is you're thinking. But…I guess I can at least offer some courtesies." Korr gave a small smile and stepped through the doorway.

Dex took a moment to put together what Korr was saying but it all came together once he realized what was in the room just beyond them.

It was a large room, most likely an old hanger. A handful of robots moved around, hard at work. But what caught Dex's eye was a magnificent, though slightly bruised and worn out, white cone-shaped ship, with a viewport that took up most of the bow and a long antenna that looked like it could serve as the world's largest rapier. In front of him, stood the *Silent Horizon*.

"H-…How did you get this?"

Korr stood off to the side, so as not to obstruct Dex's view. "As I said, I go in with full force. I can't say I saved it completely though."

Dex walked up to his ship and ran his hand along its hull.

Korr continued. "When my robots got there, It was crawling with Zar-Mecks and technicians of the Emperor's army. Chances are, whatever information your computer had is in the hands of the Empire now. But with the bulk of the Empire's forces focused on the main entrance of the outpost, getting the ship out was the easy part."

"Korr…I…"

"I know it's not a fleet," he raised his hands apologetically. "But, maybe you can get your bearings from there."

Dex couldn't speak. He only stood with eyes wide, and a smile slowly crawling across his face.

Korr waited a moment for a response, then when he knew it wasn't coming, said quietly "You're welcome, by the way. It was no trouble."

When the lump in Dex's throat disappeared, he burst, "Korr, this is mighty fine! Just…well, real damn swell." He laughed to himself in disbelief, then took a step closer to the *Silent Horizon*.

"I don't know how to thank you."

Korr slapped Dex's back, the cyborg hand hitting harder than Dex had expected. "All I ask is that you don't rat me out when you get caught."

They laughed together.

"Never, Korr. For something like this, I owe you my life."

"Keep it. Better yet, give it to your girl."

"Right!" Dex stepped closer to his ship but kept his attention on Korr. "Guess I better get going then. Don't wanna keep the missus waiting!"

Korr just smirked. "Well, I wouldn't recommend going off just yet."

Dex gave him an inquisitive look.

Korr stepped past Dex and motioned his hand toward the robots. "My crew took a look at your ship. They relayed to me just before we got you aboard that your ship is, outdated, I guess we could say."

Dex knew he agreed but still gave Korr a look of offense.

"All I'm saying," Korr continued, "is that compared to our tech, your planet has a long way to go. I admire your determination to save your wife, but there's no way in Maoul you'll catch up with an Empire ship."

The disappointment returned to Dex's face. Korr recognized it and was quick to save himself. "But! But I guess we could shift course."

"To where?" Dex asked.

Korr motioned to the nearest junkyard bot. The bot hobbled over to his master and Korr ordered, "Bring a message up to the bridge computer. Re-route for Reechi. Moorak City."

Without a word, the bot nodded and hobbled away.

Dex couldn't help but be amazed at the set-up Korr had. "What's Reechi? Is that a planet?"

Korr smiled. "Yeah, one of the oldest ones in the Empire."

"Sounds like they'd have a big presence there. Nowhere else we can go?"

"Only other option is Areeno. Desert planet without much

activity. But that's *much* further out of the way."

Dex considered his options. "So you do have allies out on this...Reechi?"

Now Korr had to laugh. "No! Ha ha, I wouldn't call them that. If they knew who I really was I'd never be able to set foot on any civilized planet again. I just have good enough cover. Definitely not allies, but I know some people that can help you out."

"So Reechi's close to wherever they're taking Lacy?" Dex asked.

"If all things go well, you should be at the Heart of the Void within a day or so."

Dex knew well enough to be grateful for even a slim chance of hope. "I don't know how to say thank you, Korr."

Korr raised a single hand in protest. "I do," he said. "All you need to do for me... is leave me out of it. I can bring you there, introduce you to a contact, but if anything goes down, I'm out of there, and you never knew me. Deal?"

Dex nodded.

"Great. Want me to show you where you can bed down?"

Dex looked back at the ship. "I think I'll be fine once I'm in my old bunk again."

Korr motioned towards the ship as if to say, *be my guest*.

6. Transport

Three hours after the interrogation, a pair of Zar-Mecks arrived at Lacy's cell. Her immediate thought was they had come to escort her to her death and pushed herself up against the wall.

"FOLLOW," the Zar-Meck said.

She jumped at the command, her fear of immediate punishment for disobedience overpowering her fear of possible termination, and followed the villain out of her cell.

Hooking a right, they walked about a hundred feet, then turned left through a door, crossing a foot-long platform into a small glass room. It was clear by looking through that no part of the room made contact with the shaft the room was in. It was just floating there like an elevator unattached to cables. And that turned out to be just what it was.

When they stepped in, one of the Zar-Mecks put its hand up against the wall. On contact, a faint blue light rippled across the glass. The room moved to the left a few feet, then dropped suddenly down the shaft at full speed.

Lacy could feel herself getting lighter, the elevator moving faster than she was falling, but her captors stayed perfectly cemented to the ground. She also realized that, although she knew she *should* be floating, her boots stayed firmly on the ground.

Within moments, they fell into an imposing spherical room, with portals littered across its walls covering nearly half the surface area. Other elevators came and went, reaching the center of the room, turning, and shooting up another shaft. They all moved with such precision of speed that there were no cars waiting or jamming up. As they reached the center of the sphere, the elevator came to a stop and Lacy's momentum attempted to force her to the floor, but the Zar-Mecks at her left and right held her up. When they grabbed her she realized something.

There's no gravity here, she thought to herself. *This must be the center of the moon!*

Just as quickly as they reached the core, the elevator rotated itself and shot upwards through another shaft.

They rose for almost as long as they'd dropped, and soon Lacy saw a light growing larger above them. When they passed through the top of the shaft and came to a halt, Lacy was amazed and terrified by what she saw.

The elevator parked itself along a wall, facing towards a hangar bay Lacy assumed was larger than the National Mall in D.C., and from one end to the next were rows upon rows of hulking saucer-shaped transport ships. Both Zar-Mecks and humanoid beings like the Analyst were moving with purpose, boarding ships, loading them up, off-boarding, or unloading them. Smaller ground transports were scurrying about, usually carrying large, clunky robots that looked like they'd been through hell and back, or other Zar-Mecks and machinery that didn't fare much better. Above the hanger was no ceiling. Instead, Lacy could see clearly into the sky through a transparent but grainy blue screen. Small saucer-like ships were constantly dropping into the hangar through the screen, dropping scraps of the robots and Zar-Mecks down onto ground cars, then flying back up and out of sight.

As the elevator doors opened, the Zar-Mecks next to Lacy pushed her forward in the direction of the closest large ship.

Approaching an entry ramp, Lacy saw at its base the Analyst.

He stood firmly with his hands behind his back. His face betrayed no hint of emotion. When they met, he raised a hand in dismissal for the Zar-Meck. "That will be all," He told them, and they turned to leave. He then shifted his attention to Lacy. "Mrs. Prullen, I'm greatly looking forward to our journey together."

"Where are we off to?" Lacy asked, trying to speak with pride, not as a prisoner. "I thought you were to have me terminated."

The corner of the analyst's mouth dropped the slightest bit, but Lacy could discern the annoyance he was struggling to hide.

"And dissected." She added to deepen the wound.

"New orders." He said plainly. "You will be brought to an

audience with the Emperor. So, given that you'll have at least another day or so to live, I decided we shouldn't waste the time we have to learn more about your planet and…" he looked her up and down quickly. "…people. Now please, follow me." He turned and walked up the ramp.

Lacy hesitated a moment, and the Analyst could feel it.

"Now is not the time to run," he said and swiveled his head to look at her through the corner of his eye. "I can't kill you but I can make you suffer. Again."

The memory of the chair returned to her so strongly that she almost felt the pain return. Lacy agreed it would be best to cooperate. She would bide her time and wait for the right moment to make her escape. With a deep breath, like she was about to jump off a cliff, she took a step onto the ramp, closer to her fate.

Her room was slightly more accommodating than the one she was forced into back at the outpost. In this one, she at least had a small bed, a toilet, and a window stretched across the width of one wall. It curved upwards from the floor, and she watched its ascent into space in that way.

Barely out of view at the top of the window, she watched the blue film warp around the ship as they passed through it. From the sky, one would never realize there was a base hidden under the planet's surface. The blue film was gone, and all she saw was the planet's surface and the damage from the battle. Lacy realized then that the blue film was a cloaking device.

As the transport ship drifted off, Lacy sat on the bed staring out into space, legs wrapped in her arms. Her body told her to lie down and get the comfortable rest she'd been dying for, but her mind told her to wait just a little longer. Maybe since she didn't see Dex when she boarded the ship, he made an escape. That would explain the loud noises and the battlefield she'd just seen. Any moment now he'd be flying in to rescue her. No one came for her.

No ships swooped in to rescue her. Dex was lost, and as much as she fought against it, a nagging thought crept into her mind that she'd never see him again. No, if she was ever going to taste freedom again, she'd have to get it herself.

Some time passed and a small ash-black robot, no more than

two feet tall delivered a tray of food to her room. The robot held it up above its small dome-shaped head like an offering but made no noise.

She took the tray out of the robot's arms, and it walked away on two stubby legs. The door slid shut behind the robot. Lacy didn't even have time to say thank you.

The meal was a stew in green broth. None of the "vegetables" were recognizable, and the meat in it looked like beef but had the taste of ham with way too much salt. It was hard to eat at first, but the smell was at least decent, and this was the first meal she'd had since being taken prisoner. She'd wished after all the time taking meal pills, her first would be something closer to a five-star restaurant seafood platter, but this would have to do.

When she finished eating, Lacy placed the tray at the base of the door, and almost instantly, the little robot returned to collect it. This time, while the door was opened, even though it was only momentarily, Lacy focused on any other sounds in the hallways. Thankfully, there were none.

For the rest of the day, Lacy sat by the door. She kept her mind focused on any and all sounds outside her room but heard nothing all day until somewhere between six and eight hours later, a light stomping quickly approached her room. Lacy put her ear to the door hoping she could make a guess at the size and speed of whatever it was outside. Whatever it was, it was definitely small. The suspense didn't last, as the door opened and Lacy fell onto the little ash-black robot, spilling a tray of oatmeal-looking food back onto the robot's body.

Lacy's body lay perfectly centered on the threshold of the door. Immediately she realized she was alone in the corridor, save for her personal waiter. The heat of the moment took her, and she was on her feet, sprinting in whatever direction she happened to be facing. Yet, with freedom being possible, maybe even probable, she stopped and turned at the sound of beeping behind her. She saw the waiter robot trying to brush the food off of its body and eyes, but struggling with its thick claw-shaped hands. It might have been the high notes the beeping hit, but something told Lacy it sounded as if the robot was pleading for help.

She looked down the hallway in the direction she'd been running, then back to the robot. To the hallway, then to the robot, who was now slumped against the wall with its small arms hanging by its side in defeat.

"Dammit," Lacy said to herself and walked back to the robot.

Kneeling to the robot's level, Lacy unrolled her right sleeve and wiped the food off its eyes.

At the sight of Lacy, the robot jumped to attention and spun around to pick up the tray it had dropped. Almost all of the food had fallen off of it, but the robot held it in an offering to Lacy anyway.

"Thanks but I'll find something else," she said, trying to show some kindness in her voice. *Maybe this little guy can be won over*, she told herself.

The robot looked at the tray, then back up at Lacy, shoving it slightly in her direction.

"No really, I'm all right. You brought a big breakfast." *Or was that dinner?*

The robot lowered its arms. Its head also tilted down, and it let out a low, sad "boooooooo."

"It's not that I didn't like it!" Lacy said, worried she'd hurt its feelings. "I'm sure this was very good too, but I'm not hungry. So why don't you run along back to where you came from?" She stood up and started to walk away, but the robot tottered around to get in her way, still holding the tray.

"I mean it! Go on!"

The robot said nothing but motioned the tray toward her room.

"Gonna tell on me if I don't go back?" She asked.

For a moment, the robot stayed silent, then out of nowhere, let out a deafening alarm.

"All right! All right! I'm going!" She said, and her door opened like it had been listening to their exchange and was waiting for her command.

The robot silenced its alarm and offered the tray again.

Lacy swatted the tray with the little bits of food still clinging to it, out of the robot's hands. "Fine. But don't run off. There isn't much to eat anyway. You can take it back in a sec." She walked into the room and the robot followed behind her. "That wasn't an invitation but, fine. Make yourself comfortable."

The robot walked to the foot of her bed and waited for her to sit down.

"Got a spoon?" She asked the robot, who didn't answer.

Lacy told herself the food was meant to be eaten without utensils in this part of the universe and scooped it up in her fingers, then shot it back like an oyster. This time the smell did nothing to save her from the bad taste. When her tray was cleared, she handed it back to the little robot waiting at her bedside, who took it happily.

The robot beeped twice, then raised an arm in a gesture like a salute towards Lacy.

Lacy, in return, looked at him curiously. "What's that?" She asked.

The robot dropped its arm and looked back at Lacy blankly.

"You got a name, little guy?" Lacy asked.

Again, the robot beeped twice.

"Well, I'm not calling you beep-beep."

The robot shook its body as a whole and waved its hands, unintentionally letting small bits of food fly off the plate. It then pointed to the top of its chest, where Lacy noticed three horizontal slits were clogged with the food she spilled onto him.

"Oh, golly!" She exclaimed and dropped to her knees to dig out the crud. "I'm sorry, is this your speaker?"

The robot gave a short beep in reply, which Lacy took as a yes.

"All right there. Not perfect, but feeling any better?"

Instead of a reply, the robot stepped back a few inches and a panel just below the speaker popped open. The gears and circuitry were all afuddle with gunks and bits of wet food.

Lacy knew where she was. She was captive on a transport ship of a more than likely, malicious empire, being taken to her death. She could trust no one on this ship and should take any chance she could to escape. *But...*she thought, *this wasn't someone.* This was a robot. Programmed to act a certain way. Maybe it could be re-programmed. Back on Earth, robotics was only just starting to blossom into something not just exciting, but reliable. The technology of this world was all alien, literally, to Lacy. But at the end of the day, wasn't it just another computer? If she could tend to the *Silent Horizon*'s technological needs, she could tend to her new soon-to-be companion too.

"Okay little guy, this might take a bit. I'm gonna shut you down but I promise you'll be back to your old self in no time." Lacy held out a hand to shake.

The robot looked at her hand, processed what to do next, and went with its first guess. It handed her back the tray.

7. Creatures of the Nebula

Korr had laid out a fresh set of clothes for Dex on his bunk in the Silent Horizon. Beside them, folded up with the helmets on top were the scarlet P.E.S.s. Dex would have felt more comfortable wearing either those, or his own uniform, but reason told him if they were going out in public, it'd be safe to blend in.

After a quick shower and shave, Dex dressed himself in the loose-fitting, long-sleeved blue shirt and the black pants with a yellow strip down the side, that Korr had left for him. He then tucked his pants into his new boots, also courtesy of Korr.

After getting dressed, Dex removed the belt and holster from his P.E.S. and wrapped them around himself. Then, for what he'd come back to the ship in the first place, he opened the storage container to grab his blaster. As he reached for the blaster, he noticed something else further back. Dex paused for a moment, then grabbed the bottle of wine he and Lacy had been saving to celebrate a successful mission.

For a moment, the world around him went silent. The bustle of robots working in the hangar outside his ship no longer existed to him.

Dex sat in the Captain's seat and stared at the label. He and Lacy had gone to the commissary together strictly as teammates the night before their flight out from "Grand Central" Space Station. Lacy wanted to go for the most expensive bottle they could find, given that they wouldn't have any other expenses for the foreseeable future, but Dex assured her that by the time they finally drank it, it wouldn't matter to them how expensive it was. When they got to the register, Dex gave a few quick glances around like he'd lost something.

"Everything okay, Captain?" Lacy asked.

"Yeah...hold on." Dex checked his pockets like he was looking for his wallet. "Hold on one second, I think I forgot something." Without letting Lacy get a word in, Dex jogged back into the aisles.

Lacy stood alone at the automated register in confusion, as the machine repeatedly asked her for payment.

In less than a minute, Dex had returned with a second bottle of wine. "Most expensive one on the shelf." He said with a smile and scanned it through the register.

"If you're this indecisive, sir, maybe they should have picked someone else to lead this mission." She said with a laugh.

Dex pulled out his military ID for the register to place the charge in his name. "You'd really want to kick me off the mission over a bottle of wine?" He asked playfully.

"Of course not! I was thinking more along the lines of swapping roles. I'll be the captain, and you take a demotion." Lacy said as they stepped out of the commissary, into the large concourse that circled the station.

Dex's eyes widened in feigned surprise.

"Only in responsibility, not pay. Don't worry."

"Well I'll have you know, this wasn't indecision at all. That first bottle is still for if we find a new world."

"When," Lacy interjected.

"Sure. *When* we find a new world. This bottle is for something else."

"Oh?" She stopped.

"At the risk of making this mission terribly uncomfortable... what are you doing tonight?"

Lacy lost her breath and almost dropped the cheap wine she was holding. "Golly, I mean, Dex...Captain!" She corrected herself quickly. "Don't you think...tomorrow being the mission..."

"I think," he cut her off, "tomorrow being the mission, why waste tonight?"

"Hmmm...maybe you're not my type."

He stepped in closer. "Maybe I am." He almost raised a hand under her chin, hoping to tilt her head up for a kiss, but she stepped back.

"I think sir, this is not the time or place for this kind of behavior."

Along the inner wall, the station monorail pulled up and rang a bell to signal the doors were opening.

At the sound of the bell, Lacy grabbed the expensive bottle of wine out of Dex's hand. "Thank you, Captain, but I should really be getting ready for tomorrow," she said and skipped over to the monorail.

"Wait a sec!" He called and followed her. "You can't just take *my* wine too."

She stepped into the car, and when Dex tried to follow she blocked the entrance. "If you want it back…meet me tonight."

Dex took a moment to realize what she had meant, and the doors began to close.

Lacy rushed out the rest of her request. "Twenty hundred! Observati-" The doors cut off the rest, and the monorail rushed off to its next destination.

Dex stood alone, awestruck, and without a single bottle of wine in either hand. But he knew one thing. He had about three hours to get ready.

That night had been magical. Dex didn't know how formally he should have dressed. Although he tried calling Lacy to see what she was thinking, he got no reply and struggled between his formal military wear, decked out with half a decade's worth of awards and ribbons, or something more semi-formal. Or maybe she wouldn't dress formally at all. He ended up going semi-formal to be safe. It was the last time he'd have an opportunity to dress up until they returned home from the mission, and even if Lacy wasn't getting all done up, at least she would still appreciate the effort he put in.

When he arrived at the elevator to the observation deck, he was greeted by a security guard. "Sorry, sir. Deck's closed tonight."

"Oh? I was supposed to meet someone here. Has anyone come by? A woman, maybe half a foot shorter than me?"

"What's your name sir?" The guard had asked politely.

"Captain Dex Prullen."

The security guard stood aside and the elevator door opened. "The room is yours. Like I told the lady, you have another…" he looked down at his watch, "Fifty-two minutes now."

"Thank you," Dex said as he stepped into the elevator. "Make it count!" The guard offered as the doors closed.

The elevator shot up quickly to the observation deck, a large room that marked the highest point of the space station. Most of the station's residents called it the "park," as it was decorated with artificial trees, grass, ponds, automaton birds & squirrels, and walkways. The domed wall and ceilings doubled as both windows and screens, so the view could be changed to one resembling earth on a summer day or night if the residents were feeling homesick. Tonight, as the elevator opened, Dex saw the windows were not just clear but zoomed in to enlarge the sun.

In front of the window, Lacy stood on a picnic blanket with a wine chiller. She was wearing a conservative, deep green dress that ended just below her knees and fell on the edge of her shoulders. Her hair for once was let down from the bun she had to keep it in while on duty, and was now lightly curled, and resting just above her breast. Around her neck, she wore a small, silver magnifying glass necklace. But what caught him still, was the blue of her eyes he'd wanted to fall into since he first met her.

From the moment Dex saw her standing by that window, he knew his life had changed forever. Dex Prullen was in love.

Dex strode towards Lacy, attempting to walk with a semblance of swagger. He hadn't been on a date since they were assigned to Grand Central to prepare for this mission, and even before that, none had stood out as exceptional nights. He'd almost forgotten how to carry himself and hoped that, even though Lacy probably only thought of this as a fun last hoorah before they left the comfort of their solar system, she'd see the sincerity in his heart.

As he approached her, Dex took her hand in his and politely kissed her fingers.

Lacy gave a small giggle.

"Too forward?" Dex asked.

"No," she laughed, "I promise I won't tell Major Haxley."

Dex smiled self-consciously, worried he'd looked like a fool. "You look lovely," he said.

Lacy looked down and pinched the sides of her dress by her thighs and gave a little twirl. "You think? I figured, you know, last night and all…why not dress up a little? And you…Captain…" she said nervously.

"Dex," he politely corrected.

She smiled, "And you, Dex. You look very handsome."

"Thank you." He said with a light, very light, bow.

They both stood there for a moment awkwardly, giggling to try to relieve the tension, until Dex took the lead for the night and held Lacy's hand, walking closer to the window. "It's very lovely out there tonight," he said. "How'd you manage to reserve this place?"

"Oh, I have my ways." She said playfully. "Major Haxley. I spoke with him earlier. He doesn't hold a lot of sway with the station's command, but he knows people who know people."

"And he had it sorted out in just a few hours?"

Lacy pursed her lips and rolled her eyes. "Well…not exactly. We may have been waiting for you to ask for a few weeks now."

Dex gave a confused look.

"The Major and I have known each other since I was in college. He helped me get into this program. A very old friend."

"Huh." Dex's face shifted to suspicion. "I see."

He let his hand drop from Lacy's, then turned and stepped slowly along the window with his hands held behind his back, not so discretely glancing back at her.

"You see what?"

"No no. Don't worry I understand everything now."

Lacy followed.

"Dex what are you-"

"Captain." Dex corrected, but he couldn't hide from Lacy a smile poking through the facade as he said it.

She began to catch on to his game. "Okay, *Captain*. What are you now understanding?"

He stopped, and without turning his body, looked over his shoulder. "Can't say. It's classified." He then began pacing again.

Lacy scrunched her face in annoyance. She stomped after him and pulled him by the shoulder to turn him around. "Captain Prullen if we're supposed to be a team I don't think you should be keeping secrets like this."

"Okay, *Lieutenant*. I see now why I was selected for this mission."

She crossed her arms. "Oh, you do?"

He paced now back towards the picnic blanket. "I'm just here for my good looks aren't I?"

"Excuse me?" Lacy stopped in her tracks.

"You figured, 'Well if I'm gonna be stuck in space with someone for who knows how long, I might as well bring someone…irresistibly attractive.'"

"More like irritably."

"So you convinced Major Haxley to assign me to this mission because you just couldn't bear leaving me behind while you got stuck with some wet rag like…I don't know, Captain Deshaun."

She laughed. "A little off course there, sir."

"But only just a little. So I'm still slightly on, right?"

Lacy stepped closer. They were both brightly illuminated by the blazing sun just outside the window, but still, the brightest thing in the room to Dex was her eyes.

"Well, I can't say I picked you for the mission. But don't think they didn't take our preferences into account."

He stepped an inch closer. "So I am your type then? And this isn't just a fun night before we sail into the unknown?"

She stepped in and tilted her head up. Lightly, she said, "It doesn't have to be, Dex."

Dex held her cheek in his right hand and placed his left on her side. "Then I'll be sure not to waste it, Lacy."

At that moment the universe filled with miraculous sights. The sun let out a solar flare, and an asteroid shot straight through its loop. Many people made a wish on that shooting star. On Earth, a new robotic design was completed that would soon change the face of the planet. Deep in the furthest reaches of the universe, a star collapsed and formed into a black hole. But in the observation deck of the "Grand Central" Space Station, the only event that mattered in the whole universe to Dex and Lacy was that first kiss they shared.

They sat for the rest of the night on the blanket, drinking their cheap wine and making predictions of what they would find beyond the stars. Dex made a promise that night, unspoken, that no matter what the mission demanded, nothing would ever happen to

Lacy.

* * *

Dex sat alone at the console, with the (*now overpriced*, Dex told himself) bottle of wine he'd bought the night of their first, and only real, date. His face was red with heartbreak for Lacy and anger towards their captors. All he wanted to do was smash the bottle against the console and scream out all the hatred he felt towards the things that stole his wife away. But Lacy wouldn't want that. He knew if it was her in his position, she'd pull herself together and carry on. Whether that meant going after him or flying back to Earth to report what happened, she'd carry on.

Dex wiped a single tear away, the only one that managed to escape, and stood. He placed the bottle back in the cupboard where it belonged, grabbed his blaster, holstered it, and exited the ship.

When he stepped off, a junkyard bot approached him. "Korr would like to speak with you. It's safer on the bridge."

"Safer?" Dex asked. He assumed he'd have at least a little while longer before the Empire caught up with them if they ever did at all.

He followed the robot out of the hanger, down a series of hallways, and up a short elevator to the bridge.

The room was large, about three hundred square feet, with rows of computers and empty seats along its walls. The front viewport, Dex could tell, wasn't a window at all, but a screen. Through it, he saw they were flying through dark clouds of green and purple. Asteroids floated by them, and every so often, lightning stuck and boomed through the ship. And in the front of the room, was a large, makeshift terminal, connected by wires taped to the floor and ceiling, leading to the computers surrounding the room. Korr Montori sat at the terminal, with his hands broken up into their cybernetic counterparts, speeding rapidly from one gear, lever, or keyboard, to the next. Though Dex couldn't see from where he stood, Korr's eyes were rolled towards the back of his head, deep in concentration flying the ship.

Dex's escort left the two of them alone, and as the door shut,

Korr asked, "Like the work we did on your ship?"

Dex walked towards Korr. "I'm very much appreciative, Korr. I thought when I crashed I'd be spending the next week doing repairs."

"Well, repairs aren't all my boys did. Come on, take a seat."

Dex looked to the wall of computers and grabbed the first chair closest to him, dragging it over to Korr's terminal. When he sat, he asked, "What do you mean?"

"Remember I said your ship seemed a little outdated?"

Dex nodded. Lightning flashed and thunder boomed outside.

"We're still headed for Reechi, but we did what we could. Those patches on your hull are more durable than whatever it is you had before, and we had to completely rewire your antenna. So that should have a bit of a stronger signal too now."

"Wow…thank you Korr!" Dex could almost hug the cyborg but didn't want to interfere with his steering.

"There was one other thing. I'm not sure why, maybe it's just a cultural thing wherever you come from, but there wasn't any weaponry on your ship."

"Well, we weren't searching for a fight. We set out to find new unexplored worlds. From our satellites and telescopes, we found nothing to suggest…well…THIS!"

Korr gave Dex a look to say, *are you kidding me?* "Well congrats, we installed what we could. It's not much but if you've got someone tailing you, you'll at least have some defenses."

"And what if I'm the one tailing someone?"

"I wouldn't recommend going on the offense against the Zar-Meck starfighters. Especially in a ship like yours."

Dex sat back in his chair. He knew Korr was right but was still annoyed. It was one more obstacle in the way of getting Lacy back. "If I can't attack them head-on, how am I supposed to get her back at all?"

"You want my advice?"

Dex nodded again.

"My advice is you don't. Turn tail and go home."

Dex's blood started to boil at the suggestion but tried not to let it show.

"But I know that's not what you're going to do, so next best I guess. Here's what I recommend. When we get to Reechi, I'll set you up with a guy I know who can get you a better engine. One capable of hitting just past hyper speed. I'll make you up some credentials before we get there to help you blend."

"What about my ship? If I'm going to the Empire home world, won't they scan my ship? They'll shoot me on sight, or take me prisoner!"

"Most likely," Korr said plainly. As he did, the ship gave a jolt. Dex grabbed onto the terminal for stability. "Don't worry, probably just some baby jrahk-birds. Anyway, remember how I said I get by because this ship doesn't exist? You'll have to cloak your ship, which, you're welcome. Taken care of."

"How's that?"

"You pretend you're someone else. Empire checks for clearance codes on every spacecraft. I have a team that scans Empire frequencies for working, low-profile codes. There aren't many but we make it work. I'm sure I can spare one or two for you."

"Fair enough, thanks," Dex said. "Guessing I gotta work it out myself from there?"

Korr shrugged. The ship shook again, this time harder.

"You said that's a baby…whatever?" Dex asked, gripping tightly to the console. "What happens if we come in contact with a fully grown one?"

"We won't," Korr said matter-of-factly. "The older they get, the lazier. Children take care of the hunting, while the parents sleep in larger asteroids."

"What do they eat?"

"Mostly small organisms. This nebula is filled with plenty of little creatures. But ships they usually leave alone. I travel through here all the time. Never had any real problem with them. The trouble is the nebula messes with the ship's internal computers. That's why I gotta be up here. Even my bots down there have a habit of going haywire sometimes." Another thud, again, tougher than the last. "Jeez, these guys are really annoying today."

Above them, they heard light thumping.

"Is that…" Dex began. "Yeah, it's climbing on the hull.

Weird."

Dex sank in his seat. "Korr?" He asked.

"Yeah?"

The baby jrahk-bird began scratching at the hull.

"How often do you travel through here…with non-robot passengers?"

The realization slowly hit Korr Montori. After years of pirating, traveling through the nebula had become just another thing with no second thought. When he set the course for Reechi with Dex, he played it out like any other trip.

The scratching became more violent until the jrahk-bird began outright clawing away at the hull.

"All right, it's just a baby!" Korr told himself nervously. "Hold on Dex, might knock into a few asteroids here!" Dex did as he was told, and Korr's mechanical thumb extended to hold down a button on the console. "Listen up guys!" Korr's voice boomed through a speaker across the ship. "Secure yourselves, it's gonna get a little wild in here and I don't want to have to scrap you later!" Korr lifted his finger off the bottom.

"Anything I can do Korr?" Dex spoke through shaky vocals. The ship had picked up speed, and they saw asteroids coming out of the clouds at a deadly rate The sounds of asteroids bouncing off the hull rang through the ship.

"I don't think so, buddy. Don't worry we'll be fine!"

As Korr spoke, a harsh scratching sound like claws on the world's largest chalkboard pierced their ears.

"On second thought! Get on the guns!"

Dex shot his head around to all the surrounding computers.

"Upstairs!" Korr shouted through another screeching. "Down the hallway, on the right about thirty feet down. Climb up!"

Dex was on his feet and rushed out of the bridge without wasting a moment. He climbed the stairs Korr mentioned and found himself standing on the ship's hull, in a long domed hallway, that ran around the middle circumference of the ship. It was through the dome he saw the jrahk-bird, clawing its way through the hull, throwing metal scraps out into the nebula.

Nothing about this creature said "baby." The jrahk-bird was

massive, nearly forty feet from the end of its tail to its hawk-like beak. Out of its back were two sets of wings, the larger ones in front had a wingspan that tripled that of the creature's length. The second was half the size of the first, that branched off into another pair of clawed hands at its forearm.

It had no legs, but huge talons where the legs should have been, and the base of its tail was armed with a barbed stinger.

Dex, at seeing the beast, was frightened.

Along the wall of the dome, about every five feet were large turrets, with double-barrel heavy laser guns and muzzles sticking out just past the wall. Dex ran to the one closest to the creature, grabbed the trigger, and after firing once at the jrahk-bird, was thrown to the ground by the recoil.

The shot was missed but it was enough to get the bird's attention. It stopped clawing and looked at him, then began to climb.

Dex rushed back to the turret, fixed his footing, and aimed for the jrahk-bird's chest. With a loud blast, Dex was nearly thrown off his feet again but managed to hold on and watch the impact of the twin blasters. They failed to penetrate the jrahk-bird's hide but the damage was done. Dex saw the blast ripple and burn holes into the beast.

The jrahk-bird regained its grip on the ship and charged towards Dex.

Just then the ship rotated hard to starboard. Dex held his ground, as best he could. He watched as an asteroid rolled across the hull into the jrahk-bird, crushing its larger left wing. The bird screeched in pain.

A weak spot, Dex thought. He rotated the turret to the injured wing and fired a third time.

The blaster bolts seared straight through the wings and sailed into the nebula, disappearing quickly into the gasses.

"Yes!" Dex shouted in triumph. "Not gonna be on the menu today you big dumb bird!"

The jrahk-bird gave Dex a discernible evil eye and pushed itself off the hull, flying into the nebula.

Over a speaker, Dex heard Korr's voice. "Nice shot!"

Dex looked around for a terminal to speak into.

"Don't worry about it," Korr's voice said. I can see and hear you through the camera feed. Listen, there's a strap just below the turret. These things are meant for the Zar-Mecks with stronger footing. Straps should help a bit."

"But it's gone! I got it!"

Back by the ladder, some of the smaller junkyard bots began climbing up and arming themselves against the wall.

"I got it, didn't I?"

"You got that one, but mommy's gonna be pissed when her baby comes home with a busted wing."

Above them, a shadow nearly four times as big as the baby jrahk-bird flew past them. The small bots hanging on to the turrets did what they could to aim upwards.

"Korr please tell me we're almost out of this damn nebula."

"Got a little ways to go still, Dex."

Dex took a deep breath and said to himself, "Don't worry Lacy, I'm still comin'."

The shadow passed over them again, this time headed to the rear of the ship. The beast was stalking its prey.

Just then, the bird crashed down on the rear of the ship. Nearly all of the bots were thrown off their guns, and Dex was tossed up into the ceiling, and then crashed down hard on the floor. The wind was knocked out of him and he struggled to regain his breath. From behind, one of the bots helped him to his feet, then placed Dex's hands on the turret, before patting his arm in a "good luck" gesture.

Dex tried to turn the turret, but the bird was too far down for him to get a good shot.

The bots down the line were all firing at rapid rates to get the bird off their ship. But they, like Dex, were not Zar-Mecks and with every blast, when one bot was thrown off the canon, another would take its place.

The jrahk-bird took the blaster bolts in stride, and with one swipe of its claw, demolished the rear of the gunner's line dome, as well as a good chunk of the hull.

"Dex!" Korr screamed over the speaker. "Dex get down here!"

Seeing no other option, Dex did as he was commanded. He

ran back to the ladder and watched asteroids fly by, slamming into the jrahk-bird and bouncing off like rubber balls.

Climbing through the shaft, Dex heard the screeching of the creature as it tore its way through the bots.

Back on the bridge, Korr was doing all he could to avoid the asteroids in his massive ship and shake off the jrahk-bird.

Dex ran up behind him. "What else can we do? Your firepower is useless against that thing!"

"It's not useless!" Korr shouted back in frustration(at the situation, not Dex). "I just don't have enough hands!" Korr dove the ship downwards, avoiding a large asteroid."

"Wait a sec…" Dex said quietly.

Korr rotated to port, and lightning flashed across the screen.

"I have an idea!" Dex shouted and jogged back to the hallway. "Just give me cover! I'll distract it!"

"Dex! Dex wait!" Korr shouted after him. But it was too late. Dex was running back down to the hanger.

From the moment Dex was in his old Captain's seat, he felt like he'd never left. The ship powered up smoothly, and with the assistance of one of the junkyard bots, Dex flew out of the hanger.

The controls felt smoother in his hand than before. Though he'd been piloting it for over a year, he'd never flown in conditions like this, with such sharp turns needed at a moment's notice. He turned the ship upwards towards where the jrahk-bird was attacking and when it was in his sights, aimed for the beast's wing. It was raised to send another blow to the hull. Dex pushed the speed as hard as he could without losing steering and shot the *Silent Horizon* through the wing. It cut through like paper.

The jrahk-bird let out a howling screech and refocused its attention on Dex's ship. With a leap, it gave chase.

Korr radioed in to the *Silent Horizon*. "Dex! What are you doing?"

"It's me it wants right?"

There was a pause.

"Right?" Dex asked again as he swerved his ship this way and that, always just barely missing a bite from the jrahk-bird's mighty beak.

"Dex I can't let you sacrifice yourself! This is my fault, getting you into this!"

"You think this is a sacrifice?" Dex asked. He didn't realize it, but he was smiling now. "I got a wife to get back to. To hell with dying!" Dex piloted the ship through a donut-shaped asteroid. The jrahk-bird crashed into it, trying to squeeze through, but it was too big, crawled around it, and continued its pursuit.

"Listen, Korr, I need you to try to get under me. When I say, pull up. And HARD!"

"Ok. Got it!"

Dex zipped from asteroid to asteroid, hoping their crashing into the bird would slow it down or weaken it, but the beast was too strong and gained on him. When the jrahk-bird was right on top of him, Dex finally saw what he had been hoping for.

"See that asteroid up ahead?" Dex asked into the radio.

"Asteroid? Dex, that's a moon!"

"Okay, so you see what I'm talking about, good!" The *Silent Horizon* jolted forward. "Jeez, I just got this thing fixed!" Knowing it might cost either him, Korr, or both of them, their lives, Dex pushed the engine so hard he lost any maneuverability with the ship and forced whatever angle of descent he could. "We're coming up!" The *Silent Horizon* took a small dive and just barely skimmed the surface of the asteroid, with the jrahk-bird following just meters behind.

"NOW!" Dex shouted into the radio, "Do it now!"

Below the beast and the *Silent Horizon*, Korr pulled up hard, and with a crunch that felt like it reverberated through the entire nebula, crushed the jrahk-bird between his ship and the asteroid. The jrahk-bird was ground up hard on its surface, leaving nothing behind but bits of mangled flesh, guts, and bones to drift through space.

Korr and Dex shouted out cheers through their radios. The bots left on the gunner's line gave no cheer. The six or so that hadn't been crushed simply returned to their posts.

8. New Friends

Lacy closed the panel on the small waiter robot's chest. She sat on her bed waiting for any signs of life. It balanced motionless for a moment before she heard its motors begin to hum again.

The robot looked up at her.

"So," she began. "Let's try this again. You got a name little guy?"

The robot stared through its small sensors, then looked down at the floor, and up again. "No." It said bluntly in a voice that teetered the line between robotic and organic.

Lacy was shocked at the realization her efforts pulled off. "Ha! You can talk!"

The robot said nothing but continued to stare.

"Okay, well, you need to have a name. What do you think? What should we call you?"

The robot looked around the room, presumably in inspiration. After a moment, it gave up and shrugged its arms.

"Hmmmm. How about…" Lacy thought. "Flash?" She asked. All that came to her head was the conversation she'd had with the Analyst, but then a sci-fi film popped in that she'd reluctantly seen with her college friends years ago. "Or what about Gort? No that's a silly name."

The robot started to lean to one side as if he were either bored or confused.

Lacy jumped. "I got it! Robbie!"

The robot perched itself straight upwards again.

"You like that one, Robbie?"

"It will do," replied Robbie, the robot.

Lacy stood. "Great! Robbie, it's nice to meet you. My name is Lacy. Lacy Prullen, and soon you'll meet my husband Dex. Now, how about we get out of here?" She started to walk to the door, only to be cut off by Robbie, who shooed her away with his arms up. "What's the matter?"

"You're not supposed to leave," Robbie said.

"I know I'm not *supposed* to, but I'm going to anyway. And you're coming with me!"

Robbie shook his whole body this time.

"Error. No. Wrong. My duty is in the ship's kitchen. Your duty is here."

Lacy put her hands on her hips. "My duty is *not* in here. My duty is with my own ship with my husband Dex. Now are you coming along or not?"

Robbie raised his claw to his chin, mimicking a pondering look.

Lacy looked down at him, tapping her foot to show her growing impatience.

"You gave me a name," Robbie said.

"What?" Lacy asked.

Robbie stepped a little closer. In his short existence, he had only ever been assigned to the transport ship, delivering meals. Before meeting Lacy, he hadn't even been a 'he,' he'd been an 'it.' His orders at all times were, "Bring this to so and so" or "Deliver this to room whatever." Not once in his memory bank could Robbie remember a, "Would you *please* bring this to so and so," or "Do you have the time to deliver this to room whatever." It had never registered until now, Robbie had never been asked to choose for himself. "You gave me a name," was all he said, as he reached out both claws and held Lacy's hand.

Lacy kneeled to meet Robbie at his level. "Your call buddy. Wanna tag along? I don't think I can find my way out of here alone."

Robbie stayed silent and stepped towards the dirty food tray that lay next to Lacy's bed and picked it up. His old programming told him to take the tray and return to the kitchen to wait for the next meal. The thing was, it wasn't pushing him anymore. He felt no drive to do as his programming told him. With the tray in his hand, he shuffled over to Lacy. "Escape pods are three levels up."

Lacy beamed. "You're coming?!" She shouted with excitement and hugged Robbie. Knowing he was her only chance to escape, she thanked him.

"We will have to ask permission from one of the Bridge Officers. I'll show you to the bridge." Robbie stepped into the hallway and took a sharp left, followed closely by Lacy.

"Hold on Robbie, if we go to the bridge they'll know we're trying to leave!"

"Correct. But, escape pod bays are locked unless there is an emergency, so we will need permissions."

"Robbie, hold on."

Robbie stopped and turned around.

"Listen, these people can't know we're leaving. Got that? We're prisoners here, they don't want us to leave. So we gotta be real sneaky."

"If they won't allow us through, we cannot go. The bays will be locked."

Lacy looked around the curved white hallway they stood in, hoping for an idea to come to her. She was lucky to get a small robot to deliver her food, but if any of the Zar-Mecks had been around or seen her now, she'd be back to square one.

"You said they open for emergencies right?"

Robbie nodded.

"How extreme does it have to be?"

Robbie said nothing but tilted his head to the side.

Lacy sighed and kneeled.

"If there's a fire in my room, would they open the escape pod bays?"

For his answer, Robbie's left claw over extended outward revealing tubing that, Lacy presumed, flowed up his arm. With the claws extended, a puff of CO_2 shot out.

"Great. I've got a mobile fire extinguisher."

At the remark, Robbie shifted the tray to his left hand and over-extended his right claw outwards to reveal the same-sized hole. This time, a flame shot out nearly four inches.

"Okay, that's not too bad. Any other tricks I should know about going forward?"

Robbie thought hard, wanting to live this first day of freedom to the fullest. For once he could put his gadgets to good use, be creative, and try new things. He could explore tools he'd never tried before. This was his moment to show he could be his own robot. Robbie put the tray down gently and then shuffled a few inches back from Lacy. Slowly, he rested his claws on the floor and began shifting his weight towards them, more and more until…

"Wow…" Lacy said, unsure how she should react. "A handstand…neat." The confusion and lack of enthusiasm were clear in her voice.

Robbie lost his balance and fell to the ground with a loud crash reverberating through the empty hallway. "Was that a trick?"

She couldn't help herself. Lacy let out a small laugh at his eager question. "Yes, Robbie, I guess it's a very good trick. But I don't think it will help us very much."

Robbie re-oriented himself and let out a small sad whine.

"At least not right now!" She saved herself from hurting his feelings. "But maybe later, you can show it off to everyone and they'll all really love it."

Robbie clasped his claw hands together in excitement. "I also have this!" He spread out his hands and the once blocky claws extended out their tips into sharp inch-long knives. "Sometimes the cargo I am assigned to deliver food to gets aggressive."

Lacy's eyes were wide in surprise. "Well…glad you didn't think I was…aggressive."

The knives retracted. "You were. But I couldn't see."

Lacy stood up. "Uh huh…well, little guy-"

"Robbie," he corrected.

"Well, *Robbie*, I think I've got a plan to set off the alarms. Do you think anyone would suspect anything if you went back to the kitchen now?"

"No," Robbie said bluntly.

"Okay great! Think you could head back there to grab me something quick?"

Robbie sat silent for three seconds, processing. "If it's small."

"Wonderful. Do you know what propane is?"

Robbie shot his body to say no.

"Damn. Okay, when they cook in there, they use gas to fuel

the fire yeah?"

Robbie nodded.

"What I need from you is a canister of that stuff, propane, as we call it. Bring it back here and we'll blow a hole in the hull."

Robbie grabbed his tray and stepped back quickly in shock. "I think we need permission for that too," he said.

Lacy couldn't help but smile. "Robbie, no more asking permission. This is what we have to do. Don't worry, we'll be safe about it."

If Robbie had more than one eye, he would have raised one of his eyebrows to tell her how strange that sounded. But who was he to disagree? She had just granted him his freedom and in his programming, he'd do what she asked. "Okay. I'll be back in a minute." Without any pleasantries, Robbie waddled away down the hall towards the kitchen. "But I think it's a strange idea!" He shouted back down to her.

With Robbie occupied, Lacy decided the best course of action would be to scope out the path they would take to get to the escape pod bay. Robbie had said it was three floors up, but that wasn't much to work with. Within the context of first seeing the transport, and how tall the rooms were on her floor, she assumed it couldn't be less than fifteen stories high. Twenty at most. But it was wider than it was tall. She knew she was in the lower half of the ship, and if it curved upwards towards the center, then three floors up would probably put the bays along the outer perimeter of the ship. And for all she knew, Robbie might only have referenced the closest ones. Based on what he said, she'd have plenty of ground to cover and try not to lose her bearings, without straying too far from her little friend.

She stepped off again the way Robbie had been leading her. After about thirty feet, nothing. She began to jog. Another forty or fifty feet, still nothing. She ran. She ran as fast as she could, but no matter how far she ran she remained in the same empty white hallway.

Her heart began to race. She was trapped. *I can't get out. There's no way out!* Her thoughts screamed.

Just then she heard a screeching down the opposite end of the hallway.

"Robbie?" She called.

The screeching continued but it was muted by the sound of…

"Blasters," Lacy spoke the words out loud. She ran back to help Robbie. "I'm coming! I'm over here!"

The sounds of Robbie's running and Zar-Meck blaster fire grew louder. When he rushed into view, Robbie came dragging a massive propane tank behind him that was scratching up the floor! Before she could say anything, a blaster bolt zoomed past Lacy's head. She dived to the ground, Robbie shooting past her, and saw three of the Zar-Mecks following behind.

"PRISONER! GO BACK TO YOUR ROOM!" Shouted one of the Zar-Mecks.

Lacy had spent too much time in captivity, especially being bossed around by those things. She jumped to her feet and dashed after her friend.

"Robbie!" She shouted.

"You wanted this!" Robbie shouted back without stopping. "I don't know what to do next! We passed your room!"

"Forget my room! Toss it in another!" Another bolt grazed her hair but continued past her.

As he waddle-ran, Robbie unscrewed the canister to let out a small hiss of gas. He then stopped at the first door that opened for him as Lacy ran past. The room was empty, and Robbie had no moral dilemma tossing it where it wouldn't hurt anyone. As soon as it was out of his hand, he raced to catch up with Lacy.

Lacy stopped and turned when she heard the metal clanging. "Light it!"

"Oh right!" Robbie said and turned quickly to go back to the room. But it was too late, the Zar-Mecks were in his way.

"HALT SERVICE BOT"

Lacy stopped running at a point in the hallway where the curvature shielded her, and listened. At that moment she believed her plan had been compromised.

Robbie didn't feel the same way. This was still his first day with free will, and he didn't want to give it up that easily. His left claw extended and he sprayed out a thick cloud of CO_2, then dashed away before the Zar-Mecks knew what happened.

With the Zar-Mecks distracted, Robbie was able to make it back to the room, overextended his right claw, and set alight the gas that had leaked out. He then quickly shut the door and raced back towards Lacy.

Reaching her, he shoved Lacy as hard as he could through the door she didn't know she was leaning up against. As the door shut, he told her, "That wasn't fun."

Then the blast came.

The transport shook momentarily, but on the other side of the door, Lacy and Robbie could hear air rushing through the hallway, out into space.

"Think that's enough to open the bays?" Lacy asked.

"Only if we get there soon enough." Robbie put his claw up against the wall of the small room they were in, and a faint blue line rippled outwards. They began to ascend. Lacy thought about the three Zar-Mecks being sucked out into space. She knew it was unlikely, but she prayed to God that they were the same three that had captured her and Dex. As she prayed, the ship's alarms went off.

"HULL BREACH." A speaker boomed through the elevator, and presumably, the whole ship.

Lacy looked down at Robbie. "You ready for real freedom?" She asked.

Robbie clapped his claws together as he jumped up and down in excitement.

"Yeah, me too buddy." She said softly.

The elevator doors opened on a similar hallway, but this time, the far wall was littered with windows facing out into space. This time looking out, she had lost all interest in what mysteries it held. She resented the possibilities that lay outside the window and wanted just for this mission to end. "Come on," she said to Robbie. "Let's get to those pod bays."

As she began to step off, Robbie held an arm out blocking her, then touched the wall to close the elevator door, and held his hand there.

"Hey, what the he-" she began but Robbie cut her off.

"Shh." He said quietly.

Outside the elevator door, they heard footsteps drawing near, and stopped outside the elevator. Whomever it was, began tapping vigorously on the wall outside, trying to call the elevator.

"Blast," an organic voice said. "Elevator must be busted. Try the next one!" The footsteps resumed and whoever it was, now ran away.

Lacy looked down at Robbie. A chill ran down her spine at the thought that they were about to be found, but Robbie was shaking hard.

"You okay little buddy?" She asked.

"If they catch you, you go back to being a prisoner. If they catch me…I get shut down."

Lacy was silent. She gave the robot freedom but hadn't considered what it meant for him if she screwed up.

When the footsteps sounded far enough away, Robbie took his claw off the wall and the elevator door opened. "This way," he said and turned left. "They should be just overrrrr…here!" He stopped and a door opened to a room littered with cylindrical pods hanging from the ceiling. "This is it!"

Robbie rushed to the first pod. It opened for him as he approached. Since it hung down to about a foot off the ground, Robbie struggled to pull himself up into it, but once in, quickly found himself comfortable in one of the escape pod's seats.

Lacy smiled at the little robot. She was ready to feel the same sense of freedom he'd had since coming into her life.

"Well done Ms. Prullen." A cold voice sounded from behind one of the pods, and the Analyst stepped into view. "Please, by all means, step into the pod." He gestured towards the pod Robbie sat in.

Short-lived freedom.

Robbie jumped out of his seat and stood at the pod's portal to see what was going on.

"Robbie burn him!" Lacy commanded.

Robbie's right claw opened up, but the Analyst calmly held out his hand. "There's no need. Robot," he directed his attention to Robbie. "Code 1-9-5-5."

Robbie's claw closed.

"You may have your escape." The analyst said to Lacy. "I

won't stop you but I'll tell you now, it won't last."

Lacy backed away towards the door, but it wouldn't open behind her.

"If a crew abandons its ship, there's only one destination programmed into the pods. So really, you'd just make a slower trip to the destination you're already headed to." The Analyst drew closer.

"You're wrong," Lacy said sternly. *I'll re-route it*, she thought to herself. "Nothing in the universe will bring me an inch closer to your dictator!"

The Analyst chuckled as he closed the distance between them. "Let's just pretend you managed to divert course. Where would you go? Home? Back to your planet Earth? You'd die of starvation before reaching it. Or! Maybe one of the empire's planets? They'd turn you in in a heartbeat. You have nowhere to run."

They were merely inches apart from each other, with Lacy up against the wall looking up at the Analyst. "Dex will find me."

Without hesitation, the Analyst said smugly, "A dead man would have a hard time finding anyone."

Lacy wanted to scream and beat his face in, but she choked. She felt tears coming and held them back. "You lie!"

"I'd be happy to show you the security footage. His escape failed. His body splattered into a million pieces against the surface of our outpost. Now, do you think anyone will come? The choice is yours." The Analyst stepped aside and motioned towards the pod.

Lacy took a single step forward. *He can't be dead. I know he can't...but if he is.* Lacy was frozen. For a moment in time, she truly believed all was lost. If Dex was truly gone, why should she keep fighting? She could live without Earth. She could live without any form of civilization, for what it was worth. But she couldn't live without Dex. If he was gone, *maybe it was time to give up.* The thought came and went in a flash. *Dex wouldn't give up like that, he'd fight for me even if I'd died!* She stepped off towards the pod, but a hand grabbed her wrist.

"As I thought. You seem to have some senses at least." The Analyst said. "We've really got a lot to learn about your species." Lacy tried to pull away but the Analyst was too strong. She knew she'd be beaten and any moment now, if they weren't already, more of the

Zar-Mecks would be closing in on her. If she couldn't have her freedom today, at least one person could. "Robbie go!" Robbie leaned out of the pod and reached for his friend, "But Lacy!"

"Just go! Be free!" Lacy yelled as she fought against the strength of the analyst. With her free hand, she punched the Analyst square in the face.

His skin began to radiate yellow but his grip on her held tight.

"Lacy! Come on!" Robbie yelled.

"Get out of here!" Lacy called after him. The door to the hallway opened and Zar-Mecks began pouring in, surrounding Lacy and the analyst.

Robbie wanted to fight. Doing as he was told again made him feel like he was back to being just another soulless robot. But he knew the battle was lost. The defeat was taken harder than Lacy would have realized, but he closed the pod door and ejected into space.

As the Zar-Mecks closed in on her, Lacy watched Robbie's escape pod be sucked into the ceiling, then with a *pop*, sent into space. She stopped fighting, and let herself be taken prisoner again. At least you've got your freedom, little buddy, she told herself for comfort.

9. Reechi

The rest of Dex and Korr's journey through the nebula continued without hindrance. While Korr's robots did repairs to the hull, Dex slept in his bunk on the *Silent Horizon* in the hanger bay.

He dreamed of Lacy. He dreamed of them floating together in space. Lacy's head was tucked into his chest, his arms wrapped around her as he kissed her forehead. There were no sounds, just the beauty of space and the distant stars illuminating them. Lacy looked up into his eyes and spoke, but the words were incomprehensible. He knew she was speaking, but her mouth didn't match what his mind knew she was saying, but he could sense fear in her. Dex held her at a distance, trying to ask what she meant but his voice couldn't escape his lips. A cold presence came over him and they were both gripped by a large hand. Dex and Lacy were spun around, and his entire field of view was engulfed by scarlet. No discernible features could be made out, but the being they stared at seemed to be constantly changing shape, staring at them with infinite eyes, probing them from all directions. No longer were they in space but in a vast, barren, murky brown world. A voice boomed and shattered his mind. Dex felt his soul escape him and flee toward the being. As it did, his insides were lit on fire. His eyes and brain melted. Dex screamed but the cries were lost as he fell into a void with walls made of rotting bones that bled and laughed at his suffering.

Dex woke up with cold sweats. The voice of the being from the dream echoed in his mind, but he still couldn't make out any of the words.

The sound of his comms device snapped Dex to attention.

"Dex," Korr's voice spoke through the comm. "If you're awake, come on up to the bridge. We're almost out of the nebula. Wanna figure out a plan for Reechi."

Dex swung his legs off the bed, then was up and rubbed his eyes.

After a moment, Korr called again. "You there? All right, keep sleeping." Dex stood up and walked over to the console to pick up his communicator. "Yeah, I'm up. Be there in a few. How long's it been?" He tossed the communicator on his bunk and started getting dressed.

"You've been out almost three hours. Everybody sleep that long where you're from?" Korr asked with humor in his voice.

Dex's eyes widened in surprise as his head popped out through his shirt collar. He grabbed the comm. "Korr, that ain't even *half* a night's rest where I'm from." He could almost hear Korr's shock from the silence over the comms. Dex laughed to himself. "I'm on my way now." He grabbed his belt with holstered blaster off the opposite bunk as he left his ship.

The bustle of the hanger bay was much calmer now than when he had first stepped into the hanger. Dex assumed Korr had his robots fully staffed on ship repairs.

When Dex arrived back on the bridge, the first thing he noticed was the thickness of the nebula had decreased. Here and there were black spaces, and while there were still plenty of asteroids, they were able to see much further out. Even the sound of thunder was less frequent.

"Good sleep?" Korr asked from his control panel.

Dex walked towards Korr and grabbed a seat next to him. "It's nice to be back in my own bed. But I've felt better."

Korr gave him a look. "So, not a good one then?"

"Just some bad dreams."

Korr's fingers were broken up, messing with a dozen switches and buttons at once, but his attention was focused on Dex. "Tell me about them."

Dex rested his elbow on the console and rested his head in his hand. "I already lost it. Just some…" he paused and thought hard. "Red. All I can remember is red."

Korr eyed him hard. "Red? Just red?"

"Yeah, red. Maybe a bit darker, crimson or scarlet."

Korr sat back in his chair and looked out into the nebula.

"Computer, think you can navigate from here?" An affirmative beep sounded from the console. Korr's mechanical fingers formed back into his normal-looking hands, then he turned to give Dex his full attention. "What you saw, was a vision of the Emperor."

Dex looked confused. "H-...how do you know."

"His empire has little religious imagery. But scarlet is His color. I don't know if you've noticed yet, but you won't be seeing the Emperor's colors anywhere."

Dex scoffed. "You can't just outlaw a color. That's ridiculous!" But he thought back to when he and Lacy were first taken prisoner. The Zar-Mecks had ordered him to remove his P.E.S. because 'none could wear the Emperor's colors.'

"When you're a god, I think you can outlaw whatever you please."

Dex calmed at the remark. "He may be a god here. But not one with a 'capital G.'"

"What does that mean?" Korr asked. "On my planet," Dex began, "we have many gods."

Korr nodded, "Yeah I remember. You said they usually don't come down?"

"Yeah. Well, most of these gods, how do I put this? They don't do a whole lot. They kinda just exist in league with groups of other gods. They've got their own areas of expertise and report to higher-ups. Gods with a 'capital G,' or titans."

"And which ones come down to your people?"

Dex leaned back. "Well, none of those little G's have come down to *my* people. But there is one that most people accepted. Now that one's a God with a capital G. He runs the whole show. Doesn't report to anyone higher, and oversees all."

"So in your eyes, our Emperor is a god without a 'capital G?'" Korr asked.

"Buddy I don't think your Emperor is either. As you said, evil is two sides of a coin. I think you've got a demon running your show."

"Not my show. I'm the only one that runs my own. But by the sound of that dream, he might be running yours soon."

"What do you mean?"

Korr spoke gently. "What I'm saying is, the Emperor's looking for you. That dream, vision, whatever you want to call it, he's sending out his signals. If you're not already in his grip, he'll find a way to bring you in. You better keep tight security on that brain of yours, before he locks in."

"Then what happens?"

Korr breathed out deeply. "You'll have to let me know. Do you know how often I've met people like you? People that haven't turned heel at their first chance?" He stood up and walked towards the view screen.

Dex followed after him. "If you don't know, then half the stuff you just said could be nonsense. What are you, tryna scare me away from him? Scary superstitions aren't going to stop me from saving my wife."

Korr stayed facing the screen. "Dex, all I know is the Emperor always gets what he wants. I've done what I can for too many poor souls caught in the Emperor's grasp. They might be saved, but in the end, it just delays their planet's downfall. You may get out of this alive, but your planet's fate is sealed."

Dex put a hand on Korr's shoulder. "I understand." Maybe Korr was just trying to scare him, or maybe he was telling the truth about the extent of the Emperor's power. One thing though was certain to Dex. Korr had spoken from the heart and wanted to help his new friend. "But I don't believe I've doomed my planet. Lacy was always the optimistic one, so maybe that's just her rubbing off on me. She wouldn't let our mistakes destroy our planet. She'd want me to make sure the Empire never found Earth. But I can't do that without Lacy by my side, and there's still a chance for her."

Korr looked at his friend. "I admire your spirit. Maybe one day I'll find a woman like your Lacy."

Dex patted him hard on the back and smiled. "I hope you do Korr."

The skies cleared outside the view screen and in the distance, a small orb appeared.

Dex studied the orb. "Is that it?" He asked.

Korr nodded. "Reechi. Fifth planet of the Empire of the Void." He exhaled. "Guess we'd better start planning. We'll be there within the hour." Then to the screen, he said, "Computer, zoom in on Reechi."

The screen did as it was commanded and the image of the planet blew up so they could see it clearly. Dex's eyes widened in awe.

Reechi was a series of rings, one on top of the other in a more-or-less sphere shape, with a small star in the center. The planet was orbited by a purple moon, a quarter of the size of the planet.

"This can't be real…" Dex said in a hushed tone.

Korr laughed. "Oh, the wonders you'll see in these parts. If it weren't for the Emperor, I think you'd actually like this place."

"How about you send me postcards when Lacy and I get out of here?"

Korr shrugged. "Yeahhh…I don't know what that means."

With his hands on his hips, Dex dropped his head and shook it. He then sighed deeply. "Okay, how about we start planning? What do I need to know?"

"Let's discuss this over a drink." Korr turned to leave the bridge, heading back for the dining area they'd first talked in, and Dex followed. "First things first. This ship doesn't exist, and neither do I. At the first sign of trouble, I'm out. All I'm here for is to get your foot in the door."

They passed through the bridge door and walked through the hall. Dex asked, "And no one's going to question an Empire ship just…hanging out?"

Korr brushed the question away by waving his hand in the air. "I've got the proper codes. They're frauds, but unless we call attention to them, they should go unnoticed. Our biggest issue is you. You look enough like a taouron, but your eyes give it away."

"Taouron?" Dex asked.

Korr stopped, turned around, and gestured to himself. "My kind. You said you're called a human right?"

Dex nodded, and they continued walking.

"By the way, do you glow?" Korr asked.

"I…I don't even know what that's supposed to mean." "We taouron glow when our emotions run high. So try not to get too worked up at any point. It'll be suspicious."

"And my eyes? I feel like that's more of a giveaway. Do you

have contacts I could borrow?"

"I wish. Honestly, the only option I can think of at the moment is a transplant, but we don't have time for it."

"How long would it take?"

Korr stopped again at the threshold of the kitchen. "Are you serious?" He eyed Dex hard.

"If it helps me get back to Lacy."

Korr rolled his eyes and entered the kitchen, walking towards the cabinets with the drinks. Dex took a seat at the table. "Too long," Korr said. "By the time you were ready to see again, your girl would be long gone. For now, we'll just have to hope my guy doesn't pay you much mind. Just keep your head down and hopefully you'll be fine. But if they don't we'll fly back up here and I'll bring you half the distance to the Heart of the Void." As he spoke, Korr warmed up their drinks and joined Dex at the table.

"What if things go south?" Dex asked. "I know, you're out. But how will you get back here?"

"I've been around the block plenty. I'll find a way out."

"And security forces? What am I up against?"

"The Emperor's army patrols every planet. We may run into the Zar-Meck on the ground. If you come into contact with them in flight, you better hope that new engine works."

Dex pursed his lips. "Fantastic."

After a moment of silence, Korr slapped Dex's shoulder and said, "Don't worry. I'm sure all will go well."

"You really think so?" Dex asked, unbelieving.

Without missing a beat, Korr said with a smile. "No. Not a chance in Maoul. But for as stupid as I think your goal is, I admire it, and I hope you succeed."

Dex gently nodded his head. "Well...let's not put this off any longer. Here's to Lacy." He raised his drink in a toast, and Korr joined him.

For the next thirty minutes or so, Dex and Korr prepared the *Silent Horizon*. Korr's bots had filled it with fuel, and Korr input the coordinates for the Heart of the Void. He also ordered his robots to stock up the ship with provisions and new tools to replace the ones lost at the outpost and a few new ones including a jarrmin box and a small personal comm device. Dex checked his blaster's charge. Having never been used, the batter pack was full, and he had two spares.

Korr pointed out to him that he'd be arrested on sight if he was seen with a blaster on his hip. Dex took off his jacket and converted the holster, along with a spare belt, into a gunner's strap on his left side, hanging from his shoulder. With his jacket on, the blaster was totally concealed.

"No open carry," Dex said. "Your Emperor guy would hate America."

"Is that one of your planets?"

"No, it's on earth, but a totally different world."

Korr also advised Dex to keep the scarlet P.E.S. and Zar-Meck suit hidden away, in case his ship is inspected at the port.

"Arrested on sight?" Dex asked.

Korr only nodded.

One of the smaller bots entered the *Silent Horizon*. "Sir," the robot said. "We are approaching the planet. Are you ready to descend?"

"We are," Korr replied.

"Good luck," the robot said, then turned to face Dex. "Don't die." It then promptly left the ship.

Dex took his seat in the captain's chair, and Korr sat in Lacy's. Dex thought it felt wrong, someone else sitting in her seat, but tried to brush it away. It wasn't like he was replacing her.

The engines rumbled and the two of them flew out of the hanger.

As Reechi came into their view, Dex was again taken aback in awe. Small ships flew all around the planet and through it. The surface of the planet's rings was a light brown and had lakes and oceans scattered throughout that sometimes fell off one layer, to the ring below it. Since the rings were constantly shifting, sometimes the water would flow directly into the sun.

Korr told Dex all planet life was maintained on the outside of the rings, while mining was done on the core side. Valuable minerals were Reechi's main export for trade, and though it was incredibly dangerous, the finds on the rings closest to the core made Reechi one of the richest planets in the empire.

Looking out towards the purple moon, Dex saw one of the Empire's ships orbiting it.

"The moon is the military's outpost," Korr told him. "That's a capital ship. Heavy with ground troops, and starfighters."

"Is Reechi expecting war?"

Korr shook his head.

"I think they're just on the lookout." Korr gave Dex a look that filled in the rest.

Dex felt a chill run down his spine. They couldn't know where he was this soon, but he knew this mission just got harder.

Korr used the *Silent Horizon*'s radio to call in their arrival. "Moorak City Port six, requesting landing."

The two men looked at each other as they listened to the radio feedback. Dex was clearly more nervous than his companion, and the looming capital ship did nothing to quell his fears.

After only a moment, a dry-toned voice responds to them. "This is Moorak City Port Control. We don't see any registration on your ship. Maintain your current course. Please identify and send over clearance codes."

"Port Control, I acknowledge. This is a private shuttle, two passengers. You'll find all you request through our clearance codes. Transmitting now." Then to Dex, "Where do I send them from?"

Dex pushed buttons on the computer and turned it over to Korr. "Are the codes on a drive or something?"

Korr pulled out a small, inch-long gold stick, with a small needle on the end. "Can your ship read this?"

"I…I have no idea what that is. Is this all you've got?"

From the computer, "private shuttle, please send over your clearance codes. If you need assistance we will send out a port security officer."

"Damn!" Korr slammed his hand down. "You should have said something!"

"Me? You're the one that had everything worked out! Try your robot…hand…thing!"

Korr looked at his hands and thought.

The port controller spoke again through the radio. "Private shuttle, we are sending someone to assist you."

This time, Dex was the one to jump to action. "Port control, that's not necessary, we are transmitting now." Dex eyed Korr hard to say, get a move on! "We just came out of the nebula and had an issue with a jrahk-bird. Messed with our system a bit."

Korr observed the ship's disc drive and worked to figure out a configuration his hand could take to transmit the data. As he did, Dex waited impatiently for a response from the port control.

The voice came back much warmer with a deep exhale. "I hear that." It said. "Buddy of mine was flying through two weeks ago and they're still working out the kinks in his ship. We'll hold on the assist, hope y'all are doing okay."

Korr figured it out, and using himself as a converter, uploaded the clearance codes onto the ship's computer.

"Oh yeah we're just dandy," Dex said.

Korr shot Dex a confused and somewhat disgruntled look. He quietly shouted "Dandy? What is that? Don't say your weird Earth words!"

"Transmitting the codes now," Dex said, then turned to Korr. "I don't know what is or isn't a word here give me a break!"

They waited for a response. It felt like hours, and Dex could swear the capital ship was headed in their direction. He felt the dead stare from the Zar-Mecks on him. A nagging thought in the back of his mind told him the port control alerted the ship to Dex's presence and any moment now they would be blown out of the sky. He looked over to his companion and saw that even Korr's fists were balled up tightly in fearful anticipation.

The radio sounded again.

"You are clear for landing. Set a course for Port six, Bay twelve. Glory be to Emperor Armourus."

"Glory be," Korr said, and Dex repeated. They both let out a deep sigh and laughed once the radio signal was closed.

"Guess we should have planned a little better," Korr said through a laugh.

"Yeah, next time, I'll make the plan, and you just tell me how we can make it work," Dex said. "Why does the Empire even have these."

"Interplanetary travel is highly restrictive unless you're on

Empire business, or work for the military in some way. Good way to keep an eye on everything."

Dex piloted to their destination, taking directions from Korr. Moorak city was large, covering a huge swath of land, but none of the buildings were very tall. The landscape on this ring was a bland brown, with little vegetation, and rivers broke up most of the city into smaller districts. The streets were packed with citizens, driving around in fancy hover-cars, or cruising above the city in larger yachts. Far off, Dex watched a shuttle launch from the ground, and fly off to another ring.

Dex told him, "That's how a lot of people get from one ring to another. It's the public transportation."

As they touched down in the port bay, the roof closed in over them, sealing them off from the brownish-green sky.

Dex looked over at Korr. He hadn't expected to be sealed in.

"You'll be fine. I'm sure," Korr tried to reassure him, but Dex understood what he meant. No more we, in Korr's words. He'd gotten Dex through and was one step closer to bailing. Dex said nothing in response.

Korr got out of his seat, but Dex stayed. "You coming or what?"

Dex replied, "If we're trying to not get me caught, I was thinking maybe I should stay with the ship."

"Not getting caught means not acting suspicious. Hiding in the ship and not checkin it with the port officials is suspicious. Me hiring a guy to put a new engine in a ship that isn't mine is suspicious. Acting like you belong here isn't. Let's go."

Dex reluctantly stood and followed Korr.

"Let me take the lead," Korr instructed. "My guy is a few blocks from here, so don't-" Dex interrupted.

"Yeah, I know. Don't draw any attention."

They exited the ship and were greeted by a short being. He stood about four feet tall, with thick, hairy arms that reached nearly to the ground. His feet were round like suction cups and uncovered by shoes. The man had a round jaw, and tiny blue eyes on his hugely protruding forehead. Instead of ears, there were two inch-deep holes on either side of his head, with small antennas lining the insides.

Though the man looked like a small beast, he dressed as formally as Dex would expect any public servant to. He spoke with a gruff but polite voice. "Welcome to Moorak City. Identification was transmitted with your codes but due to policy I still have to ask some security questions."

"Happy to oblige," Korr said with a smile.

"Great," the port official said and grabbed a tablet hanging from his belt. "Are you carrying any produce or liquids not approved by Empire customs?

Korr shook his head.

The official typed onto the black tablet. Dex saw nothing on the screen but saw lights reflecting in the official's eyes.

"Are you transporting any unregistered firearms?"

Again Korr shook his head.

The list carried on with the same questions Dex was asked at any customs checkpoint at an Earth airport. After a dozen or so, the official apologized for making them wait and let them proceed.

Dex and Korr left the hanger bay and Dex was at a loss for the number of different species he was seeing.

Korr told him, "There are about two hundred intelligent species living on Reechi. That guy back there is one of the natives, a raestien."

"Interesting," Dex said to himself.

The cries of the city were loud. Hover-cars zoomed by at breakneck speed. The blocks were a mix of sturdy, well-maintained commercial buildings and ramshackle bazaars, with people shouting at each other to buy their wares or taste their foods. Strange scents floated everywhere and crept into Dex's nose. Some were appalling and some were better than anything he'd ever smelled before. Even with the bad, he wanted to try it all and hoped that one day he'd be able to try these foods without being hunted by the Emperor's army.

As they walked through the streets, Dex took in all the strange sights, while trying not to look out of place. He saw all different types of species and made mental notes to ask Korr what each one was if they had time later. The most common species he saw were the raestiens, and by the look of it, they made up most of the working class. In most of the storefronts or restaurants they passed, it was the raestiens that did the serving.

The next largest group of species Dex noticed was the taouron. He couldn't tell if they were held in a higher societal tier than the raestiens, but the trend he saw was their clothes were usually a little more formal than that of the other species. At least, they did by his Earth standard.

With each step, Dex paid less attention to trying to be inconspicuous and soon tripped on a sidewalk. Before he hit the ground, Korr reached out to grab him, but someone else stopped his fall and his blaster fell to the ground.

"Watch where you stepping, citizen." A voice said from behind Dex and pulled him back to his feet.

Dex's eyes widened in shock seeing his blaster fall from the holster and quickly grabbed it back up and slipped it into place. He then turned around to thank the person who saved his fall but went cold and pale at the sight of them.

"Are you feeling okay, sir? Do you need a doctor?" The Zar-Meck asked.

Korr began to back away.

Dex dropped his head a little and looked at the ground. "No sir, I'm fine. Thank you."

The Zar-Meck gave him a once-over. "Mind your step now," he said, then carried on.

A bead of sweat formed on Dex's brow. When he turned to find Korr, he saw him standing more than five feet away. Even though he knew Korr was ready to ditch him, he still felt disappointed. "Don't worry. I know not to give them your name." Dex continued walking without waiting for a response.

They carried on in silence the rest of the way to Korr's connection.

10. Tools from the Empire

Lacy sat in a comfortable armchair in the Analyst's office. He sat in an elegant chair behind the desk that separated them. It had been nearly thirty minutes of him reading from his tablet in silence, and her waiting for him to acknowledge her. She'd tried talking to him when she was escorted in, but no matter what she said, he never so much as looked at her.

At one point, a woman came in carrying a mug of something that smelled to Lacy of cinnamon. The analyst took the mug, thanked her, and she left the room without either of them acknowledging Lacy.

Lacy saw this as a test and decided not to give it. She felt confident in her decision when the Analyst eyed her, then returned to his tablet to type more.

Growing incredibly impatient, Lacy started patting the arms of the chair at a slow, steady pace. The Analyst didn't stir. After a few seconds, she upped the pace and looked around the room nonchalantly. She then noticed the Analyst's eyes twitch the slightest bit like he was beginning to look at her, then changed his mind. *So I do have your attention?* She thought to herself. Lacy slouched in her chair and began to hum a melody of an old popular earth song quietly.

The Analyst didn't move.

Instead of a hum, Lacy began to whistle. *Who isn't annoyed by whistling?* She asked herself.

The Analyst moved again. This time, he didn't stop himself from looking at her. He studied Lacy for a moment.

Lacy stopped and met his gaze. Their eyes were locked. Who would speak first?

Lacy didn't want to lose this battle of wills. Just because she was a prisoner on this ship, didn't mean she had to be a prisoner to him too.

His mouth began to open, but then…he returned to his tablet and smiled.

Frustrated and dropping care as to what would happen to her next, *at least it would be something,* Lacy stood up. She at least expected one of the Zar-Mecks to rush in and throw her back into the chair, but nothing happened. She walked around the office, a large room filled with antiques and murals she didn't understand. Lacy looked back at the Analyst and saw he was deep in thought with his tablet, so she began touching the antiques, waiting for a response.

Almost all of them, she quickly realized, were variations of the same figure. Ranging from crudely made clay figures that looked like they were made by a child to, pieces of high art that belonged in a museum, depicting a scarlet figure with a golden head. Some of them were posed in menacing or aggressive ways, while others radiated with a sense of warmth and care.

The murals were the same. On one side of the room, in a style that reminded her of ancient Japanese art styles, the scarlet being appearing to be leading an army against strange grey-green monstrosities. On the other side of the room, a mural showed people gathered around the being like he was Christ giving the sermon on the mount.

Lacy looked back at the one with the army and reached out to touch it. She extended her fingers to trace the scarlet figure on the canvas, but a centimeter away from contact, the Analyst spoke up.

"That will be enough of that," he said.

Lacy jumped in surprise and looked back at him.

"Please, Mrs. Prullen, have a seat." The Analyst gestured towards the armchair.

Lacy hesitated a moment. "I'm glad I have your attention," she said.

The Analyst said nothing but motioned to the chair again. She walked over to his desk and took her seat again.

"Now, Mrs. Prullen-" the Analyst began, but was interrupted by Lacy.

"No."

The Analyst raised an eyebrow. "No…what, Mrs. Prullen?"

"You can address me as Lieutenant," she remarked sternly. The Analyst cleared his throat.

"As I recall, you stated yesterday that you wished to be called 'Mrs. Prullen.' Am I wrong?"

"That *is* my name. But until I know yours, you can call me Lieutenant, and I'll address you by your rank as well."

The Analyst was silent again, and after a moment of staring, he returned to his tablet, tapped it a bit, then gave Lacy his attention. "I have no rank. My name is Jaskek Dreed."

Lacy hadn't expected such a complacent response. She nodded her head in an *'okay then...'* gesture. "So you're not military then?"

"Our military has officers and the Zar-Meck. In terms of rank, Mrs. Prullen, we don't have any. There is the Emperor and his people."

Lacy nodded again.

"It seems your people take a different approach to this. If I understand correctly, your husband holds command over you?"

Lacy pushed her tongue against the inside of her lower gums in annoyance. "Only on paper. Don't you guys have marriage here?"

Jaskek studied his tablet. "But it says he's a Captain, which according to your ship means he is in charge of you."

"Have you listened to our logs too?" Lacy asked.

"Yes."

"Then you should know that our rank only determines how much we're paid."

"I disagree. Listening to your *husband's* logs, as you have very few, it appears to me as he is the one giving orders."

"We have different roles. He flies and I keep the ship in the air. He comes up with ideas, and I tell him how we can make it work. It's fifty/fifty, like a healthy marriage should be."

"Hmm." Jaskek typed more on his tablet. "I guess that brings us to why I called you here. You, like your ship's records, are very inconsistent. I can't imagine your mission going smoothly if you weren't respecting the foundations your people set for you."

Lacy shifted her posture. "Our mission was perfect until you showed up."

"Was it not you that landed on our outpost?" Jaskek replied

sharply.

Lacy didn't say anything.

Jaskek scrolled through his tablet. "Last time we spoke like this, we discussed your ship's historical documents. Specifically, their lack of consistency. Tell me about them."

She knew if she wanted a way out of there, she'd have to work with him. Just enough though to keep him hooked. Lacy knew Jaskek would throw her to her doom once there was nothing left to learn. She thought hard about her next move, and Jaskek did his best to hide his impatience.

"Don't you have legends around here?"

Jaskek raised an eyebrow.

"You know," Lacy began. "Myths? Fables? Stories of heroes that fought off evil or scary stories to spook little kids?"

"Of course," Jaskek said. "It's a core foundation of the Emperor's teachings to pass on his history to the next generations."

Lacy fixed her posture and sat up, leaning slightly toward the Analyst.

"I'm not talking about history. Don't you ever make stuff up? Golly, don't you people ever have any fun?"

"Why would we seek to confuse our youth? Is it not important on your planet to educate your children?"

Lacy sighed deeply in annoyance.

"Of course we do! We also let our people be creative!"

Jaskek exhaled and typed something onto his table with his eyebrows raised. "This seems like it would lead many people astray from the truth. But...your world hasn't been educated. Once the Emperor's forces find your planet we will remedy this."

Lacy rushed to find something to say but was cut short in her thoughts.

"In our talk, you called these stories 'fiction.' Fabrications of reality, it sounds like. Your ship's database was absolutely filled with..."

"Movies," Lacy interjected. "And books."

"Yes, books I know, and we have plenty of those. And 'movies,' you call them, we have similar mediums, although the term you use is strange. So... simple-minded."

Lacy shrugged off the condescension. "It works, doesn't it?"

"Hm. Regardless, you claim your people are encouraged to be creative and that's the best you come up with."

He's looking for a reaction, Lacy thought.

They eyed each other for a moment, patient to see who would break the silence. But while Lacy thought she was making the officer's job harder, every move, and lack of, was just more information Jaskek was happy to work with.

"These characters and stories are made up," Jaskek began again. "They never existed, yet from what we could find, the volume of 'fiction' in your database strongly outweighs the...let's call it 'non-fiction.'"

Lacy nodded sarcastically with a smile. "Creative."

Jaskek pursed his lips and carried on as if not being criticized. "This tells me that earthlings value their own fabrications more than dealing with reality. Tell me, is your world dying?"

"Excuse me?"

"The only logical explanation for this is that life on your world is so terrible, your people are trying to escape it. Which would make sense for why you and your partner were attempting to flee this 'Earth.'"

"No it's not like-"

"Were your people dying?"

"No!"

"Famine? Plague?"

Lacy opened her mouth but was quickly interrupted.

"Was it war?"

"No, we-" Lacy became flushed with annoyance.

"I found in a scan of these stories a strong uptick in the use of the word 'war' in the last decade. Upon further research, I found many of these stories are all referencing the same event. It's strange, all of these fictional stories share nothing in common except for one major event. Explain this to me."

"See, there was a war. There were a few. But even when it was over some people couldn't escape it." Lacy thought about what Dex had told her about his father, how after the war he would be plagued by nightmares and claimed he was back on the front lines. Even by the time the *Silent Horizon* began its voyage, no one knew how to help him.

Jaskek relaxed a bit. Lacy was sitting straight up stuck in her thoughts.

"These stories were sometimes the only help some people had to get by. When Dex and I left Earth, things were getting better. In fact, life was the greatest we'd probably ever known as a race. But whenever things were bad, we would watch these movies, and see these heroes that had the same struggles as us. They would overcome and for a little while it gave us all hope for something better.

"But they didn't accomplish anything. They weren't real." Jaskek was blunt and demeaning in his response.

"It didn't matter to the people watching these movies. I can't really explain it better than that. Film wasn't really my thing-"

Jaskek cut her off. "So, what you're saying is you don't know what you're talking about?"

"No! That's not at all what I meant! It's like…it's like music! You have music here at least right?"

Jaskek's continued monotonous tone was irritating Lacy to a point where she could kill him just for hearing another bland word. "Yes of course we have music." Then with pride in his voice and a slight glow in his skin, "We have the grandest operas in the known universe!"

"About your Emperor I suppose?"

Returning to the monotonous tone, "Well naturally."

Lacy huffed. "Well, I'd bet our music is a little more interesting."

The tone of Jaskek's voice shifted again. "And why would you say that?" The shift was not in pride but in…curiosity? Lacy thought to herself. Jaskek for the first time in their appointment put down the tablet. By the way he did so, Lacy guessed it was an unconscious gesture. She thought, *he's not asking for his report anymore. I've got him.*

"Sometimes," Lacy began, "people connect more to things that aren't just a story. Sometimes, it's an emotion itself that people need to connect with. If you've done your research on our ship, have you listened to 'Rhapsody in Blue?'"

Jaskek tilted his head to the side quizzically.

Lacy humphed, then reached across the desk between them, grabbing Jaskek's tablet before he could react. "How does this thing work?" Lacy asked.

Jaskek calmly stood up and held out his hand. "Safety measures," he said. "You can't. That tablet is assigned to me, and me alone." He tapped his temple with his free hand. "Special lenses. Only I can read what's on there."

Lacy pursed her lips and handed the tablet back. They both took their seats.

"Now," Jaskek began. "What was the name of that song?"

"Rhapsody in Blue."

"Hm. Strange." Jaskek's words were blunt again. He tapped on the screen, then looked as if he were scrolling. Lacy saw the lights flicker in her eyes. "Here we are." He lay the tablet down on the desk, and the music began.

An oboe hit its notes rapidly for the first few measures, then crescendoed high and fell.

Lacy kept her focus on Jaskek. His eyes wouldn't stray from the tablet, and he showed no sign of emotion.

The strings assisted the melody and the trumpets made their introduction. The volume remained low for a few moments.

Jaskek leaned in and stroked his jaw in concentration. "What is going on in this? What's the-"

Lacy shushed him.

Jaskek gave her a look of annoyance, then went back to the music.

At a minute in, the piano entered. The music briefly swelled, then exploded into a symphony!

Unprepared, Jaskek gave a slight jump. He tried to hide it and conceal his face from giving anything away, but Lacy saw all she needed. His skin, though incredibly faint, glowed.

The music continued, flowing between moments of the powerful orchestra blasting into a party, and low moments of the piano stealing the show in softer, rapid solos.

Lacy tried to keep her concentration on Jaskek's subtle shifts in his expression, the intensity of his glowing skin, but soon enough even she was swept up in the music. It was because of this she knew she'd picked the right song.

Two and a half minutes into the song, the piano player's fingers danced rapidly across the keys. Jaskek's skin was illuminating more, but still lightly, and pulsing almost in sync with the music. Two minutes and fifty seconds, the music's tempo increased. Lacy could see in his eyes that Jaskek was enthralled in the music. The tempo slowed down momentarily at three minutes in and then, another explosion of the brass instruments!

Lacy's own heart was racing. Partially for Jaskek's reaction, but mostly for her own love of the piece. But it was cut short.

Jaskek shot out his hand and turned the music off, then tapped another unknown button on the tablet.

Lacy sprang to her feet in a mixture of annoyance and mild anger. "What was that for?!"

The illumination of Jaskek's skin dulled but didn't entirely fade. "That's enough of that. You'll be escorted back to your room, now."

The door in the rear of the room opened and a Zar-Meck entered. It walked briskly to Lacy's side and grabbed her by the arm.

"I will send for you when we arrive at our destination."

The Zar-Meck began to pull Lacy away. "You liked it!" She shouted over her shoulder, trying to pull herself away from the Zar-Meck. "Admit it! You loved that music!"

Jaskek stayed seated and refused to look up from his tablet or say a word as Lacy was removed from his office.

* * *

Hours later, Jaskek stood in his small quarters, looking out at the Heart of the Void. Ahead of him was his emperor, his god. He hadn't expected to return so soon after receiving his first assignment.

Jaskek could feel his heart beating heavily. Since his appointment with Lacy, the melody she'd played for him was stuck in his head.

Stepping away from the window, he walked over to the door to his quarters and looked into the hallway. It was empty, but he still made sure that when he closed his door it was locked. Until they reached the Heart, Jaskek would not be disturbed.

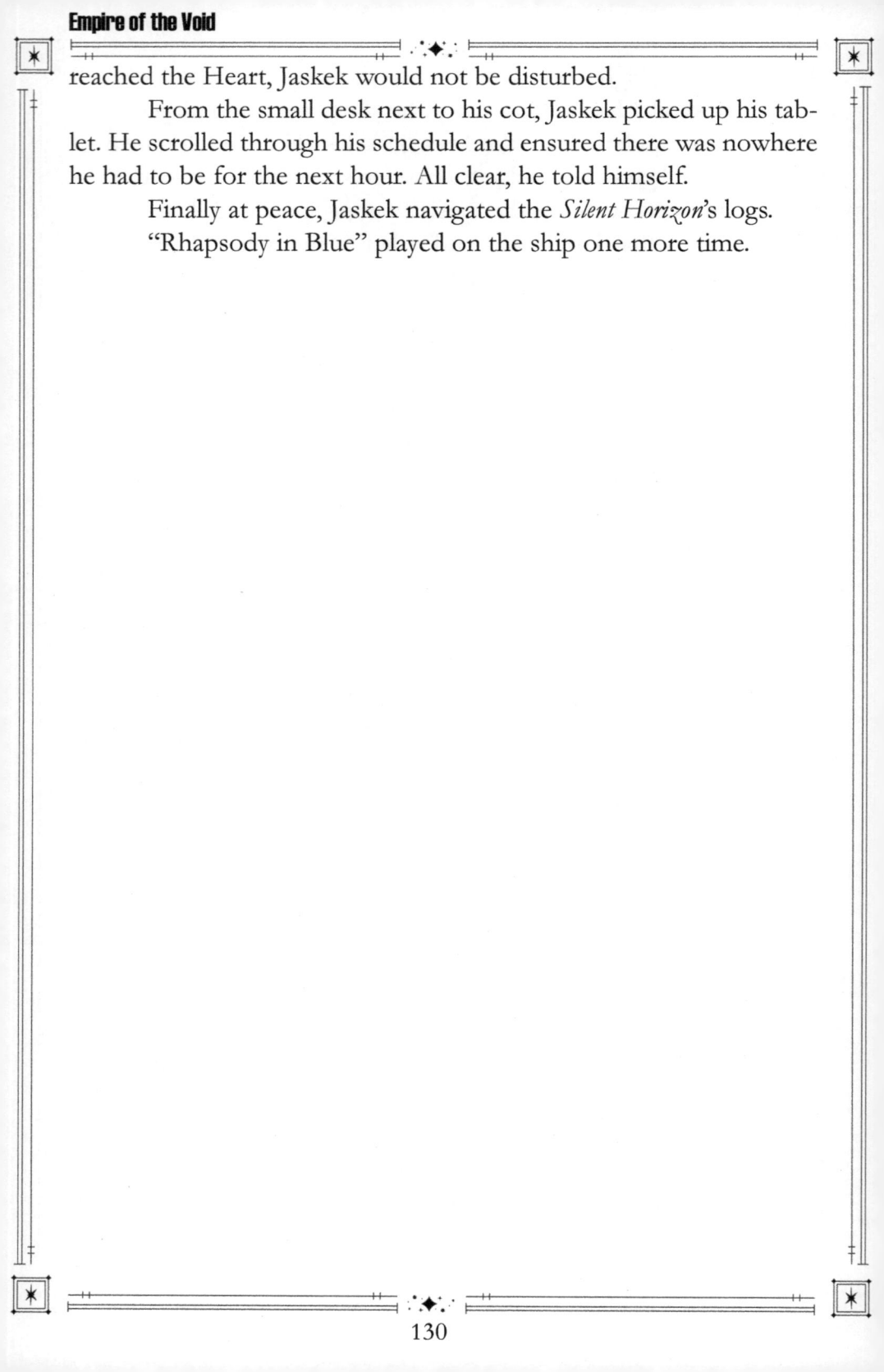

From the small desk next to his cot, Jaskek picked up his tablet. He scrolled through his schedule and ensured there was nowhere he had to be for the next hour. All clear, he told himself.

Finally at peace, Jaskek navigated the *Silent Horizon*'s logs.

"Rhapsody in Blue" played on the ship one more time.

11. Trouble on Reechi

The mechanic's shop took up a large chunk of the block. The front of the building was mostly open garage doors, with a sign overhead written in a language Dex didn't understand. He assumed it was just the name of the shop.

Dex and Korr walked into the shop, where species of all kinds, though mostly raestiens, were tuning up speeders and hover-cars.

Korr tapped on one of the worker's shoulders, a small, blue-furred creature with bug eyes. "Is Hwaq around?"

The bug-eyed creature spoke in an alien tongue, that came out in rapid nasally bursts. Waving at them to follow with mechanical arms serving as extensions to its naturally stubby arms, led them through the shop.

They made their way into a cluttered office, where an overweight raestien sat behind a desk. He was reclined with his feet up on the desk, and eyes closed. It smelled to Dex of car exhaust. He struggled to hold back a cough.

The bug-eyed creature walked around the desk and shook him awake.

"What! What is it?" Hwaq shouted in a gruff voice and sat upright in his chair. He looked around and saw Korr. "AH! Korr Montori! Good to see you!" Hwaq reached over across the overcrowded desk. Dex assumed he was going to shake Korr's hand, but instead, Korr wrapped both his hands around Hwaq's fist and bowed his head.

"Glory be to the Emperor."

Hwaq pulled his hand away and slumped back in his chair. "Glory be," he said. "Go on now, have a seat." Hwaq then turned to the bug-eyed creature. "Don't you be havin' a job to get to?"

The bug-eyed creature threw up its stubby arms, muttered something in its species' tongue, and left. As it did, Korr took a seat across the desk from Hwaq. There were no other chairs, so Dex stood in the corner, where a shadow just covered his face.

"Those bohtith, biggest slackers in the known universe. I've had that guy on my payroll for nearly fifteen years. Would've fired him years back if it weren't for their darn union."

Korr feigned agreement. "I hear ya Hwaq. Used to have one of them on my crew. Thank the Emperor I don't have to tolerate unions on my ship."

They both laughed. Dex stood where he was with his arms crossed, not making a sound, trying to stay unnoticed.

Hwaq wiped away a tear from his laughter that hung on his over-extended forehead. "So Korr, what can I do for ya?"

Korr flashed the mechanic a dashing smile, "Straight to the money with you, as always."

"Well. If you stopped by my place once in a while, said 'hi' to my family, or stayed for dinner, it'd be different. But this is my shop."

Korr threw up his hands in defeat. "Fair's fair," He said. "Maybe next time I'm in town you can make me some authentic Reechian food. How is Laqqa by the way?"

"Good, my friend. She just delivered our seventeenth kid."

Dex barely held in his surprise, but Korr acted like it was just another thing. He said, "Congrats my friend. The Emperor has definitely bestowed his blessings on you."

"And I'm grateful for it every day."

"Good…good," Korr began. "Well, I guess as a little bonus to help out with the newborn, I've got a high-paying job for you."

Hwaq fixed his posture in the chair.

Korr gestured, without turning, to Dex. "My friend here needs a new engine for his ship. Hyperdrive."

Hwaq raised an inquisitive eyebrow. "Mighty tall order. What do you need one of those for?" He stared down Dex.

Dex looked at Korr.

Korr looked at Dex and gave a slight nod of the head toward Hwaq.

"My wife," Dex said bluntly. "An anniversary present."

"Uh-huh...she must be high maintenance, taking a hyperdrive to impress her!" He laughed.

"She's worth it, I can assure you," Dex said calmly.

Korr turned back to Hwaq and began to speak, but was cut off by Hwaq.

"You do know these hyperdrives don't come cheap?"

"I can manage." The cool never faulted in Dex's voice.

Hwaq pursed his lips. "It'll take some time to get ahold of one."

Without hesitation, Dex said, "Give me the price." Hwaq looked over at Korr. "I'm not liking your friend's attitude. Not the most polite guy, is he?"

Korr looked back at Dex for a moment, then returned to Hwaq. In a low voice, he said, "Look, the guy's under stress. It's a last-minute thing, marriage is falling apart, and her dad hates his guts."

"Wonder why," Hwaq retorted with his eyes on Dex.

"Listen, it's a one-time thing, then we'll be out of your hair." He looked up at Hwaq's bald head. "Office, at least. Just do it for me? I'll even bring some apps to dinner."

They both leaned back in their chairs. Hwaq considered for a moment the cost of the operation. He then clucked his tongue and offered Dex his price. "50,000 credits. I can get it installed in three days."

Dex had no sense of the value of anything on Reechi, or anywhere in the Empire for that matter, but acted like it was just another thing. "80,000."

Hwaq was shocked and confused.

Korr couldn't believe what he'd heard.

Dex continued. "80,000, get it installed today."

"Listen taouron, we ain't got hyperdrives just lyin' around. If you want it done today, it'll be closer to 100,000."

"85."

A smirk appeared on the raestien's face. "98."

Dex dropped his arms and stood up taller. "85. I've seen your garage. There are plenty of your guys just hanging around I'm sure one of them can spare some time to find a hyperdrive."

Hwaq glanced at Korr as if to ask for advice. Korr just shrugged. Looking back to Dex, Hwaq offered "95."

Dex stepped a little closer, the shadow ending just above his nose. "Work with me a little. 87."

"You want a hyperdrive today, someone's either gonna get scammed or paid off. 93."

Dex stood his ground. "88. My girl's dad has a nice fleet of yachts that could use an upgrade. I wouldn't mind referring you." Dex gave a smirk.

Hwaq liked the sound of rich clients. And with seventeen kids to feed… "89 and it's a deal."

In joy, Dex let the smile loose and stepped out of the shadow holding out his hand to shake on the deal. "Knew you'd come around.

Hwaq looked at Dex and his outstretched hand in confusion.

Korr hid his rising fear.

Immediately realizing what he'd done, Dex curled his fist. "Pardon, got excited."

Hwaq maintained his confused look but wrapped his hands around Dex's fist. "Glory…be…to the emperor…" he said slowly, then released his hand.

Dex cleared his throat and stepped back. "Glory be."

There was a terrifying moment of silence for Dex and Korr as Hwaq sat in his chair staring Dex down.

Dex and Korr straightened themselves.

"You're an odd fellow," Hwaq said, pointing at Dex. He stood. "But I like the size of your pocketbook. Let me see what my boys can do." Hwaq shuffled his way around the desk and out of his office, closing the door behind himself.

As soon as they were sure no one would hear them, Korr jumped to his feet. "What in Maoul is wrong with you?"

Dex stood his ground. "I'm in a rush. I don't exactly have time for courtesy."

"We're walking a thin line as it is, Dex. You're lucky he didn't notice something was up when you reached for him with…whatever that was."

"It's a handshake. Like your weird fist-grip thing."

"Whatever it is. You're sticking out too much. If he said one-hundred, you should have stuck with that! You're already costing me a fortune what's a few thousand credits more!" Korr dropped his hands on his waist and paced the small office, facing away from Dex.

"At least you're only risking money."

Korr turned sharply. "What was that?"

Dex said nothing as the office door opened and Hwaq walked back in. Under his breath, Dex told Korr, "I'll pay you back somehow, don't worry."

Hwaq didn't hear them. "All right," he said. "Looks like we'll be able to get your ship's engine installed today. I just *happened* to get an offer from an old friend for a decently priced hyperdrive."

"How long do you think it'll take?" Dex asked.

"What, is the party tonight?"

Without hesitation, Dex said yes.

"All right, give me four hours or so. Where's the ship?"

An hour later, the three of them were riding in a hover-truck back to the spaceport. A hyperdrive was secured in a trailer attached to the rear. How Hwaq obtained it, Dex didn't want to ask. He knew he'd been pestering him enough, and how lucky he was to still be on a good track to get to Lacy.

It must have been the haggling, but during the brief drive back to the port, Hwaq lightened up a bit to Dex. "You from Wiccar too?"

Not wanting to engage too much, and not wanting to be rude, Dex looked out the side window as he talked. "Born and bred."

"Nice, I've always wanted to take a trip out there," Hwaq began. "I've seen photos of their oceanside cliffs. AbsoLUTELY gorgeous. Been thinking about taking my wife there for a second honeymoon. First was on the third moon of Areeno. I tell ya, for a desert planet, some of its moons are incredibly beautiful. You been out that way?"

Dex tried to give a sense of interest in his voice. He appreciated all Hwaq was doing, and the fact that he was probably being genuine right now. It made Dex feel even worse about avoiding eye contact so hard. "Not yet. Not a fan of the desert. Gonna try to avoid it as long as I can."

Hwaq scoffed. "Well I tell ya, if you don't check out its moons, you're missing out."

As they talked, Dex kept mental notes of how many Zar-Mecks they passed on the street. By the time they arrived at the port, he'd seen six. It wasn't many, and he thought he could make an escape from just six, but he knew better. That had only been one small section of a single street. If something happened, there would be dozens of Zar-Mecks all over him.

When they arrived at the spaceport, a taouron security guard waved them through.

"I do plenty of jobs here," Hwaq said. "At this rate, I should just be contracted with the port. They could at least refer me or sumthin', I don't know." They rode around the open bays slowly, avoiding docked ships and port workers. Many of them waved to Hwaq or jokingly cursed him for his driving.

"All right where's yours?" Hwaq asked.

Dex scanned the bay. "That one, just past the yellow junker."

Only when they approached the *Silent Horizon* did Dex realize that it may be too different from the style of all the other ships in the port. He hadn't seen anything that resembled it and was sure Hwaq had seen nearly every kind of spaceship ever made.

"Well, would you look at that..." Hwaq said quietly to himself as the three of them exited the hover-truck.

Dex and Korr shot him a look.

"Where'd you get this beaut?" Hwaq asked Dex without taking his eyes off the *Silent Horizon*.

Dex looked at Korr, who mouthed something that Dex couldn't understand. "Uh...a friend. Custom build."

Hwaq looked at Dex quizzically. "Come on... I gotta know. I haven't seen a ship like this since I was a kid!" He walked under the ship and ran his fingers along the hull. "It's just like the prototype at the universal fair, what was it, thirty years ago! Sleek futuristic design and everything."

Dex thought of a response quickly. "Where do you think I got the idea for the make? My girl's dad is a collector. Remember the yachts I'm sending your way?" He knew he was getting too close for comfort, but figured if he cozied up to him, talked his language, he'd put himself at better odds. Dex walked alongside Hwaq and smacked him on the back. "Get this job done in decent time and maybe I'll let ya take a spin."

Before Hwaq could turn to look Dex in the eye, Dex had turned away, walking back in Korr's direction.

"Nah nah, now don't be messin' with me now, kid."

"Get started and we'll see!" Dex waved a dismissive hand in the air, then addressed Korr quietly. "How'm I doing?"

"I won't lie buddy, you've got me on the edge of my seat. But…" he looked past Dex to Hwaq who was now unfastening the trailer from the hover-truck. "Under other circumstances, I'd say you'd fit in just fine on my ship."

Dex smiled. "Maybe one of these days. If life ever calms down."

"Hope it does. But where would the fun be in that?"

They both laughed. "Korr, you and I have very different ideas of fun."

Hwaq pulled the hovering trailer around to the airlock of the *Silent Horizon*. Dex jumped ahead of him to open the door. "Thanks, kid," Hwaq said.

Looking at the size of Hwaq compared to the engine he lugged in *and* the one he'd be taking out, Dex was amazed at the strength raestiens must be capable of.

After Hwaq was through, Dex called over to Korr. "Why don't you take a walk? Get yourself a drink or something. Can't be fun being cooped up in that ship all day."

"Yeah, you'd know huh?" Korr shouted back.

Dex said nothing but just smiled with a nod, then followed Hwaq in.

* * *

Korr walked around Morak City looking for a bar. He wasn't thirsty, just needed somewhere to get in on all the latest rumors.

Through his first three drinks, nothing stuck out to him. Conversations ranged from a new world being inducted into the empire, to the affairs of the miners on the flip side of the planet's rings.

Even if Korr didn't hear anything about Dex and Lacy, he could at least keep his ears open for potential jobs.

Korr watched Zar-Mecks patrolling the streets. He was waiting for a sign that they were alert to Dex's presence. Eventually, he told himself it was just paranoia. For as strange as Dex had acted, it wasn't enough to tip anyone off.

When almost an hour had passed, he paid his tab and headed for one of the local bazaars. If rumors weren't being shared at the bar, Korr was sure he could find some there.

* * *

While Hwaq worked on the engine, Dex read up on the preliminary report the *Silent Horizon* created for Reechi. He studied the ringed-planet system, how they rotated within each other, and the moon outpost that orbited it.

The readouts weren't incredibly detailed. It let him know the general size and density of the masses, as well as levels of organic life. What he got told him that Reechi's entire surface was heavily populated, save for a handful of lakes.

Using what he had, Dex made new files on the ship's computer for all the things he'd seen in this part of the universe. He updated the *Silent Horizon*'s map to include Reechi(with Morak City and the places they'd stopped), the Nebula, and the outpost. Though he hoped he'd never have to return to any of these places, Dex knew it'd be best to have them documented and memorized. After inputting those planets, he gave Korr a quick call, and asked for the coordinates of the Heart of the Void, just in case. He also made detailed records of the new species he'd encountered. The officer in him said if he and Lacy ever made it back to Earth, they'd want humanity to be prepared for what could one day knock at their door. Personally, though, he knew he couldn't risk the same ignorance on other civilized planets as he had on Reechi. If he showed up at the Heart of the Void without gaining a basic understanding of how this culture worked, as well as what kinds of creatures operated in it, both he *and* Lacy would be doomed.

Working silently, Dex hoped Hwaq had forgotten about his presence.

From the moment Hwaq started his work, he hadn't spoken

to Dex. Though Dex wasn't paying Hwaq much mind, he heard every so often Hwaq questioning the parts of the *Silent Horizon*'s engine. They were small things like, "What the hell is this?" spoken in a disgruntled murmur.

One of Dex's worries was that the hyperdrive wouldn't be compatible with his ship, but thus far, Hwaq gave him no bad news.

After the first two hours, Dex decided he needed some fresh air. As he walked down the hallway to the airlock, Hwaq called out to him. "Heyya, Dex, right?"

Dex stopped and looked into the engine room. Tools and engine parts were everywhere, but the new hyperdrive looked to be fitting in just fine. "Yeah?" He asked.

Hwaq rose to his feet and wiped his hands on his pants. "Said this was a custom build right?"

"Mhmm." Dex nodded.

"Huh, never really seen a make like this before. Anywhere." Hwaq looked around the room once, then back to Dex. When their eyes locked, Dex quickly dropped his head and rubbed his eye.

"You all right there?" Hwaq stepped a little closer.

"Yeah, just uh…got something in my eye."

"Ah, that's annoying, lemme get a look," Hwaq quickly jumped over to Dex.

Dex threw up a hand between them and began speed walking out to the airlock. "No don't worry, got it!" He said as the door opened. "You just, finish up and I'll get your payment!"

As the airlock shut behind him, Hwaq began to shout back, but his voice was cut off.

Once a few yards away from the *Silent Horizon*, Dex pulled the comm device off his waistline and called Korr. "Korr, this is Dex. You copy?"

After a moment, he heard. Back, "Yeah buddy, I'm still here, what's up?"

Dex glanced back at the ship and saw Hwaq unloading the old engine down the ramp. "Might wanna start heading back. Look's like you're friend is finishing up, and I am more than ready to get out of here."

Through the comm, Korr asked, "You think he's onto you?"

Dex turned again, away from his ship. "Not yet, but I think he's getting suspicious." As he said this, Dex heard a ship zooming by overhead. He looked and saw a small saucer, that looked like a miniature version of the Zar-Mecks capital ship. "How we looking on Empire presence out there?"

In a hushed tone so Dex had to raise the comm close to his ear, Korr said, "If I had to guess, empire forces around here are on the lookout. There's more patrols out walking than when we got here, but I wouldn't say they know you're here. I'll start heading back though."

"Copy. See ya soon." Dex slipped the device back onto his waistline.

Another saucer passed overhead, and Dex looked up.

Without Dex noticing, Hwaq had appeared by his side. He too was looking up at the sky. "Don't usually see their starfighters coming down like that. Wonder what's up?"

"I try not to think too hard about it," Dex told Hwaq. "Sometimes it's just not my place to get involved. Engine done?"

Hwaq turned his head to Dex. "Just about. Wanna start up your ship for me? Make sure it's actually connected?"

"Sure thing." Dex walked briskly back and into his ship. His heart began to race. So far no trouble, and they were almost clear. Before entering, Dex noticed Hwaq wasn't beside him. He looked back and saw the small raestien shuffling around one of his pockets and pulling out a comm device similar to the one Korr had given him. Dex entered the *Silent Horizon* but didn't let the airlock close. Instead, he listened to Hwaq's conversation.

"Laqqa, you hear me?"

A pause.

"Laqqa...Laqqa I'm in the port I can't hear ya too well."

Another pause, this one longer.

"Can't be!" Hwaq grunted into his comm. "Yeah thanks for the warning, I'll be on the lookout don't worry... No, don't mention it to the kids they'll just get worked up...Don't worry I'll be fine! I'll see you in a bit." Hwaq put his comm device away. It was a few seconds before Dex heard any footsteps, then quickly raced to the ship's console.

Dex rushed to start the ship's engine, hoping, praying that Hwaq had everything right.

The *Silent Horizon* gave a familiar whirr and hum as the computer systems booted up.

Hwaq's voice from behind asked, "Everything running okay?"

Dex shot his head around. "Yeah!" A bead of sweat began to form next to his temple. "Yeah, just uhmmm, gotta give the ship's computer a moment. Then we'll try the engine." Dex pursed his lips and gave a quick nod."

Hwaq was standing in the threshold of the hallway. His huge arms hung low next to him. Dex could see slight twitching in his fingers.

Trying to ensure the situation remained calm, Dex added, "I'm impressed with your turnaround time. Sorry for hassling you earlier."

Hwaq stepped a little closer, walking slowly. "I understand, don't worry. We've all got places to be. 'Specially with all the Zar-Mecks around."

Dex did his best to suppress his nerves, but it felt like his whole body was shaking. "Can't mind them too much if you haven't done anything wrong, right?"

Hwaq was almost at Dex's feet.

They heard another saucer zoom overhead, this one sounded louder.

"Ah!" Hwaq exclaimed, pointing out the *Silent Horizon*'s window. "Look at that, they're act'lly landing."

Dex turned quickly and saw one of the saucers landing in the bay next to them. The sweat was coming more intensely.

Before he had time to turn back around, Hwaq's bulky hand grabbed him by the jaw and spun him around. "Knew something was off 'bout ya!"

Their eyes were locked and Dex couldn't turn away. Hwaq stared at his human eyes. "This honor will be better than anything you could've paid me."

The jig was up. Dex attempted to push Hwaq's arm off, but the raestien was too strong. Instead, Hwaq pushed him deeper into the seat and covered Dex's mouth with his spare hand. "If ya know what's good and right, you'll just come with me to the port security. This don't have to be a problem." He talked as if trying to console Dex.

But Dex hadn't come this far to give in now. He tried desperately to fight back, but Hwaq was too strong, and his grip was getting tighter. Dex's jaw felt like it was about to snap. He started kicking out his legs, hoping to hit something, anything! Hwaq stood his ground, and shouted at him to stop fighting with him until Dex realized...

I have a gun.

Dex reached into his coat, pulled out his blaster, and fired.

Hwaq stumbled back, letting go of Dex. He clutched the instantly cauterized wound on his left side. It missed any vital organs or bones, but seared flesh and fat.

They were both in shock.

Dex had never fired the blaster outside of the range before and had prayed he'd never have to use it. Even now, after he'd fired the blaster and knew the stakes, he wanted to toss it aside. He wanted to apologize but then saw the rage in Hwaq's deep blue eyes.

Hwaq screamed and charged Dex.

Dex threw himself out of the chair and onto the floor, keeping his blaster on Hwaq.

Missing his target, Hwaq's fists came down hard on the ship's console, mashing the buttons. More parts of the ship activated, and in the back room, the engine began running.

From the floor, Dex backed up to the wall and aimed at Hwaq's chest. "Just go home, Hwaq! Go back to your family, you don't have to be a hero!"

Hwaq was in a frenzy. He swung again laterally at Dex, attempting to knock the blaster away.

Dex fired another shot and Hwaq's massive hand swung into him. The blast lodged itself in Hwaq's right shoulder, but that only angered him more.

The blaster went flying across the room, landing on the portside bunk.

Without a weapon, Dex was momentarily lost for what to do, and that was all the time Hwaq needed. He grabbed Dex by his jacket and swung him in a full arch overhead, smacking him back on the ground.

Dex couldn't breathe. Before he knew it, Hwaq's hands were coming down again. This time onto his chest. Dex rolled to the left and was up against the bunk, blaster only a few feet away. He tried to get to his feet and make a break for the blaster, but as soon as he was up, Hwaq had him by the ankle and yanked. Dex fell, smacking his face into the *Silent Horizon*'s hard floor. The next attack came so suddenly, Dex didn't even realize one of his front teeth was chipped and lying on the floor.

Hwaq held him by both legs now and stepped to the left, swinging Dex like a bat, at full force into the framing of the starboard-side bunk. The frame made contact across his core. Whatever wind he had managed to take back in was quickly knocked out.

Dex wheezed.

Hwaq dropped Dex's legs. "Ready to turn yourself in?"

Dex fell to the floor, wanting the fall to continue into unconsciousness. He coughed, and small flecks of blood hit the floor. Dex took a deep breath in, and let it out slowly.

"I didn't want to do this," Hwaq said. "I don't want my kids to worry if their dad's gonna come home tonight."

Dex attempted to rise to his feet. They wobbled and he collapsed, but he tried again, holding onto the bunk's frame.

"But we have a duty," Hwaq continued, watching Dex's feeble attempt to stand. "I serve the empire to protect my kids. To protect my wife."

Dex was on his feet, leaning against the bunk. "Then you should understand-" he took another deep breath. "...why I can't let you take me. Wouldn't you choose your family over the empire?"

Hwaq was shocked at the question. Without hesitation, he said, "It's because of the empire my family prospers. I owe everything to the Emperor, no matter what that means. Now come with me. You can't win this one."

"I'm sorry Hwaq. I really am." Holding on to the top frame of the bunk, Dex jumped and swung his feet up four feet in the air, kicking Hwaq hard in the face with his heels.

Hwaq tumbled back onto the floor, hitting his head on the console. His mind went blank for a moment, brain hemorrhaging, and when he opened his eyes about five seconds later, Dex was on the opposite side of the room with the blaster in his hand.

"I won't kill you Hwaq. You'll still get your pay. Somehow, I promise I'll send it." He looked out the window and saw two Zar-Mecks patrolling the bay with batons. "Just get off my ship! Go back to your wife and kids!" Dex's face had gone red. He was desperate. Looking outside the window again, he saw the Zar-Mecks looking at his ship and gesturing something. Others appeared further back. Even worse, they heard the airlock open and heavy footsteps walking toward them.

Hwaq rose to his feet. "I would die before I abandoned my emperor!"

Dex knew what he had to do. He dropped his arm slightly and fired twice.

Hwaq collapsed and gripped his knees, screaming in agony.

Worried the Zar-Mecks heard, dex crouched down and rushed to Hwaq, grabbing him under the arm and dragging him. "Just go home! You fought well, and you're no less honorable. Now just let me be!"

Not wanting to give up, Hwaq bit Dex's arm.

Dex gritted his teeth through the pain and continued to drag. "Do that again and I'll blow your teeth out!"

Just outside the ship, Dex heard the voices of two of the patrolling Zar-Mecks. One of them said, "This looks like the one from the alert."

Dex dropped Hwaq, still gripping his knees in pain, in the ship's hallway. "Screw it. You're either off my ship now, or you get sucked out the airlock."

An artificial voice called to him, "Identify yourself!"

Dex slowly turned his head. The two Zar-Mecks were standing on the ramp just outside the still-open airlock. Dex cursed to himself.

The Zar-Meck closer to Dex spoke next, "That's the one." He raised his baton. "By order of the Emperor, you are under arrest."

Dex knew he could be bested by just one Zar-Meck in terms of speed and agility. It'd be pointless to try to draw his blaster on them. If only he had…

Way past the Zar-Mecks, standing in the shadows up against the bay's walls, Dex saw Korr.

A smile almost found its way onto Dex's face at the sight of an ally, but then Korr was gone. He'd disappeared into the shadows at the first sign of trouble as he said he would.

Dex's heart sank. *This might be it. At least one way or another, I'll probably be closer to Lacy.*

"Step slowly," the Zar-Meck commanded him. "Just exit the spacecraft and don't try anything."

From the ground, Hwaq cried out, "Thank you! Oh, thank you, glory be to the Emperor!" Hwaq propped himself up on his elongated hands and attempted to crawl toward the Zar-Mecks.

They commanded him, "Stay where you are citizen!"

But Hwaq didn't listen, he was too overjoyed at being rescued from the evil alien. "I knew you'd get him! He tried to kill me!"

The Zar-Meck's attention was focused on Hwaq, and Dex seized the opportunity he saw. He walked slowly behind the injured raestien, feigning surrender, and just before crossing the threshold, slammed the emergency airlock button. The door slid down fast on Hwaq's feet. Dex heard the screams of the mechanic and felt pity, but knew it had been his only option short of killing him. The Zar-Mecks stepped over Hwaq and banged on the door, demanding Dex open it.

Not wanting to waste any more time on Reechi, Dex ran to his seat and took control of the ship. It took only a moment to get the *Silent Horizon* off the ground. Dex had no way of knowing but prayed Hwaq's feet had been unstuck before they took to the air. For the Zar-Mecks though, he couldn't care less how far they fell from.

Blaster fire began shooting past his ship from Zar-Mecks on the ground.

Dex reached across to where Lacy should have been sitting and smacked a series of buttons. The computer screen pulled up a window showing a rear view from the back of the ship. Dex saw the port shrinking in size and blaster bolts coming his way. The aim was close, but the Zar-Mecks failed to hit any part of the ship that would do serious damage.

The ground forces weren't his only obstacle though. Flying

into view from his front and back were numerous Zar-Meck starfighters.

Dex banked hard to port, flying level along the planet's ring.

The Zar-Meck starfighters adjusted course and began firing. Blasts zoomed past the *Silent Horizon*. Dex pushed the ship as hard as he could to outrun the starfighters, while zipping up, down, left, and right to avoid their blasts.

While struggling to stay in the air, Dex tried calling Korr on his comm. "Korr!" He shouted, "Korr, where'd you go!" but there was no answer.

Coming up fast, another of the planet's rings was making its rotation straight through Dex's trajectory. Dex angled the *Silent Horizon* downward to avoid the land mass and flew across the lower crust.

The starfighters stuck to him but fired with more intent, and less often. Glancing up at the crust, Dex saw miners watching the action play out. Not wanting to put them in harm's way, he revolved the ship around the crust, and skimmed the side of the mass, before angling back up toward space.

Dex knew he wouldn't be able to shake the Zar-Mecks until he could activate the hyperdrive, but with the number closing in on him, he couldn't focus enough attention on getting it ready. He had to find a way to cut them down!

As if he were just a player in a sick game by the universe, the Zar-Meck capital ship slid into view directly ahead of him. Dozens of Zar-Meck ships flooded out of it in his direction.

A million ideas raced through his head. None of them made any sense. There was no way one man could fight off a whole fleet! He glanced back down at the rear view screen and an idea came to him.

Rotating the ship in a hard 180 degrees, Dex shot the *Silent Horizon* back down to the surface. Blasts from the six or seven starfighters that were now in front of him hit the ship's hull, but Dex was already cutting through their ranks.

The Zar-Mecks made a quick turn around and were joined by the dozens that came out of the capital ship.

Facing the planet's core, Dex saw exactly what he'd hoped for. The closer they got to the core, the smaller the rings were. They rotated slower, but the gaps between them were much more narrow. Dex didn't have the firepower to fight the Zar-Mecks but had enough flight experience to stand a chance in these conditions.

His heart raced faster than ever as he committed to the new plan.

As the battle ensued overhead, civilians watched and cheered on the empire forces. They cursed the ship that stood against the mighty Zar-Mecks and cried in sadness when the first starfighter crashed into an oncoming planetary ring.

"One down!" Dex cheered to himself.

He was rapidly coming up on the planet's inner rings. Dex intentionally flew as close to, and in and out of as many rings as possible.

Little by little, the Zar-Meck starfighters backed off. They wouldn't risk jamming themselves up or bottlenecking in the tighter spaces. While most still followed closely and blasted away at Dex, some of the ships in the rear broke off and flew around longer paths to try to cut him off.

One of the starfighters was successful and came up on Dex's starboard side fast.

Dex gritted his teeth and jerked the ship hard to starboard, crashing against the oncoming starfighter, sending it careering onto a ring's surface.

As Dex flew past the planet's core, he was nearly blinded by its intensity. He had to squint his eyes, but held his hands steady on the controls, maintaining a path he hoped would lead him to safety. To make matters worse, the blaster fire was once again intense. For now, the Zar-Mecks didn't have to worry about firing on civilians, though Dex believed they would have taken it as an honor to be killed in the crossfire if it was to catch the Emperor's prisoner.

The *Silent Horizon*'s computer rang in alarm. The hull had taken serious damage. If Dex was ever going to make his escape, it would have to be now.

In a leap of faith, Dex ignored the blaster fire raining down on him and activated the hyperdrive. He heard the engine whirring louder in the back. Not knowing when or if it would actually be ready, he watched the skies until all the rings were out of his way. He quickly input the coordinates for the Heart of the Void.

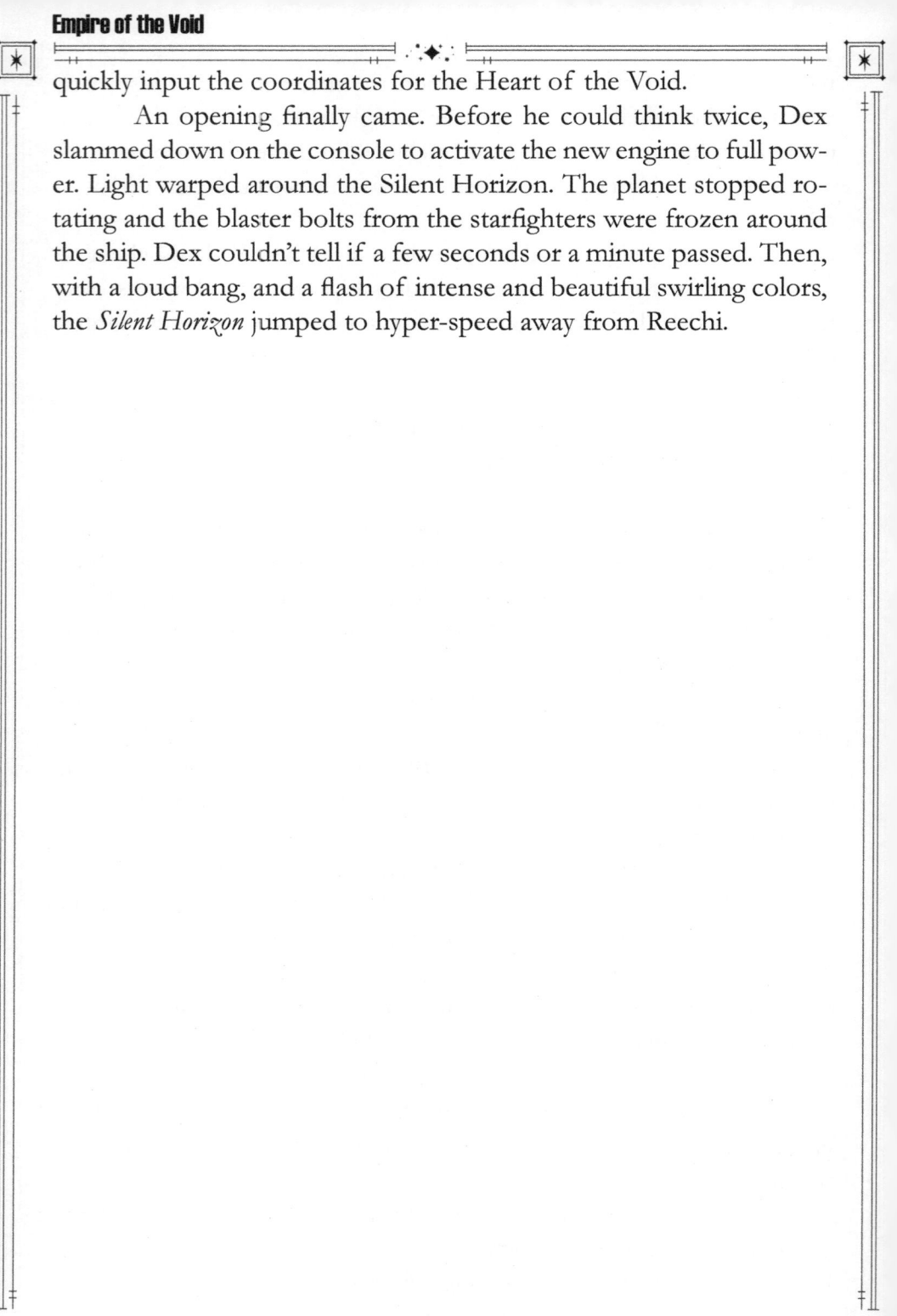

    An opening finally came. Before he could think twice, Dex slammed down on the console to activate the new engine to full power. Light warped around the Silent Horizon. The planet stopped rotating and the blaster bolts from the starfighters were frozen around the ship. Dex couldn't tell if a few seconds or a minute passed. Then, with a loud bang, and a flash of intense and beautiful swirling colors, the *Silent Horizon* jumped to hyper-speed away from Reechi.

12. An Audience with the Emperor

The transport ship began its descent to the surface of the Heart of the Void. Lacy saw as she was being escorted out of her room by a pair of Zar-Mecks armed with blasters, a massive golden hand next to the planet, and could only wonder what it was.

Minutes later, she knew they were close to the exit by the noises echoing down the hallway, and the stronger presence of Zar-Mecks and officers walking around intently.

As they approached the exit ramp of the ship, Lacy was amazed at what she was seeing. In front of her, past the tarmac, the transport lay on, was a grand skyline of magnificent gold and brown pyramidal skyscrapers. Reaching well over three thousand feet into the air, they were elegantly swirled, and many had bridges that connected to other pyramids. Beautiful vegetation grew off of and cascaded down the structures.

It looked to Lacy like she had just stepped into El Dorado on a massive scale. But what grabbed her attention more than anything else on this new planet, was the castle in the sky. From where they stood, Lacy assumed its base must have been at least a square mile. Because of its distance and height, she couldn't discern what the structure looked like, but she knew it was the Emperor's palace. This idea was solidified by what was behind the planet. She understood now what the golden hand she saw was.

The Heart of the Void was held in the hands of the Emperor. A massive statue of the Emperor in his scarlet robes floated in space. The spikes of its golden head grew out and over the floating castle like rays of the sun. The Emperor truly created a godly image for himself above these people.

At the moment, there was only one thing missing. Lacy looked around for someone. She and her Zar-Meck escorts stopped at the bottom of the ramp as if they were waiting for further instructions.

Not wanting to talk to the Zar-Mecks, Lacy waited for a real person to walk by. Presently, an older gentleman with a similar uniform to Jaskek walked down the ramp and past her. "Hey you!" She called after him.

The Zar-Meck to her right smacked the butt of its blaster into Lacy's side. "Silence prisoner!" It commanded.

Lacy nearly keeled over, but the officer intervened. "That won't be necessary," he said with an upity voice. To Lacy, he asked, "What is it you want?"

Lacy looked up at the officer. "Where's Jaskek? He's been in charge of me."

"Hm." The officer grunted and pulled out a tablet. "Making friends are we? I wouldn't get too fond of anyone." He stopped scrolling on his tablet, and he scoffed. "Excuse me," he said and promptly returned up the ramp.

Lacy turned to watch him almost speed-walk toward another officer. She couldn't tell what he was saying but knew something was very wrong by the way the upity officer was gesturing as he spoke.

The Zar-Meck to her left spoke next. "Look forward." It said bluntly.

She did as she was told and turned to face back toward the city, taking in its incredible beauty. Behind her, she continued hearing a muffled but agitated voice of the officer, then footsteps walking down towards her.

After a moment, the officer returned to her and let out a deep, annoyed sigh. "You will be coming with me."

"Is Jaskek not coming?" Lacy asked.

The Zar-Meck to her right tensed its arms to strike her again, but the officer raised his hand to ward it off. "Officer Dreed is indisposed. In light of that, I have been informed you will be under my supervision. Now if you will, this way." He turned from her and tapped something on his tablet.

The Zar-Mecks nudged her forward. A few seconds later, a small topless shuttle landed in front of them.

The four of them boarded. There was no pilot on the shuttle, instead, the Officer tapped another button on his tablet and they took flight toward the floating castle.

Though the wind was loud as they flew through it, Lacy still called to the Officer. "You got a name?"

He didn't hear her.

Lacy began to stand, but the Zar-Mecks extended their arms over her legs.

"Where do you think I'm gonna go?" She asked, and they brought their arms back in. Lacy stepped forward two rows to be behind the Officer. "Hey!"

He turned and shot her a look. "What are you doing?"

"What's your name?"

He scoffed. "That's none of your concern," the officer said, then turned away from her to face ahead.

Lacy tapped him on the shoulder.

"I'm Lacy."

Without turning his head all the way, the Officer said. "I don't care."

With the palace-city looming ahead of them and the cold presence of the three Empire cronies around her, Lacy began to realize she was missing Jaskek. Not in a way that she wanted to hug him if she saw him again, but at least he was someone to talk to. Even if it was just for her own gain.

She sat the rest of the trip out in silence, gazing down at the city below. She watched the citizens and vehicles going about their business, oblivious to what was going on above their heads.

As far as Lacy knew, she was the first human being to step on a civilized world outside of the Earth's solar system, yet no one on Earth would ever know, and no one below her would ever care. Though the realization was crippling, she fought to keep her head high, and her being, dignified.

Lacy could now see the palace-city's design. The architecture was reminiscent of the hanging gardens of Babylon, continuing the theme of blocky, but regal with many grand parapets that hovered above the main structure. Everything about the palace-city proclaimed majesty to all who gazed upon it, but to Lacy, it only proclaimed her doom.

The shuttle pulled up along the edge of the palace-city base to a courtyard, where they were met by a tall, elegantly dressed, purple alien.

Lacy didn't have to be told to get off the shuttle and helped herself. The Zar-Mecks followed behind her. The officer began to stand but was stopped by the purple alien.

"You will not be needed here," the purple alien said in a deep, wisened voice.

The officer nodded his head, and silently tapped on his tablet, sending the shuttle off to their next destination.

The purple alien stood at least eight feet tall. He had a long, flat face, with a chin that curled upwards with a horn adorned with rings and engravings. Its eyes were long and angled upwards, giving them a naturally intimidating look. His hair grew out of just the very top of his head. It was very long and ornately braided with gold strings wrapped in it. He wore an ornate green robe that hung loosely with an open chest and trailed off behind him. The only decoration on his clothing was a pin similar to the one Jaskek wore on his uniform.

"I suppose it's time for your Emperor to meet me." Lacy's phrasing didn't go unnoticed by the tall alien.

"From here you will only speak when the Emperor commands you." The alien scowled. "It will be less painful that way. Now, follow." He turned slowly and the Zar-Mecks shoved her into motion.

Walking through the palace-city, Lacy couldn't help but admire the architecture and decor. Other members of the purple alien's species populated the palace. Lacy observed them tending the hanging gardens, wiping windows, and cleaning the walkways. Everything was so pristine, to a point where it looked like the aliens lived only to clean and manufacture the place. She also noticed that as her party walked near one of the service aliens, they tried to hide how they cowered from Lacy's escort.

While it was technically one building, many of the rooms had open walls and ceilings, and hallways were bridges from one room to the next. Some were small, while others were nearly fifty feet long. Lacy could look over the railing of one of the bridges and stare down at the city below. That is, if her guards let her stop to stare.

After a few minutes of walking, they reached the center of the palace-city. Across the largest bridge yet, like crossing over the Hudson River, she gazed upon a beautiful golden pyramid, with rays shooting out of its peak, just as the statue that wrapped around the planet. Beyond the bridge, the Emperor waited for her.

* * *

On the Heart of the Void's surface, officers and Zar-Mecks were preparing the ship for its return to the Royal Void Outpost. On the way, they would be delivering supplies to other outposts on their route and disseminating updates about the new "human" species that had found its way into their empire, via the notes of one of the Empire's analysts.

With all the bustle going on to prepare for their next voyage, no one paid much mind to a memo that came through to the hanger supervisor about a Zar-Meck starfighter that had been stamped for decommissioning. The ship in question would promptly be removed from the hangar and left for ground control to deal with.

The starfighter was shuttled across the tarmac to a new hanger where it would be dismantled, and salvageable parts would be shipped to the factories on Gallach.

In the new hangar, before a crew could begin their job of dismantling the starfighter, an officer from the Emperor's Army called their attention.

"Is this one the starfighter from RVO-19?" Jaskek asked the crew chief.

A taourun responded, standing at attention, appropriate for addressing an officer. "Yes Sir. Just got brought over."

Jaskek walked slowly down the length of the circular starfighter.

"Is there an issue, sir?"

Jaskek stopped and slowly did an about-face to look back at the crew chief. "From whom did you receive the order to dismantle this ship?" He slowly walked back towards the crew.

The crew chief looked curiously from Jaskek to his crew, then back to Jaskek. "I uh...I should have the memo here." He snapped at one of his crew members, who promptly ran off out of sight, and returned with a tablet. The crew member handed it to Jaskek who scrolled through.

Jaskek said nothing and expressed no emotion. Half a minute passed before he stopped scrolling. Lights danced in his eyes.

"Everything all right sir?"

Jaskek shot a glare at the crew chief. "Don't touch this starfighter. By order of the Emperor." He started walking towards the hanger's exit when the crew chief stopped him.

"Excuse me, sir!" The chief called. "I don't mean to pry, but our order was to dismantle this ship."

Looking over his shoulder Jaskek replied plainly, "You're welcome to carry out your tasking if only you don't wish to ever meet the Emperor's grace." Without another word, Jaskek left the hangar.

The starfighter wasn't touched again by the crew, nor were any reports sent back to the transport ship. All anyone knew, was that they did exactly as they were told.

***

As the great doors of the pyramid opened, the tall alien waved the Zar-Meck guards away. They did as commanded without a word.

Lacy watched them leave, wondering if she would be able to make her escape.

"They will not be far," the tall alien said as if reading her mind. "Come. He has waited long enough for you."

Lacy turned her attention back to what lay beyond the doors. The hallway she stared into was lit by floating torches, but they failed to give off enough light for her to see how deep the hall went.

The tall alien walked in.

Lacy was hesitant. The Zar-Mecks would no longer force her, but she had nowhere to go. She knew her doom lay down the hall, but after all this time…a nagging feeling told her she had to at least see the Emperor, the man or beast that enthralled nearly the entire known universe to his will.

She looked back one more time and saw one of the servants across the bridge looking at her. Faintly, she could have sworn she saw the creature shake its head.

Lacy took a deep breath and decided it was time. If she was to meet her fate, she'd do it head-on.

The doors closed behind her as she entered the pyramid.

Lacy quickly caught up to the tall alien. As they walked, the torches floated alongside them, lighting the way.

"Budget doesn't cover any more lights?" Lacy asked, knowing she probably wouldn't get an answer.

This was proven correct by a few moments of silence. "I mean you'd think, Emperor of the universe and all that, he'd keep the place a little more, modern."

Still nothing.

"So how'd you get this job? Good references or…nepotism?"

The tall alien remained cold and stone-faced, but said, "you will not have such tongue when you gaze upon his glory."

After what felt like minutes of walking, the hallway ended and Lacy found herself in a massive empty room. The tall alien held out a hand to tell her to stop walking.

The floating torches that followed them were still the only sources of light in the room, and Lacy began to feel a punishing, cold emptiness consume her. She'd never been afraid of the dark, but something about this room made her soul freeze.

In a hushed tone, the tall alien said to her, "You are about to experience a great honor. Treasure this moment." He then called into the darkness, "My Lord! I humbly bring you the Earth woman!"

When she looked up at him, he'd already disappeared back down the hallway like a ghost.

Lacy was now truly alone.

Then from the darkest corners of the room a million voices called to her in unison, "I have waited eternities for a being such as yourself."

Lacy shrank at the voice. In the depths of her soul, she was terrified but refused to let it surface. *I will not fear him*, she told herself. Whether Dex would come after her or not, she had to be strong. If not to survive long enough for him to come, then for his memory. With the strength the thought of Dex gave her, Lacy spoke back to the voice. "I am truly sorry for the length of the wait, and applaud your patience. If I had known of your greatness sooner, I would have flown slower."

Suddenly, the room lit up. Lacy's eyes took a moment to adjust, and when they did, she almost thought blindness would have been preferred. The room was even larger than she could have imagined from the look of the pyramid. She stood on a ledge that wrapped in a perfect circle around an impossibly deep, black pit. Pillars of fire were spread along the ledge, illuminating the surrounding walls constructed of brown rotting bones of millions of different alien races. The ground she stood on was a deep, sandy maroon. Out of the pit, a platform rose. When it reached a level plane with Lacy, something began to take shape.

Lacy watched as red and gold colors swirled together, and formed creating a scarlet robe, arms, golden hands, and a golden head with rays that shout out like a sun. The Emperor stood before her on the platform over fifty feet tall. There was no face, yet Lacy could feel eyes piercing her.

"Wh…who…what are you?" Lacy's voice shook. It was the same image of the shine she's seen before, but her mind saw something her eyes couldn't, and she had never known fear like this before.

"My children call me Emperor Visconos Armourus, yet I have no name that mortals can truly comprehend. From eons beyond when time was conceived, I am the hand that will grasp all infinities!"

Lacy was speechless. The thundering voices echoed in her mind. Behind the solid golden facelessness, she wanted to believe she saw movement. The gold ebbed and flowed like oil under the scarlet robe, and shined brighter with the columns of fire reflecting off of him.

"From the moment you entered my domain, I felt your presence and needed you," the Emperor continued. "Now that you are here, I must savor this moment."

In the pit far below, a secondary platform began to rise up to the ledge.

"Come forward," the Emperor commanded.

Without a thought, Lacy began to step forward, but then

caught herself and stopped. Her guard had been down, and she felt the mysterious powers of the Emperor trying to work within her. Looking from the platform to the Emperor, she defiantly took a step back. "With respect, I did not travel here just to be ordered around by a tyrant!"

The flame column burned brighter and cooked the room as the Emperor's voice boomed louder through her head. "Come forward, insolent creature!"

Lacy felt like a hook was stuck in her chest, pulling her toward the platform. She wanted to grab ahold of it and rip it out. Mustering her resolve, she fought against her body's urging, and fell to a knee, refusing to walk.

The flames calmed down to their original state. "You have true strength in you," the Emperor said calmly. "Is this why you were sent to my Empire?"

Lacy raised her head to stare down the giant. She breathed heavily, feeling like she'd run a marathon trying to fight off his control of her. "I…I was sent here…" She fought to control her breathing. "I was sent here to tell you to go to hell!"

The Emperor paused for a moment as Lacy rose to her feet again. "I will enjoy consuming you."

"I should let you know, I won't go down easy," Lacy told the Emperor bluntly.

"We shall see. You will be prepared for my feast. Your sacrifice will mark the beginning of a new age for my empire." While the Emperor's voice boomed through the room, vestiges of terrifying creatures began to float along the sides of the room, looking down on Lacy. Two were the faintest bit recognizable, horrible skeletal caricatures of the taouron and the race of purple aliens she'd seen working around the palace city. They were all dressed like royalty in magnificent gowns. The common physical trait they shared was skullcaps that burst violently outward in terrible sharp and barbed horns, and dark eyes filled with malice and misery. It was only now Lacy saw, the Emperor's robes weren't just a deep scarlet. They weren't even blood-red robes. It was itself…blood. Flowing and wet, dripping into the pit below, blood. "You will serve in my world as an emissary of your race. My army will find your planet and subject your people to my reign, and through you, their sacrifice will strengthen my Empire a thousandfold."

The tall alien reappeared behind Lacy and placed a long three-fingered hand on her shoulder.

Lacy didn't even flinch. She couldn't fully comprehend what the Emperor had threatened her with. Lacy only knew it was terrifying, but she refused to let her fear show. "If you find my planet, you will also find an end of your empire. My people are stronger in spirit than any other race in this universe. We will not fall easy."

The Emperor ignored Lacy and spoke next to the tall alien. "Tarnascus, my loyal servant, prepare for a feast and gather up worthy offerings."

Tarnascus the servant fell slowly to his knees, then clasped his hands hands together above his head in a salute. "I will do as you command. Glory be to you, my Emperor."

The Emperor said nothing but waved them away with his huge golden hand.

Tarnascus rose and turned Lacy to walk back down the hall.

Lacy looked back over her shoulder at the Emperor and the court of phantasms as the flames started to dissipate. Though losing his illumination, the Emperor remained a haunting image.

13. Dex Arrives

The *Silent Horizon* pulled out of hyperspace in an empty sector of space.

Dex wiped the sweat across his brow and thanked God he was still alive. Before moving on to the next task, Dex gave himself a moment to just relax in his chair and compose himself.

After a few moments, he let himself laugh, then opened a new log on the ship's computer.

"Day… what is it… four eighteen? Seventeen? Jeez, I don't know. If anyone back on Earth ever hears this… you won't believe what I've just been through. Word of advice, if you head in the direction of the coordinates attached to this log, bring lots of guns. I recently escaped a planet called Reechi…" Dex recounted the story for the log, having fallen into his natural Captain-y rhythm. He gave a brief synopsis of the people he met on Reechi, the different aliens he saw, the Zar-Meck attack, and Korr…

"Korr…" Dex whispered the name. "Korr you bastard." Without a proper closing, Dex ended the log and turned to the ship's radio.

"Korr! Come in Korr do you hear me!" Dex waited a moment for a response, then double-checked to make sure he used the right signal Korr had given him.

A minute passed and Dex received no response. "Korr I know this signal works, now answer me, you coward!"

Dex waited another minute and was momentarily relieved to receive a response until the words came through. "You knew what was coming, don't start playing dumb now."

"Don't you think it was a little late to back out Korr?" Dex asked angrily. "Hwaq saw you with me, think he's gonna keep quiet?"

Almost instantly, Korr responded. "I don't think he's gonna

say anything to anyone. Ever."

It took Dex a moment to realize what Korr meant. "You didn't..." "I laid out my cards plainly, Dex." Dex stood and paced alongside the console, leaving the radio signal open.

Korr continued to speak. "I truly am sorry it came to this." There was a hint of sincerity in his voice. "Hwaq was a good friend of mi-" Dex shouted into the radio, filled with anger. "So you murder your friends now?"

"Would you rather it be you?"

Dex stopped pacing and dropped his hands onto the console. "And why wasn't it?! He had kids! You just met me!"

Korr let out a deep breath that Dex heard faintly through the radio. "I've known Hwaq for a long time. But his loyalty to me is beat out a hundred times greater by his loyalty to the Emperor. Maybe under enough suffering, you'd turn me in, but even now..."

Dex stared at the speaker waiting for a response.

Korr sounded exhausted when he spoke again. "Don't ask me for more help Dex. You've got your hyperdrive, just go home. There's still time. Forget your girl. It's not worth the suffering the Emperor will put you through. Even if you did get her back, the two of you will never truly be free of him."

Dex took a moment to compose himself. His heart beat rapidly at Korr's words. He looked around the cabin at the empty bunks. The one that hadn't been used for over a year, and the one Lacy should have still been in. Dex turned back to the radio and said, "I'll suffer through anything the Emperor throws at me. I'll spend eternity running from or fighting the Empire. They can shatter my bones again, and a million times over, and rip my soul from my body. But I will save Lacy. Even if the Emperor takes me, I *will* save her."

"Dex, please-"

"Korr, I'm going to face him." Dex began to input the coordinates for the Heart of the Void and let the computer map a course. "I might die, but you could at least give me a fighting chance. If you truly believe the Emperor is as evil as you say, at least we'll go down doing something good for the universe."

Dex waited for a response, but Korr wouldn't give any. After a moment he smacked a hand on the console. "Come on you son of a bitch! If you're doing nothing with your life do you really wanna live forever?!"

Still, Korr wouldn't answer.

Dex fell into his chair and realized he wouldn't win Korr over. "If you change your mind…just don't keep me waiting too long." Without waiting for a response, Dex closed the line.

As he prepared for the launch to hyper-space, Dex ran through the ship's computer looking for any problems the new engine may have caused. So far everything looked fine. No alarms had gone off. The only thing that stuck out to him was the *Silent Horizon*'s fuel level. The initial journey out into Empire territory had cost them little fuel, having only used it to accelerate them to cruising speed. Powering the rest of the ship took minimal effort from the engine. Looking at it now, based on how much fuel he had spent from the jump out of Reechi, Dex guessed he would only have enough fuel for two or three more jumps. *As long as it's enough to get back to Earth*, he thought. Even as the thought came out, he knew he didn't believe it. "As long as I can get Lacy back," he corrected out loud.

Everything was now set. The *Silent Horizon* plotted a course for the Heart of the Void, and the engine was ready. Time slowed as light wrapped around the ship.

As the fabric of the universe was pulled open in front of Dex, a voice called out to him. It was incomprehensible and had a tone of calm questioning like Dex's presence was uninvited but not unwelcome. In an infinitesimal moment that lasted an eternity, an image shot into Dex's mind of a vast green landscape, sliced into tiny elevated islands by thin rivers.

Before he could study the scene, the vision was gone. Dex could no longer hear the voice. He was back flying through hyper-space, watching the colors of the stars swirl together as he zoomed past them.

The computer estimated the trip would take just under two hours. Dex thought this was plenty of time to formulate a plan. The biggest problem though, was Dex had no idea what he'd be going up against.

He assumed that if this was the Empire's home world, defenses would be incredibly high. If he went in guns blazing, he surely wouldn't get remotely close to the planet's upper atmosphere. Even if he tried to go in stealthily, he wasn't sure if his clearance codes would still work.

Regardless of how he would initially approach the Heart of the Void, Dex knew that he would eventually find himself fighting again. This thought scared him too. He'd been up against the Zar-Mecks twice already. On the ground, he wasn't fast or strong enough to face them without help.

Dex then realized *I may not have the speed, but I think I can GET the strength!* Rummaging through the storage above the starboard side bunk, Dex found the black cube of Zar-Meck armor.

As if readings his mind, the cube didn't move until Dex knew he was ready to let it cover him again. The warm and relaxing feeling took over Dex. His vision was covered only for a moment before the purple visor appeared over his eyes.

Dex looked around the *Silent Horizon*'s cabin, getting a feel for the suit. The purple tint felt off-putting to Dex, and again, the suit read his mind. The visor's tint shifted to a transparent white.

So, it can recognize what I want it to do! Dex thought to himself. He spoke aloud, "All right, give me a gun!" Dex shot his hand up like he was drawing a blaster, but nothing appeared.

"Come on!" He re-drew his hand in a similar way the Zar-Mecks swapped out their weapons. "Just give me a weapon!" As the word was spoken, a screen appeared on the visor's heads-up display. A list of weapons and images of them popped up. He saw the familiar blasters and batons the Zar-Mecks carried, as well as others such as small grenades, short swords, and daggers.

Dex locked the image of the blaster in his head, then quick-drew the weapon out of his armor's thigh like he'd seen the Zar-Mecks do. It clicked for him that the suit needed specifics for what it could conjure up.

On the right side of the heads-up display, he saw an outline of his body, with a note to the side labeled "Armor capacity." It was currently at 93%. *Did those bots give me a busted suit?* Dex let the blaster assimilate back into the suit, and he saw the armor capacity rise to 95%.

"Of course," Dex told himself. "Suit can't be perfect."

Dex tested out the other weapons, seeing how much they took away from the suit and how they felt in his hands. The closest he'd ever come before this to sword fighting was playing knights with his cousins as a kid. Dex knew fighting with bladed weapons would be the last resort.

Recognizing that the suit was fluid, he wondered if he could focus on where the armor should cover more heavily, or if he could retract parts of it. Dex mentally commanded the suit helmet to retract, but was disappointed when nothing happened. The suit was capable of only so much, but it gave him a leg up he hadn't expected.

Dex made a mental note to try to get one for Lacy too if they had time during their escape.

With the suit explored, the only thing left for Dex to do was figure out a plan of attack.

* * *

After leaving the hangar, Jaskek put in a call for a shuttle through his tablet. But before he could complete the request, a shuttle arrived with an Imperial Officer sitting in the front.

"Officer Dreed, what are you doing out here?" The officer inquired.

"Classified, Officer Orbek," Jaskek replied without hesitation. "Regards the prisoner."

Orbek stepped up and out of the shuttle. "Is the prisoner over here, Dreed?" His tone was hard.

"No, sir, I-"

Orbek interrupted, "No! She's already up in the palace because I had to bring her. Now, I'll ask again, what are you doing out here?"

Jaskek remained calm, standing tall with his hands clasped behind him. "As I said, sir. Classified."

Orbek harrumphed and stepped closer. "If you're looking for re-assignment to Mascoadon, I'd be more than happy to file the request."

"Officer Orbek, how much time have you spent with Lieutenant Prullen."

"What's that, Dreed? Lieutenant Prullen?"

"As I thought." Jaskek stepped closer and hardened his face. He towered over Officer Orbek, with his flesh beginning to illuminate. "You know nothing of the prisoner. You have no idea what her kind is capable of. No one does, except me! I have *witnessed* what they can do. The chaos they can create! What I'm doing here is greater than anything you could possibly dream of sacrificing for the Emperor. Compared to what I have to do you'd look at Mascoadon as a pleasure trip! Now stand aside, Orbek."

Orbek watched madness dance in the young officer's eyes. He stepped back closer to the shuttle. "I think, Officer Dreed, you need to return to your training. It seems your first duty station was a bit more than you can handle."

Jaskek closed the distance again, and let himself calm down, so the glow left his skin before he spoke. "Or you are too old to see a bigger picture."

Orbek was pressed against the shuttle door, standing in Jaskek's shadow. "The only order for the prisoner was to bring her to the Emperor. There is no danger Officer Dreed. Now come with me back to the ship. We'll sort everything out there." Orbek opened the short shuttle door and stepped through, never taking his eyes off Jaskek.

There was a pause between the two officers. They eyed each other intensely until Jaskek stepped aboard.

"Good," Orbek said. "Now sit."

Jaskek did as he was ordered, taking a seat in front of Orbek.

As the shuttle took off for the short trip to the transport ship, both taouron felt the tension in the air. Orbek felt grateful to be sitting behind Jaskek, not wanting the analyst to see that his skin was now glowing lightly.

In the row ahead, Jaskek was looking around, studying the ground below them as if searching for something. Orbek was growing more and more unnerved at his behavior. Jaskek then looked up to the palace-city floating above. A small fleet of shuttles were flying towards it.

Orbek spoke, attempting to add levity to the tense feeling he had. "The Emperor surely isn't wasting a moment with this prisoner.

Those must be the offerings for the sacrifice."

"Reroute the shuttle, Officer Orbek."

"What was that?" Orbek shouted to overpower the wind blowing past them.

"Reroute the shuttle. Take me up to the palace."

"Officer Dreed, right now your duty is-"

Before another word escaped him, Jaskek had jumped back, riding the wind to give him a boost into the row of seats behind Orbek. With lightning speed, Jaskek placed his hands around Orbek's head and snapped his neck.

The officer's lifeless body fell to the floor of the shuttle.

Jaskek knew this was the moment his fate was sealed.

Taking out his tablet, Jaskek rerouted the shuttle to the Emperor's palace-city.

* * *

After deciding on a "plan," Dex took to practicing his swordsmanship. Dex played back clips of Errol Flynn films, studying his footwork, and how he held his sword. Dex knew it was by no means the best training, but with the limited time he had, Flynn's movies were the only thing he could come up with. Between clips, he would practice against one of the P.E.S. suits he had propped up against the back wall. Giving no resistance, it was still one of the toughest enemies he'd ever fought.

Half an hour later, he sheathed the Zar-Meck sword back into the suit and told himself matter-of-factly, "Yeah, I'm gonna die."

Now, the Heart of the Void was approaching. Dex pulled the *Silent Horizon* out of hyperspace.

The sight of the Empire's home world left him in awe. Dex gazed upon the Heart of the Void. He was amazed by the magnitude of the statue that looked to be holding the planet in its hands. Equidistant from the planet and statue were three massive black holes, constantly pulling the world, maintaining a perfect balance of its place in the universe. Dex felt that if there were a center of the universe, this place must be it.

Time for taking in beauty was cut short. Rapidly approaching on the *Silent Horizon*'s radar was a small object.

Dex pulled up imaging on the ship's computer and saw a small pod hurtling towards him.

Angling the ship so the rear blaster Korr installed could be properly aimed at the pod, Dex waited for a prime opportunity to fire. But as it got closer, he knew something was off. The pod looked nothing like the Zar-Meck starfighters and was making no attempt to hail him or fire. Furthermore, the computer read no signs of life coming from the pod. Dex kept his guard up, sensing it could be a ploy. At this distance, he would have already been spotted by the pod, so Dex decided to be the one to make the first move.

"Unidentified craft…identify yourself or I will fire on you," Dex called into his radio.

After only a moment, as if expecting the call he heard back a very plainly stated, "Robbie."

Dex was taken aback. Firstly, he expected more of a fight before anyone gave themselves away, and also, *what are the odds of someone being named 'Robbie' out here?* "Sorry…"Confusion held heavy in his voice. "Say again?"

Again, "Robbie," very politely and plainly was all that came through.

Dex looked at the radar screen. The pod was still coming in fast in a course that would soon fly past him. "Okay…Robbie, I need you to slow down your ship or I will be forced to fire on you."

"Please don't."

"Excuse me, what?"

"Please don't fire."

Dex didn't know what to say. The pod wasn't arming up or slowing down. It just continued to cruise.

"I don't know what I'm doing."

Dex was at a complete loss.

"Robbie, are you from Earth? How did you get out here?" Seeing the pod wasn't slowing down, and not wanting to let it reach the Heart of the Void, Dex flew into the ship's path. He planned to stay in the ship's path, ready to blow it out of the sky at any moment.

"My friend put me in this pod. I don't know where she is. I think the officers got her."

This guy just sounds like a scared kid, Dex thought, and then it clicked. An Earth name and his friend was a woman. "Okay, Robbie, who was your friend? What was her name?"

"Lacy Prullen." Dex laughed. A tear of joy welled in his eye. "Lacy?! Where is she now?"

There was a moment's hesitation before Robbie responded. "I am unaware of her location. She only instructed me," Then in a recording of Lacy's voice, Robbie played back over the radio, "Just go! Be Free!"

Dex's heart leaped at the sound of Lacy's voice. He tried to speak, but his voice was lost in shock. Dex wanted to sit and treasure the moment for as long as he could, but the *Silent Horizon* and Robbie's pod were still on a direct course for the Heart of the Void.

"Uh-Okay-Robbie…Robbie listen you have to slow down your ship."

"I am unable to pilot this craft."

"Well, you have to try Robbie. Is there a control panel in there?"

Robbie took a few seconds to respond. "Yes."

Of course, there is. He's talking to me somehow, Dex thought to himself. "All right great, look around for something labeled thrusters. See 'em?"

Another few seconds passed. "No."

"Damn." Dex ran his hands through his hair in frustration. "All right, here's what I'll do. I'm going to try to manually slow down your pod. From my reading, it doesn't look like your thrusters are on. Say a prayer for us buddy!"

As Dex prepared his maneuver, Robbie called back again. "A prayer."

Dex didn't understand what Robbie meant, or if he heard him right, but he brushed Robbie's words aside.

Lined up perfectly with the pod, the *Silent Horizon* began to slow, closing the distance between them. Dex hoped that if he slowly added resistance to the pod, he could slow them both down without damaging either ship. Once they came to a halt, Dex would use the spacewalk suit to retrieve Robbie. The hardest part would be bringing Robbie back onto the *Silent Horizon* if he didn't have a suit of his own. Realizing this, Dex called the pod to ask if he had a suit, but was cut off too quickly.

"I will come to you. It will be easier."

"Wait, Robbie what?"

Instead of receiving an answer, Dex saw through the rear-view camera feed the pod of Robbie's shuttle open. Air rushed out, and along with it, a small ash-black box.

Dex shouted into the radio, "Robbie! Robbie are you okay?!"

No response came.

"Robbie!" Dex threw himself out of his seat and rushed to get dressed in the spacewalk suit. He was dressed and ready in under thirty seconds and trudged along in the heavy suit down the hall of the *Silent Horizon* to the airlock. Passing through the first door, Dex hooked up the oxygen line, and as he initiated the de-pressuring, he could have sworn he heard a knock at the door.

Dex brushed the ridiculous thought from his mind and waited impatiently for the de-pressurization to finish. The moment the hissing sound left the room, Dex heard the knocking again.

"Hello?" Dex asked towards the door. "Robbie is that you?"

He waited for a response that wouldn't come.

Dex reached out to open the door, realizing only too late that he didn't have his blaster accessible.

The door opened and holding on to the left side of the door with a tiny claw hand, dangled Robbie, the small ash-black robot.

"Robbie?! You're a…a robot?"

"May I come in?" Robbie asked, sounding like a scared child.

"Y-…Yeah, I mean yes! Come on!" Dex reached out and grabbed the robot.

Dex closed the door behind Robbie, then re-pressurized the airlock. "How did you get over here? I saw you fly away!"

Robbie didn't speak, but instead sprayed a bit of his extinguisher from his left claw as he'd demonstrated for Lacy before.

"Good to know," said Dex, taking off his suit helmet. "Well, Robbie, it's nice to meet you." He grabbed Robbie's claw to shake it, and the small robot's arm flailed about.

"I don't understand your kind. You must be Dex. Lacy's partner."

Dex let go of Robbie's claw and began to escort him back to the main cabin. "I'm her husband, yeah. And I need to get back to her. I think she's down on that planet."

"She is. I think she's dead now." Robbie spoke so matter-of-factly, but Dex had come too far to believe the robot.

"She's not dead. Not yet." He began to undress from the suit.

"How do you know? Have you seen her?" Robbie began to shuffle around the room, inspecting the alien craft.

"No, not yet, but I believe she is."

"But you're not certain."

Dex, now sitting on the ground, pulled a foot out of one of the pant legs and threw the suit on the ground. "I *am* certain. I refuse to believe she's lost."

Robbie dropped his attention from the contents of the scarlet P.E.S. he'd been studying and looked back at Dex. "You're very strange Dex Prullen."

"You're the one to talk."

Robbie stepped closer to Dex. "You and Lacy are both very strange."

Dex finished undressing and laughed lightly as he hung the suit back up. "Yeah, she's a weird one. One of a kind. There's no one like her in the whole universe, and that's why I know she's still alive."

"I highly doubt there's no one like her."

Dex walked back towards the front console but didn't take his eyes off the robot following him. "Have you ever met someone like her?"

Robbie stopped in his tracks. He thought of Lacy helping him pick out a name. It was the first time any living being or intelligent machine had asked for his thoughts on something. "No. Never."

"I thought not." Dex took his seat and regained control of the ship's navigation. "So do you believe me?"

Robbie pulled up next to Dex. "No. She is most likely dead."

Dex glanced down at Robbie and gave the robot a hard look.

Robbie shrank away half a foot. "But…there is clearly no convincing you. In her memory, I will help you go die too."

"Whatever. Come on up here little guy." Dex picked the robot up and placed him in Lacy's co-pilot seat. "We're not gonna die though."

"If you say so. What is your plan."

Dex breathed out deeply. "Well...I'll admit it's not great. I'm assuming she's on her way to, or with the Emperor now. So I'll look for a palace or castle or whatever, fly in hard and fast, hop off the ship, grab her, hop back on the ship, and fly off, hoping and praying the whole time we don't get blasted to smithereens."

Robbie stared blankly at Dex, then out into space towards the Heart of the Void. "We are going to die."

"I'm all ears if you've got any ideas."

The robot looked back and forth between Dex and the Heart of the Void, then shook his head. "I have no plans. All I know is where Lacy would be."

Dex beamed. "Why didn't you say so?!"

Robbie didn't know what to say, he only shrugged.

"Well, where is she?"

"All sacrifices are brought to his palace. It floats high above the planet's surface, in the northern hemisphere, under the crown of the Emperor."

"You mean that huge statue surrounding the planet? That's *the* Emperor?"

"Some cultures in the Empire believe that to be the Emperor himself."

"And is it?"

Robbie and Dex both stared ahead at the great statue holding the planet. "It is possible," Robbie said. "The first peoples of the Empire believe it is."

"Great," Dex said plainly. "At least he doesn't look like he'll bother us too much on the surface. Think you can navigate the ship to the palace?"

"I am not programmed for flying."

"That's fine I just...wait. Of course! Robbie, I need you to fly this thing!" Dex looked half mad with excitement.

Robbie shot a glance at Dex. "What? Dex I said I am not program-"

Dex waved his words away. "I don't care what you're programmed for. I need you to fly. Look all you need to know for now is this; right here controls movements up and down. Next to it, here, is left and right. Push this one in to go faster, pull it out to slow down. I don't need you pulling any crazy stunts, just keep this baby in the air for as long as possible okay?" Dex's heart was now beating heavily with excitement. With a co-pilot(even one that had never flown before) his odds increased greatly. If things went well, the *Silent Horizon*'s flight assistant should work wonders for Robbie.

"I cannot fly."

Dex's smile began to fade.

"But I will try before I die."

Dex clapped his hands in triumph. "Yes! Okay! Awesome, thank God. Here we come Lacy."

"Strange person," Robbie said to himself.

Dex accelerated the ship faster toward the planet. "All right, I have some old clearance codes on the computer. I'll submit those when we get close to the planet. Should be good enough to at least get us through."

Robbie said nothing, but Dex could feel him wanting to be negative about their chances.

"What do I do if the Emperor's Zar-Mecks get on the ship?"

"I think you'll be fine Robbie."

"Should I have a blaster?"

"Robbie it doesn't even look like you have fingers. How would you pull a trigger?"

Robbie looked at his claws, then dropped his arms, letting his body fall back against the seat in defeat.

"Just try to shake them off, okay?"

"Okay," Robbie said quietly.

"You are so weird," Dex said to himself.

As the *Silent Horizon* drew close to the planet, the ship was hailed just as Dex had expected. A port officer requested their clearance codes, and this time Dex didn't hesitate to send them.

The response from the port officer took much longer than they had on Reechi, but after about two minutes, they were granted permission to land and instructed where to go.

"All right, when we get closer to the ground, I need you to point me in the direction of the palace," Dex instructed. "Once we're on top of it you take the steering. If we can land, great. If not…I'll figure something out."

The view of the main city came upon them, but Dex wouldn't let himself pay it any mind. He had to stay focused on the mission.

"Over there," Robbie pointed out towards the palace-city, hovering far off in the distance.

Dex jerked the *Silent Horizon* off their course and flew fast towards the palace-city.

Over the radio, the feminine voice of the port officer called to them. "Remain on your course or you will be taken out of the air. This is your only warning."

Robbie reached out to grab Dex's arm. "Dex I'm having second thoughts about this."

"Too late!"

The palace-city was approaching rapidly.

Over the radio, the port officer called them again. "Dex Prullen, whatever you are planning, you will not succeed."

Dex and Robbie stared at each other in disbelief.

Nearly on top of the palace-city now, Dex saw a squad of Zar-Mecks waiting for them with blasters ready.

"All right Robbie, your turn to fly. Take us in low."

"What? Dex, I cannot fly!"

But Dex was already on his feet and slammed down on the flight assist button before running to the port side bunk to grab the cube of Zar-Meck armor which encased his body the moment his fingers made contact. Dex wrapped his rigger belt around his waist, then prepped two grenades. "You ready little guy?"

"No!"

Dex was already headed for the airlock as Robbie shouted at him. "Remember, keep me low! I have a comm to the ship just stay alert!" The door slid shut behind Dex as he entered the hallway and rushed to the airlock.

Already he could hear blasts from the Zar-Mecks ricochetting off of the *Silent Horizon*'s hull and felt the ship shake more under the control of Robbie's piloting.

The airlock opened as they passed over the squad, and without hesitation, Dex dropped both grenades out to the platform below.

The Zar-Meck squad was thrown by the blast in every direction. One had even been knocked off the platform entirely, falling down to the planet's surface.

"Robbie, you hear me?" Dex called over the comm.

"I hear you," he heard back.

"I need you to make another round. And get lower!"

The *Silent Horizon* turned for another pass and dropped another thirty feet.

Dex mentally prepared himself as the platform approached. They were still a good twenty feet up, but the Zar-Mecks were getting back up.

Blaster ready in one hand, and a grenade ready in the other, Dex jumped down to the palace-city.

14. One Heart to the Next

Lacy stood with feet locked into place on a hovering platform, facing a mirror in a large, domed dressing chamber at the peak of a large tower. Vines and flowers decorated the pillars holding up the roof. From her vantage point, she could see nearly all of the palace-city below her but refused to give its beauty any attention or praise.

Lacy was being dressed in a magnificently detailed scarlet gown, embedded with beautiful gems along its long sleeves and the trim of the even longer train. One of the tall purple aliens who referred to themselves not as a species, but as Children of the Void, a thin woman named Rassmenda had helped her dress and covered any exposed skin on her hands, chest, neck, and head with thick crimson paint that emphasized her bone structure while embellishing with elaborate detailing, and flowed naturally into the design of the dress. Rassmenda took her time in every aspect of the dressing and painting, ensuring the fabric fell in just the right places, shining the gems, and fixing the jewelry that hung around Lacy's neck, off her ears, and out of her hair. The final piece was a haunting, and simultaneously gorgeous, skeletal crown.

Rassmenda carried it delicately by the two largest of the many thick horns that protruded out the sides. From its furthest point side to side, the crown was three feet wide and extended that length in height. A hundred gold strings dangled from piercings in the crown.

Lacy kept her eyes forward, looking back at herself. She maintained a strong, sturdy expression. For all the admittedly beautiful and impressive work Rassmenda put into preparing her, Lacy refused to express any recognition.

The crown was gently placed on Lacy's head, and she noticed the paint on her face blended seamlessly with the coloring of the horned bone crown. Rassmenda pulled the jewelry in Lacy's hair through open slits of the crown and placed them strategically to hang down along the sides and back of her head.

"You are about to receive a great honor," Rassmenda said gently. It was the first thing she had said since Tarnascus passed Lacy off to her. "You will stand high in the Emperor's court for all eternity. A queen and mother, delivering your children into the world beyond of our Emperor."

Lacy studied the crown, thinking of the similarity it had to the headdresses of the ghostly figures she saw in the Emperor's hall. The Emperor's words were mysterious, but she gathered that she would be converted into some kind of deity, trapped in a terrible undead existence. Now with the crown and body paint, she feared a physical transformation too. If it went through, *would it be painful?* She thought, *is there any turning back? If not...how will I be able to keep fighting him?* Her heart beat heavily at the thought.

Rassmenda took a step back and assessed her work. "You are ready. The Emperor will be rejoiced to have you in his court." Lacy attempted to calm her heart. "I will rejoice when the Emperor dies."

Rassmenda dropped her head, fearful of Lacy's words. "You should not speak as such," she said quietly. "You are a gift unto the universe, serving a greater purpose than you could have ever wished. Only one of each race will ever be accepted into the Emperor's court. You will have power over all your peoples."

Lacy turned her head slowly to face Rassmenda, focusing on balancing the crown. "But the Emperor will still have total control over me. Won't he?"

"There is no one greater than the Emperor. He has wonderful control over all of us. You have the gift of being close with him on a level our simple minds cannot begin to comprehend."

"No tyrant has ever been a great person," Lacy snapped at the woman.

Rassmenda jumped back in shock, and for a moment, Lacy felt a twinge of guilt. This life was all the alien had probably ever known. Lacy wouldn't have been surprised if Rassmenda had never even stepped foot on the city below.

Lacy turned back to the mirror. "I hope one day you leave this planet. I hope you see the universe. You'll see there is so much more than this box you live- HEY!"

She had moved so silently and quickly, draping a cover hanging from either side of the crown to hang in front of Lacy's jaw. Though it didn't cling to her face, it absorbed all sound escaping her mouth. Lacy couldn't pull it off no matter how she tried. Even when it was pulled up to reveal her mouth, it still absorbed her words. The cover emitted a short-range field that blocked any sound from passing around it.

"You will blaspheme the Emperor no more. Come, it is time for the feast." Rassmenda left the room, walking to a staircase that wrapped around the tower. The platform Lacy was stuck to followed after, staying to the side of the staircase.

Off in the distant skies, something passed through the clouds. Lacy saw it briefly, hoping it was Dex but knew it was nothing more than a bird.

At the bottom of the tower, two lines of mixed alien races wearing matching scarlet togas. At the head of the precession stood Tarnascus, wielding a large golden staff, and another Child of the Void to his left. This one looked similar to Rassmenda and kept her head hung low. She wore a white gown that matched the styling Tarnascus' robes.

Lacy's hover platform fell in place between Tarnascus and the lines of sacrifices. Rassmenda took her place to Tarnascus' right.

"Mermorrum," Tarnascus said to the woman to his left. "You may begin."

Without hesitation, Mermorrum's head shot up, eyes focused on the Emperor's pyramid ahead, and bellowed deep, alien words. Lacy had no idea what they meant, but they were repeated by the people behind her in perfect unison.

Tarnascus stepped off toward the pyramid. The ritual had begun.

Mermorrum let out another cry, followed by another repeat by the alien sacrifices.

It sounds like a prayer, Lacy thought.

As Mermorrum began her next chant, an explosion roared in the distance. Tarnascus and the two women next to him didn't react, but Lacy and the rest of the sacrifices turned to try and see what was going on.

Dex! Lacy thought, *it has to be Dex!*

There above the rooftops by the edge of the palace-city, Lacy saw the *Silent Horizon* being hit by blaster fire. She couldn't help but beam with excitement. Turning back to Tarnascus, she yelled, "You hear that?! Didn't I say he'd come!" forgetting entirely she was muted by the face cover.

The Pyramid drew closer. Lacy turned back once again, attempting to catch another look at the *Silent Horizon*.

* * *

Dex landed on the solid ground of the palace-city. The three remaining Zar-Mecks were back on their feet, firing at the *Silent Horizon* as it passed overhead. Before the Zar-Mecks could notice him, Dex threw the grenade he'd dropped down with. The moment it hit the ground, it blew up, tearing chunks of the Zar-Meck's armor away. Dex raced over to the downed Zar-Mecks and blasted one in an area of exposed flesh.

The others were too fast. They were up on their feet guns ready.

With his free hand, Dex picked up the body of the dead Zar-Meck, using it as a shield. The suit he wore helped a little, increasing his speed and strength, giving him just enough of an edge on these guys.

Dex sidestepped to the right, blasting the nearest Zar-Meck so rapidy and intensely, one would have thought he carried a machine gun.

With the third one down, Dex threw his Zar-Meck shield at the remaining enemy, then charged, knocking him down. Dex took three precise shots to break the armor covering the Zar-Meck's chest, then a fourth to end its life.

With all of them defeated, Dex stepped back and gave himself a moment to catch his breath. A flash on his heads-up display told him he had taken damage. The suit's power was now down to 78%.

Dex pulled his comm device off his belt and called to Robbie. "You all good up there, little guy?"

"NOOO!" Robbie shouted back immediately. "I THINK THAT THIS IS FEAR I FEEL!"

"Are you going down?!"

"No! I don't like flying!"

"Okay, you'll be fine Robbie. Just keep that ship in the air, I won't take too long." Dex clipped the comm back onto his belt and scanned the roads around him.

There were no identifying marks or directions. Using one of the vines hanging from the top of a nearby building, Dex climbed to the roof to get a better view.

Off in the distance, he spotted the Emperor's pyramid. "Robbie! That pyramid, is that the Emperor?"

"Yes, Lacy will be there!"

Dex didn't waste time responding. He was running across the roof, jumping from one building to the next, trying to avoid slipping through alleys that would send him falling to his death below.

Five rooftops later, a blaster bolt shot through the air, slamming into Dex's leg as he jumped from one roof to another. The impact slowed his momentum, and he was able to just barely grab onto a vine that hung on the side of the building.

"He fell!" A Zar-Meck voice shouted!

A second voice responded. "Go confirm! If he's dead, he's dead. But if he's alive orders are to bring him to the Emperor."

Dex tried to pull himself up but stopped when he heard heavy footsteps racing toward him. He looked around for other options and saw a footpath about fifteen feet to his right. If he could swing over to the path, Dex figured he'd be able to lose the Zar-Mecks within the city and would have greater cover.

Using the vine to swing, Dex ran across the wall and jumped when he couldn't swing any further.

Dex landed on the center of the narrow footpath and dashed through a narrow hall with a vegetated trellis roof.

"It looks like he fell!" The Zar-Meck called.

"No! He's down here!" Another shouted, and blaster bolts ripped through the greenery.

Dex took cover against a wall and prepped two more grenades.

Blasts shot down sporadically throughout the crammed hall. There was no one point the Zar-Mecks were firing from. Dex could tell he was completely surrounded.

In a bid for more time, Dex tossed the grenades through sections of the roof that had been completely obliterated. When the explosion rocked the hall and surrounding buildings, the Zar-Meck firing halted briefly, and Dex took off.

As he approached the end of the hall, opening up to a beautiful garden and pool area, Dex found himself trapped again.

A Zar-Meck was waiting for him, sword drawn.

Dex raised his blaster to fire, but the Zar-Meck caught the bolt with his blade.

Right, Dex thought, *I don't have time for this.* A thought passed to use another grenade, but they had been depleting his suit's power level quickly, and he'd need it as a shield more than anything. *But what would one more hurt?* Dex drew a grenade and tossed it in the Zar-Meck's direction. Without hesitation, the Zar-Meck grabbed the grenade and tossed it back with incredible speed.

Dex tried to flee, but the grenade blew up, knocking him off his feet.

Before Dex knew it, the Zar-Meck was on top of him, bringing down his sword. Dex drew his blade and blocked the attack.

A second blow came down swiftly, with much more force behind it. Dex dodged to the left and rushed to his feet. A follow-through came that slashed across Dex's back. The suit took most of the damage, but Dex still felt the force behind the swing and was pushed up against the wall.

Dex turned quickly, seeing the Zar-Meck coming at him in a lunge. Dodging the slightest bit to the right, the blade missed. The Zar-Meck crashed into Dex, who sliced the villain's hands with his own blade. The Zar-Meck dropped the sword and jumped back, avoiding Dex's upward slash. Blasts from the far end of the hall shot toward them. Dex refused to let the Zar-Meck swordsman retreat or retake any advantage. He swung madly as the Zar-Meck drew a new sword from his suit, then beat down continuously, keeping the

Zar-Meck pinned against the wall. Dex's body was tired, and each swing came with a heavy breath, but the adrenaline pumping through him kept Dex going until a blow came down so hard and fast that it sliced off the Zar-Meck's sword hand. Without a second thought, he stabbed the Zar-Meck in the chest.

With the blasts flying too close for comfort, Dex escaped down the hall into the garden. The tip of the pyramid began to peak over the buildings. Dex got his bearings and ran at full speed towards Lacy, shooting at Zar-Mecks as they neared him. When passing a bridge, Dex dropped a grenade to destroy it, hoping to slow down his pursuers.

Now, even with the sounds of blaster bolts zipping through the air, and explosions going off left and right, Dex heard chanting coming from the Emperor's hall.

"I'm almost there, Lacy," he said to himself.

The closer Dex came to the pyramid, the more enemies came down on Dex. Constantly switching between his blaster for enemies on rooftops and at distances, and sword for up-close combat, Dex was quickly adapting to the suit's mental command system, but his power level dropped steadily.

After passing a number of towers and courtyards, dodging the onslaught of Zar-Meck blasters and grenades, Dex came to one of the wide bridges that met the pyramid on the other side. Surrounding the pyramid was the entire population of Children of the Void that resided in the palace-city. There were hundreds, all kneeling with their hands clasped in reverence above their heads. Dex heard a low mumbling coming from the crowd.

The ritual procession was entering the pyramid, still chanting their prayer to the Emperor. Standing tall on her platform above the rest of the sacrifices, Lacy was in clear view of Dex.

"Lacy!" Dex called.

Lacy turned at the shout and saw Dex across the bridge. "Dex! Dex I'm here!"

Rejoiced and motivated at the sound of her voice Dex took a step onto the bridge, but as he did so, half a dozen grenades fell to the ground ahead of him. A moment of shock took over. Dex froze and was then thrown backward by the force of the explosion. He was momentarily in a daze, ears popped and head spinning. When he came to, Dex saw the bridge completely destroyed and the large doors of the pyramid shut.

Dex tried getting to his feet. Suddenly, someone grabbed Dex's arm and pulled him hurriedly into a nearby building. "Listen Captain Prullen, we don't have much time."

* * *

Jaskek's shuttle pulled up under the palace-city. The echoes of the battle above told him he wasn't far from the action, but still at a safe distance for the time being. He hadn't expected Dex to make it to the planet, but no one else would be causing that much chaos.

Using a low-hanging vine, Jaskek pulled himself up onto a walkway, then sent away the shuttle with his tablet.

If the Zar-Mecks' attention is on Dex, I should have no problem intercepting the ritual procession, Jaskek thought. He still walked quietly, checking every corner for Zar-Mecks to be safe.

Knowing how rituals worked, though never seeing one in person, Jaskek wasn't worried about running into the Children of the Void. All he had to worry about was not getting caught in the crossfire.

With every building he passed, the sounds of blaster fire and grenades drew closer. Even when he ran away from the battlefield, the threat of getting stuck in it would catch up to him.

Jaskek's luck ran out when he took a wrong turn and came upon a Zar-Meck hiding in a corner, waiting to ambush Dex.

The Zar-Meck turned, hearing Jaskek's footsteps. It raised its blaster and aimed at Jaskek's head. In a powerful voice, the Zar-Meck commanded, "Officer Dreed, you are not permitted to be in this area. Return to your post!"

Jaskek stiffened himself. "Stand down soldier. And lower your weapon when speaking to an officer."

The Zar-Meck's voice amplified and it took a step closer. "RETURN TO YOUR PO-"

Its words were cut short. Dex had run past behind it, seeing a Zar-Meck and not wasting an easy hit.

The Zar-Meck fell forward towards Jaskek, then spun to catch the already-gone human.

With his attention diverted, Jaskek rushed up behind the Zar-Meck, grabbed its blaster, and aimed it under the Zar-Meck's chin. The Zar-Meck fought hard, trying to pull and shake Jaskek off.

Maintaining his hold on the Zar-Meck, Jaskek pulled the trigger repeatedly until the armor was cracked and a bolt entered its head.

The lifeless body fell to the ground and Jaskek felt no remorse. He only grabbed the blaster, then peaked around the alley corner to see if Dex or any other Zar-Mecks were there.

A group of footsteps quickly approached. Jaskek hid quickly against a wall as Zar-Mecks passed, giving orders through comm devices for where to cut Dex off.

"The human cannot get to the palace. Destroy the bridge if need be."

Jaskek doubled back to find an alternate route to the pyramid until he too found himself looking upon the wide bridges. It was only a moment after he'd come out into the open that a bridge a hundred feet or so to his left was destroyed. Jaskek watched Dex's body fly backward.

Jaskek looked towards the bridge to his right but saw a pair of Zar-Mecks attempting to hide on a rooftop, ready to shoot anyone that got close to them. He ultimately realized, his best chances to get out of there alive were with Dex.

Ignoring the blaster fire that was sure to come his way, Jaskek dashed over to Dex's momentarily incapacitated body, using the smoke and dust from the bridge explosion for cover, and dragged him into the nearest building, a huge spiraled tower. Blaster bolts struck the ground all around them, and once in the building, Jaskek shut and barricaded the door.

Kneeling over Dex, Jaskek said hurriedly, "Listen Captain Prullen, we don't have much time."

The palace-city then ruptured like a small earthquake. Jaskek had no idea where it came from. Grenades couldn't have made such an impact.

Dex looked into Jaskek's taouron eyes. "Korr? Is that you?"

He asked in a daze.

"I'm a friend of your wife, Lieutenant Prullen. We can still save her but you have to do as I say. Can you stand?"

The world began to clear again, and Dex rose slowly to his feet.

"Yeah," Dex said. "I…" The realization hit that he didn't know the man that dragged him. His heads-up display identified Jaskek as an officer in the emperor's army. Dex quickly drew his blaster. Jaskek swiped it aside. In a flash, Dex adapted, summoning a sword from the suit in his left hand and brought it up to Jaskek's neck.

"Calm down Captain Prullen," Jaskek spoke boldly, not giving away a hint of fear for the blade at his throat. "I am the only way you will get your wife back."

"Oh yeah? How do I know I can trust you? You a friend of hers?"

"No, far from. Chances are she'll kill me once we find her."

"Then why would you help her?"

Jaskek took a moment to think, knowing the wrong word would bring him death too quickly. "Because whether for her own good or out of kindness she helped me, even though I was sending her to her death."

Dex lowered his blade slightly and considered. "You stay in front of me. I still don't trust you, so the moment you make the wrong move I won't hesitate to kill you."

"I could have left you to die by that bridge."

"You could also be escorting me to my death for your own glory."

"Do you really wish to waste more time arguing?"

"Fine, what's your plan?" Dex dropped his sword to his side.

Jaskek looked around the room for inspiration and glanced at the staircase that rose to the top of the tower. He then rushed to the window and opened the shutters the littlest bit. "Come here," he commanded Dex. "How far do you think that gap is?"

Dex looked through the window. "Sixty feet. Seventy with the distance from this building." He looked at Jaskek and tapped his suit's helmet. "Lotta cool gadgets up here."

Jaskek backed up towards the stairs. "So I've heard."

A squad of Zar-Mecks crossed in front of the window and began banging on the barricaded door.

Jaskek commanded Dex again, "Quick, drop some grenades on the floor here. But do NOT detonate them, then come to the top of the tower."

Dex didn't question Jaskek. He summoned six grenades from the suit and carefully but quickly lay them down on the ground, then raced up the stairs behind Jaskek.

At the top of the tower, Dex asked, "What's the grand plan?"

Jaskek was lying on the floor, but quickly got up to grab Dex and pulled him to the ground. "Stay low! The Zar-Mecks have got those bridges covered. We'll never get across going over them. So we'll have to make our own."

"What?"

"Get ready to jump. We'll detonate those grenades and ride the tower. It's tall enough to cross the gap."

"You're insane! What about the people down there?!"

"The ones praying your wife has a good death?"

Dex paused, then, "You're right. I'm sure they'll move. All right let's do this." He summoned two more grenades and watched in his heads-up-display, the power level drop down to 8%. The suit was no longer covering his whole body. What was left had consolidated around his torso, and even that felt thin.

The first grenade he dropped down the tower steps. "Let's pray this works," he told Jaskek.

Jaskek said nothing, only harrumphed.

It took a few moments, but as the Zar-Mecks inevitably broke through the barricade, the grenades waiting to meet them detonated.

Jaskek and Dex felt the tower rumble and begin to fall. At the first hint of sway, Dex primed and rolled the second grenade off the ledge in the direction away from the pyramid.

"What are you doing?" Jaskek asked nervously.

"Fixing your plan."

The grenade detonated halfway down the side of the tower. The blast was strong enough to shift the tilt of the falling tower in the direction of the pyramid.

Zar-Mecks on other rooftops began shooting in their direction, hoping a stray bolt would find a target.

On the pyramid side of the bridge, the Children of the Void could no longer ignore the sounds of battle. Many turned to see what the latest explosion had been and ran when they saw the heavy bricks of the tower falling towards them.

Dex thanked God for their fleeing. Even in his anger towards the empire, he'd wanted to avoid death where he could, save for the soulless Zar-Mecks. They could burn for eternity for all Dex cared.

"Get on the roof!" Dex shouted at Jaskek as the tower came closer to the ground.

Before Jaskek could struggle to get up, fighting against the speed of his fall, Dex had grabbed onto the ledge of the far side window and was pulling himself onto the outer wall. Jaskek climbed through just in time, and they both jumped off onto the solid ground of the palace-city as the tower crashed down and tore away a piece of the pyramid.

Dex rolled away from the crash. Bits of what was left of the Zar-Meck suit tore away as they scraped across the ground. All that remained of the suit was the blaster.

Children of the Void we fleeing to the far side of the pyramid and trying their best to keep the prayer chant alive.

"Hey! Jason! Or whatever your name is! You okay?" Dex called through the cloud of dust and rubble that rose around and above the ruined tower.

"It's JASKEK! I'm fine! Legs are killing me though."

Dex coughed up some of the dust. "Welcome to the airborne."

"What?"

"Nothing, army joke, doesn't matter. How do we get in?"

Jaskek began climbing over the tower to get to Dex. It's just over here."

The two of them raced towards the great doors of the pyramid. Children of the Void watched them, mumbling their prayer, trying to figure out if they should intervene.

"The Emperor is in danger!" Jaskek announced to them. "Open this door so we can save him!"

Without hesitation, the crowd of aliens rushed to the heavy

doors and pulled them open.

"Thank you! You shall be well rewarded!" Jaskek said, and the two of them ran into the hall. He then said in a hushed tone to Dex, "Dumb aliens."

* * *

Lacy's heart raced, but she tried to maintain a stoic expression.

I will not fear him, she told herself repeatedly.

The chanting had only grown louder since entering the pyramid and continued down the dimly lit hallway that felt like it went on for miles.

Up in front of the procession, over the sound of the chanting, Tarnascus began his own prayer to the Emperor.

"Great Lord of all worlds and being, we bring to you these sacrifices! Your devoted followers who give their souls willingly, so that we may live closer with you, and in your spirit."

The precession began spilling out of the hallway, into the Emperor's great hall. The pillars of fire were already lit, illuminating the horrific walls of dusty, rotted bone. Phantasms of the Emperor's court began to fade into existence. One grotesque horror show for every species of alien that offered itself to the Emperor and a reminder of what Lacy suspected was waiting for her.

I will not fear him, Lacy told herself again. *I will not let him take me.* She tried to listen without turning her head, for any sounds of battle outside the pyramid, but the walls were so thick, nothing came through.

Tarnascus continued with his prayer. "Great Lord of all worlds and being, we bring to you this woman!"

The three Children of the Void, Tarnascus, Rassmenda, and Mermorrum, approached the edge of the bottomless pit and knelt, then raised their arms in a salute.

Towering above the pit, with his robes of blood, and crowned head that shined as the sun, the Emperor beckoned his sacrifices closer.

"This woman is brought before you," Tarnascus continued

his prayer, "so that your reach may grow, and other peoples may know your embrace."

Mermorrum ceased her prayer and sliced her left hand upward to signal the others to cease as well.

There was a moment of silence in the pyramid.

Lacy looked around and saw that she was the only one without her head down. The Emperor took notice of this.

"Why do you not honor me, Earth woman?" His thousand voices boomed through the great hall. The Children of the Void and all sacrifices shivered in fear and worship.

Tarnascus approached her and removed the cover over Lacy's mouth that was silencing her. He then quickly returned to his place along the edge of the pit.

Lacy felt a shiver too, but only of fear, and repressed it. The eyes of the phantasms cast their glower down on her.

No, not hatred, she thought, *that looks like...anger? No...disappointment.* The only look she could relate it to was her father, giving her the, "I'm not mad just disappointed" speech. *But why?* The weight of the crown bore down on her.

"SPEAK WOMAN!" The voices of the Emperor again threatened to rupture her ears.

The others in the room looked like they wanted to shield their ears and antenna, but would never block out something as holy as the voice of their god.

"I..." Lacy started, stifling the tremble in her voice, wanting to speak boldly. *I will not fear him.* "I honor no one...who feeds off the suffering of others! I will not give in to a tyrant who only lives to kill! I know what you are. You are all that is wrong and evil in this universe! You are not a god, you're a demon!"

Everyone kept their heads down.

"If you will not honor me, then you WILL fear me!" The sound of his voice shook the entire palace-city.

The aliens in the room struggled not to fall flat on the ground, and Mermorrum nearly fell into the pit. But Lacy, locked onto the hovering platform, was unmoved and stood tall.

Proudly she declared "I do not fear you!"

"We shall see." The Emperor's voices returned to a bearable

tone. "Tarnascus, I am ready to accept your offerings."

Tarnascus stood slowly, "As you command, my Lord." He turned to the group of sacrifices, now helping themselves to their feet.

As he turned, a platform rose from the pit to the ledge.

Tarnascus welcomed the sacrifices forward. "There is nothing nobler, nothing greater any of you could do with your lives than to serve your Emperor in this way. The children you leave behind will be proud of you, and one day, you may look back through the eyes of the Emperor, and watch them do the same."

The sacrifices walked to their deaths.

Lacy refused to give up hope. Dex was only just outside and she knew it. *He's probably running down the hallway now.* But there were no footsteps behind her.

The platform looked like a large dinner plate. The sacrifices were all raising their hands towards the Emperor, like small children wanting to be lifted into their parent's arms.

The pillars of fire now burned brighter. The Emperor grew larger and raised his arms out toward the people on the platform as if to receive them.

"I thank you for your sacrifice," he told them. "You shall all receive my greatest gift."

The sacrifices began to cry out in their alien tongue. They praised the Emperor and reached out, hoping to touch his massive golden hands. Some were even climbing over each other in an attempt to get closer.

"Be still! Now is the time to join me!"

The platform hummed. Instantly, the people calmed. They felt the Emperor's power move into and through them. The Children of the Void were silent, their eyes locked on the Emperor.

Lacy watched, worried as to what would happen next.

In a low hum, Tarnascus, Rassmenda, and Mermorrum began to pray.

Lacy heard the cries begin again, but this time…something was off. It was subtle, but it no longer sounded like cries of worship. No…these people were in pain.

Quickly, the cries became screams of terror! The phantasms

watching the sacrifice were taking a more solid, but still slightly transparent form. Their dark eyes were rolled to the backs of their heads. And though the Emperor had no facial features, there was a surely defined look of pleasure emanating from the emptiness that should have been his face.

For once, Lacy had to shield her eyes from the horrors she was witnessing. The screams of terror ate away at her heart.

Throughout the suffering, the prayers from the three Children only grew louder, as if competing with the alien's screams.

For half a moment, the building shook again lightly. It was the only moment, Lacy saw, that Rassmenda and Mermorrum flinched throughout the ceremony. Lacy couldn't tell if something was wrong, or if the power coming from the Emperor was affecting them too.

When the screams stopped, there was a terrible silence in the room. Lacy held her tear-soaked hands over her eyes. She felt a coldness wash over everything.

Slowly, she pulled her hands away from her face. The sacrificial platform descended, and Lacy only caught a glimpse of a horrific mass of mangled bodies. Tarnascus stood before her with his hand out to escort her toward the pit.

"It is time," he said in a soft, but still firm voice.

The locks on her feet released. Lacy looked back to the hallway one last time. Still no sign of Dex. She turned back and met the Emperor's eyeless gaze.

"If you take my soul, I swear to you, you will not have me as a prisoner. You will have me as an enemy, fighting you for eternity." Lacy extended her hand and allowed Tarnascus to lead her to a new, smaller platform that rose out of the pit.

The Emperor welcomed Lacy to her doom with his arms wide.

"It will be an interesting eternity spent together then," was the Emperor's only reply before the next part of the ritual began.

Tarnascus began a new prayer. After every verse, Rassmenda and Mermorrum would repeat him. Every verse was louder than the last.

The platform Lacy stood on began to glow and she felt a strange energy flow into her.

Her heart raced. *I am not afraid.* Her eyes were locked onto the Emperor's face.

The body paint on Lacy's hands and face began to radiate with heat. She could feel it molding into the dress, crown, and her flesh, accentuating the features it had created. The energy force she had felt was now shifting to pain. Lacy gritted her teeth and clenched her fists. She even let a tear escape her eye, but she would not scream for mercy, or look away from the Emperor.

Tarnascus' prayer echoed around the hall but was drowned out in Lacy's ears by her internal screams of pain.

Suddenly the prayer was cut short.

Mermorrum let out a gasp of shock and fell into the pit.

Lacy felt relief from the pain. She broke contact with the Emperor and turned. Tarnascus' tall frame concealed her vision of the hall, but two blaster sounds rang out. He fell to his knees, writhing in pain.

Walking boldly towards the pit were Dex and Jaskek.

"Lacy!" Dex called to her.

Lacy's voice was stuck in her throat. She was overjoyed at the sight of him and let the tears flow. "D- Dex!" Without wasting a moment, she leaped from the platform to the ledge of the pit.

Dex ran to her, reaching out for her arm as Lacy's foot slipped on a loose rock.

"Don't worry, I got you!" Dex comforted her as he helped Lacy to her feet.

Behind them, Jaskek had Rassmenda stuck up. "Don't make any moves," he warned her.

"WHO ENTERS MY HALL!" The voices of the Emperor roared.

Jaskek fell into shock at the realization he was in the presence of the Emperor. His skin illuminated brightly.

Dex held Lacy in his arms as he looked up at the Emperor, trying to avoid being stabbed by her hulking crown. "Lacy, we have to get out of here! We're running out of time." T

hey started shuffling back to the hallway, hand in hand.

"Jas! Come on let's go!" Dex smacked Jaskek's shoulder as they ran past him.

"Rassmenda, my servant, stop them!"

Rassmenda was frozen, unsure of what was happening. She thought, *how could anything like this happen in the Emperor's presence? How could someone do this to god?* But she was not one to keep the Emperor waiting. Putting the Emperor's word before her ineptitude, Rassmenda ran after the trio and grabbed Lacy's arm.

"Please!" She cried, "You don't know what you're doing! It is a gift! A gift he's giving you!" Tears streamed down her face as she pleaded with Lacy. For how thin her frame was, she had incredible strength and dragged Lacy and Dex back to the pit. "It is a gift!" She cried again.

"Let me go!" Lacy demanded.

Dex aimed his blaster at her with his free hand. "Let her go!"

Rassmenda, unconcerned with the blaster, only cried and pleaded, terrified of disappointing the Emperor.

Dex fired a blast into Rassmenda's leg. She fell to the ground, and quickly helped herself back up, continuing dragging Lacy, as if it was no more than a slight inconvenience. A trip over a rock almost.

Jaskek was yelling at Dex to take care of Rassmenda.

Dex was yelling at Rassmenda to let Lacy go. He didn't want to have to kill her.

Rassmenda was yelling at Lacy to come with her.

Lacy was sick of the yelling, and especially of being dragged this way and that across the universe by this god-awful Empire. In a burst of adrenaline, the pulled herself in towards Rassmenda, tilted her head down, and lunged the crown through the woman's stomach.

Rassmenda's eyes widened in shock. Blood flew from her mouth. She let go of Lacy's arm, taking the crown with her.

Lacy's hair fell down her shoulders and back, gold hair pieces dangling with it. She said tensely to Dex, "I…cannot begin to tell you…how much I hate that damn woman."

Dex and Jaskek didn't know what to say.

"Are we going or what?" Lacy asked and picked up her dress.

Dex began to speak, but Jaskek intercepted. "Yes, right now. I have a ship that can pick us up." He began tapping on his tablet for the Zar-Meck ship he'd docked in the hangar to fly to his location.

The three of them started running again down the hall.

Empire of the Void

"Wait no, we have a ship!" Dex said. "Hopefully it's still in the air!" He pulled the comm device off his belt and called to the *Silent Horizon*. "Robbie! Robbie you there?"

"Robbie?!" Lacy thought Dex showing up had already made her as happy as possible, but this was a great surprise.

"Yeah, I'll explain it later!"

The door was just ahead, and thankfully still open. Jaskek ran through first. The Children of the Void were still waiting patiently outside.

"Not to worry," Jaskek assured them. "The Emperor is fine!"

The Children of the Void gave a communal sigh of relief.

"Now if you'll please step aside-" Jaskek cut himself short when a grenade landed at his feet. "Back!" He ordered Dex and Lacy.

The three of them fled behind the great pyramid doors for cover from the grenade. When it blew, the Zar-Mecks couldn't care less for the Children of the Void they had slaughtered. They had their orders.

"Lacy, take this." Dex handed off the Zar-Meck blaster to Lacy and drew his own from his holster.

"Dex, you know I'm terrible with these."

"Yeah well, maybe the range was just an off day."

For the second time since being taken prisoner on Prullen-1(RVO-19 for the Empire), Lacy let herself laugh. Even after almost being turned into a demonic being, and now being under fire by soulless embodiments of evil, she was with Dex again. If this was the end, it would be a good one because they were together. She pulled him in for a kiss.

Dex was caught off guard, his head still in the battle, but he let himself enjoy the moment. He wrapped an arm around her, and placed his other hand on her cheek, pulling her in close.

The kiss washed away all the pain they had endured since parting. All things wrong in the universe were temporarily set right as they embraced.

When the kiss ended, Dex looked into Lacy's eyes. Something was different.

"Lacy...your eyes..."

Lacy's eyes were still primarily blue, but looked like they were dotted with tiny stars and galaxies. They shined in magnificent tiny colors as never before. Dex gazed into her new eyes that were a sea of space.

"No time you two," Jaskek interrupted. "My ship's almost here."

Dex came to, and turned to Jaskek, "Hold on, how well can you control your ship from here?"

"What do you mean?" Jaskek peeked out the door, and a blaster bolt shot past his head. He quickly returned to cover.

"Can you target the Zar-Mecks with that thing?" He pointed to the tablet. "If you can take out the Zar-Mecks, we can make an easy getaway to our ship."

Jaskek thought about this plan. "It's worth a try. But we'll only have a minute before the Zar-Meck's figure out what's going on."

"Great! That's enough." Then into his comm, Dex asked, "Robbie? Come in buddy. What's your status?"

Static for a moment, then "THERE'S A FIRE WHERE HAVE YOU BEEN?!"

Dex sighed in relief. "We're ready for exfil." To Jaskek, "Where should I tell him to meet us?"

"West side landing pad. We'll have to be fast."

"I'm planning on it," Lacy said. "Anything to get out of this dress."

Dex called Robbie again. "Listen, pal, we're gonna meet you at the WEST. SIDE. Landing pad. You got that?"

"I TOLD YOU I CAN'T FLY! I DON'T KNOW WHY I HAVEN'T CRASHED AND THE SHIP IS ON FIRE!" Robbie sounded hysteric.

"You're fine, Robbie." Dex tried to calm him down.

"I AM NOT!"

Lacy took the comm. "Robbie it's me, Lacy!"

Immediately his tone changed. "Lacy?! It's you? Really? Hello friend! I told Dex you were dead! I'm glad I'm wrong, for now!"

"That's great. Listen, I believe in you okay? You can land the ship."

"I will do my best," Robbie said with sincerity, not wanting to let Lacy down.

"You both ready?" Jaskek asked.

Dex and Lacy raised their blasters to give an affirmative.

"Good," he peaked out past the door again. "Because it looks like my ship's here."

A Zar-Meck starfighter flew across the rooftops and began blasting any living thing it saw.

"Let's go!" Jaskek shouted and rushed out the door.

Lacy followed after him, but Dex held her back. He puffed up his cheeks, and she did the same, and they blew out together as their lips met.

"Guppie kisses," they whispered together.

"I love you," Dex said.

"I love you too," Lacy replied.

"COME ON!" Jaskek shouted.

Dex and Lacy rushed out the pyramid doors, blasting anything that resembled a Zar-Meck.

The starfighter gave them adequate cover. Enough at least for them to cross the bridge without it blowing up, and once they were running through the halls and alleyways of the palace-city, all they had to do was keep up their speed. Jaskek was in the lead, followed by Lacy, and Dex in the rear.

Zar-Mecks continued to blast at them from rooftops, and some were waiting to ambush them from behind corners.

A swordsman jumped out from behind the trio as they stepped onto a long, but narrow bridge. He lunged at Dex, who instinctively dodged out of the way. Lacy dodged too as the swordsman's blade charged toward her, and together, she and Dex shoved the man off the bridge.

In pushing the swordsman, Lacy nearly pushed herself off the narrow bridge. Dex grabbed her and pulled her in. "You okay?" He asked.

Lacy nodded quickly, heart racing.

"Look out!" Jaskek called to him from the far end of the bridge.

The couple looked up and saw two Zar-Mecks about to fire. They jumped back to solid ground, avoiding the blasts that came down so heavily it destroyed the bridge.

Dex and Lacy took cover.

"Lacy, you take the left I take the right."

"Got it."

"Ready, now!" They poked out of their cover and began blasting at the Zar-Mecks.

The Zar-Mecks ducked, and under cover fire, Jaskek climbed to the roof.

Seeing Jaskek on his target, Dex shifted fire to the Zar-Meck on the left.

Jaskek, sneaking up on the enemy, rushed the Zar-Meck and threw it off the roof.

Dex and Lacy hit their mark simultaneously. Two blaster bolts, one to the chest, and one to the head, sent the remaining Zar-Meck flying back with its helmet shattered.

"It's clear," Jaskek called to them.

Lacy eyed the distance of the chasm between them. "It's too far! We won't make it!"

Behind them, in the direction of the pyramid, more Zar-Mecks were running towards them and opened fire.

The *Silent Horizon* flew overhead.

Dex looked around for new routes, knowing there was absolutely no time to spare.

"I think I have an idea. Hold on!" He wrapped an arm around Lacy and grabbed a nearby vine. "Always wanted to do this," he said, almost to himself.

Lacy didn't question him. She only held on for dear life as he swung the two of them across the chasm. Blaster fire raced past them, and Lacy did her best to fire back with the arm wrapped around Dex's front.

He let go when they made it to the other side and tumbled to the ground. Jaskek was already back down in the hall, giving them cover fire as they got to their feet.

"Landing platform is just over there," Jaskek said.

Dex and Lacy ran together hand in hand, with Jaskek firing back at the Zar-Mecks.

When they approached the landing pad, the *Silent Horizon* was touching down. It was in terrible shape, scarred by blaster burns all over the hull. The airlock was still open from before and smoke was escaping from it.

"Jesus, he wasn't kidding," Dex said.

Lacy was the first one onto the ship. Dex swapped roles with Jaskek, laying down fire while he boarded. Dex boarded last and sealed the airlock.

His eyes burned from the smoke in the cabin, and all three of them were coughing.

"Are you all on?" Robbie's electronic voice called to them.

"Yes!" Lacy coughed twice. "Yes we're here! Let's go!"

Robbie pulled away from the platform and zoomed into the upper atmosphere.

Lacy rushed to her co-pilot seat and brushed Robbie to the side. "Thanks, Robbie. I'll take it from here."

Robbie hopped down from the chair and attended to the fire burning from the starboard side bunk with his reserve extinguisher.

"What happened Robbie?!" Dex gestured to the flame as he walked through the cabin to his seat at the main console.

"You did not close the door. A stray blast got in as I flew away."

Dex shook his head as he took a seat. "All right, party's over. Prime the engine. This heading." He pointed to a random spot on the map.

Jaskek was looking over his shoulder. "That's not where Earth is."

Lacy glanced over at Dex. "He's right. Why aren't we going to Earth?"

Dex kept his focus on the console. "We need to throw them off. If we take a straight shot to Earth, they'll follow our trajectory. We'll be dooming the whole planet. Plus we can drop your friend off somewhere safe." He thumbed Jaskek, whom he'd felt hovering too closely over his shoulder.

"What?" Lacy asked with a bit of revulsion. "He just helped us escape!"

Something exploded outside the ship.

Dex toggled through the computer's displays and brought up the rear-view feed. They had company.

"Lacy, a rear turret is installed. I need you on that."

She slid into officer mode for a moment and manned the turret. "Roger captain." Then, back out of the officer's tone, "but we can't just leave him now!"

"I agree," Jaskek said. "I won't be able to show my face in the Empire again until I've brought back something to prove myself."

Dex caught him without either of them noticing. "Until." The word Dex had been expecting to hear.

"Baby," Dex said to Lacy, "Change of plans. I need you piloting."

Lacy's gaze rushed back across the console in confusion. "Wait! Wait Dex, what?!"

Before anyone knew what was going on Dex was on his feet and socked Jaskek in the face.

Jaskek fell back and hit his head on the floor.

"Dex what are you doing?!" Lacy screamed, then rolled the *Silent Horizon* to the left as a Zar-Meck straighter careened towards them, firing repeatedly.

"He's not here to save us. He just wants to be the first to the prize." Dex kicked Jaskek while he was down.

"Dex stop!" Lacy cried, but couldn't pull herself away from the controls. The Zar-Mecks were hammering down on them hard. She could barely dodge their attacks.

"Wait!" Jaskek coughed up blood. "Okay! I'll admit..." another cough as he got to his feet, propped up by the port side bunk. His skin began to glow again, flickering like a beating heart. "It's true. When I first found you that was my plan. But things changed!"

"See!" Lacy insisted.

Dex looked at his wife, still unsure.

"I can see now," Jaskek continued. "I don't need *both* of you." He had feigned the level of pain he'd felt, grabbed Dex's blaster, and drew his own, aiming at both of the earthlings. "Just need one of you to operate this ship."

"Lacy, don't try anything," Dex told her, with his arms raised.

"Now for all the work we put in to save her, I think it's only fair Lacy is the one that gets to come with me."

A voice in the back of the room asked politely. "Can I come

too?"

The three of them all turned their heads to see Robbie in the back, swaying back and forth lightly, holding his claws like a child asking for dessert.

With Jaskek's head turned Dex punched him in the gut.

Jaskek dropped the blasters and staggered back. A moment later he lunged at Dex shoving him up against the console, with his hands around Dex's neck.

Dex countered, knocking Jaskek's elbow down to break the contact, then punching up into his jaw.

Jaskek's glow beat more intensely. He intercepted Dex's next blow, threw a punch into his gut, then twisted his arm, throwing him to the ground.

"Robbie help him!" Lacy called to the robot who sat unsure in the corner.

Robbie perked up at hearing his name but was unsure of the right action to take. On one claw he wanted to help his new friends, and on the other was an officer in the Army he had served for his entire existence. His programming told him one thing, but deep down under all the circuitry, another voice told him something else. The voice that won was his own. *I have a choice now.*

Robbie rushed to assist Dex. His right claw was overextended, ready to flame Jaskek.

Seeing the robot rushing, Jaskek only had to give a light kick to knock Robbie onto his back.

Robbie flayed his arms trying to get himself back on his stubby feet.

"I have spent too long being a bystander of history," Jaskek said. "Earth will fall to the Emperor. But I will at least have a taste of your world before handing it over to him."

Dex was on his feet, arms raised, ready to throw down. "You think you'll be welcomed back after what we just pulled?"

"The Emperor cares for worlds, not individual, replaceable lives. In time I will prepare your world for his arrival and be welcomed back as a hero! My debt paid off! I will be honor-"

Dex cut him off with a jab to the face.

The retaliation was swift. Jaskek rushed Dex, grabbing him by the neck and throwing him to the ground.

The *Silent Horizon* rattled under more blaster fire as Dex's head hit the ground. He couldn't breathe, it felt like his lungs collapsed.

Every moment Lacy tried to turn her attention from the battle she was facing against the starfighters to help Dex, another one came in, pinning her in her duty. Instead, of leaving her post, Lacy barrel-rolled the ship hard to the left. Dex and Jaskek rolled around the cabin with the contents of the overhead storage.

Dex was hit in the head by something small, and when Lacy leveled out, Jaskek was back on top of him, ready to choke Dex out.

"Should have taken me back with you!"

Then, over the radio, a voice came in. "Dex do you realize how many bad guys you've got on your tail?"

"What the hell is that?!" Lacy called.

Jaskek looked out the window, then quickly back at Dex before he could be caught off guard again. A Zar-Meck transport ship was hovering over them, with starfighters pouring out. "Those aren't Zar-Mecks. You've got some friends huh?"

Unable to hold herself back anymore, Lacy jumped from the controls to Jaskek and pulled him off Dex with her arm around his neck.

Jaskek thrashed at her, trying to pull her off, but Lacy was so full of rage towards everything to do with the Empire, and reveling in her chance to get some payback, nothing could pull her off of him.

Dex struggled to regain his breath.

With what little focus he had, Jaskek reached for one of the blasters on the floor under the ship's console. He was going to risk getting to Earth without either of them.

Dex grabbed the first thing he could find. The small object that hit his head in the barrel roll.

The jarrmin box.

Dex pulled himself on top of Jaskek and slammed the box on his face. The force alone was enough to shatter bone, and the pain shot through all of Jaskek's being.

Jaskek aimed the blaster at Dex.

Lacy pulled tighter on his throat.

Dex activated the box.

As the medical device numbed and pulled back the flesh on his face, Jaskek pulled the trigger of the blaster.

Dex fell back in pain, ripping the jarrmin box off of Jaskek's face.

Within seconds, Jaskek went from feeling incredible pain, to shock, to death. He lay fleshless-facedown on the floor of the *Silent Horizon*.

Dex and Lacy were both sweating hard in the rush of the action. Her body paint was starting to wash off and run. She wiped it off her face, unsure what to say next.

Looking down at Jaskek's corpse, she thumbed the transport ship just outside. "Um…" she tried to say. "That. You should look."

Dex pulled himself up, then helped Lacy, and they returned to their seats.

Again, the voice over the radio. "Dex! Are you there? Fix your flight path you're headed straight for me."

Instinctively, Dex angled the ship away from the transport, then responded to the call. "Korr? Is that you?"

"Who in Maoul else would it be?" Korr responded enthusiastically.

Dex and Lacy looked out the window and at the rearview feed. Small unmanned fighters from Korr's ship were fending off the Zar-Meck starfighters.

Dex laughed, "What changed your mind?"

"Don't get me started. But I will say, if I'm gonna die, might as well be for the right reason. And a blow to the Emperor himself seems like a pretty good reason."

Lacy took over the radio. "I don't know who you are, but thank you!"

"Appreciate it," Korr said. "Now let's catch up later. I have a hangar open, and not a lot of fighters left on the battlefield. So get in here and we'll be off."

"You got it Korr," Dex said, then gave a command to Lacy. "Power down the hyperdrive engine."

"Hyperdrive?" Lacy asked.

Dex shrugged. "Call it an anniversary present."

The *Silent Horizon* flew around the perimeter of Korr's ship, looking for a hanger entrance. Zar-Meck fighters pursued them, which were pursued by Korr's fighters.

"There it is!" Lacy called, pointing to a small opening in Korr's ship. "The hanger."

"I see it, diving now!"

Dex angled the ship down and began a fast approach to the hanger. It was going to be a close call, but the Zar-Mecks on his tail were too close.

Just a few seconds to freedom, when out of nowhere, a Zar-Meck fighter made a suicide run across their path. Dex had to pull up sharply to avoid a crash.

"Korr I missed my chance!" Dex called through the radio. "I'm coming around for another pass!"

"No!" Korr called back immediately. "I'm too low on fighters. We've got two Empire battleships approaching from the city. I can't cover you much longer. Just get out of here!"

Dex wanted to argue, and he could see in Lacy's eye she did too, but they both knew they weren't going to last long enough for another run. Alarms were blaring left and right in the cabin, screaming at them that the *Silent Horizon* had taken too much damage.

"We're sorry Korr," Dex said. "Lacy, prime the hyperdrive."

Korr's remaining fighters were doing all they could to hold the Zar-Mecks off.

"Lacy what are you doing?!" Dex shouted. "

Just wait! We need something for this!" Lacy raced to find something in the computer's library. "Here!"

Throughout the ship's speakers, "Pines of Rome" picked up where they had stopped after crashing on Prullen-1.

"Lacy are you serious right now?!"

"Trust me! I have an idea." As the triumphant climax of the song played, Lacy rerouted the output to play through the radio as well.

From the other end of the radio, Zar-Meck transmissions argued with each other about what they were hearing.

"That should throw them off for a moment."

Dex scoffed playfully. "All right, enough of the games. I need you to prime the hyperdrive."

"Roger Captain, I'm ready to be out of here."

The *Silent Horizon* raced across the top of Korr's ship, while on the underside, the Empire battleships drew in closer and began opening fire on Korr.

Korr abandoned his ship's bridge and fled for the nearest escape pod. The ship was shaking violently under the heavy canons of the Empire's fire. He could barely stand as he dragged himself through the halls.

Dex angled the *Silent Horizon* upwards again towards space.

"Engine ready?" Dex asked.

"Ready."

A thought stuck Dex suddenly. The ship's fuel levels. "Wait!"

"We don't have time to wait Dex!"

"Lacy, we only have enough fuel for one jump, wherever we go, we might not make it back to Earth…" His voice began to die out, not just fade away.

All around the ship, Zar-Meck starfighters and drones from Korr's ships blasted away at each other. Laser beams crossed across the *Silent Horizon*'s windshield. It would take only one unlucky blast to blow them out of the sky. Yet the only thought in their minds was the choice between safely escaping to an Earth they would doom, or flying off into the further reaches of uncharted space, where any sort of peril and adventure would await them.

Korr's ship met its ultimate fate in the skies of the Heart of the Void, with flaming debris raining down around them, crashing into Zar-Meck ships before assaulting the ground below. The pieces missed Dex and Lacy as if only by fate, and in that moment, the answer was clear to both of them.

Without plotting a course, Lacy reached out to the center of the console and activated the drive to propel them in whatever direction they were meant for.

The universe slowed, then froze around the *Silent Horizon*. Light began to wrap around the ship. The music swelled triumphantly. Dex looked into Lacy's eyes. Lacy looked into his. He put a hand on her cheek, and they leaned into each other. As their lips met, the *Silent Horizon* made its jump into the unknown infinity of space. Captain Dex and Lieutenant Lacy Prullen, two astronauts from Earth, began their next adventure together, happy again in each other's love.

Epilogue of Book 1

Tarnascus entered the throne room accompanied by a taourun, Romek Amari. The two of them fell to their knees by the pit's ledge. They bowed and gave their salute to the Emperor. "How may we serve you, my lord?" Tarnascus spoke for the two of them in a bold and respectful tone.

Emperor Visconos Armourus appeared on the platform above the center of the pit. His voice boomed through the pyramid as he spoke. "You and Zar-Mecks have failed me, Tarnascus."

"My lord," Tarnascus' voice trembled slightly. "He was given aid by a traitor. He had help fro-"

"SILENCE!" The Emperor's voice rattled the entire palace-city. "I care not for your excuses. For three hundred years you have served me. It seems as though your service has run its course. Step forward, and show your bones."

Tarnascus rose slowly and stepped closer toward the ledge. His legs were healing fast from the shots the Earthling had taken at them.

To the side of the Emperor, a phantasm resembling a horrifyingly disfigured Child of the Void appeared.

"Please…my lord…I…I beg you." Before him, a platform from the pit below rose to the ledge.

"Tarnascus, I condemn you to suffer in Maoul."

Tarnascus stepped onto the platform, tears streaming down his face. "I only wished to serve you…"

Romek continued kneeling, eyes to the ground. Unless the Emperor commanded him, he did not wish to witness the suffering Tarnascus had begun to endure. The screams of pain and holy terror were enough to last an eternity in his memory.

When the screaming stopped, the Emperor shifted his attention to Romek Amari. "The Earth beings have escaped and I now task you to hunt them down."

A tear fell from Romek's cracked green eye. "I am...honored...Lord, that you would choose me for this holy mission. I will be merciless in my hunt, Lord. I will earn this duty." Romek let his hands fall to the ground and looked up at the Emperor's imposing golden head. The platform with Tarnascus' body had been replaced with a clean one.

"RISE!" the Emperor commanded.

Romek was on his feet quicker than he realized and stepped onto the platform. Almost instantly his muscles began to ache, and his head felt like it was about to cave in.

"I grant you my powers, Romek. Fail me, and you will never pass beyond this universe. You will be lower in my eyes than the multitudes of worlds I have obliterated, and you will suffer more than all combined."

Romek screamed. His bones cracked. His muscles spasmed and exploded under his skin. He wanted to claw out his eyes that had felt like they were melting, and leaking into his nose, mouth, and lungs. Romek tried to fall to the ground but the Emperor commanded him to rise, and through all his pain, Romek couldn't say no to his god. He stayed on his feet, which stung as if he were standing on molten glass shards.

Romek wanted to die. He wanted to throw himself off the ledge and dive headfirst into the abyss, obliterating himself on whatever lay however far down there, but the voice of the Emperor bade him stay standing where he was.

As quickly as the pain came, it left him. Romek was allowed again to fall to his knees. His body was intact, eyes whole where they belonged, but something was different about him. In his core, he felt new energy welling up. His muscles were bigger, and he had a greater sense of his surroundings. In fact, all of his senses registered much more than before. Looking at the ground around him, he saw the dust and dirt vibrating.

Romek again looked up at the Emperor.

The thousand voices of the Emperor ripped through Romek's mind. "Go now, my servant. Do what must be done for the sake of my Empire!"

Intermission

Aboard the Brighter Day

1

Captain Silvers never much cared for the Lieutenant assigned to her ship. Although Lieutenant Taylor was a worthy spacefarer, there was a lack of chemistry between the two officers. During mission coordination, their personality assessments had been an almost complete match, but they could tell during breaks in training in the weeks leading up to their departure, there just wasn't chemistry between them. Not so much as had been between Captain Mitchell and Lieutenant Leone, and nowhere near as much as Captain Prullen and Lieutenant Carradine. Regardless, the pairing was only a contingency in case something went wrong during the mission and they couldn't return to Earth. At that point, Silvers supposed they wouldn't care about "chemistry" anymore. If they had to survive alone on a new planet, then that would be the mission, and she would do her best to lead them.

For six months, they'd drifted through space. Though the view never changed, if Captain Silvers was on her shift, her eyes would be glued to the viewport or radar. When it was Lieutenant Taylor's shift, she would check in once an hour, on the hour.

"Lieutenant, do you have anything to report?" She would ask.

"No, ma'am. Clear skies as always."

"Very good. Let me know if anything turns up."

"Roger, ma'am," Taylor would say, and wait for her to return in another hour. That was life aboard the *Brighter Day* until they were ambushed by the "tear."

Alarms rang throughout the ship. Captain Silvers jumped out of her bunk and was in her seat in a flash, not even bothering to dress over her skivvies.

"Report!" She ordered Taylor.

Taylor looked from one screen on the console to the next, pressing button after button and inputting commands to the computer, to get a solid reading. "I'm not sure Captain. It looks like the computer's picking up some kind of electrical storm dead ahead, but nothing on radar and nothing visible."

The spacecraft shook violently.

"What the hell was that?" Captain Silvers' head shot hard in Taylor's direction.

"I'm picking up atmosphere, Captain. I don't know how, but the computer says we've entered atmosphere. And we've got gravity!"

Captain Silvers felt herself lifted out of her seat, while Taylor felt himself pulled into his harder, like they had just launched into space again. Anything not strapped down in the cabin began shooting around the room at breakneck speed, complying with a strange, selective gravity.

Outside of the ship, space dust amassed around them, and lightning strikes struck in brilliant scarlet colors.

"I'm losing control, Captain!" Taylor gripped hard on the help, trying to maintain a steady flight.

"You're relieved, Lieutenant!" Captain Silvers took over flight controls before Taylor could object. "I need you to ensure hull and engines are okay."

Lightning streaked across the viewport of the ship, blinding them and erupting in a sound like nails on a chalkboard that tore through the cabin. Small dark dots began carpeting the viewport and running away like-

"Rain! Captain, are you seeing this? We've got rain!"

"That's not rain!" Captain Silvers rebuked her Lieutenant. "Rain isn't red!"

She was right. Upon closer look, Taylor saw the cosmic liquid more closely resembled blood.

"My god… what the hell have we flown into?" Taylor asked the universe.

The ship jerked, sending everything inside toward the hull, regardless of the inconsistent gravitational pulls.

Taylor felt like all of his internal organs rushed to his head, and nearly blacked out. He fell back into his seat, attempted to compose himself, and shouted, "Captain, I think we've been hit!"

"That's ridiculous, Lieutenant! There are no masses out there,

it's just a storm! We'll be fine, just have to get out of this."

The cosmic rain rattled against the ship's hull and another thud hit the rear of the ship.

"Captain, what-" Taylor was pulled to the side hard, with an awkward tug of gravity. "Agh! What do you mean 'just a storm?' Something's out there!"

"Calm down Lieutenant! I see a path out of this!"

Dead ahead, the two could see a clear patch of space. The rain was so heavy on the viewport and hard to see past, but their eyes were sharp, and Silvers was determined to get herself to safety.

"Almost out! Almooost oooutt!" She said to convince herself more than anything Taylor assumed.

Just before they crossed the threshold of the storm, a final gravitational attack came upon the ship. It was so violent that both of their seats were torn up from the floor and thrown about the room. Taylor was jettisoned toward the back of the cabin, spinning rapidly as he was, but struck the back wall chair-side. His head whipped back and he was out cold. Captain Silvers' chair was thrown upwards into the cabin sealing. She didn't pass out but felt the weight of the heavy chair doubled, no, tripled by the chaotic gravity, pinning her legs and neck to the ceiling. For a moment she thought her neck had snapped. There was a momentary burst of pain across her body, then nothing. All she knew was she couldn't breathe. Her cheek was pressed hard against the cold metal ceiling. Her mouth was open, and she tried desperately to suck in air, but her lungs burned as she did so. Fear took over her. Her fate was nearly sealed.

For a brief instant, something came over Taylor and Silvers. Their vision and minds opened wide. Voices flooded into their ears, and vast landscapes left impressions on their eyes. Vivid colors and sounds, greens and reds, soft and chaotic, called to them.

The *Brighter Day* continued its course, and moments later, escaped the storm. The ship's artificial gravity kicked back in, and the crew dropped to the floor.

It was a long moment before Taylor was able to register anything going on around him. It was slow, and at first, all he could feel was pressure building in his head. As he sat up, he felt a warm trail of blood oozing out of his nose. Taylor slowly raised a hand to wipe the blood, feeling like this was the first time he'd ever used the limb. The next thing he noticed was a distant call by Captain Silvers. She was screaming her lungs out, but it sounded no louder than a whisper a thousand miles away compared to the ringing in his ears.

Taylor clumsily unbuckled himself from the seat and took his time standing up, holding onto anything within arm's reach for support.

Captain Silver's cries became louder, and finally comprehensible to Taylor. "Lieu- lieutenant! Help me! Get over here! Lieutenant!"

Taylor's vision now began returning to him. Anything further out than his hand was a complete blur. Overall shapes, colors, and light he could make out, but nothing solid. And the harder he tried to focus, the more his head pounded. He let Silvers shout another two or three "help me's" before trying to walk.

With Taylor's first step, the *Brighter Day* shuddered. Taylor collapsed and blocked out whatever it was Silvers was shouting now.

I'll get there when I get there, Captain! Calm the hell down!

Taylor grabbed onto the back panels of the starboard bunk and hoisted himself up. As he did so, nausea hit him with a violent punch in the stomach. Vomit threatened to force itself out, but Taylor held it back.

"Lieutenant! I need you here! I- I can't feel anything! I can't get up!"

Taylor's vision faded to black. His legs threatened to give again, and the vomit in his throat couldn't be held back much longer.

The bunk was right there. He could lay down, *sleep it off*, he told himself. Taylor planted his hand on the coarse green blanket. *I'll sleep it off and be better in a few hours. My shift is over... I can... I can sleep...*

Taylor's body gave in. He fell forward onto his bunk. Just before his eyes closed, his vision came back into focus.

Captain Silvers lay on the floor, bleeding out from her legs. They looked like some had hacked into the back of her knees with an axe. Her neck was almost entirely purple with bruises. No part of the Captain's body moved, except for her eyes and mouth. She managed one more, "Help me!" before sleep took Taylor away.

2

I'm going to die here…

My legs… my arms… my god, my neck! I can't feel anything! I can't move anything!

Is that…

Oh my god… blood! I'm bleeding!

"Lieutenant! Get out of that bed and help me! Help!"

Remain calm. You're a Captain. You must compose yourself. Breathe…

Calm…

That's it…

Don't lose control. Collect your thoughts. You'll figure this one out. Lieutenant Taylor will come around eventually.

Lieutenant…

I don't know what's come over him, why he's abandoned me like this…

I've been a good Captain. I've been fair to him, treated him well. I've done all I could for him. And this is what I get! He doesn't know how lucky he is to have been on my ship. Those other crews have all probably lost their minds by now, but I've kept us from going mad! They've all probably given up already. Months alone in space. They've probably all shacked up and turned tail.

That's why…

That's why he's leaving me to die…

Because I put the mission over selfish wants? The pairing was for emergencies. They didn't send us up here to mate! But he doesn't care anymore. It's been so long, and he isn't strong enough anymore. He's been wanting me since the start, and now that's clouded his judgment. He's leaving me to die out of spite! Either that or…

God…

He's only waiting. Waiting until I can't fight back. There's medical equipment right above his head. I don't know where the blood's coming from, but

I can assume it's my legs. I may never walk again, but if only he wasn't so spiteful he could save the rest of me.

He'll probably keep me alive. Keep me in my bunk… or in his!.. and have his way with me.

I'll have to find a way to protect myself. Even if I can't move, I'll have to stay on guard.

I can bite him! If he gets close enough after mounting me, I can bite his throat!

But then how will I get home? I still need him for that…

I'll have to be patient. If there's even the littlest bit of sense in him, doubtful there is, he'll turn the ship around. Once we're on the right path, I can…

But how will I survive?

If I can't move, I can't eat…

Even if I had food right here next to me for six months, my body would rot, sitting in one place.

I need him. I need to suffer through him. If I can hold myself together for just six months, we'll make it home. He'll be reported and held accountable for his actions.

But… but we can't turn back. Not entirely. We discovered something. A major cosmic phenomenon! We have to study whatever that was before we can return home. This mission, now more than ever, cannot be wasted.

I will be patient. I'll be strong. For the…

For the betterment of the human race on Earth and…

and the colonies, I will…

I will be…

I w-…

be…

strong…

* * *

Taylor awoke hours later with the worst hangover of his life. It felt like he'd been asleep for days after having been hit alongside the head with a ten-ton baseball bat. The pressure was still there, but the ringing in his ear was gone. Taylor opened his eyes, and this time, everything came into focus much more quickly, but it still took him a minute to notice Silver's pale body on the floor.

"Captain!" Taylor shouted as he threw himself out of his bunk. His brain followed behind with a three-second delay, and when it caught up, rattled violently in his skull.

Captain Silvers looked such a pale grey, she could have camouflaged with the floor, had it not been for the pool of blood she lay in.

Taylor searched her body for wounds and discovered two large gashes in the backs of her knees. Below the knee, the skin had started to decay. Taylor knew he would have to amputate if there was any chance she would pull through.

"Captain! Captain, wake up!" He patted her cheeks, and almost shook her head until he saw the bruising around her neck. Instead, he dropped his head to her chest and listened for a heartbeat.

Silence...

Terrible silence...

Come on, Captain! Pull through!

Bump... Bump bump...

Taylor jumped back in surprised joy. "Captain! You- you wait right here! I'll help you!" He rushed back to the bunk and dug around the storage container above it, looking for a medical box. It was in the furthest back corner, behind all the home comforts he'd brought with them.

The medic box had most of what he needed, tourniquets, gauze, antibiotics, probiotics, pain relievers, cannulas (*this will come in handy*, Taylor told himself), everything he needed except for something to cut major limbs with. The only thing he could think of that could work, as messy as it would be, was his entrenching tool, a multi-purpose, collapsible shovel. It wasn't made for cutting, but if someone was desperate enough, they could make it work. And in the moment, the crew of the *Brighter Day* was desperate enough. The last thing he needed was the ship's laser-cutter tool. The tool was meant for ship repairs, or cutting open foreign materials for study, if ever were found, but it burned hot enough that Taylor thought it might be able to cauterize the Captain's wounds.

Taylor tied the tourniquets above both of Silvers' knees. The blood had already mostly stopped flowing, but if the "surgery" Taylor was about to put her through woke her up and blood began pumping again, she would surely be lost.

Taylor gripped the e-tool in both hands, raised it up, and swung. He winced as it drove into the Captain's kneecap, expecting her to wake up and scream in pain, but there was no movement. Taylor then yanked the e-tool out of her knee and swung again. Two swings later, the legs snapped off. Taylor swapped the e-tool with the laser cutter and began an attempt to cauterize the wound.

At first, he went directly. The short beam cut thoroughly, but only mangled the meat in her leg. Taylor stopped quickly and readjusted his plan, as well as the beam, instead holding it parallel to the wound. Grazing just the surface with the side of the beam, Taylor made slow but effective process. Once the right leg was completely cauterized, he wrapped the stump in gauze and moved on to the next leg.

With the right technique down, Taylor was able to make quicker work on the left leg. After wrapping the left stump, he checked the Captain's heartbeat again.

Thank the Lord, still beating, he assured himself.

Next step, Captain Silver's needed blood. Taylor prepped the needles, cleaned them with rubbing alcohol, and inserted them into either end of the cannulas. Although he was sure of her blood type, he double-checked her dog tags. Type O+. A match with his. Taylor sighed in relief at the small blessing, then began the transfusion.

Though no medic by any means, the four crews of the Wider Universe mission all received advanced life-saving training. Brain surgery was out of reach, but with enough rest, Taylor was sure he'd done well enough to bring Captain Silvers back around.

* * *

"*Brighter Day* Captain's log, day 197. This is Lieutenant Taylor reporting in Captain Silvers' stead." Taylor recounted the day's events in the log, hoping that as he did, answers would come to him of what it really was that they had experienced.

"As of now, I have found no explanation for the 'storm,' as we're calling it. It's hard to even make assumptions without totally disregarding any laws of physics. When the Captain wakes up, we will discuss turning around. With the state she's in there is no chance we can carry on the mission. We set out here to find something that could better the human race, and though I don't believe this mission was in vain, I don't think it was in the cards for this ship. I hope the other crews are having better luck than we are.

"This is Lieutenant Taylor, report complete."

Taylor sulked in his chair, looking out of the viewport into the emptiness of space. Everything was so calm and peaceful, with no sign that anything out of the ordinary had happened to them. The whole incident could have been a dream. Maybe he had fallen asleep at the helm. He'd turn around and sure enough Captain Silvers was still lying in on her bunk. Except a few key details were different. Captain Silvers *was* on her bunk, but her legs below the knee were not accompanying her. The blood stains on the floor also hinted that this might just be real.

But he could block it out. For as long as Taylor stared out the viewport, he could pretend nothing happened. He could carry on the mission as normal. It would be the return mission, and he would tell their commander, Maj. Haxley, back on Earth that nothing was found.

"But you were only supposed to return if nothing was found in five years, not six months," Maj. Haxley would rebuke.

"Oh, has it only been six months back down here? That's so strange! Well, you know how time works up there. It doesn't!" Taylor would laugh, and the three of them would walk to one of the many bars in the "Grand Central" Space Station for a drink.

The three of them would walk.

No, two of us…

Taylor was pulled from his daydream when he realized he was no longer looking out of the viewport but at the bloodstain on the floor. Then from the bloodstain, the amputee.

Some color was returning to the Captain. She no longer had a pale grey hue, but it was far from radiant.

For a moment, Taylor considered trying to wake her up. She needed fluids and food to recover. Taylor ultimately decided against it, thinking it better to let her get a little more sleep, as long as she didn't show any signs of deterioration.

Taylor would occupy himself with other tasks for the time being. First, he realized, he should ensure the ship was in good condition after the storm.

His biggest concern was the hull strength. If there was a problem with the engine or life support, there would have been a notice on the computer. Hull damage wouldn't be reported unless it was significant. There would only be a durability percentage shown if requested down to 75%. When Taylor checked, he saw it sit comfortably at 88%.

The report showed there were minor impacts scattered across the outer hull, presumably from the lighting strikes or dust scrapping across like sandpaper.

"Wonderful," Taylor said to himself. "Everything ship sha-"

A noise from the ship's rear, and the computer read 87%.

Taylor leaned in closer. Was it a trick of his eye? Had he read it wrong at first? No, it dropped.

It's nothing, he thought. *Just a stray asteroid drifting along…a stray asteroid.*

Another noise echoed through the ship, like something pressing against the hull.

Taylor stood and turned toward the hall. Although was quiet again, a sinister energy fell over the *Brighter Day*. They had left the storm well behind them, but it had left its mark, and a presence followed close behind the ship.

The sound of slow pressing rumbled through the ship again. Taylor jerked his head to check the computer. Still 87%, but this was clearly no trick of a distressed mind.

Taylor walked slowly across the cabin, listening intently for any hints as to what the mysterious sound was. With every step, he felt colder. Not on his skin, but in his heart. It felt as though his willpower, his soul even, was shying away from whatever it was causing the sound.

As he approached the doorway to the hall, the sound rumbled again, and Taylor could feel soft vibrations under his feet. He knelt down and placed his head against the cold floor. For a moment, he could only hear the beat of his heart. It quickened the more he thought about it.

Breathe, sonny. Just breathe, take a deep breath.

Taylor pulled back from the floor and postured himself upright. He took a deep breath in and let it out. Another deep breath in, and slowly let it out, again and again until his heart calmed. Once ready, he lay his ear back down against the floor.

All was now silent. No more rumbling or pressing.

It was all in your head, you big chicken, Taylor condemned himself. Just to prove it to himself, Taylor knocked on the floor.

Before his hand was raised from the second knock, the vibrating returned underneath him. Taylor almost pulled back but heard something this time. For a moment, it sounded like something slid across the lower hull. It was smooth, not at all like a jagged asteroid would sound. This sounded to Taylor like a creature, crawling slowly on its stomach. He would have to bring this to the Captain's attention.

"Captain!" Taylor gently shook Captain Silvers' shoulders. "Captain, wake up!"

Silvers hesitantly opened her eyes but couldn't focus on her Lieutenant. "Li- Lieutenant? What did-..."

"Yes! Yes, it's me! Thank god you're back!"

"Lieutenant... what did you do to me?" Her voice was weak but brimming with contempt.

Taylor looked for the right words, but nothing came to him.

Silvers wanted to reach out and grab her Lieutenant by the throat. She tried with all her willpower, but her arm refused to move. She spoke again, with more strength in her voice. "I can't feel anything. What did you do?!"

"Ma'am, I did all I could," he looked at her stumps, wondering if she knew already that he cut them off. *Maybe she wasn't completely unconscious when I did it. Maybe she felt the whole thing, or saw like in an out-of-body experience!* "We made it out of the storm, but your legs, I had to... I had to amputate. They were already-"

Silvers cut Taylor off. "Lift my head, Lieutenant."

Taylor did what he was ordered without hesitation.

Silvers winced as pain stabbed her in the top of her neck. It cut off so suddenly, she could tell the exact inch where paralysis began. When she saw the stumps, she held in her terror, determined to stay mentally strong as the officer of the ship and leader of their mission.

With the damage reviewed and accepted, Silvers nodded as best she could, wordlessly ordering Taylor to lower her head.

"I did the best I could Ma'am. You'd almost completely bled out."

"Are you well rested, Lieutenant?" The contempt and spite were strong in her tone. It again took the words out of Taylor's mouth. "Did you hear me? I asked you a question."

"I... I... I did all I could..."

"I saw you, Lieutenant." Every time she said 'Lieutenant,' it felt like an insult, like his rank alone was cause for condescension. She continued, "I saw you look at me as I lay there in pain. You could have saved me. But no, you needed your rest, *didn't* you?"

Taylor took a half step back.

"What did you *do* to me while I was out? You took my legs and left me paralyzed. How else did you violate me? You never even dressed me. Have you just been staring this whole time? Or did you seize your chance when I couldn't say 'no!'"

"Ma'am, I-" Taylor's arms were raised halfway in surrender. His voice trembled in embarrassment. Her voice was so filled with conviction that he felt guilt for a sin he didn't commit. "I didn't do anything like that! Honest! Here, I'll get your clothes!"

Taylor jumped to open the storage container above her bunk and grabbed a set of trousers and a blouse.

As she was dressed, Captain Silvers asked in a restrained voice, "What's our current course?"

"No change, ma'am. I thought it best to wait until you were conscious until I make any changes to the course."

It was the answer she had hoped to hear, but she still felt spite for her subordinate. "And if I hadn't come back? Would you just be drifting until you ran out of fuel?"

"No ma'am." Taylor knotted Silvers' pant legs so they wouldn't dangle, then adjusted her so she could sit up in the bunk.

"Then what *have* you been doing?"

"I ran checks on the ship. Just making sure we were okay after the storm."

Silvers looked down at her legs. "Hm. No damage I hope."

"Nothing major." Taylor knew it was the wrong way to say it as soon as the words were spoken, and Captain gave him a glare to make sure of it. Nevertheless, he continued as if the look didn't stab his little remaining pride. "We've taken some damage to the hull. Down to 87% strength. And ma'am, I don't know how to say this, but I think there's something on the ship."

"What are you talking about?"

"I heard something. It sounded like it was sliding across the hull."

Captain Silvers rolled her eyes. "It's just an asteroid."

"I don't think so, Captain," he said, trying to sound respectful. "It was too smooth. An asteroid would bounce once and fly off."

"Then it bounced off."

"Silvers it-"

Her eyes hardened on the Lieutenant. "It's *Captain* Silvers. If there were something near the ship, radar would tell us."

"Not if that something was *on* the ship." He knew the infliction in his voice was risky but needed to convince her. "The radar has a minimum distance. It's not going to register something within a few inches."

"How about this? You suit up and go check out whatever you think you've heard." A half-cynical, half-annoyed smile spread across her lips.

Taylor took a step back in amazement at her stubbornness.

Silvers continued, "Listen to me, Lieutenant. We flew through a storm. We're going to turn the ship around and investigate. Afterward, we will return home and report our findings. But for right now, you need to get your head together. I can see the damage report from here. 87%? Go have a look, and then fix my seat. I may not be able to move, but by god, I'll still be at the helm while conducting my duties."

A moment passed in silence.

Taylor was so sure of himself. So sure of what he'd heard. But Captain Silvers looked at him with equal conviction.

Captain Silvers nodded toward the computer, egging him on.

With his eyes locked on the Captain, Taylor walked slowly over to the computer. Only when he approached it did he turn his head.

Captain Silvers didn't even have to wait for a response or see his face to know what was going on in his head.

"Now, fix my seat, and let's get back to the mission." She said with a sneer. *I've lost my body, but at least he still knows who's in charge.*

Taylor couldn't pull his eyes off the reading.

88%.

Taylor raised his hand to the back of his head. The storm, the gravity attack, his head slammed against the wall at a thousand miles an hour. Something must have been knocked loose. Tricks must have been played.

"Roger, Captain," Taylor said softly. "I'll get right to work."

About twenty minutes later, Taylor had found a way to weld Captain Silvers' chair back to the floor. She grinned as he carried her from her bunk to the helm, reveling in the power she still had on the ship.

Maybe he didn't do anything to me while I was unconscious, too scared to try, Silvers contemplated. *But he has six months to try, and his mind could be failing. I'll have to stay on alert.*

Taylor took his seat next to the Captain.

"Preparing a new course, Captain" he announced. "We should be back at the incident location in about five hours."

"Very good. While we wait, why don't you clean up this mess? A blood stain on the floor when we return won't look good."

"Roger, Captain."

For the next five hours, Captain Silvers kept him busy with menial tasks. He cleaned every surface a dozen times, took inventory of their gear, performed maintenance on the engine, whatever she could think of to keep his mind from wandering.

While Captain Silvers felt comfortable in her seat at the helm, Taylor was in the engine room wondering if the rumbling he heard were the machines around him or the sound that had latched onto them since the storm.

The sliding. The pressing. It was low, almost imperceptible under the whirring of the engine, but Taylor was sure it was there.

He lay on the ground, with his ear pressed to the floor. If only he could pinpoint where it was coming from, or what direction it was moving it. Would it ever go to the front of the ship? Climb onto the antenna on the *Brighter Day*'s nose? He could get a good look at it, and with the Captain stuck in her seat, she wouldn't be able to deny it. Taylor just had to get it to move in the right direction.

Using a nearby wrench, Taylor began banging on the floor. The ringing of metal on metal erupted in the small room and rattled his brain. A headache began to brew, but he'd power through it. He hit the floor three times, then got up and peeked his head out into the hallway. Taylor expected a verbal lashing from the Captain but heard nothing from her.

Good, she thinks I'm still working, he thought.

Back with his ear pressed to the floor, Taylor listened for the sound of movement. Whatever it was had moved a few feet to the starboard side.

Taylor moved with the sound and began banging again a few inches behind where he thought the cause of the sound was residing. Though his ears were on the ground, he kept his eyes on the Captain. If he was caught screwing around, he'd never hear the end of it.

Through slow in progress, Taylor was certain the thing under the ship was going where directed. Better yet, it moved faster every few feet. By the time they reached the hallway portal, the thing was darting towards the front of the ship.

Taylor jumped to his feet and ran after it shouting, "Captain! Captain, look outside!" Taylor ran so fast he nearly crashed into the console, but it was worth it.

Wrapped around the base of the antenna was their stowaway. The thing was so dark it was nearly imperceptible against the backdrop of space, but Taylor could just make out some details.

The thing was thin but long. It looked almost like a bone with the thinnest layer of sinewy flesh barely holding onto it. Taylor could almost make out a claw holding on to the antenna, but it was too far away and too dark to be sure.

He knocked on the viewport, hoping it would move again and give him a better understanding of what he was looking at. The thing reacted to his rasping and slowly sulked away back to the lower hull.

"No! Get back here!" he screamed, then turned to the Captain. "Did you see it? I told you it was there!"

But the Captain didn't answer.

Taylor saw she was asleep and was filled with anger. He grabbed her by the shoulders and shook. "Captain! Wake up damn it!"

Captain Silvers didn't stir, and Taylor realized she had gone pale again. She hadn't eaten since before the storm and was losing her strength again.

Taylor hardened his resolve and was determined to keep her alive if only to show her the creature and prove he wasn't going mad. He grabbed a bottle of meal pills from the cabinet by the side of Captain Silvers' bunk and forced two down her throat. The pills were only recommended for one every six hours, but this seemed like a good exception. Taylor knew she might feel sick later, but as long as she was alive, he hoped she'd be grateful. After the pills went down, Taylor filled a canteen and made her sip. Most of the water leaked out of her mouth and down her neck.

"Come on Captain," Taylor begged. "I know you've still got a little in you."

Air escaped Captain Silvers' lips. Then, "Lieutenant…"

"Yes! Yes, Captain? What is it? How are you feeling?"

"Why can't you just let me sleep?"

Taylor fell back into his seat. He could wring her neck he was so full of her.

Captain Silvers turned her head toward Taylor. Her eyes were so heavy, they barely looked open at all.

"Did you finish your tasks in the engine room?" she asked.

Taylor rolled his eyes in frustration and saw another set looking back at him through the viewport. He almost thought they were stars, they were so small and pure white. Two tiny dots against the endless sky. Were it not for the faint outline of a misshapen skull he would have ignored them. But there they were, staring at him, mocking him.

Taylor jumped to his feet and pointed at the eyes. "There! Captain, look! I told you something was out there, just look!"

Captain Silver tried to lean in, forgetting her paralysis, and only if to humor Taylor.

"Come here, help me, Lieutenant."

Taylor did as he was told, and rushed to prop her up.

"Look, do you see it?"

"Lieutenant, I have no idea what I'm looking for."

"It's right there, by the antenna. Two white dots, clear as day."

Captain Silvers sighed deeply with impatience. "Lieutenant, all I see are white dots. You'll have to be more specific or get back to work."

Something came over Taylor then. The constant condescension, the menial orders, the lack of respect and gratitude he'd received throughout the mission, it was all coming to a head. Without thinking, Taylor threw Captain Silvers out of her chair.

As she fell, with her head turned in his direction, Captain Silvers attempted to bite Taylor. She missed his hand but clenched her teeth on his pinky.

Taylor yanked his hand back, and blood burst from his hand as the opposing forces ripped the finger off.

Captain Silvers hit the floor and spat the finger out.

"You bitch!" Taylor shouted. "Everything I've done for you! I saved your goddamn life! You'd be dead without me!"

"I'd still be able to walk if I had a better crewmate!" She lay facedown, unable to turn herself over. "You're insane Lieutenant! You've lost it out here! You're seeing things like your boogeyman!" She spoke calmly now, doing her best to sound like a respectable leader. "If I can keep my composure like this, no legs, no arms, nothing but a head, you can get your shit together."

"It's not in my head, and I'll prove it!" Taylor stomped to the back of the cabin where their spacesuits were stored.

"Lieutenant! Lieutenant, what are you doing? Get back here!"

"I'm going out there, Silvers. I'll prove there's something on the ship."

"You will do no such thing until you pick me up!"

"Huh, right. I think you can lay there until you learn to show a little respect for your *crew*."

"Lieutenant! Lieutenant!" Captain Silvers kept screaming and ordering him around as Taylor dressed himself. He refused to acknowledge her until he came back with proof.

Taylor twisted his helmet on, and Captain Silvers' words became muffled. It was easier to ignore her.

Each step down the airlock hallway felt like a mile. Each step disturbed him more. Each step was a reminder that he was disobeying orders, and the mission was falling apart. Each step was one closer to an unknown entity. All signs told him he was making a mistake.

It doesn't matter, Taylor told himself. *I have to prove this.*

Taylor found the end of the oxygen tube and raised it to lock into place in the hall. It would provide him air and ensure he didn't drift away from the ship while on his spacewalk.

As he began to twist, a voice found its way into his helmet, clear as day. Taylor froze.

"Samuel, please come back." The Captain.

It was the first time he'd been addressed by his first name since well before the mission began.

Samuel Taylor looked down at the glove of his space suit. The white fabric was turning red with his blood.

"Samuel… please… I need your help."

It could have been a trick. Something in her voice though latched onto a part of his heart that had been neglected and discarded a long time ago. There was tenderness in it. Sincerity. A stable shake that told him tears preceded the words.

It wasn't fear or loss of adrenaline that kept Taylor from going outside. It was bravery. Bravery *not* to give into fear. Bravery to have compassion for the Captain, and humility to accept it from her.

Taylor lifted his helmet off of his head and undressed from the bulky spacesuit.

3

Fay Silvers lay in her bunk with her head propped up by pillows so she could see out of the viewport. She had backed off from giving commands for a while. Her crewmate recommended rest and a fair amount of fluids. She complied happily and left Samuel Taylor to his duties.

"We're coming up on the incident location, Fay."

"Very-..." She stopped herself short in an attempt to stop herself from sounding so Captain-ly. "Wonderful," she said instead. "Skies still look clear to me. Do you see anything on the radar?"

Taylor shook his head. "No signs of disturbance. Storm's long gone."

Silvers pursed her lips. "Hm. Disappointing. Well, we've had a good run, right?"

Taylor swerved his head so fast he may as well have broken his neck and joined the club with Silvers. "Just like that?" he asked with a laugh.

Silvers nodded. "I think my last order will be... set a course for home."

"Aye, Captain." Taylor gave a fake salute and prepared their new course until something hit him. He stopped, thought for a moment, then rummaged through different computer programs.

"What are you doing over there?" Silvers asked.

"Just a moment. I had an idea."

Silvers waited a few seconds for a follow-up, then asked, "Would you like to share?"

"I just want to scan for chemical readings. If there was a storm, electrical reactions, and dust clouds, then even if it's dispersed there must be some evidence floating around on molecular levels.

Whatever those are may be clues to what happened. And look! Picking up something!"

Excitement overcame both of them. Their eyes met again and they said simultaneously, "This is it!" Everything their mission and strife had been about was about to pay off. All they needed now were samples.

In no time, Taylor was dressed again in the blood-stained spacesuit, equipped with gear to collect the gasses floating around the *Brighter Day*.

Silvers wished him good luck and safety as the airlock cycled. For half a moment, she even thought about blowing him a kiss.

If only I could.

Stepping out into space was like taking his first breath all over again. Once all the sounds of the ship were muted by the vacuum of space, he could have believed he stepped into an entirely different world.

No time for gawking. I have to do a comms check, he reminded himself.

"Fay, do you read me?"

The call played through the ship's speakers. It was set up so Silvers wouldn't have to move or press any buttons to speak with him.

"I read you. Try to make it a quick trip. I think I'm finally getting homesick."

"Okay, okay, I'm working on it." Taylor laughed and turned around to face the ship again.

Coldness returned to Taylor's heart. His smile disappeared as he saw a sinewy black substance had enveloped and slithered across the surface of the *Brighter Day*.

Book 2

Lost World of the Void

15. Flight of the Silent Horizon

Fire erupted from the engine room and began to spread throughout the rear of the *Silent Horizon*.

"Robbie! Help us out!" Dex barked orders at the small ash-black robot. The two of them held back the flames of the overworked hyperdrive engine; Robbie with his extinguisher claw, Dex with the ships'.

Music blared over the crew's shouting. Lacy tried shutting it off so she could think, but one alarm sounded after another and got in her way on the computer. *Fire in the engine room! Fire in the airlock! Life support critical! Fire in the greenhouse! Engine critical!*

"Dex, hurry up! This whole ship is about to blow!" Lacy cried.

Any moment now their atoms would be dispersed into the universe, flying at the speed of light in a million different directions. Dex and the robot pushed on, holding back the flames.

"Dex! The engine!"

"I know, I know! Vent it!" Dex called back.

"Vent is offline! System's totally fried!"

"Damn! Can you shut off the airflow?"

Lacy checked the few remaining controls they had. Sweat dripped from her brow into her eyes. "It'll have to be a complete life support shutdown."

"All right, I'm getting there!" He shoved the robot closer to the engine room door. "Go on, you worry about the engine, I'll get the hall!"

"It is too hot in there." The robot said matter-of-factly.

"You'll be fine!" A burst of flames shot out through the doorway, inches from Dex's face. The heat was overwhelming. "You're strong, you got this! Just go! Fast!"

"I am not." He tried to back away, but Dex pushed him fur-

them in.

"I believe in you, go!"

Robbie processed the chances of success. He had a light but tough metal shell. There was a high chance his circuits would melt, but there was also a guarantee that the ship would be destroyed if he didn't act.

"I will g-"

"Great!" Dex cut him off. "Shut it down, Lacy! And hold your breath!"

Robbie wobbled as fast as he could into the engine room and flailed his extinguisher arm every which way, attacking the flames with extreme prejudice.

Lacy deactivated the life support and rushed to grab an oxygen tank from their space suits in the rear of the cabin.

The flames ate up the remaining oxygen in the ship. Dex held his breath as he and Robbie fought off what remained of the fire. When he couldn't hold his breath any longer, Dex rushed to join Lacy. They took turns breathing through the tank and prayed Robbie would be able to clear out the room.

Between breaths, Dex called out to the robot. "Robbie, how's it looking?"

"Fire is out. There is no air. I cannot breathe."

Lacy's eyes went wide and rushed to save him. "Robbie!" She screamed and dropped the tank into Dex's hands.

"Lacy, wait!" Dex grabbed her by the arm.

"He's going to…" she struggled for air, "die in there!"

Dex took a deep breath from the tank, handed it back to her then held up a finger, telling her to wait.

Robbie stepped out from the airlock hall. "It is a good thing I do not need to breathe. The fire is clear."

Dex gave the robot a thumbs up, then patted Lacy on the shoulder, signaling her to turn the life support system back on before his face could turn a deep blue.

The crisis was averted for the time being. Battle scars from their escape from the Empire displayed themselves proudly on the *Silent Horizon*. The outer hull was heavily damaged, streaked with laser burns from the Empire's Zar-Meck starfighters. Ash from the fire caked the ceiling of the airlock hallway, engine room, and the artificial greenhouse. The newly installed hyperdrive had been activated too frequently and it was taking its toll. In the main cabin lay the corpse of the faceless Imperial officer, Jaskek Dreed.

Robbie offered to move the body out of the way. He'd been freed from his Imperial programming by Lacy, but still felt discomfort at seeing the body.

"Where would you like me to put this?" Robbie asked, holding up the foot of the corpse.

"Over in the hallway, buddy. We'll dump him when we pull out of hyperspeed."

Robbie nodded in acknowledgement then struggled to pull the corpse into the *Silent Horizon*'s hallway.

"What do you say we get this...stuff...off you, dear?" Dex traced the backs of his fingers down Lacy's scarlet-painted cheeks.

She was adorned in a magnificent scarlet sacrificial dress, with beautiful jewels around her neck and in her hair, and her skin was painted in such a way as to exaggerate her bone structure. She didn't know for certain, but in seeing phantasms of the Emperor's court, and the way the alien Rassmenda talked as she prepared Lacy for sacrifice, Lacy believed that the dress, jewels, and painting were meant to merge into her being, decaying her natural beauty into a horrible skeletal image.

"Yes, please," she faux-pleaded Dex, then laughed. "It's a lovely dress, but I don't think red's my color anymore. And I could do without all the extra."

Dex held a smile but was still unnerved about the circumstances of the escape. Lacy's eyes had always been blue, but they were strikingly different now, and Dex didn't think she had yet realized this.

She stood up to walk to the head to change, but Dex, staying seated, gave her pause. "Are you feeling all right?"

Lacy turned slightly, with a quizzical smile. "Perfect, darling." Her starry eyes shined brightly. "Why do you ask?"

They'd escaped the Empire but the lights swirling in her eyes told him they hadn't left it behind. These moments should have been sweet between them, and as much as Dex wanted to let them be so, his better judgment told him this should be addressed.

"I need you to see this," he said as he jumped from his seat, closing the small gap between them, then took her by the hand and walked with her into the head. "Do you see?"

They stood in front of the mirror together. Lacy leaned in and raised a hand to her face, touching the cracking paint, too distracted to notice her eyes.

"See what? Do you think I'm having a reaction to this stuff? I don't feel irritation or anything."

"No, I mean your eyes. Look." Without giving her a chance to look deeply, Dex grabbed a face towel that hung next to the sink, ran it under the water, and handed it to her. "Maybe it'll be easier to see without all that crud off your face."

Lacy took the towel and wiped. With the paint gone, she was now able to see what Dex had been talking about. To her, it didn't pop out as much as it had for Dex, but the stars in her eyes couldn't be ignored.

As she inspected the abnormality, Dex asked her again, "You sure you feel fine?"

"Yes," Lacy said, slightly annoyed at his insistence, but still patient. "I'm sure it's nothing, just… I don't know. Something in the food maybe."

Deep down she knew that wasn't it. As strange as this adventure had been she knew the most likely answer to this mystery had to do with whatever had been interrupted in the Emperor's hall. The failed sacrificial ritual.

"After you shower, I want to do a scan. Just to be safe."

Lacy nodded but didn't say anything. Now that it was obvious to her, she only wanted to ignore it. The thought of keeping a piece of the Empire inside her disgusted her. At least with Robbie, he had no loyalty to the Emperor. But this… thing… she knew was a piece of the Emperor himself.

Dex gave her privacy as she undressed and cleansed herself of the previous days. They both knew how precious those moments were after coming out of the field from a training event and how necessary it was to have a warm shower and soft bed all to themselves for a few minutes. This had been much more stressful than any training event.

As she showered, Dex turned his attention to the corpse in the hallway.

Robbie had been busy cleaning the blood off of the floor and struggled to comprehend why more continued to slowly leak out of Jaskek's torn-open face. The smell of dead flesh was beginning to seep through the doors and would have to be dealt with quickly.

"Move over little guy," Dex said as he knelt beside the robot.

Dex looked the body up and down. Their sizes weren't far apart. Dex was slightly bulkier and an inch or two taller, but a spare Imperial uniform wouldn't be bad to have in Dex's wall locker. Just in case.

Robbie had also placed Jaskek's blaster on the corpse's chest.

Dex reached for the blaster and held it up for Robbie to see. "We don't want to get rid of this kinda stuff, got that?"

Robbie shifted his weight to the left. "Why?"

Dex felt like he was talking to a child. "Because things are probably going to get harder from here. We have to conserve whatever gear we can. So, when we find stuff like this, tools or whatever, we might need to keep it."

"But it is not ours."

"I don't think he's gonna miss it." Dex looked down at Jaskek's skinless face. Another small stream of blood trailed down his neck and the side of his head. The shock alone must have been enough to kill the Imperial officer.

Robbie reached out to put his claws over Dex's hands. "You should give it back. He might want it when he wakes up."

Dex almost laughed, "Robbie, do you think he's..."

"He might still be alive. He is still making fluids." Blood pooled around the robot's feet.

Although Robbie couldn't directly show any emotion, Dex could see the look of innocence in his lenses.

"All right, how about this? We'll drop him off as soon as possible, and if he's somehow still alive, I'll give him all his stuff back. Okay?"

Robbie straightened. "That is fair."

"Now you just, um... go stand guard outside the head and

make sure no one hurts Lacy."

The robot saluted Dex and shuffled away.

"And don't salute me!" Dex called after Robbie as the door shut between them.

With the robot gone, Dex slipped the blaster into his waistline then picked up the medical device Korr had called a jarrmin box. It was still open and active from their fight. Having a strong idea of what would happen next, Dex mentally prepared himself for the horrific sight to come, and then deactivated the medical device. Jaskek's face fell from the device, onto where it belonged on his head, though, rotated almost a full 180 degrees.

Dex wanted to vomit but knew the look of his vomit seeping into Jaskek's bloody skull and facial muscles would only make him sicker. But that thought also made him want to vomit.

From the shower, Lacy thought she heard Dex shouting in the hall.

"Dex? You okay?" She shouted through the walls.

"Fine!" He called back, wiping the bile from the corner of his mouth. The body had to go. Fast.

He stood back up, jarrmin box in hand, and was about to leave when he noticed another object on Jaskek's hip. It was one of the data tablets Imperial officers carried on them. Dex made a quick pass to grab it then rushed out of the room, escaping from the rank smells before a headache could overcome him.

"Is he awake yet?" Robbie asked.

Dex walked back to his seat at the console and answered Robbie without looking at him. "Not yet buddy. But I'm sure in a few hours he'll be just fine. Get on back to the controls. I want to find somewhere to touch down before we don't have fuel left to even land." He followed close behind Robbie back to their seats.

The *Silent Horizon*'s radar wasn't programmed to detect anything while moving faster than light speed. Dex hoped though, that with the new antenna Korr installed, they wouldn't have any issues.

Lacy finished showering, dried herself, and dressed in her skivvies. Her Planetary Exploration Suit and olive jumpsuit had been confiscated by the Empire. Save for the scarlet dress, her wardrobe wasn't carrying many options.

"Hopefully wherever we land has a Macy's." She joked with Dex. "Let's see what we've got," Lacy scoured through the storage bin above their bunk. "This could be a nice outfit." She pulled out a light blue nightgown that fell just below the knee and held it up in front of herself.

Dex spun in his chair and traced her figure with admiring eyes. "Lovely, darling. But not quite the right outfit for going out."

Robbie turned as well and gave Lacy a once-over. "Dex is right. That won't give you any protection in space."

"Thank you, Robbie," Lacy laughed, then to Dex, "It's this, that hideous red dress, or I go out in my undergarments."

Dex considered the dress but remembered the words of the Zar-Meck when they were first captured.

The Emperor's colors.

"The nightgown should be all right."

As if on cue, a beeping rang from the console.

Lacy draped the gown over herself and asked, "Are we coming up on something?"

"Looks like it," Dex said, reading off of the computer. "Can't make out any details. The ship can't tell if it's a planet or some floating debris."

Lacy walked up behind him and put a hand on his shoulder. "Think it's worth it to check out?"

Dex took a deep breath and thought. "Way I see it, we've got three possibilities. One, it's nothing. Not enough gas left in the tank to jump again, and we've burned too much to get back home off of just cruising. Dead in the water. Option two, my preferred option, it's a habitable planet. We land safely and start an early retirement."

"And the third option?"

Dex opened his mouth, but it was Robbie who answered. "The Empire is very large."

Lacy watched Dex, waiting for a response. He only shrugged in agreement.

"So do you think it's worth it?" She pushed again.

"If it's even a five percent chance of that early retirement, it's one hundred percent worth it. All right crew, please ensure you are strapped in safely as we are beginning our descent." Dex flicked some buttons on the console.

"Mind if I sit here, Robbie?" Her graceful aura made it impossible to deny any request.

"I will not be able to see if I move."

Lacy rolled her eyes. "You can sit on my lap, how about that?"

Without waiting for a response, Lacy picked up the robot and sat down placing him on her lap like a child.

"Coming out now. Who wants to put bets down? I bet retirement."

"I second," said Lacy.

"I do not know what any of that means," said Robbie.

The *Silent Horizon* dropped out of light speed.

"What is that?" Dex and Lacy asked.

"What is it? I cannot see." Robbie attempted to pull himself up on the console for a better view. "Oh, that. That's a spaceport. Private. Non-military by my data."

"Is it safe?" Lacy asked.

"It is for me."

16. The Spaceport

"What's the point of a spaceport like this when these people have hyperdrives?" Dex questioned their robot companion. He flew the *Silent Horizon* along the edge of the spaceport looking for a place to dock.

"Not everyone is so fortunate to own one, I would think," Robbie answered.

Dex and Lacy studied the array of ships docked below them. Many were dinky little things held together by scraps. They were about the same size as the *Silent Horizon*. The two Earthlings found a sense of familiarity looking at them. The view wasn't too far off from the spaceports of Earth's solar system. The difference was that only the richest of Earth and its colonies could afford personal cruisers. Here, it looked like spacecraft were as common as automobiles, and the used-spaceship business was booming. In another section of the port, separated from the smaller craft, Dex and Lacy noticed larger cargo vessels, but nothing like the Empire's saucer-shaped military ships.

"Robbie, do you have any idea where we are?" Lacy asked.

"I do not know exactly. But if I had to guess, I would say we are close to the current outworlds."

"What do you mean current?"

Without taking his visual sensors off of the view, Robbie said, "The Empire is always expanding. I have never seen spaceports like this. I wonder what it will be like."

"I'm sure you won't have to wait long for an answer. Keep your eyes open for a spot to land. I haven't been hailed yet for clearance codes. Must be a free-for-all all."

"There," Lacy pointed to a spot a few hundred meters away. "Looks like that's open. Slow down, you'll see it."

They came upon a spot, a tight squeeze between two crafts that looked to be this part of the universe's answer to a Ford Pickup. As they dropped down onto the landing platform, they could see the thin blue film of a shield pass by the viewport.

Dex commented, "Doesn't seem like the safest idea, does it? Jump too high and you float out into space."

"Worth it for the view, isn't it?" Lacy asked.

The *Silent Horizon* came to a halt.

"No music this time?" Dex asked as he powered down the ship.

Lacy laughed. "I don't think a gas station warrants the same celebration as your heroic save."

"I wouldn't call that heroic, Darling. It's what anyone would have done for their girl."

The sound of the engine whirring faded away along with the rank smell coming from it.

"Call it what you will," Lacy rose from her seat and kissed Dex on the cheek. "You're *my* hero at least."

Lacy stepped away, running her fingers along his shoulders, and Robbie lowered himself from the console to where she stood.

"And what about you, little buddy?" Dex asked.

"You have almost gotten me killed. Twice. I have only known you a few hours."

Dex waved off the comment and rose. "We'll call it undecided then."

"Do we have a plan?" Lacy asked with her hands on her hips.

"No plan yet. Just goals. More than anything, we need more fuel."

"I'd agree, but from the sound of the engine, it seems like that should be our first priority. I wish I could fix it on my own, but I know nothing about this drive you had installed."

Bang! Bang! "Hey in there! You checking in or what?" A warbly voice called to them from the rear of the ship.

"Damn! What do we say?" Lacy directed the question at Robbie who only shrugged.

Dex stepped forward and unclipped the data tablet from his belt. "I think I've got an idea." He fumbled with the device, trying to activate it. "How does this thing work, Robbie?"

Robbie looked from Dex to Lacy in confusion.

"You were a part of the Empire, weren't you? You should know how this works!" Dex demanded.

Robbie took a step back from everything. "I worked in a kitchen."

Again, the dockworker banged on the airlock door. "I don't want no freeloaders on my dock. Y'all gotta check in or I'll have to call security!"

Lacy rushed into the hallway and shouted back, "We'll be just a moment! Engine problems!"

Dex joined her to flesh out the excuse. He called through the door, "We had a leak! Smells toxic! Just got to take care of that first and we'll be out!" Then to Lacy, "I've got one other idea."

A minute later the airlock opened. The dockworker was shocked to see an Imperial officer standing in the doorway and almost fell back. He held out his fists and tilted his head down. "Glory be to the Emperor. I wasn't aware Imperial presence was expected today."

Lacy looked at Dex who hid just out of sight with his blaster at the ready. She'd argued against it, but Dex wasn't willing to get caught that easily. With her eyes, she implored him for guidance. Dex did his best to demonstrate the greeting he exchanged with Hwaq the mechanic, and mouthed 'glory be.'

Returning her attention to the dockworker, a four-armed wolfman creature, Lacy placed her hands gracefully over his fists and replied, "Glory be… and carry on." She began to turn away and close the airlock behind her, but the dockworker closed the distance between them.

"E-excuse me, ma'am! I'll need your ship's ID."

From the corner of her eye, Lacy saw Dex, standing over the body of Jaskek, positioning himself to blast the worker. Their escape from the palace-city was more than enough violence than she had ever wished to see in her life. She wouldn't let this creature be the next casualty of their escape. Lacy had to think of something fast.

Without turning to face the worker, Lacy pulled up the data tablet and pretended to operate it. "That won't be necessary," she said. "Sanction… two-one-one-alpha. Under Imperial directive, this craft is to go undocumented until mission completion." She then turned with flair to look the creature in the eye. He stood almost two feet taller than her and had to crouch to fit his head into the threshold. Lacy knew he could tear her apart in an instant if she let up the littlest bit in the act. Maintaining her cool was all that mattered. She tried to speak with confidence, but when the words came out, it was a compassionate warning, not a threat. "If you know what's best for your safety, you'll forget you ever saw us here."

The dockworker had been raised to give complete devotion to the Emperor. His parents had been hard workers on the docks, and though he'd tried to find a way off the spaceport he'd lived on his whole life nothing ever came of it. He never saw the moons of Areeno like he'd hoped to, but day in and day out, he'd been grateful to the Empire and his god. He'd heard stories about worlds discovered by scouting missions of the Empire's army. He knew how lucky he was, even if his life was regulated to a dinky spaceport, and the protection he had here was thanks to the Emperor and his army. The dockworker had complete respect for, and devotion to, the Empire.

"I apologize, ma'am. I never saw anything." The dockworker took a step back and off the steps of the airlock.

When his footsteps were out of earshot, Dex came out from his cover.

"Nice quick thinking, darling," he said with a smile.

She didn't return his energy. "Were you really ready to kill him?" she asked bluntly.

Dex looked at her with confusion. "I- I guess? He could have gotten us caught."

"You don't know that. He doesn't know anything about us."

"Lacy, we can't pay for parking. We don't have ID. Zar-Mecks would be all over us in seconds if he called them."

"You don't know he would have done that." She stepped closer toward Dex to stand by her point. "*He* didn't with me," Lacy said, pointing down at Robbie, who looked up at them like a confused child.

"You got lucky with him. Not everyone out here is going to be like that. Trust me, they'll turn on you quick out here." Dex hol-stored the blaster in the gunner's strap under his jacket. He made way for the airlock and said, "Now let's go. I'm thinking we could hitch a ride on one of th-... Lacy?"

Lacy sat on the starboard side bunk. Her head hung low.

Every moment not spent looking for a way out of the spaceport was a second wasted. A second closer to being discovered. The captain in Dex wanted to call her to his feet, but everyone in the cabin knew deep down those days were past. He knelt down at her feet and took her hands, unsure what to say next.

"We're not on Earth anymore, Dex."

He nodded.

"So, stop thinking the people here will be the same. I know you lost hope for back home. Don't lose hope for the rest of the universe."

"If you have hope, then so will I." Dex leaned in and kissed her cheek.

* * *

Dex and Lacy took their first steps off the *Silent Horizon* and halted to look around. The dockworker was completely out of sight.

"Wait here, Lacy," Dex held out a hand and walked over to the edge of the dock. He looked over the edge into the emptiness of space below them. *This will be perfect*, he told himself. Jogging back to the ship, Dex and Lacy grabbed Jaskek's corpse, carried him to the edge of the dock, and tossed the body. Robbie followed and watched the corpse fall.

Once off the public docks, Dex and Lacy swore they had never seen any place so busy. Robbie took the lead in case a sign for a mechanic was written in an alien language, but they struggled to keep an eye on the small robot. Every step they took was a bump into another alien. The claustrophobia was bad enough, and on top of that the artificial air of the space station had a stale synthetic taste to it like they were breathing in static. Lacy held on tight to Dex's arm so as not to lose him. The only positive to the crowds was no one looked twice at the humans. At a glance, they could easily pass as taouron, even if it was no longer the most common species in this part of the Empire. Many of them didn't even notice the uniform Lacy wore.

During Lacy's time in captivity, she had only seen taouron and the Children of the Void. Now she was seeing a plethora of strange creatures. Some she found terrifying, others cute. "What's that?" She'd ask Dex. "Have you seen others like them yet? Wow, that's a funny-looking guy!"

"Lacy, keep your voice down. I don't know what they're called."

"I'm sorry, I just think they're interesting. What kind of people have you met out here?"

"Not- hey excuse me!- not many. I didn't waste a lot of time finding you. OOF!" Dex was pushed to the side by a ten-foot-tall, broad-chested grey alien that looked like it could bench press the *Silent Horizon* without breaking a sweat.

"Watch it, twerp!" The behemoth threatened.

As it turned and continued walking away, Lacy asked, "What about that one? Do you know what that's called?"

Dex rubbed his arm. He could already feel it bruising. "Yeah, it's called an asshole."

They continued walking until Robbie pointed out what looked like a garage. The sign was in a language they couldn't understand. Even Robbie admitted he wasn't one hundred percent sure. Lacy led them in anyway while Dex stood watch by the entrance.

The garage was almost deserted, save for two wide-eyed and pale aliens in the back watching something on a strange flat television device. To Lacy, it looked like they were watching some alien sporting event.

"Excuse me! Could one of you please help me?" he asked politely.

Neither of the two aliens took their eyes off the screen.

"Excuse me!" She called again to no response.

"Hey," Dex whispered then said with a smile, "You're an Imperial officer. Act like one."

Lacy composed herself and tried to find the right tone. "Eh'HEM! You two! I require assistance!"

One of the pale aliens turned and smacked the other's arms

when he realized who was speaking to them.

"Glory be to the Emperor!" They said in unison, with their fists held together and heads bowed.

"Glory be to him," Lacy said, hands raised. "Are you two busy?" She asked then in her usual tone.

"No, of course not," they said. "Never too busy to serve the Emperor." Perfect unison.

"Only one need speak, thank you." She laughed and raised a hand to her head. "You two are going to give me a headache."

Dex shot her a look of warning. *Be careful*, it said. *That might be the norm.*

The pale aliens struggled to comply. One began, "We-e ap-po-lo-"

Then the other, "-gize. H-how c-"

"an w-"

"we ass-"

"-ist you?"

Lacy looked back and forth between the two, absolutely bewildered.

"I um… I need a fix. Hyperdrive. You looked like a garage. Can you help?"

The pale aliens nodded together, then struggled to speak as Lacy requested.

"We a-"

"-re, yes. But-"

"Our sist-"

"-er is-"

"Okay, you know what," Lacy cut in. "I'm very sorry. Talk however you wish. I'm sorry."

The pale aliens glanced at each other again, like this last request was stranger than the first. They had never before been asked to talk one at a time as twins with a shared consciousness and never would have expected an Imperial officer to cater to them.

They began once more in unison, "Our sister would be the one to help you. Unfortunately, she just left for a job."

"When will she be back? I'm in a bit of a rush."

The pale aliens drew back as if afraid, "Please forgive us, but she is gone. She took a job on a cargo vessel."

Lacy dropped her hands on her hips. "Fantastic. Is there anywhere else a girl can get a hyperdrive fixed?"

Dex and Robbie waited outside patiently for Lacy. Dex kept a low profile but kept a lookout for any wandering eyes. Billboards above shops were broadcasting the news of the Empire and Dex knew it was only a matter of time until he saw their faces flashing for the entire spaceport to see.

Aliens would approach him, peddling one good or another, or asking for spare change. Dex waved them off without a second look. At one moment with an exceptionally pushy vagrant, Dex considered opening his jacket to flash his blaster but knew better.

When Lacy came out, she had a look of mixed emotions on her face. "Doesn't look like we have a ton of options."

"That sounds better than none. Can we get it fixed?"

"Not here. They wouldn't give me anyone else that could fix the engine. But they *did* try to set me up with their sister who can. Problem is she's flying out soon. We'd have to hitch a ride along with her on a cargo ship."

Relief washed over Dex. "That's a lot better than I thought you'd say. All right, great. Where's this ship?"

"Dex, what are you talking about?"

Dex looked around, checking again for onlookers, then led Lacy and Robbie into a nearby alley. He spoke quietly. "Think about it. If this cargo ship is big enough, we can get the *Silent Horizon* loaded and have this girl work on it. We'll be moving again and have far less eyes on it. Then when she's done, we bail! Head straight back to Earth before anyone gets wise and warn everyone!"

Lacy considered the plan. Dex was right, there were too many eyes on them here. If they pulled it off right, there would be no trace of them to lead the Empire back to Earth.

"Okay, let's try it."

"Great! Just try to keep up this persona a little while longer." Dex playfully bumped the bottom of Lacy's officer cap.

Robbie did his best to lead them to the dock the twin aliens mentioned. The commercial docks were easy to find. It was the signs in alien writing that gave them trouble. The docks were less populated than the port town. In place of people, robots carried cargo on and off ships. Only a handful of organic beings were working by their vessels, and mostly only directed the robots where to drop their loads.

The appearance of an Imperial officer, a small robot, and a civilian was more noticeable now. To the relief of Dex and Lacy, the attention they received was 'glory be' and invitations to book passage on other ships.

"Y'all headed over Lo'Stall way?"

"First class transport here! We'll get you to Reechi in no time!"

Dex whispered to Lacy, "In another world, you might actually like Reechi."

She whispered back, "Darling, that *is* another world."

They laughed quietly to themselves and listened for someone to shout out a planet called 'Taranok' as a destination.

"You don't think we missed the flight, do you?" Dex asked.

Lacy shook her head. "Those guys didn't sound like I had to be in the biggest rush. I'm sure we've got time."

Robbie halted his waddling and asked, "Which dock are we looking for?"

"I think he said, section nineteen, dock thirty-three," Lacy answered.

"Yes, I have found it then. It's that one," Robbie pointed to a spacecraft the size of the Empire State Building. Standing at the base of the gangway was a squad of six Zar-Mecks and an Imperial officer.

Lacy froze where she was. "Dex, we need a new plan."

Dex gave her a light shove. "I'd agree, but we've been here too long as is. You've got this, *ma'am*."

She shot him a mean glare in return for the comment.

"I'll be just a few paces back if things go south."

Lacy pulled Dex to the side, behind a cargo container. "You go this time. You keep sending me out to do this stuff, it's your turn now!"

"Lacy, *you're* the one in the uniform. You've been around them more than I have. All you have to do is get them out of the way." Dex brushed a group of loose hairs back behind her ear. "Gotta have hope, right?"

She rolled her eyes and conceded. "Not too far behind me, okay?"

"I won't let anything happen. I promise." Dex puffed his cheeks for one of their guppie-kisses. It always worked to put Lacy at ease.

After the kiss, Lacy stepped out from behind the container and approached the enemy. Robbie wobbled at her side.

"You there!" She called to the officer, pretending the Zar-Mecks didn't exist. "I require assistance."

The officer moved to attention and opened his mouth to speak but Lacy was intent on not letting him have a moment to even think about the situation.

"There's a scuffle at dock thirteen. Drunkards roughing up the dockworkers. My troops need backup. Go!"

The officer and his Zar-Mecks showed no intention of following her orders. Instead, the officer looked Lacy up and down and noticed how uncouth her uniform was. The pin on her blouse was that of an analyst, not a security team. Something was very wrong here.

"Understood, ma'am." The officer said. "Would you please join me inside so we can discuss this further?" As he gestured toward the cargo ship, the Zar-Mecks slowly circled around Lacy.

Fear threatened to take over her. Dex was too far behind her to give her a look of encouragement, and she didn't think he'd be fast enough to react to the Zar-Mecks.

"We do not have time for games… sir. Civilians need our assistance."

"Of course," the officer said with a smile. "And we'll be there momentarily. Please, step onto the ship."

The Zar-Meck closed in on Lacy. She could sense Dex about to make his move. It wasn't just a feeling, but a voice, Dex's in the back of her mind but clear as day. He was telling himself to intervene.

There are too many civilians here, she thought. *Someone's going to get hurt!*

"Send your troops now, or innocent people will die."

"Well now, we wouldn't want that. Come along," he said sternly and reached out for Lacy's hand. The officer saw something then in Lacy's eye. He hadn't initially noticed how they sparkled as if filled with galaxies, but now it was impossible to ignore how vibrantly they swirled. A feeling overcame him, an unwavering drive to do as she commanded him.

"Troop, to dock thirteen. On the double." The officer and his Zar-Meck marched away from the gangway without another word.

When the coast was clear, Dex joined Lacy and kissed her on the forehead. "What'd I tell you? You've got a way with words."

17. Voyage to Taranok

A taourun crewman leaned against the hatch at the top of the gangway, smoking a pipe. He perked up as soon as he saw Lacy approaching and he raised his fists together. "Glory b-"

"Yeah, yeah, we get it. Glory be and all that." Dex dismissed the crewman. "You taking passengers on this boat?"

Lacy spoke up next, sensing the confusion of the taourun. "Last minute change of plans. We're taking the place of our counterparts." Past the hatch, she saw civilians walking around. "A lower profile is all. Zar-Mecks don't instill the best sense of comfort in public, do they?" She tried to sound friendly in asking it.

"I suppose not." The crewman answered hesitantly. Never before had an Imperial officer spoken to him like that before. Was this a genuine nicety this officer was giving him, or was this "low profile" cover for investigating what they would be doing on his ship? Either way, he knew better than to argue. "Please, come aboard. Captain should be back soon, and we'll be off."

"Very good," Lacy said as she stepped through the hatch. "Carry on," she smiled politely at the crewman.

Dex helped Robbie step through the hatch, then asked the crewman, "Who can I talk to about getting cargo loaded?"

The crewman's face contored in annoyance as if to say, *Great, first a change of crew now more cargo right before takeoff?*

"What's the load? Not much time before we go, but if it's small it shouldn't be an issue."

"Our ship. Docked over in civilian parking. Dock nine."

"The civilian... parking?"

Dex leaned in and winked. "Low profile, remember. Let's just get that moved and we'll have no trouble. Don't wanna have to tell the ma'am."

"Of course, sir. I'll make sure someone gets on that right away."

Dex slapped his shoulder with a "Good man," then took off to follow Robbie and Lacy.

Right away, Dex and Lacy knew they'd made the right choice with the cargo vessel. Organic lifeforms were in short supply. The ones that were on the ship were not so different from their robotic counterparts, rushing from one task to the next, not paying much mind to what was going on around them. All that mattered to the crew was a successful lift-off from the spaceport. It looked as though Dex and Lacy would be able to ease up a little on their secrecy. Lacy still received acknowledgment in passing from the crew, organic lifeforms, and robots alike. Dex on the other hand was all but ignored. Thankfully, on the few instances where they asked anyone if they'd seen a pale woman with big eyes, no one recognized them as anything other than taouron.

"Pale lady? Twins right? You mean the ullullu broads, right?" One of the crewmen, a bulky reptilian alien, tried to help Lacy. They stood in a hallway so narrow that the reptilian alien took up nearly the entire width of the place.

"Yes, I think so. Have you seen them?" Lacy asked.

"Tryin' to stay away from them, but yeah, I've seen 'em. Those weirdos are in the cargo hold running inspections on your gear."

"Of course. As they should be," Lacy reverted back to her fake officer tone. "Thank you for your help, civilian. Carry on."

The reptilian man bowed his head with respect and let them squeeze by him before leaving to carry out his own tasks.

"What do you think the Empire's carrying on this ship? Why not use their own transports?" Lacy studied the contents of the cargo hold with great interest.

"I'm not sure. I thought there was a warship ready on every planet."

"Maybe they're working overtime now. Looking for a few lost earthlings," Lacy laughed at herself. "As if they would stop everything to find two people."

"You never know," Dex shrugged. "That Emperor guy seemed to really like you."

"Oh stop, Dex," she playfully hit his chest.

"I'm just saying, it looks like you made an impression on him." He reached out and took her arm, then spun her around to look into her eyes. "And it looks like he made an impression on you too." His voice dropped low and gained some concern. "Are you sure you're feeling all right?"

"Yes… I feel perfect. To be quite honest," she glanced over her shoulder to make sure no one was within listening distance. "Maybe something is different, but only because I feel much better than I expected after everything we've been through."

The cargo hold wasn't difficult to find. It was the largest room and right in the center of the ship. Smaller vessels flew above the cargo ship, lowering their loads through the huge opening in the roof.

"Looks like everything is working out for the best. We might actually have a shot out of here." Lacy pointed up. They saw the *Silent Horizon* being lowered in slowly.

"Wonderful. We can get it fixed and hide out in there until we get wherever we're going. Let's just find this mechanic."

"Two grey girls," Lacy reminded. "Mostly humanoid. I think that's them."

Just a few yards ahead, they saw the two ullullu girls working on a machine. As they approached, Dex realized there were dozens of the same type of machine all over the cargo hold.

Something going on on this Taranok? he asked himself.

"Excuse me! Hello!" Lacy called out to the girls. "Are you Ja'laa?"

"Yes." The ullullu girls answered in unison.

"Okay, you're Ja'laa, and you are?" Lacy asked, pointing to the other girl.

"Ja'laa."

"Right, sure." A smile spread across Lacy's face the likes of which the ullullu girls had never seen on an Imperial officer. The smile was infectious.

"Your brothers sent me. I have a ship that needs repairs. See that one over there?" She pointed to the *Silent Horizon*. "The hyperdrive needs repairs. And fuel too if you can scrounge some up."

"Yes, ma'am. Fuel may be sparse, but we can get on it right

after we complete our inspections on these generators."

"No," Lacy cut in. "No, I'm sorry but this needs to be a priority."

"We apologize, but we were instructed to finish our inspections before lift-off. We can attend your craft once we're done."

Dex's voice sounded off clearly in Lacy's mind again. *Convince them otherwise. This is more important.* Whether it was what she assumed he was thinking, or a whisper that really did escape his lips, Lacy knew he was wrong.

With her smile somewhat faded but still holding strong, Lacy conceded. "Very well. You're admirable workers, and the Emperor is proud of you."

The looks of excitement on the ullullu girl's faces were almost comical. But to them, there was almost no greater compliment they could receive directly from Imperial forces. The girls fell to their knees and held their fists high. "Thank you, ma'am. We will never fail the Emperor. Our lives are for him."

Dex rolled his eyes.

Lacy looked around nervously, worried that the girls would attract unwanted attention. She stepped back. "Yes, well… get back to work and come to my ship when you've finished. Okay?"

"Yes, ma'am," the girls affirmed. As they raised their heads, Lacy was certain she could see tears of joy in the women's massive eyes.

Dex grabbed Lacy by the arm and pulled her away in the direction of the *Silent Horizon*, "Let's go, darling," he whispered. "These girls give me a bad feeling."

Lacy turned away from the girls. "That's just how these people are raised. You can't blame them."

"When how they were raised gets us killed I will. Come on."

Even when they were out of sight of the ullullu girls, they could still hear them raving about the honor they'd been given.

The *Silent Horizon* was still being placed when Dex and Lacy came to it. Crewmen were reorganizing crates to make room for it.

"Hold it now! Just wait! You're gonna crush this stuff!"

"What kind of ship is this anyway? You ever seen something like this?"

"Not once. Must be a new model of Sterlissens."

"No, it's too small for Sterlissen."

Dex leaned into Lacy. "I don't like all this chatter."

"You're worrying too much." She chided him.

"And you don't worry enough."

Lacy harrumphed and stepped forward toward the loading crew. "That's enough of that yap, gentlemen. The type of craft Imperial officers fly is of no concern to you."

Dex couldn't help but smile at how well she was playing into her role. "You'd almost think she were a real Imperial," he said to Robbie.

No response came.

"Robbie?" Dex looked down and around him. "Robbie, where'd you go?"

Behind crates and back by the ullullu girls, there was no sign of the small robot.

"Damn!" Dex rushed back to Lacy. She'd successfully silenced the crewmen and was sure they wouldn't speak of the *Silent Horizon* again once the loading was done.

"Lacy, have you seen Robbie?"

"No, I thought-"

"He's not. I don't remember seeing him since we boarded."

Lacy cursed to herself. "We can't leave him behind. He'll be scared without us!"

"Lacy I think the more important thing is if the Empire gets ahold of him, he could tell them everything."

"That's not what's important. He's our friend, not an accomplice we have to keep quiet."

The crewmen finished loading the *Silent Horizon* and were beginning to look at them again. What civilian in their right mind would talk to an officer like this?

Dex noticed their looks and demanded, "Back to work. This doesn't concern you." Then to Lacy, "Wait on the ship for the mechanics. I'll go find Robbie."

"Dex, wait!" She reached out a hand for Dex.

"I'll be fine. Just wait in the ship."

They both knew it was the right move. Unless they found

another uniform for Dex to wear, they couldn't keep acting like an officer and civilian were treated with the same respect. For all the Empire would like to pretend there were only two classes, the Emperor and his people, it was clear from their interactions that no one really believed it. In moments like this, though, Lacy didn't care so much what the *right* move was. The last time she and Dex were separated it was almost deadly.

She did as she was instructed anyway and waited in the ship. Through the viewport, Lacy kept a close eye on the goings on of the cargo bay. The crewmen slowly finished loading the cargo, a clear sign that lift-off was approaching.

Dex rushed to trace his steps back through the narrow halls of the vessel. He looked in every nook and cranny big enough to fit their small friend. Whenever he knew there wasn't anyone from the crew around, he'd call Robbie's name. Intuition told him Lacy gave him a name uncommon to this part of the universe. The slightest misstep he took would make it obvious that he wasn't from around here.

After making his way back to the gangway they entered from, Dex eventually found his way to the upper deck, a spacious area with floor-to-ceiling windows that gave the illusion of a promenade deck. From the cargo hold to the upper deck there'd been no sign of the robot ever coming on the vessel. At the very least, he'd seen enough of the ship to know a general way around the place.

He's gone, Dex told himself. *Little guy wandered off the ship. Probably back to where we parked.* "Lacy's gonna kill me."

Dex leaned against the window. His head rested on his arm as he looked out over the spaceport and the starry sky beyond it.

"In another life…"

The cargo ship rumbled. The engines were coming to life. One more inch closer to freedom. But something wasn't quite right, and it wasn't their missing friend.

The gangways were being disconnected, but from further down along the docks, people were running towards them. Six Zar-Mecks and an officer. Dex couldn't hear them through the glass, nor read their lips from that distance, but he knew exactly what they were saying. "Hold it! Stop that ship!"

Dex had to move fast. The outer hatches would already be closed for departure, but it wouldn't be hard for the Imperial squad to get one open for emergency boarding.

Without hesitation, Dex booked it for the bridge. There wasn't much time. He turned left, right, sprinted down the hall, crashed through aliens and robots alike. Dex was so focused on getting to the bridge, he didn't notice he'd tripped over something until he was facedown on the ground.

"Dex? Are you alright?" A metallic voice asked.

Fear hit him first. The Imperial troop had made it aboard and found him already. But the Zar-Mecks would never address him as 'Dex.' He shot his head around and saw Robbie standing with his dome head cocked to the side.

"Robbie, what the hell are you doing here?" he shouted and rose to his feet.

"I was lost so came back to my post." Robbie pointed toward the room they stood next to, the ship's galley.

"Don't run off again! Get to the cargo hold, now!" Dex was off again. Robbie tried to speak, but Dex only ordered him, "Get moving!"

It was a short exchange, but one that Dex knew could have stalled him just enough to doom them all. When he got to the bridge, he wouldn't have time to be diplomatic with anyone.

Dex stepped through the door to the bridge, his hand hovering above his blaster. His finger twitched with violent anxiety. From there he could see most of the layout of the upper deck through the viewport. It wasn't much different from earlier models of nautical cargo vessels on Earth. It could almost be a replica of one from back home except it was over twice the size and had a shield surrounding it.

Three aliens of varying races sat at the helm. There was no clear indicator of who was the pilot, co-pilot, or navigator. Moreover, who would be in communication with port control? As long as they continued not to notice his entrance, he could wait and hope to cut in right as they called.

"All systems good to go," one of the aliens said to the team.

The one in the middle of the helm flicked a few buttons. The cargo ship lurched upward. Dex almost lost his balance and grabbed onto whatever was nearest and stable. They were finally moving away from the dock.

A head turned at the sound of Dex's stumble. A trio of eyes from one of the aliens turned and noticed Dex. "What are you doing up here? Who are you?"

Before Dex could answer, something buzzed on the command console, followed by a staticky voice. "Cargo Liner *Venture*, this is Port Control, how do you read?" The third alien raised a hand, presumably to press a button to send a message back. Dex jumped forward and found his target.

"Captain needs you. I've been sent to hold your post." Without giving the crewman a chance to refute, Dex bumped him out of the seat and took his place. "Said it's an emergency," he continued with concern in his voice. "I wouldn't want to keep him waiting."

"Did he say what was wrong?" The crewman asked.

"No, but I can tell ya he wasn't on cloud nine, that's for sure." Dex turned his attention to the ship's radio and held down the button he saw the crewman reach for. "This is Cargo Liner Venture, I copy." He didn't raise his finger off the button.

The alien he'd replaced began to speak again, but the three-eyed commanded him, "Get going Slorn. Don't want another pay cut, do ya?" He and the first alien laughed together. Dex joined in to keep up the act.

Slorn backed up a few steps and then jogged out of the room. "Damn, Jorra's gonna ring me again!"

Once gone, the three-eyed alien nudged Dex. "Hey, be honest. Captain didn't need Slorn, did he? Don't worry, I won't say nothin', just as long as you know how to update the tower once every few hours." His face showed no sign of hidden meaning.

The first alien humphed. "Waste of space anyway."

Playing into it, Dex tried to read the room and fake a smile. "I used to run navigation on my last job. This junker's got me stuck in the cargo hold, though, and let me tell you, it has not been a highlight of my career."

"I hear that," the first crewman said. "What's tower calling about, anyway? They call back yet?"

Dex threw up his hands strategically, feigning surprise, but was sure to keep a finger pressed down on the comms button. "I don't know!" He lied, "Maybe they called into the wrong ship. I'm sure if they really need us they'll call back. Hey, you guy's ever been to Areeno?"

* * *

Lacy studied Ja'laa, the ullullu girls, as they worked on the hyperdrive. She tried to learn as much about its mechanics as she could in case they had another incident. Based on what Dex had filled her in on, they'd become too reliant on Imperial mechanics to get them out of a jam.

To the surprise and delight of Ja'laa, Lacy had repeatedly offered to help them wherever they needed.

"No no," they would say. "You work hard enough already to serve our Emperor."

"You're too kind," Lacy would respond, making the girls blush.

Things were running smoothly, but she still worried about Dex and Robbie. The only thing that kept her mind at ease was the fact that no one had begun blasting them yet.

* * *

"Hey, let me check the radio," Kerjan, the three-eyed crewman, reached over toward Dex.

"It's alright! It's working fine!" Dex argued.

"That's the problem, you've got your finger still on it."

Dex looked down, pretending to be shocked. "What? Oh… golly I thought that was how this thing worked! Back on my last job, that's how it was!"

"What kind of ship was it?" Quey'Ten, the other crewman, challenged.

There were no more lies Dex could spin to get out of this one.

The crewmen stood. "Don't make any trouble," Kerjan said

with his hands raised to grab Dex. "We've had our fair share of stowaways on this boat. We know how to handle your kind."

From this point on, all Dex could do was hope Lacy would be understanding. He jumped up and back a few steps. Fast as a gunslinger from the movies he'd been raised on, Dex brandished his blaster.

The instant his finger left the comms button, a shrill voice cried through the radio. "TO YOUR LOCATION! I REPEAT! ZAR-MECK STARFIGHTERS ARE EN ROUTE TO YOUR LOCATION! PREPARE TO BE BOARDED! MAINTAIN YOUR COURSE!"

* * *

"I really can't thank you two enough." Lacy almost held out her arms to hug Ja'laa, but switched it up last second to shake their hands instead. They were still confused but went along with it. As they stepped off the *Silent Horizon*, Lacy added, "If there's anything the Empire could do for you, please feel free to ask!"

"We could never ask anything from you, ma'am, nor the Empire. The Emperor has given us all we need in this life. Oh! We're sorry little one!" Ja'laa kicked something on accident and turned to see a small, ash-black robot knocked over.

"Robbie!" Lacy jumped down from the airlock threshold to help him up. "I'm so glad you're safe!"

Robbie stood back up on his feet and said, "I wish people would stop kicking me around."

"We'll try to be more careful buddy," she rubbed his dome head like a puppy.

"Please forgive us, ma'am!" Ja'laa begged. "We did not see him! We didn't know he was yours!"

"It's all right," Lacy laughed. "Just an accident is all."

Robbie looked up at the ullullu girls. "Are these the mechanics you were looking for?"

"Yes, Robbie. Meet Ja'laa." She gestured to both of the girls.

Robbie looked from one to the other, then said, "Thank you for helping us escape the Empire."

The smiles that had persisted on Ja'laa's face since first meeting Lacy could not have shifted to anger any faster. "Traitor! Heathens! *HELP!*"

The cargo hold that had previously felt empty quickly flooded with life. Right on cue, alarms rang throughout the cargo ship.

* * *

Kerjan lunged for Dex's blaster. Dex dodged to the left and slammed Kerjan's face with his elbow.

"Don't mess with me, Quey." He aimed the blaster at the other alien. "I've had a really bad week already." The Hollywood gunslinger was gone. In his place, a real one. Dex's back was up against the door.

"There's no way off this ship, Korr, if that's even your real name."

It was the only one Dex could think of in time that would fit in in the Empire.

"I think I'll find a way. Just stay away-"

An alarm rang throughout the ship. A deafening *wwwWW-WEEEEEEEEEEEEEEOOO!*

Dex shifted his gaze to the right and saw Kerjan hunched over the command console, with his hand smacked on a black-and-yellow striped button.

The door slammed shut behind Dex and locked tight.

"There's no use to that blaster anymore," Quey-Ten said. "You'll go peacefully with the Zar-Mecks. Just don't hurt us. It won't help you."

Dex looked from Quey-Ten to Kerjan, then to the glass viewport. He switched up his aim and fired on the glass.

"Stop!" Quey-Ten shouted and jumped in the way of the blaster fire. A laser beam shot through his shoulder and Quey-Ten fell to the ground in pain. The whole attempt had been in vain. Not only did he shoot someone, but the laser beams didn't even shatter the glass. They only left small holes that caramelized around the edges.

Dex looked around for something heavy. For half a moment,

he considered tossing Kerjan to break the glass. After all, neither one of them would have a problem killing Dex, why should he care about their safety? But no, that was too cruel. Instead, he grabbed one of the chairs, took a step back from the console, and threw it as hard as he could at the place his blaster fire shot the glass. The entire pane shattered and Dex jumped up on the console.

It was a five-story drop down to the upper deck with nothing soft to land on if he jumped. Down below, everyone was running this way and that, shouting to each other about what was going on with the alarm. Off in the distance, Dex saw the outline of Zar-Meck starfighters approaching the cargo ship.

He looked back at the helm, wondering if he could shut off the artificial gravity from there. *No, not on a ship this big. That'd be somewhere by the life support or engine.* There had to be another way down.

Off to the right, Dex spotted a pipe. Whether it was sewage, oxygen, or noxious gases, it didn't matter. It was his only bet back to the cargo hold. Dex jumped down onto a small ledge just below the viewport frame and sidestepped twenty feet to the pipe.

From below, he heard someone shout, "Did you see that?" Then someone else, "Up there! By the bridge!"

Dex kept shuffling until he reached the pipe, then held on tight and slid down. Crewmen were ready to meet him at the base, but Dex was also ready with his blaster.

"Back away! All of you!" he shouted, flagging the entire group in one long spread of his blaster. But it wasn't Dex who needed to tell them to move.

The Zar-Meck starfighters, four of them in all, descended onto the cargo ship.

* * *

The first crewman to come to the aid of Ja'laa was a hulking grey alien with four arms. The very same that had bumped into Dex in the spaceport village.

"She's a traitor! Both of them!" Ja'laa shouted.

The four-armed creature grunted acknowledgment. It was no longer a concern that the woman was wearing an Imperial officer's uniform. A traitor was a traitor.

Lacy's eyes went wide with fear. The crewman was nearly twice her size, there was no way she would be able to fight him. She grabbed Robbie by the claw and pulled him toward the ship. Robbie's other arm was at the same time yanked by the brute, with three times Lacy's strength.

Robbie slipped from her grip, and Lacy spun to shoot at the crewman. One long green bolt fired from the Imperial blaster, searing the crewman's side.

The brute dropped Robbie, and instead swung its massive arm at Lacy, knocking the blaster out of her hand before she could fire again. With his swing, the crewman caved with the pain in his side.

With only a moment before the brute picked himself back up, Lacy grabbed Robbie again and they rushed into the *Silent Horizon* sealing the airlock behind them just as the hulking crewman closed in. Undeterred, he began banging on the door, and from the sounds of it, was attempting to tear the thing down.

Please, God, let Dex be on his way back! Lacy prayed.

"I don't think they meant to help us escape," Robbie said, leaning against the door like his body weight was enough to hold back the crewman.

"They weren't! Hold him back! I'll get the engine running," she rushed to the front of the cabin, hoping Robbie would have enough sense to torch the brute if he got through.

Lacy activated the *Silent Horizon* and was grateful Ja'laa had been good at her job. The engine hadn't sounded this healthy since they first left Earth.

Lacy's optimism failed to extend to Robbie. He was sure that any moment now the crewman would burst through the door and crush him without a second thought.

"I think I liked the galley better," he told himself.

*   *   *

Dex jumped behind the first piece of cover he could find. The Zar-Meck starfighters landed just between him and the cargo hold opening in the upper deck. Without giving him time to plan, ramps descended from the starfighters. Zar-Mecks rushed out of their ships and Dex opened fire.

Laser beams traced over Dex's head and shot into the crate he took cover behind. He ducked down to avoid the fire but couldn't get back up. The Zar-Meck volley was too heavy, he was completely pinned. A blast shot through the corner of the crate. Wood exploded and splintered, scraping his left cheek. But it gave Dex an idea. Maybe there was something in the crate they were transporting that could help him.

He elbowed an already chipped segment of the crate and pulled back the board. Nothing! Just some alien fruit by the looks of it. Of course, it'd be too convenient for his first choice of cover to also be his salvation.

To buy time, he shot wildly over his head, knowing he would only stall the Zar-Mecks if he was lucky. Their armor was too thick to get a lethal blow in one hit.

From the sound of the blaster fire, the Zar-Mecks were drawing closer. Dex had to move fast, within the next few seconds if he was going to survive at all. It was then that a realization hit. They weren't aiming to kill him; they only wanted him pinned. Dex and Lacy were meant to be prisoners.

That's my advantage! Dex knew, or hoped, that the worst they would do was wound him if they weren't close enough to grab him. The thought gave him an ounce of optimism. Risking a glance over his shoulder one more time, Dex caught a glimpse of the loaders the crewmen had been using to lower cargo into the hold.

Dex took a few quick breaths, forcing adrenaline into his system, and shot off in the fastest sprint his legs could push, firing wildly in the direction of the Zar-Mecks. Their reflexes were quick, and their aim reliable, but Dex was right. They were careful not to make a killing blow. The shots landed around Dex's feet and past his legs, all only centimeters off of their target. As soon as he was close enough, Dex jumped into the loader and forced it into action, drifting sideways towards the cargo hold.

The loader was slow, but Dex only had to make it a few meters.

The Zar-Mecks tightened their shot group. Blasts hit the loader's outer frame at the height of Dex's chest. Dex fired off a few more rounds, then threw the loader off the ledge into the cargo hold. Looking below, he saw a crewman banging on the airlock of the *Silent Horizon*. Dex steered the loader closer to his target and fired a round at the crewman to get his attention.

The shot hit its target, burning into the muscles on his back. The crewman turned around and saw the loader descending on him and tried to flee. But Dex was filled with vitriol and shut off the hover system as the loader found its mark directly over the crewman.

Dex jumped off the loader and onto the roof of the *Silent Horizon* just before the loader crushed the crewman beneath it.

"Hey! Watch it, twerp!" Dex shouted as the crewman screamed out his last breath.

From above, blaster bolts rained down on them.

Dex rushed across the hull to the bow and slid down onto the viewport.

"Lacy! Open the airlock!" He shouted through the glass.

The smile on her face when she saw him made him momentarily forget all the terrible things they were going through.

She mouthed back an affirmative, then thumbed towards the head of the ship, confirming it was open.

Dex jumped off the hull and ran under the ship to reach the airlock. A blast grazed his arm, burning a small hole through the jacket Korr had given him. He ignored the pain, boarded the ship, and closed the airlock behind him. The instant it closed, Lacy pulled the *Silent Horizon* up.

"What took you so long?!" Lacy demanded.

Dex rushed to the bow and jumped into his seat. "Oh, you know me. Just making friends." A quick volley of laser beams rang across the hull. "Okay, maybe not *friends*."

With Lacy piloting the ship, Dex pulled up the controls for the rear turret.

"Hyperdrive is ready. Back to Earth?" Lacy asked.

"Baby, I'm really thinking Earth isn't an option if we can't lose these guys. Besides, it doesn't look like those girls exactly topped us off."

The *Silent Horizon* shot out of the cargo hold but was immediately cut off by a Zar-Meck starfighter. Lacy banked hard to starboard and leveled out. Dex fired off a few rounds at their pursuers but missed all of them as the Zar-Mecks dodged the shots with sporadic evasive maneuvers.

"Watch it!" Lacy shouted. "You'll hit civilians!"

"Lacy, I don't they're exactly innocent anymore, they tried to get us killed!"

The hyperdrive notified them it was ready, and Lacy didn't hesitate to activate it. They were free again temporarily from the Empire, but it wasn't as victorious as before.

Lacy glared at Dex. "It's not their fault. That's how they're raised out here."

Dex leaned in and said sternly, "Darling I don't care how they're 'raised' when it's your life on the line. You had no problem with it when I was breaking you free!"

"That was different and you know it! You've been more than ready lately to kill anybody who raises the slightest inconvenience." She stood from her chair and paced back and forth in the cabin. "I'm worried about you, Dex. I don't want this to be the person you turn into."

Dex didn't know what to say. He thought of Hwaq, the mechanic on Reechi, how quickly he'd turned on him. Not even Hwaq's kids mattered more to him than the Empire. No amount of reason could change Hwaq's mind. Dex could argue this to Lacy, but he knew it wasn't the right time. In his mind, Lacy just wasn't ready for the truth of the world they'd entered.

Hours passed. Blip after blip appeared on the radar, but none they wanted to risk until cabin fever crept into their anxious minds. They couldn't all be Empire. The next one to pop up would be their destination.

"Let's hope we've found our new home," he joked, hoping it would bring Lacy back into a better mood.

Lacy didn't budge.

Dex swerved his chair around and offered, "You can put on a song if you want."

She couldn't hide her smile.

"Come on," Dex laughed. "Pick something out quick. We're coming in."

Lacy rolled her eyes and walked back to her seat at the console. In silence, but grinning, she picked out a piece from 1933 by Max Steiner.

Trumpets led the orchestra as the *Silent Horizon* dropped out of hyperspace, revealing a lush green planet split in half, and only held together by planetary roots.

"It's pretty," Lacy stared, entranced by the broken world.

"Let's just hope the Empire hasn't gotten here first," Dex said. His tone matched the imposing melody of the track Lacy had selected. There was no sign of the Empire as of yet, no warships or other vessels. But the *Silent Horizon* still approached with caution toward the mysterious planet below.

18. The Lost World

The *Silent Horizon* skimmed above the trees of the lush green world.

"Looks like there's a stable atmosphere here," Dex read from the computer reports. "Plenty of oxygen. And by the looks of it, every kingdom of life except Imperial."

"How can you be certain the Empire isn't here?" Lacy asked.

"Well, I don't want to jump to any conclusions, but I bet if they were here they'd be on our tail already. Look over there," Dex pointed out the viewport. "Looks like a clearing. I'm gonna take us down."

"Finger crossed you do better than last time," Lacy joked, referencing their crash on Prullen-1.

Dex chuckled at the remark and banked the ship. "As you wish, darling. One smooth landing coming up."

As the *Silent Horizon* flew above and into the clearing. It soon became clear the trees were leagues taller than Dex and Lacy had expected.

"Golly," Lacy remarked. "They're as tall as skyscrapers!"

Darkness shrouded them as they descended. Thin streams of light poured through the leaves, reflecting off the eyes of creatures occupying the trees. Lacy stood and leaned closer to the viewport for a better look at the creatures.

"Settle down, Lacy. I don't think this ship can take on any more pets." Dex glanced down at Robbie, then back to the controls.

"I'm sure we can fit one more little guy. We *do* have a spare bed."

Dex harrumphed. "About to land. Might want to get back in your seat."

"You've got this, I'll be fine."

The *Silent Horizon* jerked as it touched down. Lacy almost lost her balance. She gave Dex a playful scowl. He shrugged off her look with a smile. "You are now free to roam the cabin. Please enjoy your new home." He stood and held out his hand to take hers. "Care to join me?"

"Ha, are you ready to make that claim already?"

"You see those trees? See how tall and thick they are?"

Lacy looked them over again.

Dex continued. "Let's say the Empire does show up here. They'd have to come down to the surface and comb the entire planet to find us. I think we'll be okay for a little while. And here, if it makes you feel better…" Dex flipped some switches on the console. "Radio signal is off."

Lacy pursed her lips and crossed her arms.

"Come on," He took her in his arms and said softly, "early retirement, remember? It's time to unpack." Dex kissed her on the cheek.

She wasn't convinced, but for the time being, agreed not to argue.

The air of the planet was sweet, clean, and warm. A very *humid* warm. It was the closest they'd felt to being back on Earth since they'd first left. The trees were like that of the redwood forest on steroids. The grass of the clearing was full and vibrant. As the sun moved overhead, greater light poured in over them. It wouldn't last long, but in the new light, the clearing looked like a garden out of a fairy tale that had been waiting for their arrival.

Dex patrolled around the perimeter of the clearing. The brush was thick around the bases of the thick trees. Small animals rustled about as Dex approached them.

Lacy watched from a distance, standing by the airlock with Robbie.

"It looks safe to me," Robbie said.

"We just have to be sure. You never know what could be out there."

Dex attempted to step through the brush to see how thick it was. The roots and branches were so tough, it was like a fortress wall surrounding them. He thought it would be great for protection, but a nuisance when they had to go out into the jungle to hunt. After a few minutes, Dex was only able to cut in about a foot with no sign of thinning out. He stepped back and reevaluated his plan.

The wall of brush was tall, maybe twelve feet high. If it was that hard to cut through, Dex assumed it'd have no problem holding his weight and deemed it safe enough to climb. He grabbed a branch and began to pull himself up.

"Dex! What are you doing?" Lacy called.

"Just getting a better look. I'll be right back, don't worry!" Dex pulled himself up on a branch. As his fingers wrapped around the alien wood, dozens of brown-and-green-skinned spidery creatures rushed out of the darkness of the brush and scattered. A group of them scurried across his hand and up his sleeve. Each tiny step they took felt like minuscule needles pricking his skin. Dex jumped back and tore off Korr's jacket.

Spiders were thrown into the air like a cloud of mist.

"What is it?!" Lacy shouted and began to rush to him.

"It's fine! It's fine!" Dex thrashed his arm and swatted at the spiders. Small beads of blood trickled down his forearm. "No worse than a paper cut." He stepped up to the brush wall again.

"Dex, wait. There could be more."

"They're gone, darling. I'm sure they all scurried away when I spooked 'em. Look." He grabbed onto the same branch. "Like I said, it's fine."

Lacy harrumphed. "Just be careful."

Dex laughed. "I always am!"

Lacy watched Dex climb with her arms crossed. She felt ready to spring into action if anything else jumped out at him. *But what would I fight with?*

Amidst her worrying, something rustled in the jungle. Dex fixed his stance atop the brush wall and drew his blaster.

Lacy jumped to her feet and backed slowly toward Robbie and the ship.

"Did you see anything?" Lacy called. "It sounded... big."

Dex kept his focus down the sights of the blaster and scanned his surroundings. Everything in the jungle was so thick that it was hard to see more than a few feet away.

"Yeah... definitely big... and definitely fast."

Something moved a few yards away at his two o'clock. Dex turned and aimed his blaster.

The shadows in the clearing darkened. Visibility dropped quickly in the jungle.

"Dex! Come down from there! Let's get back in the ship."

"Yeah..." He said, mostly to himself. "Yeah, that's a good idea." Dex slowly lowered the blaster but didn't take his finger off the trigger. He stood for a moment with the weapon at his side, hoping to catch a slip from whatever it was, hiding from them, watching them.

Dex scanned the area ahead of him one more time. The jungle was completely dead except for a set of yellow dots, looking down on Dex from high above.

For the remainder of the evening, Dex, Lacy, and Robbie heard no sign of any large creatures in the jungle around them. Here and there they heard the cawing and screeching of strange beasts from a distance. Dex stayed a while outside, sitting by a fire he'd made, listening to the nocturnal sounds of the alien world.

Lacy stayed on the ship while Dex relaxed outside. She was taking her time adjusting to their potentially new home. She'd gone camping often enough with her family when she was younger. She, her parents, and her younger brother would take trips up to the Harriman State Park for a week at a time in the summer. They were some of the best trips they ever took as a family and helped instill a sense of adventure in young Lacy. Harriman she knew was safe. A bear might wander around once in a blue moon, but they were never looking to pick a fight with a hiker. But this planet was an entirely different beast. For all she knew, anything and everything past the tree line was waiting for them to wander just an inch too far into its domain so it could pounce. It wasn't far-fetched either, to believe that something would pop out from the wood line in the middle of the night to eat them without provocation. What bothered her most was that Dex didn't seem to care.

Dex was content with his fire. He didn't care if a jungle beast jumped out then and there to attack him. Not for lack of will to live, he'd just decided that no matter what, *it can't be worse than the Empire.*

So, he sat by the fire and imagined himself with a glass of something stronger than coffee, and a cigar like the one Korr had given him.

Korr... the memory of his short-lived friendship drifted into his head. He had known the cyborg for less than a day, yet the man gave his life for Dex and Lacy.

Dex raised an imaginary scotch glass into the air. "This one's for you buddy. Wish you could be here."

"Who are you talking to?" Robbie's voice caught Dex by surprise. The robot had snuck up on Dex and sat by his side.

"No one," Dex said quietly, then corrected himself. "My own robot friend. You didn't get to meet him." He almost took a sip of his drink before realizing it wasn't really there. "It doesn't matter. Happens right? You just wander into the wrong place at the wrong time and *BOOM!..* ruin it for everyone."

"I-" Robbie began but was cut off.

"Korr, got him involved now he's dead. Hwaq, only meant to buy from him and he's dead. The people on that cargo ship just going about their business, got them killed. Oh yeah! And I think we pretty much doomed everyone on Earth!" He laughed hysterically. "How's that for a damn 'exploratory mission?' 'So long ladies and gentlemen! Good luck out there! Bring back lots of cool space stuff and try not to get us all killed! Oh, you did? Don't worry, the human race won't be around much longer to remember how you damned us all anyway.'" He got to his feet and kicked some dirt and grass into the fire, then paced around the flames. "At least we can't screw up anything here, right? No, as long as we sit in this hole until we *DIE*, we'll have no problems whatsoever. Just peachy, isn't it? Proud of me, Dad?" Dex shouted up at the sky.

Lacy stuck her head out of the airlock door. "Dex? Are you okay?"

He didn't hear her. "Wanted me to find something better, right?! Well, I found the answer! It's nothing! There's nothing better! It's the same shit on one side of the universe as the other!"

"Dex, what's wrong?" Lacy stepped down the ramp slowly, struggling to see anything in the dim light the fire emitted.

"Nothing's wrong." He finally acknowledged her. "I'm just..." He dropped his head and looked at her face. Guilt rushed over him.

They were both scared. They were both lightyears from anything they could call home and anyone who had ever loved them, and there was no way to go back. But her eyes weren't saying that. Looking into her dazzling, starry eyes, behind the fear, he saw how hard she was fighting to stay strong. Her strength could crumble at any moment if he wasn't able to fight alongside her. And here he was, wallowing in self-pity when he knew he should be grateful they were alive together.

"I'm sorry, Lacy."

Lacy took three big strides towards him and threw her arms around Dex. Tears streamed down her face and soaked into his jacket. "Don't give up on me now. Not after all we've just been through."

Dex kissed her temple and held her close with his hand holding the back of her head. "Never, darling. From one end of the universe to the next…"

Lacy pulled back an inch to meet his gaze.

"…I will always be there for you."

Robbie guarded the *Silent Horizon* as they slept that night. He'd hoped that if anything came into their area, it would be something small. His blowtorch extension was strong enough only at close range and would only be useful in scaring anything off. Taking Dex and Lacy's request to heart, he was on high alert for any sign of movement or loud noises. His arm was almost always raised and ready to attack.

Lacy opened up the ventilation system on the ship before bedding down for the night. The warm, sweet-smelling air helped her fall asleep. She burrowed deep in Dex's arms as they slept. From the instant they lay down together, all memory from the prison cells on the Empire outpost to the transport to the Heart of the Void faded.

As exhausted as he was, Dex couldn't stay asleep. Their previous trials may have been over with and out of Lacy's mind, but he saw the mark it had left on her. He thought of her eyes, how they sparked and swirled like hundreds of galaxies as if her eyes were a window to the universe. He hadn't seen firsthand what happened to her in the Emperor's presence, hadn't witnessed the ritual Korr talked about, but he didn't need to in order to know the Emperor had changed something, even if unintentionally, about Lacy in more ways than the color of her eyes. Dex thought of the voice he heard in the back of his mind on the cargo ship. The voice that was too clear to be his imagination.

She had to have been talking to me, he thought.

Lacy stirred in her sleep. Dex saw a half smile on her face and thought about what beautiful dreams she was having. At that moment he envied her.

From down the hall, Robbie's footsteps echoed. Dex sat up in bed. The footsteps were casual. They didn't warrant alarm, but situational awareness wasn't Robbie's strong suit anyway. The pacing could have said anything between 'I saw a bug and wanted to show it to you,' and 'The Empire's here and they're about to blow up the planet.'

Robbie shuffled into the cabin with his arms swinging lazily at his sides.

"What's going on, buddy?" Dex asked.

"There's a monster outside," Robbie said, still casually. "I thought I should report it."

Dex jumped out of bed, startling Lacy awake.

"Jesus, Robbie! Move with a purpose why don't ya!" He ran out in his skivvies, grabbing the blaster from the holster he hung on the starboard side bunk.

Knowing something was out there, a 'monster' as Robbie called it, the same nighttime scene he'd sat peacefully in just a few hours prior now felt like the lion's den.

Dex scanned the dark environment. The light of a distant moon only barely crept over the tops of the trees. Even if there was movement, he realized he probably wouldn't be able to register it until the monster jumped out at him from the tree line.

Two yellow dots flickered off to the side. Dex spun fast and shot off a beam from the blaster. The bolt sped through the air and faded quickly in the dark. The yellow dots disappeared. Something moved in its place, rushing to the left. Dex followed the sound with the tip of the blaster.

He stepped off a few feet away from the ship. The creature in the jungle stopped racing left and made a sharp turn upwards, climbing through the tree. Dex listened intently to the sound it made as it moved. It wasn't at all like running. It had a thumping sound. No, not thumping. It was jumping at high speed from branch to branch. The thing jumped higher and higher. It hopped onto one branch, then another, then stopped and Dex could see what he guessed were its yellow eyes looking back at him.

Robbie and Lacy waited for him by the airlock.

"What is it?" Robbie asked,

"It's by no means a monster, I can tell you that much," Dex said and dropped the blaster to his side. As he walked back to the ship he said, "Just a scared animal. Probably never seen anything like us before."

Movement to the left. Much larger this time. Dex raised his weapon again. Perhaps there was a monster lurking in the woods.

First came the sound of tumbling rocks, something rolling toward them, then heavy thudding that shook the ground.

"Dex, get back on the ship!" Lacy ordered.

He didn't listen.

Shadows moved in the jungle. Dex only noticed them briefly before the monster jumped from the wood line. Brush collapsed under its feet.

Dex fell back with the impact and fired off a short burst from the blaster. Two of the bolts hit their target. They sank into the monster's thick, oily reflective hide like they were being sucked into quicksand.

The monster lunged.

Dex dodged to the left, ducking under the *Silent Horizon*, and fired off another quick burst. The first hit the monster in the side. The monster reacted quickly, dodging the other two laser beams. Dirt kicked up into the air as it turned and planted itself to prepare for another lunge.

Up above him, the *Silent Horizon* roared to life. It sounded like Lacy was ready to bail on their new home.

The monster lunged. It was too fast for Dex to outrun. Instead, Dex rolled into it just before the monster had him in its clutches. Razor-sharp claws swatted at Dex on his roll, slicing four thin strips off his back.

Dex pushed through the pain and fired again as he came out of the roll. The shots were still nothing more than a nuisance to the monster, but it would have to do until he could find something better.

Lacy and Robbie's hurried footsteps echoed through the lower hull of the *Silent Horizon*. The monster took notice and began clawing at the ship. Each swipe at it took a thick chunk of the ship with it. It was clear to Dex that if he didn't act fast, the monster would be taking the ship out of commission indefinitely. He had to draw the thing away.

Dex shuffled backward toward the brush. He shot at the monster again, not caring if it did damage, only attempting to get its attention. Although he couldn't distinguish any eyes or facial features on the beast, one blast hit close enough to what Dex thought was a face. The monster abandoned its efforts on the ship and charged again at Dex.

There the two of them were, in a gladiatorial fight. Dex stood in the Colosseum, fighting this beast for the enjoyment of the crowd, the animal with the yellow eyes hopping from tree to tree whose presence Dex still felt. This was a match that had been rigged against him. A blaster was clearly no use and there weren't any eager audience members who would throw in an extra spear. But there were other dangerous creatures in the jungle, right in the brush for certain.

Before Dex could formulate a plan, the monster was on top of him again. It was the first decent look at the shape of the thing from the glow of the rear engines. The monster looked like a chimera mix of two or three creatures melted together. It stood on multiple legs like a spider, but they were all different lengths and sizes. The torso came up from the body like a centaur, with arms that hung down and beat at the ground like an ape. The head was nearly melted into the body, with half of it drooping lower than the rest, and having features that resembled nothing of the other side of the face. Here Dex saw that the face wasn't eyeless, there were two tiny white dots deep in the back of the socket. But there wasn't time to study its anatomy.

The monster's fists pummeled the ground in front of Dex. He lost his balance and fell on his back. The monster smashed at the ground again and again, missing Dex only by inches as he tried and failed to pull himself back up and out of the monster's range. The monster swung its ape-like arms again, its talons teasing the idea of ripping out Dex's innards.

Dex was quick, and rotated to the right, just barely avoiding another deep cut, turned over and was on his feet, bolting across the clearing. The claws tore through the brush instead of Dex. Branches, thorns, and insects went flying into the air; everything but its prey. The monster persisted and was on Dex's tail again.

Run him into the brush, Lacy's voice in Dex's head again. There was no time to debate whether it was real or not, he would do what she said.

Lacy brought the *Silent Horizon* to a hover and rotated the ship, keeping the rear pointed at the monster using the rear camera feed.

"You've got it, hun," Lacy said to herself.

Robbie sat in Dex's chair, watching the feed in fear and awe.

Dex made it successfully back to the brush wall, and before he could turn, the monster swatted at his head. Dex ducked to the side and the monster crashed into the brush. Spiders crawled out and over the monster. It was caught in the twisting branches, and the more it tried to pull itself out, the tighter it got stuck.

Dex raised his blaster again and as he pulled the trigger, the head of the monster was seared off by a massive laser beam. The body spasmed once, twice, then stilled. Dex looked back at the *Silent Horizon* in surprise. The barrel of the rear turret had the faintest glow of usage. He was frozen for a moment with the expectation of the monster springing back to life or making one final effort swipe at his throat with its razor-sharp claws.

The *Silent Horizon*'s engine fizzled out. The airlock door opened and Lacy rushed out, matching Dex in her skivvies.

"Hold back!" Dex told her. "It might not be dead."

"Might not be dead?" Lacy reiterated. "I blew the damn thing's head off!"

Dex dashed over to Lacy and stood between her and the headless monster. "You don't know how things like this work. It might not even need a head to stay alive."

Branches snapped behind the brush. The two of them looked into the darkness of the jungle. Instead of seeing the monster move, or worse, a second monster as they both assumed, they were met with the sight of dozens of glowing yellow eyes surrounding the entire clearing.

"Get back on the ship," Dex whispered. "Run. Now!"

They both stepped off but one of the creatures with the yellow eyes jumped out of the jungle, soaring through the air above Dex and Lacy and landing between them and the *Silent Horizon*. The surprise of the creature's capabilities made them stumble, but more so what shocked them, was the creature carried a spear with a serrated tip.

The creature was frog-like in form, with green skin and legs that made up nearly half of its over six-foot height. Its yellow eyes were hard like dried mud with the darkest black diamond pupils Dex and Lacy had ever seen. The creature showed signs of intelligence not just in its ability to create weaponry, but also with the pads it wore on its shoulders, the chest piece, and cloths around its waist, presumably made with tough animal skins.

Before Dex and Lacy could step back, more of the frog-men surrounded them. Half a dozen spear tips waited patiently to jab them in their throats.

The leader of the group spoke to one of their men in a deep gurgling voice, a tongue neither Dex nor Lacy could understand. On their left, one of the spearmen broke off and sniffed out the *Silent Horizon*.

Lacy almost spoke, but Dex cut her off. "Don't," he whispered.

When he spoke, the frog-man's eyes went wide. The spears pulled back a few inches. The leader exchanged a few quick words with his men, and then barked orders. He lifted his spear and stepped closer to the humans.

Lacy shook in Dex's arms, wishing she had at least grabbed her nightgown on her way out of the ship.

Dex tried to prepare himself for the worst. He was already bleeding, a wound that would probably soon become infected from venom in the monster's claws. If nothing else, he thought he might be able to get Lacy out alive. The frog-man would probably kill them right there for Dex speaking out of terms.

Instead, the frog-man looked as if it was deep in thought. Then, he puffed his chest. His mouth pursed. Sound escaped his throat. "Khhh… Kaahhhhmm."

Dex and Lacy glanced at each other in confusion. The tone of the frog-man's voice wasn't half as threatening as they'd expected, yet it was still demanding.

The frog-man spoke again. This time, there was no misunderstanding him.

"Come."

19. Captured, Yet Again

"I can't believe this," Dex complained. "We travel all the way across the universe and *still* run into the French."

"Dex! You can't say that!" Lacy scolded.

"Why not?" Dex almost continued but tripped over a root and was helped up by one of the frog-men.

They'd been traveling through the jungle for well over an hour. The faintest bit of light was beginning to creep through the treetops, although that was barely enough to see anything. Dex and Lacy could only trust the frog-men to see better than they could in the low light. As the sunlight brightened up the forest, the bright yellow of the frog-men's eyes began to dim and change to a more natural amber with black pupils.

In a small gesture of goodwill from the universe, the only goodwill they thought they would get, the density of the jungle lessened the further they walked.

Robbie had been smart and stayed on the ship when the frog-men captured them. Lacy had no trouble assuming how he was feeling at the moment.

He's terrified, she thought. *He's hiding in the head or the engine room, probably hoping these aliens wouldn't look twice at him if he didn't move. That's probably where he'll stay until- if - we come back. Just sitting and waiting in fear until he rusts and can't move! Oh golly, we have to get back to him!*

Dex's train of thought was a stark contrast. *That rust bucket better learn how to fly the damn ship and blast through these woods to save us.*

Dex looked back every once in a while with false hope to see if Robbie was coming to their rescue. Every time he did, the frog-man behind him would jab the shaft of his spear into Dex's back and groan a "Fhuh!" *Move*, as Dex assumed.

The trek wouldn't be half bad for either of them if the frog-men had at least let them dress. Walking around the jungle in bare feet and very little to dignify themselves, Dex saw himself and Lacy as cavemen from *One Million B.C.* For all the technological wonders they'd brought from Earth, and further seen in this part of the universe, mankind once again found its place low to the ground, with naught but sticks and stones for defense. At least on Earth, man had been the smartest animal, uncontested. Here there was competition, and Dex couldn't even argue the weight class of the species. Sure, the frog-men didn't have intergalactic travel like humans, but it wasn't the frog-men who were being held prisoner.

Around midday, or what felt like midday with how long they'd been walking, the party halted. Most of the frog-men scattered into the trees like hunters. The leader of the group commanded one of the men from his troop to him. This one was shorter, but broader in the chest, had thicker legs, and carried a primitive rucksack.

The supply sergeant, Dex thought.

The supply frog-man dropped his pack at the foot of the leader, and opening it, pulled out provisions wrapped in wet green & blue leaves. He handed one to the leader first, then to Dex and Lacy, then left to hop from tree to tree, handing out the rations to the rest of the party.

The earthlings accepted the provisions but were immediately revulsed. Lacy dropped hers and exclaimed, "It moved!"

Dex felt movement in his hand, too, and looked to the leader for guidance. The frog-man gave the two of them a look of offense then unwrapped his leaf. Inside was the largest beetle Dex or Lacy had ever seen, at least six inches in length. It lay belly side up with its insides exposed. Across the meat of the bug, smaller insects skittered. The frog-man shot out his tongue and picked off the insects one by one. Each time his tongue hit the beetle's stomach, the bug's legs twitched. The thing was still alive.

Dex almost threw up.

Lacy *did.*

To add to their disgust, almost rubbing in how gross the act was, the frog-man tore off a piece of the sturdy leaf wrap, and used it like a chip, with the beetle's stomach meat being the dip.

"Why does all the food out here have to be the most disgusting thing possible?" Dex asked partially to Lacy, but mostly to himself. Then, with reluctance, he opened his wrap.

"You're not *actually* going to eat that are you?" Lacy protested.

"Got anything else I can have?" He asked, eyeing her up and down.

To the bug's credit, it didn't smell half as bad as Dex expected. *I'll close my eyes and it'll just be a liver paté,* he told himself. As he took a scoop, the beetle's legs slowly closed in, in a poor attempt to save itself. Dex sucked the meat off the leaf-chip and was pleasantly surprised that it wasn't the worst thing he'd ever tasted. That's not to say it was *good* by any means. "It's edible," he consoled Lacy then spit out one of the small insects. "Just pretend it's something else."

She wanted to protest with 'I'd rather starve,' but knew better. As horrible as it was, the bug was their only option. By the time she found the will to take her first stomach-churning bite, Dex was almost done with his meal.

He put the bug to the side and asked the frog-man, "Do you have water? You know…drink?" Dex took a sip of imaginary water.

The frog-man appeared to understand. He discarded the cleared-out beetle carcass from the leaf, then rolled up the wet wrapping and wrung it out over his mouth.

"Convenient," Dex commented. He did as he was instructed. The water, if it technically *was* water for as similar the two liquids were, tasted sour. It wasn't as hard to get down as the bug had been, but the first gulp almost got stuck in his throat. Nevertheless, it was quenching his thirst.

"Dex, I can't eat this," Lacy gagged out.

Dex looked at her and saw her face was a sickly green. She was about to throw up again. "Just push through it, darling."

With stubborn reluctance, Lacy took another scoop of the beetle meat. The tiny insects inside it skittered across the meat and onto her hand. Lacy screamed and dropped the entire leaf. "No! Dex, I'm *not* eating this!"

The frog-man troop leader looked at Lacy with annoyance and said in a deep, quiet voice, "Haaaaah." He lowered his hand, a sign telling her to be quiet.

In a hushed tone, Lacy asked Dex, "Any plans yet to get out

of here?"

"Not a one. Right now, I'm just hoping Robbie will come in to save the day."

"I'll take that bet. I believe in him."

Dex gave Lacy a side-eye. "I said I was hoping, not betting on it. Here," Dex picked Lacy's lunch up from the ground. "This could be the best meal we have on this planet. Don't starve on me."

Lacy felt like a child refusing to eat her greens. It was embarrassing how stubborn she was being, but at least Green Giant vegetables didn't have worms crawling in them. *Just force it down before you can think about it,* she told herself.

Dex gave her a nod of reassurance, then she forced herself to chow down. As fast as humanly possible, Lacy tore through the beetle's insides and forced the meat down her throat. Twice she almost gagged it back up. When she was finished, there were fewer scraps on her "dish" than Dex had left. She dropped the hollowed-out beetle from the leaf and then wrung it out into her mouth as they'd been instructed. Lacy hoped that the water at least would be normal, but it became just another obstacle in this marathon of horrible foods.

"I'm sure we'll get used to it eventually," Dex tried to reassure.

Curdled over with her arms wrapped around her stomach, Lacy replied, "I think I'd rather be back in prison."

Dex laughed and rubbed Lacy's back. He took in the softness of her skin, the warmth of it, and wanted to lay his cheek on her body. *It'd been what, two days? Three, since we found the Empire?* He thought. But it felt so much longer than that since he'd been intimate with her. Even the night prior, before the monster attacked them, the emotional and physical exhaustion of their adventure was taking its toll. One that could only be paid back with a good night's sleep. Now wasn't the time either for intimacy, whether an embrace or a kiss, but he ran his hand slowly up and down her back, giving her comfort while she held back the contents of her stomach threatening to come back up.

The troop leader stood and without words or hand signals, the rest of the troop fell back into formation on the ground.

With a "Fhuh!" they were moving again. Dex and Lacy rose

with the rest of the troop and were escorted once more through the jungle.

The frog-men padded along the jungle floor. Their eyes remained fixed on their surroundings, cautious of creatures like the monster from the clearing. Even though this region of the jungle was less dense, a skilled predator could still easily hide itself from its prey. In the trees above them, a small squad of frog-men kept a lookout, hopping from tree to tree as the party advanced.

The further they walked, the more thankful Lacy became that she'd forced herself to eat the disgusting bug. Her legs were beginning to shake with exhaustion. Every so often they came upon thick roots, some taller than her by more than two feet. With no way around them, no paths the frog-men cared to bother with, Dex offered to help her over.

"Such a gentleman," she teased and kissed him on the cheek.

Dex cupped his hands at her knee, and she stepped into them. As he lifted her up, Lacy joked, "Eyes forward, Captain."

"It's not 'looking up your skirt' if you're not wearing one," he shot back with a faint laugh but kept his eyes respectfully forward.

Within the next hour, their white skivvies had acquired enough mud and dirt to be stained a heavy brown. With enough rips from snagging branches, the caveman look was rapidly becoming complete, loin cloth and all.

Lacy caught Dex's smirk at the caveman thought and probed him. "What's on your mind, Dex?"

"Me no Dex. Me Tarzan." He beat his chest like the ape-man.

Lacy laughed, the loudest Dex had heard her laugh in ages. For a moment he forgot the pain in his feet, the aches in his leg, and the spears shuffling them along the rough yet slippery terrain.

"Haaaah!" The troop leader whisper-shouted.

Lacy tried to stifle her laugh. Dex merely blew off the demand. "Yeah, yeah. Haaah. We get it."

"Haaaah!" The troop leader repeated, then after a short pause and scan of their surroundings ordered his troops, "Rhuom! Ra thaata!"

The troop dispersed into the trees. The troop leader pounced on Dex and Lacy, throwing them to the ground. They both began to protest, but the troop leader didn't need to give them another 'haaaah' to tell them to shut up, and that his act was out of protection.

The ground shook beneath them.

They were pushed deep into the brush up against the stump of a tree. The frog-man's body was spread wide across both of them, but not nearly enough to cover their whole being. Dex looked out from under the frog-man's arm. He saw nothing, but the ground shook again, harder. Something was approaching them.

The stomping drew closer. The sound of wood snapping rang through the jungle. Small animals rushed past Dex and Lacy's hiding spot, away from the sound. It sounded larger than the monster that had attacked them in the clearing, and neither of them was in the mood to pick another fight.

A familiar oily-black fist pummeled into the ground just a few feet in front of where they lay hidden. This one thicker by nearly twice the size of the one in the clearing. The arms, too, were bigger, but where they met the monster's chest it was totally different than the one in the clearing. Its head was almost non-existent, with two antenna-like eyes giving away where it should be. The leathery body slithered to be met with thin, angular legs. All the power of the monster was in its front. The monster didn't look like it was built for speed or charging, but it had a tough hide, and neither Dex nor Lacy wanted to be caught in its grip.

The antenna eyes jutted around, searching for prey.

Dex looked around at the trees above them and saw no sign of the other frog-men. Then looking back at the arm of the one on top of them, he saw why. The skin tone of the troop leader had shifted slightly to brown. It wasn't a perfect camouflage with the foliage, but Dex knew he wouldn't notice it right away unless he already knew where to look. Thankfully, the monster didn't.

It kept prowling slowly across their periphery.

Lacy tried to control her breathing. She inhaled slowly and exhaled when the monster slammed its massive fist into the ground.

We're safe, she told herself. *It won't see us. We're safe.*

Dex reached out and grabbed her arm. He was ready to run and carry her on his back if he had to, to get them out of there. At just the thought of it, he felt he could sprint all the way back to the ship.

The monster lifted a fist to take another step, then hesitated.

Dex gripped onto Lacy's arm tighter.

She almost pulled away, feeling like she'd be bruised if his hand clenched anymore.

The monster dropped its fist slowly, then turned in their direction.

This is it, Dex told himself. Adrenaline was boiling inside of him.

The monster leaned in, sniffing them out. It beat the ground once as if challenging them, unsure whether or not something was really there, but displaying its strength anyway.

"Get ready," Dex whispered as it locked eyes with the beast.

The monster then roared, shaking the trees and ground around them, and pulled back an arm like it was going to punch Dex, Lacy, and the camouflaged frog-man straight through the tree. As it lunged forward, the three of them jumped to the side. Dex and Lacy to the right, the frog-man to the left.

With spear in hand, the frog-man stabbed the monster's forearm as it passed him, missing by nearly inches.

Dex and Lacy darted into the woods, jumping over another tall root for cover.

Behind them, the troop leader shouted, "Mok Tau! Attha!"

Dex peaked over their cover and saw a rain of spears descend on the beast, all with near-perfect aim, digging into the thing's back.

The monster flailed, thrashing its arm out in a wide berth that threw the troop leader into a tree. Dex saw a green liquid splattered on the wood where his head had hit, and the lifeless body fell to the ground.

Others from the troop descended from the trees, jumping onto the monster's back and stabbing into it time after time. The beast rolled over to squash the frogs. Most of them dismounted in time and went for its scaled belly instead.

"Come on!" Dex commanded Lacy with a tug of her arm. "No need to watch the action, let's go!"

She pulled back. "We have to help them!"

"Are you crazy? Let's go!"

But Lacy was already trying to pull herself back over the root. Dex tried to grab her by the leg, but mud on her leg slid her right through his grasp.

Exasperated by her reluctance to get to safety, Dex pulled himself over the root as well.

Lacy had already picked up a spear and threw it at the monster, but it was too distracted by the small army of frog-men to notice one more spear half-lodged in its hide.

"Lacy, what are you doing?" He grabbed her by the arms and almost shook her like a misbehaved kid.

Before she could answer, the supply frog jumped in front of them. "Fhuh! You! Fhuh!" His eyes were wide with concern. There was no mistaking the desperation in his voice and the obvious use of another English word, 'you.'

"Come on, Lacy!" Dex gritted his teeth. "Even *he's* telling you!" There was no time to dwell on the language breakthrough. He instead nearly threw Lacy over the root. Dex began to climb, and the frog-man helped him, then climbed over himself.

"Come!" The supply frog beckoned, and the three of them ran deeper into the jungle.

The screams of the rest of the troop followed them, along with the thundering of the monster's fists crushing them.

They hadn't made it even a hundred feet when the sounds of violence shifted to something else. The pace of the thudding changed, and it was clear the monster's focus was no longer on the rest of the troop. The ground was rattling now, and the monster was on their tail.

"Fhu-rak! Fhu-rak!" The supply frog shouted.

Lacy's sprint faltered. Her feet fell out from under her and caught on a rock. She screamed out in pain, but before she could hit the ground, Dex caught her in his arms. He couldn't sprint with her, but he'd be damned to let the beast take her without a fight.

Sparing only a quick glance back as he picked her up, Dex saw the monster gaining on them. It was launching itself forward from its arms, shooting through the jungle like a bullet. Its oily black hide was drenched in green blood.

"Don't worry darling, I got ya," he reassured Lacy and pushed his aching body as hard as he could.

Again, the supply frog shouted, but this time not to Dex or Lacy, "Mok Tau! Kron-kaal!"

A dozen meters or so ahead, more frog-men jumped down from the trees. They beckoned the trio to them, demanding they run faster.

Dex nearly fell with Lacy in his arms when the monster landed fifty yards behind them. The supply frog pulled them both up, and the three were met by the new arrivals. They were quick to grab Dex and Lacy and throw them over a wall of root, to land on softer, dark sandy ground.

A command was shouted by the supply frog that neither Dex nor Lacy could understand and huge sharpened logs shot out of the ground.

Lacy watched as the monster was pushed back by the defenses. Most missed, serving only to scare the beast, but one sliced through its arm, dismembering it completely. The monster remained unfazed by the loss. Black ooze seeped out of its wound. The monster backed away a few feet then, and recognizing its loss, turned and ran back into the jungle.

Lacy let out a sigh of relief. She was safer now and all things considered, the pain in her foot didn't seem too bad. At least she was alive to feel the pain.

"Lacy, are you okay?" Dex asked, crawling toward her. He was barely able to pick himself up from exhaustion. The adrenaline was wearing off fast.

"I'm... I'm great!" She struggled to speak between heavy breaths. "How about you?"

He held up a thumbs up. "Peachy." His heart beat at a million miles an hour.

"Think they'll let us rest yet?" Lacy asked.

Dex looked around. With all the excitement it was easy to miss that they were no longer in the open jungle. The root they were thrown over, Dex realized, wasn't a root at all, but a wall. Within the wall they were thrown over were structures. Homes, by the look of it.

"I'm not sure, baby." He slowly rose to his feet then helped Lacy up.

A crowd began to gather around the two, and leading them was the most elderly, withered-looking creature either of them had seen before. Leaning on a walking stick taller than himself, he studied Dex and Lacy.

No one in the crowd spoke.

Dex and Lacy didn't know what to say.

It was the supply frog that broke the wondrous silence. He stepped forward and threw down his pack between the elder and the humans. The supply frog reached into the pack and pulled out Dex's scarlet P.E.S. suit.

The entire crowd gasped. The elder's eyes widened the littlest bit. His wide mouth pulled back in a weak smile. "Wel...come." He said slowly. "We have been..." He breathed deeply, "waiting... a long... long time... for... you."

20. The Mok Tau Village

Dex and Lacy sat across the village elder in a moss-covered stone hut. The air was damp, and warmed by the torches on the walls. The room was laid out like a small temple, with an altar low to the ground in front of the elder. The scarlet PES suit lay folded on the altar next to a rolled-up scroll.

The elder had held their hands as he walked them through the village. Everyone stepped out of their way, parting like the Red Sea, and gazed upon the earthlings in amazement. Some were shedding tears, but none spoke. The supply frog led the procession, holding up the scarlet exploration suit high so all could see.

"We… Mok Tau… we are…" the elder paused to breathe. He could barely keep his eyes open. "Over glad… you came. I… only wish… we had…" He took a deep breath in. The wheezing of his chest filled the small temple. "Prepared… better."

Dex looked down at the scroll on the altar. There was no way these people could have known he and Lacy would be landing on their rock.

Lacy was the one to speak up. "You've, well, prepared just fine. Thank you, and your people for getting us here safely. And we're sorry for the loss of your people."

Dex almost whispered argument to her, confused at what her angle was, but a feeble smile cracked open across the elder's face.

"They are…" deep breath in, "*HON*ored… to have… given life…" he paused again as if he'd fallen asleep, then breathed in heavily and finished, "for you."

From the way the elder spoke about them, and the set-up of the structure, Dex guessed he wasn't just the tribe's chief. Most likely, he was their religious leader as well. Everything they said would have to be very carefully thought out.

Agreed, Lacy's voice said in the back of his head.

He gave her a quick look but now wasn't the time to talk about her newfound oddities.

"How did you find us?" Dex asked. "We landed far from your village."

The elder tried to laugh. His eyes remained mostly closed but his face filled with vibrance. "The star fell... as... you said... you would..." *wheeze* "show yourself. "Our great... warriors..." pause, and slow inhale, "journey to... make... true... the signs were... right." The sentence took nearly a full minute to complete.

From behind them, Lacy heard footsteps and whispering. She turned and saw Mok Tau children peeking in. Their eyes were filled with wonder at the aliens that had come into their village.

The elder didn't seem to notice the children. "They... say me... you deef..." his face scrunched up in hard thought. "Defette... defetted..." He leaned forward and took a breath so deep it looked like his heart had given out. Both Dex and Lacy almost jumped forward to help him back up, but the elder helped himself. He continued, "defetted the... Kron-kaal."

The monster in the clearing, the Kron-kaal.

"The... cov... covat... was kept, as we... were shown."

"Covat?" Lacy asked.

"I am... sorry," the elder said with pure self-condemnation taking over his vibrancy. "I have... done all I..." *wheeze* "can to... learn... your speak... by the... dreams."

"I see," Dex said, although, he really didn't.

"You're doing just fine," Lacy said sweetly and reached out a hand to touch the elder's on the altar.

His eyes then widened with joy and vibrance taking over his face. His old heart beat so hard it almost beat right out of his chest like in the cartoons that played before films back on Earth.

"Is this really... the time? Have you... thought us worthy... of saving?"

"Y- yes, of co-" Lacy began.

Dex bumped her with his knee. "We have traveled far to be here," he said. "We haven't even yet had a moment to rest."

Lacy glared at Dex.

Blocking out her glare, Dex continued, "Thank you for your... hospitality," he said, not wanting to offend the tribe. "But you all seem like you're doing just fine on your own. You don't need us for anything." Dex tried to force himself to laugh in a friendly way as if he and the elder were old buddies.

The elder attempted to maintain his smile but was clearly confused. "I am... grat-...gratatious... you see it... as that. But..." his eyes rolled to the back of his head as he breathed in, and his eyelids went narrow again. "But our... village has... grown small. The kron-kaal attacks..." he held out his hands straight and brought them close together as he searched for the right word.

"Thinned?" Lacy asked. "Those monsters killed off your people?"

The elder nodded. "Many," he said. "Killed... many. Others... lost."

"Lost where?" Although the elder talked slowly, Lacy's expression said it was the most riveting thing she'd heard all year.

"To kill... Torro-Kaal."

A cloud overcame the room. Whether real or just in their heads, the torches dimmed as the word came out of the elder's mouth. Lacy turned to the temple door. The Mok Tau children had scurried away at the word.

"Please," she said, turning back to the Elder. "Your language is strange to us. What is this 'Torro-Kaal?"

The elder slowly rose from behind the altar, hoisting himself up with his stick. Dex and Lacy watched him as he hobbled to the back wall of the temple. Crude drawings were etched into the wall. The elder held his hand over a triangular blotch.

"Torro-Kaal," he said. "The... birther... of the Kron-kaal. This... is where she... lives. Her..."

"Lair," Lacy finished, seeing the triangle and the etchings around it as a mountain amongst trees.

Dex looked from the mural to Lacy, unbelieving that she was getting invested in the elder's babbling. She'd taken charge of the conversation and all he wanted was for her to wrap it up so they could get back to the ship.

"You... said... you would... save us." The elder slowly made his way back to his spot behind the altar and sat down. "I am... wrong... to doubt." *wheeze* "Our people... the kron... kron-kaal..." His head dropped. Tears welled in his eyes. "We were... not patient... for... you. Please forgive... me."

There was silence in the room.

Amidst the silence, the presence of the scroll demanded Dex's attention.

He spoke up, his tone challenging so as to not let the doubt be on him or Lacy. "Why do you believe it is us that are here to... help?" 'Save' almost came out but felt too definitive.

The elder reached out for the scroll.

"We have... waited... a long... long... time." The paper unfurled slowly in his ancient hands. "I listened... and saw... the dreams that... were sent." Red marks began to show themselves on the scroll. "There is no... denying..."

Dex and Lacy understood. Next to their scarlet exploration suit, was a scroll that had been in the village's keeping for maybe centuries. On the center of the scroll, as clear as a photograph, was the image of the Emperor in his scarlet robes.

* * *

Dex and Lacy sat under the awning of a hut on a small hill that the Mok Tau made up for them. The hut overlooked the small village and the surrounding wall. The number of huts greatly outnumbered that of the people walking the streets. Those who were in the village made their way toward the temple, forming a crowd around it.

Even from this distance, Dex and Lacy could see the heads of the Mok Tau turning towards them for a quick glance. Resting on a hill above everyone else, Dex and Lacy knew it would only serve to make them look more godly.

Lacy spotted two of the Mok Tau leaving the temple with clay bottles, pushing through the crowd.

Dex tried not to pay mind to any of the goings-on in the village.

"You're mad at me," he stated, trying not to make it sound

like an accusation.

"I'm not mad," she shot back.

"Annoyed then. But I know you're not happy."

"I'm fine."

Dex rolled his eyes. *There's nothing more dangerous than a woman saying 'I'm fine'*, his father had told him. "There's nothing we can do here, Lacy. They think we're gods. You really think we can live up to that?"

She said nothing, only watched as the two Mok Tau from the temple walked towards their hill, the crowd of villagers behind them.

If she didn't want to talk about what happened in the temple, Dex wanted to question her on the voices he'd been hearing. There was no denying it was more than just his conscience, and on top of the change in her eyes, something serious was happening inside Lacy.

"Do you want to tell me-"

"Why won't you help them?" Lacy interrupted and sat up, eyeing Dex harshly.

He paused, then said, "It's not our business, Lacy. In fact, we *should* already be out of here if the Empire already knows about these people."

"So, we're in trouble anyway. Why not do something about it?" She pressed.

Dex fixed his posture, making himself taller than Lacy. "Because if I only have a week left to live, I want to at least try to live that week in peace. There's nothing we can do for them anyway."

The footsteps of the Mok Tau drew nearer.

"Can't do anything if we don't try." Lacy rebutted.

"There is no *try*, Lacy."

Would your Dad have said that? This time Dex couldn't tell if the voice in his head was Lacy's or his own.

The Mok Tau interrupted their argument by cresting over the hill, pitchers held out, and crowd in tow.

"We'll talk about this later," Dex whispered to Lacy, then stood to greet the Mok Tau. Lacy begrudgingly joined him.

The Mok Tau with the bottles dressed differently than the troop that had escorted Dex and Lacy through the woods. Their faces were narrower but with bigger eyes. Their skin was a lighter green and they were dressed in gowns instead of armor. Dex's first assumption was that they were female. The taller of the two wore bangles on her wrist and had studs down the crook of her flat nose. The smaller one looked younger. It wasn't just the smoother skin or naiveté in her eyes, but the way she constantly looked back and forth between the taller woman and the earthlings as if for some visual guidance.

The taller of the two held the jug out and said, "Teek. Dreenk." *Drink,* Dex and Lacy assumed.

Dex reached out to accept the jug with a smile, but the Mok Tau woman and her shorter partner walked past Dex and Lacy, and into the hut. Dex turned in confusion to watch her, but she was replaced with the supply frog who presented another offering.

The supply frog knelt down and held the spear above his head. Just under the tip, fourteen leaves were tied. "Leaf," the supply frog said, reverence filling his voice. "To remember Mok Tau who give passage to you. Village ask you keep their soul safe."

The memory of the attack flashed in Dex and Lacy's mind, and the way the troop leader was thrown against the tree.

The supply frog laid the spear at their feet and stepped back to be replaced by a family of Mok Tau with several children. The eldest of the bunch pushed one of the children with a "Fhuh."

"I thank, for your sight," the child said and stepped back quickly.

The other children brought forward small carvings in the Mok Tau's likeness. *Like a frog-man G.I. Joe.*

"What is this?" Lacy whispered to Dex.

"I think they're their toys."

"No, *this!* All of it."

The family was replaced by another individual Mok Tau who offered a tray of jungle food.

"We're their gods, Lacy. This is better than sacrifices."

It didn't take long for the entire village to pass through. The front step of the hut was soon filled with assortments of food, weapons, toys from the children, and flowers. It was anything the people had, from a village that didn't look like it had much to offer.

As soon as the last villager had placed their offering, a single spoon, and turned to return to their village, Dex said flatly, "We can't keep this charade up." He turned and entered the cabin.

Lacy followed and said, "You can be the one to tell them otherwise. Oh! Hello!"

The women from the temple stood in the hut with the bottles still in hand. "Dreenk." The taller of the two said.

Lacy fell back half a step, thinking of the terrible meal they were given in the jungle and the sugar water.

Dex accepted the jug and nodded. "Thank you." He held out the jug for Lacy.

She whispered to him, "I can't drink that again."

"You're the one that wanted to 'help' them. Don't start offending their hospitality now."

Lacy knew he was right, and after a quick look at the eager eyes of the Mok Tau women, took the drink from Dex.

He accepted the other one from the younger woman and popped the cap open like a Coca-Cola bottle. The smell of something far from sugar water hit his senses like a brick. Dex recoiled so fast that he almost dropped the offering.

The Mok Tau women jumped back, worried they'd offended their gods.

"What is it?" Lacy asked worriedly. "Is it toxic?"

Dex went in for another smell to verify what he thought it was. "If we drink it, yeah. But it's not poison." He held it out for her to smell. "It smells like gasoline!"

The realization of what it meant hit Lacy like the smell hit Dex's nose. Her eyes widened in a mix of joy and confusion.

"More!" Dex beamed at the Mok Tau women. "Please! More, bring more of this!"

The women were clearly confused by the request but retreated nonetheless out of the hut and back to the temple.

Once on their way down the hill, the women would deliver the request to a very ecstatic village elder who would command his people to bring as much of their ritual wine as possible to the hut on the hill the gods were residing in.

"Do you see what this means?" he asked, holding up the bottle as if she hadn't seen it before.

"Dex, don't rush to-"

"We can go back! We can get back to Earth and warn them!"

Lacy placed her bottle down on a small table they stood by. "Dex. It *smells* like gasoline. It's exciting, yes, but what are the odds this stuff can actually run the engine? That of all the planets we land on *this one* just happens to have refined gasoline as a natural resource. For all we know this will most likely destroy the engine for good."

"The- the odds? Lacy, who cares about the odds? This isn't Earth! I was on a planet made up of dozens of rings, and fought a giant eagle-looking thing, in *SPACE!*" He held up the bottle again to emphasize his point. "This! This could be our way out of here!"

"You don't know that."

"But you can figure it out!" Dex put the jug down and took Lacy's hands. "Lacy… Darling," he said intently. "This could be our only chance."

She pulled her hands away then crossed the room and refused to look at him. "And what happened to 'retiring' out here? You never wanted to go back to Earth. What was it you said? 'I'm glad I made it out when I did.'"

"Lacy, that was before we knew what we were getting into!" His voice began to rise again. "We came out here as scientists, not heroes. Do you know how much science I've done on this whole mission? None! Earth was screwed when we left but it was nothing like this! I was out there Lacy. I saw the grip the Emperor has over these people. You've seen it yourself! These people have their species whole history based on a lie! Earth isn't the most innocent planet in the galaxy but at least we did away with human sacrifice centuries ago! At least the whole planet isn't controlled by a single bloodthirsty dictator. We go now, and there might still be a chance for us."

Silence filled the room. It made her sniffing back a tear all the more loud.

Dex didn't realize until too late how loud he was. How aggressively he'd shouted at her.

Moments that felt like hours passed as he stood staring at the back of her head. Lacy's arms were crossed against her chest but she refused to wipe her tears away. Neither of them wanted to be the one to break the halt in time. They could stay there forever, or until the

Empire found them again and they went quietly to their deaths with the rest of the human race soon to follow.

Ages later, it was Lacy who spoke up. "Okay," she said so softly, Dex wasn't even sure if she'd spoken at all. "I'll... I'll see what I can do."

Dex stepped forward, closing the mile-wide gap between them. Slowly, he wrapped his arms around her.

"For Earth," she said. It was a statement, but part of Dex told him her words held a challenge in them as well, like she was calling him out on a lie and waiting for him to slip up.

"For Earth," he answered back.

Dex walked alone down the hill. Lacy refused to be with him when he broke the news to the village elder.

She'll come around, he told himself. *Can't expect a girl like that to not help a lost puppy right? Hell, isn't that why you fell for her? The only one on the mission that had any positive outlook other than completing a mission? Thank God she's a far cry from Captain Silver. Thank God. Shit. 'God.' Who? The Emperor? Myself? Who the hell should I be thanking other than myself for being the only one with reason?*

He was so caught up in thought, that Dex didn't realize the Mok Tau stepping out of his way as he passed through the village.

Lacy watched from their hill and understood what Dex couldn't see. As they moved out of his way, it wasn't just out of reverence, but fear as well. The Emperor had found these people and promised them salvation from the monsters in the jungle, but it must have come with a price.

Her mind drifted to her back to her audience with the Emperor. Darkness enveloped her vision. The Emperor stood before her, looming over her with his court of demonic spirits still gazing down at her with malice and misery in their eyes. She saw the spirit of the taourun. The spirit of the Child of the Void.

"Your sacrifice will mark the beginning of a new age for my Empire."

Lacy scanned the court as the memory played out. Blood dripped slowly from their robes, but they never drained.

"You will serve in my world as an emissary of your race."

The words of the Emperor cut through Lacy as she saw what she had most feared.

"I thank, for your sight," the child had said.

Lacy's eyes opened and she found herself on her knees with her head to the treetops. Her eyes and mouth were desert dry. So dry it pained her to blink, like her face was made of brittle rock, ready to crack and fall apart at the slightest move. She fell forward and tried to catch herself, but her hands collapsed under her, and her cheek landed in the dirt.

"Dex…" She tried to call, but the words couldn't come out. "Deeeeeexx…" she tried again but only heard the wind escape her lungs.

"Your soul belongs to me." The voice of the Emperor, but not from any memory.

Her heartbeat quickened.

Her skin went cold.

Her senses were still in his temple, on the platform above the pit. The crown of bone weighed down on her head. Its sharp edges dug into her flesh. Blood pooled in front of her eyes. It leaked out of every pour and dried as scarlet tattoos on her skin.

"Your suffering shall be eternal."

Every nerve in Lacy's body exploded as it was ripped apart. Every muscle, every tendon torn. Every vein and artery sucked dry. In the presence of the Emperor, Lacy had held back her pain. Now though, there was no holding back.

Lacy's screams were felt throughout the galaxy.

21. Acts of God

When Lacy awoke she felt five pounds lighter. She opened her eyes slowly. Darkness surrounded her, save the soft glow of a candle. Her body ached but the pain was gone. Still, as she turned onto her side her muscles tensed and held her back.

"Take it easy," a soothing voice said.

"Dex?" Lacy asked.

"Yeah. Yeah, it's me, darling. How are you feeling?"

"I'm... I'm so thirsty." It took all of her strength to turn her head. Dex was little more than a faint silhouette.

"Here, drink this."

"I can't... Dex. I can't drink their stuff."

"It's water. I distilled theirs. Trust me, it's safe to drink."

Lacy reached out blindly for him. Her fingers grazed a smooth clay cup. Dex placed it in Lacy's hand and helped her close her fingers around it. She tried to sit up and Dex laid a hand on her chest. "Easy now, one thing at a time. Just take a sip first."

Lacy acknowledged wordlessly and brought the cup to her lips an inch at a time.

Most of the water spilled, running down her cheeks and neck, but a few drops wet her tongue. There was still a hint of sourness to it, but it was real water nonetheless, and moisture returned to her eyes. The shape of Dex became more defined and she could see his face again. She took another sip. It went down easier that time, bringing back more strength with each drop.

"All right," Dex said, taking the cup back. "Not too much too fast. Here, let's sit you up." He leaned in and together they helped Lacy sit up against the wall the cot was placed against. "We're really the talk of the town now." Dex tried to sound playful, but the words came out more nervous than joking.

"What do you mean?" Lacy's back tightened as she adjusted herself on the cot.

"Your episode. Everyone heard you screaming just as an earthquake hit."

If Lacy had been more awake, she would have leapt out of bed to check on the village. Now, she could only turn her head to face Dex more directly. "Is everyone okay? Is the village-"

"Everyone's fine," he reassured Lacy with a hand on her cheek. Dex's tone shifted then. "Darndest thing. Quake shook 'em all up, but not a rock out of place. Almost like it was just in their heads. And right when you have this... I don't even know what to call it."

Lacy fell back on the cot but kept her eyes on where his should have been.

"You ready to tell me what's going on, Lacy? Ever since the escape... well... just look at yourself. Look at your eyes! Something's changing inside you. These people think you're their god. Even I can't deny they might be onto something."

"Oh stop it, Dex." In a display of newfound strength, Lacy turned over to face away from him.

"Now's not the time to shut me out." No 'darling', no 'Lacy'. He sounded like they were back on Earth before the mission. Dex was speaking again as Captain Prullen. "You've been in my head for a while now. At first, I thought it was just my conscience or something like that. But it's like you're whispering in my ear." He paused to give her a chance to respond. When it was clear she wouldn't, he continued, "I know that wasn't an earthquake. So, are you going to tell me what's going on?"

For half a minute the only sound in the room was the crackle of an alien sap that lined the candle wick. If they hadn't known better, it would have been safe to assume Dex and Lacy were the only two beings on the planet. Lacy resented the silence.

"It wasn't me," Lacy said into the pillow she hugged.

Captain Prullen left the room and her husband returned. "What was it then, Lacy?"

She took a deep breath. "He's looking for me."

Dex slowly fell back in his chair. He took a moment to process what she said and knew exactly what it meant. "You're safe,

Lacy. We're safe. He can't hurt you here."

"How could you know that?" Lacy bit back, throwing her body over and propping herself up on her hands to meet him face-to-face. Her hair bounced and fell over her right shoulder. It was a small thing, but the beauty of it momentarily distracted Dex from the vitriol in her challenge.

"He did the same with me. What was it? A vision?" He remained calm asking her. "He's searching blindly. Korr, my…guy that saved us, he told me. It's like a one-way radio. It's a threat and nothing more."

"He could have killed me, Dex. He could have killed everyone in this village."

"He won't. He wants us captured. If he wanted us dead we wouldn't have made it off that cargo ship." He paused again to let her process his idea of the situation. "Look, why don't you just tell me exactly what happened? Before you passed out, do you remember anything?"

"I was… I was thinking about the throne room. Maybe not exactly a 'throne room' per se, but what else would it be? His court, I guess. I don't know if you saw them, but during that ritual, there were these ghosts."

"Yeah. Yeah, they freaked me out like all hell."

"I tried replaying that memory in my head. Something about what the Emperor said when I was there has had me thinking. And then there was the little girl. She mentioned visions of the Emperor. When I thought back, it was like an out-of-body experience. I wasn't just remembering, Dex, I was there again. The Emperor said I'd be an 'emissary' for humankind. So if there'd be one for us…"

"Then there's one for every other race under him," Dex finished her thought. "Then the frogs-"

"Mok Tau, Dex. But yes, that's what I looked for. And I was right, there was one of them in the room with us."

Dex rose. Only the smallest sliver of the right side of his face was illuminated by the candle.

"You've been in my head. Directly in my head, Lacy."

"Dex," Lacy started but didn't know what to say.

"The Emperor can only send out signals to us, but you can go both ways." There was almost excitement in his voice.

Her mouth opened again to speak, but Dex's entire stream of consciousness poured out. "Those ghosts, whatever they were, they're links. That's why he needs you. I guarantee that if he wanted to, the Emperor could look into the minds of any one of those frogs out there and see us. Because he has one trapped in his world, linking him to the rest of the race."

"His world? Dex what are you talking about?"

"Korr told me a little bit about it. This guy, whatever he is, he's like a... like a... some kind of demon from hell, or another dimension at least. Point is, he's not from here. So, he gets these sacrifices, an 'emissary' from each intelligent species to connect him with the whole race. That's how he has such control."

"If that were true, how come he hasn't found us? Like you said, he could just look into their minds and see us."

Dex almost laughed. "Because he doesn't know where to look. He can't pinpoint you, Lacy. You stole his power and he feels it, but doesn't know where from and he lashed out on everyone. I didn't feel the quake. You didn't do it to them, he did. And I'll bet that these people weren't the only ones in his Empire to feel it."

"This is... this is just crazy." She threw up her hands. "He still hurt me, Dex. How does that fit into your theory?"

Dex began to pace the room, thinking of an explanation. "Maybe that wasn't all him?"

"What?"

"Think about it. You're trying, unintentionally we'll say, trying to channel the power of a being *FAR* greater than ourselves. Like taking that first shuttle into space without any prep. Your body can't handle that kind of strain."

"But I didn't feel anything before. Like when you said I got into your mind."

"Baby steps, baby. Those were simpler things than having an out-of-body experience. You didn't even realize you were doing it."

"If it's like a muscle, it might get stronger," Lacy suggested, half to herself.

"Most likely. And eventually, he'll look in the right place."

"So... so we really do have to leave."

It wasn't what Dex expected to hear.

She continued, "Eventually, the Mok Tau will…"

"They'll either figure out the truth or we'll get them killed."

Lacy didn't argue. Her head dropped and a strand of hair fell in front of her face.

Dex sat next to her on the cot. He put an arm around her and pulled her close. Even with all the walking through the jungle, the mud, the sweat, she still smelled better to him than anything in the universe.

"When do we leave?" She asked.

"Sunrise."

"When's that?"

"I don't know," Dex laughed. "Days are a little longer here. You passed out just after noon."

"How long have I been out?"

"I'd say twelve hours."

"Huh. Long day."

"You can say that again."

* * *

At the day's first light, the two Mok Tau women from the temple walked the village elder up to the small hut on the hill. The Emperor's attack on their minds had nearly killed him. He could no longer walk with just his stick for support. The temple women held his frail arms and walked him slowly through the village.

In his pride, and want to please the gods, he refused to be carried.

Dex saw the elder approach, his eyes a dull yellow, and met him halfway. Calluses had begun to form on the soles of his feet from the previous day's walk. Each step was still uncomfortable, but the smooth dirt of the village floor made it an easier walk. "Good Morning, Roak."

"It is… good," Roak, the village elder, slowly breathed the words out. "Every… day you …" he gestured as if giving Dex a gift as he searched for the right word. But the right word in the god's tongue wouldn't come to him. He carried on, hoping the hand gesture was enough. "...us, it is...good."

"And there will be many more. Just as soon as we get back to our star."

Roak tried to smile. In doing so, his eyes shut completely. "The... gifts... they are..." As he paused to breathe, his knees went weak. The women were quick to catch his fall, but Roak waved them off with a flimsy hand. He'd waited his whole life for the god's arrival and would not look weak in front of them.

"The gifts... pre... pared. Your... humble w... warriors..." he bowed his head when he said 'humble.' "They wait... out... side," a heavy wheeze, then, "wall."

"And it's all the... the um, wine?" Even after their meeting to discuss the march back to the ship — star, as Roak understood it — Dex still wasn't clear on what they would call the gasoline. The women wanted him to drink it, but he also saw them use it as a rub on Roak's skin after the Emperor's attack. Whatever it was to them, Dex assumed it was an all-in-one ritual solution. *Great for parties and sacrifices*, he thought.

Roak nodded. "Yes. Yes... Mok Tau... they work all," he arced his hand across the sky, "dark... to make."

"Wonderful."

Again, Roak smiled. "That is... good?"

"That's better than good," Dex laughed. "It's wonderful."

"Wonder. Ful." His arms shook with joy.

"Wonderful. There you go, add that to your vocabulary."

"Vo...?"

All right, too much all at once, Dex told himself. "Don't worry about it. Thank you, again, for all the kindness your tribe has given us. You'll uh... it'll be remembered. All right?" He held out a hand to shake like he and Roak were old pals.

Without missing a beat, Roak reached out and wrapped his brittle fingers around Dex's hand. "We will... see..." *wheeze* "one another... again."

"Yeah, you'll see me in your dreams." He knew it was a rude thing to say, but at least to Roak, it'd be taken as a promise of good things. "Go back to your temple. Pray for strength in your men on this journey."

"Yes, I will… pray. Yes." Roak motioned for the women to escort him back to the temple.

When their backs were turned, Dex retreated back to the hut to gather their gear. Most of the village's offerings had already been collected by the escort party. All that was left was a small pack made of a large, sturdy leaf, strung together with twine. The pack was filled with the scarlet P.E.S. and food that Dex had inspected beforehand. No bugs or anything still crawling. Lacy had a long way to go before she was completely recovered, and arguing about what was edible wouldn't get them anywhere. Beside the pack they were left a change of clothes, still basically loincloths, but clean at least, and the spear that was presented as an offering with the fourteen colored leaves. Going out into the jungle this time, Dex didn't want to be an easy target for whatever creatures were lurking.

Lacy said very little as she dressed in her new jungle attire.

"How ya doin, Jane?" Dex asked, trying to bring her out of her slump.

Lacy shrugged off the question. "Not gonna wear the suit?"

"I don't think that shade will fit in too well with the jungle."

Lacy shrugged again. She still felt weak. Her legs were strong enough to stand on without assistance, but she took her time with her steps. For moments here and there, she looked like Roak, shuffling through the village.

"Here, try this," Dex said, grabbing something out of the pack.

"What is it?"

Dex pulled out a small brown slab. "It's like a cracker."

Lacy took the cracker and inspected it. "What's the twist?"

"What?"

"Everything out here has a weird twist. Let me guess, it's like a cracker but tastes like chicken?"

Dex took the cracker back and bit the corner off. "Just a cracker, Darling."

They ate quickly, and when Lacy was ready, they walked down to the village wall.

Even though Dex had told Roak to go to the temple and pray, he was still surprised he hadn't come back out to say goodbye. He was the only one in the village who wasn't waiting for them at the moss-covered gate.

When the gate opened, the Mok Tau chanted softly in their native tongue.

Lacy looked over her shoulder, watching the crowd. They were on their knees, with their hands to the sky. In the darkness, their eyes had turned back to a bright yellow. Lacy couldn't tell if they were looking at the ground, at the sky, or at her. She whispered, "What did you tell them we were leaving for?"

"We're considering their offerings."

It wasn't difficult then for Lacy to deduce what the chanting was for. Safe travels, and that their gifts would be accepted in exchange for the gods' service. And Dex had already decided for them. Furthermore, even though they prayed, he wasn't worried it would alert the Emperor. They were praying to Dex and Lacy, the 'almighty,' not the Emperor and his court of phantasms.

The troop was smaller than the one that had escorted them to the village. Everyone who survived the last march, including Dex's aptly named Supply Frog, was present and joined by three new additions to the troop to make nine, including the humans.

The new troop leader stepped toward Dex and Lacy, with his spear held close to his chest. "Ready," he gurgled.

"What's your name?" Dex asked.

"Boritt," he answered with his head down in reverence.

"All right, sergeant," Dex waved forward with a knife-hand gesture. "Let's get a move on while there's still some light."

Boritt's eyes said clearly he didn't understand what 'sergeant' meant, but he wasn't going to argue with whatever the gods wanted to call him. To Boritt, it could just as well be an honorable title. Dex was just happy Boritt wasn't calling out his earth-terms like everyone else seemed to enjoy doing.

Moisture hung in the jungle air like they were walking through a light misty rain frozen in time. Lacy found it soothing. It wasn't quite a shower, and it didn't have the stick or must of sweat. She could almost picture herself walking through a cool sauna. Even when a soft breeze navigated through the trees, it was a reprieve more than anything from the weakness in her legs and ache in her feet. For long stretches of their walk, Lacy could almost imagine herself somewhere else. Somewhere safer.

When they came up on the first mile or so of their journey, the troop cut right as if avoiding an invisible obstacle. Dex and Lacy both realized quickly what it was from gashes in the trees, as well as the smell of decaying animals. Not animals, Lacy reminded herself. The tribe.

The troop was keeping their distance out of respect. The land would be treated with respect and untrampled until nature did its duty, and whatever remains were left decomposed. The planet would cleanse itself.

Although the smell forced itself into Dex's nostrils, he did his best to ignore it. He would have left the spear behind or untied the feathers from it had he not been worried about offending the Mok Tau, or worse, make them think he wasn't really their god. The illusion had to be maintained until they were back on the *Silent Horizon* and far from the village.

By the second mile, the calluses on Dex's feet had torn.

They pushed through it as best they could to keep up with the pace Boritt was setting. The Mok Tau showed no sign of slowing from their pace the day before, even with the additional load of jugs. Rule number one in being a god, or at least one of the rules of being a god, must have been not to be weaker than your people. If Dex could push through at the Mok Tau's pace, he'd do it. Worried Lacy hadn't rested enough, he closed what little distance there was between them and asked how she was feeling.

"Need to slow down? I think they'll do whatever you ask."

"I'm all right," she said plainly.

"Need a drink?"

"I could go for a Pinot Noir if you're hiding any."

Thank God, a joke. She doesn't completely hate me. "I'll see what our hosts have on the menu," he laughed. "But honest, if you need to stop, just say the word."

"I'm fine. In fact, I think that episode did some good for me. I don't know if I sweat it off or what, but I feel five pounds lighter. If only our new friends believed in proper footwear I could probably walk all day."

"I don't think it was cold sweats, baby. I feel it too. I thought the world took a weight off my shoulders when you woke up, but no. I feel lighter too."

"Any ideas? Something in the water?"

"Possibly." Dex lowered his voice and said, "Just another reason to get off this planet. I don't want to get too light and float away unless it's in the ship. By tomorrow I could be flying around like Superman."

"Who says you're not Superman already?" A smile flashed across her face.

Dex laughed. "Thanks, but no." He beat his chest and made a quiet "ooh-ohh!" ape noise. "Tarzan, remember?"

"Okay, Tarzan," she said through a grin she was trying hard not to let turn into a laugh. "Why don't you just swing us home then?"

Without warning, Dex swooped Lacy up in his arms. The hypnotizing ethereal sound of her laughter sent waves of joyful energy through the darkest parts of the jungle and settled blissfully in Dex's heart. The Mok Tau troop turned in reaction to her laughter, but they were invisible, as was everything in the world to Dex but the colors swirling in her eyes.

"Okay, monkey man. Put me down," she giggled. "I'll tell you when I'm good and ready to swing."

"Sure do hope it's soon," he said, letting her get back on her feet.

"Be patient, Tarzan," Lacy said over her shoulder as she stepped back into pace with the troop.

Dex stood still, admiring his girl. Nudging a passing Mok Tau, he commented "What a woman…"

Noon came hours later than it would have on Earth's time. The troop halted, and like before, all but the leader and supply frog took up observatory positions in the trees. Everyone ate and drank in silence. Lacy pecked away slowly at the crackers, still cautious that something would be just the littlest bit off about them. Even after finishing the first one completely, she still had herself convinced something was wrong with them past the extreme dryness.

All through the morning the jungle had felt empty. Birds

chirped here and there, and there had been a few signs of life rustling off in the distance. Even though it felt safe now, though they couldn't forget the kron-kaal. Dex could all but guarantee the oily black creatures that were waiting for the perfect moment to strike. The kron-kaal was likely the reason the jungle felt empty in the first place. Dex thought back on the previous two attacks. There was such ferocity and strength in the creatures, every beast in the jungle must have been too afraid to make any noise that would attract it. At least, they were strong enough to wipe out most of the villagers.

Regardless, it was the Mok Tau's problem, not Dex's.

A few miles after their lunch break, the jungle began to grow denser. It was a clear indication they were getting closer to the *Silent Horizon*. The sun became scarcer, only peaking now through the treetops, lighting small patches of the world. Soon enough, the troop was wandering through the thick labyrinth of trees and brush, reliant on the Mok Tau's powerful eyes to find the right path that would lead them to the clearing.

Lacy held on tight to Dex's hand, afraid that if she let go of him or lost sight of anyone in the troop, she'd never make it out of the jungle alive. Dex felt the same but gave Lacy no indication, not wanting her to worry or lose faith in the troop as a whole.

When Dex saw worry flash in her eyes, he said gently, "Hey pretty lady, almost home, right?" He faintly saw her nod. "Almost there. Robbie'll be waiting, and we can take a warm shower, and sleep in a nice bed. Sound good?"

"Yeah," she rushed to agree. "Yeah, it sounds good." She squeezed his hand tighter.

Risking losing the troop, Dex paused in his tracks and brought Lacy's hand to his mouth.

With just a kiss, her spirits lifted just enough to get them through the labyrinth.

The clearing opened up to them like something out of a movie. Afternoon sunlight shone on the *Silent Horizon* like a gift from the heavens. Lacy's audible sigh of relief was enough to be comical.

Dex helped Lacy down the brush wall, then let Boritt assist him.

"Home sweet home," Lacy said, gazing at the *Silent Horizon*.

"Not quite yet," Dex said. He looked around the clearing and recognized that something was off, and he wasn't alone in this thinking. "Where's that monster?"

Off to their right, there was evidence of something large having crashed into the brush. Black goo stained the weeds and dirt, but no alien body.

Boritt appeared at Dex's side. "Kron-kaal. Tough kill. Die hard. It is…" he waved a slimy hand toward the jungle. "Out there."

"Out there? The dammed thing doesn't have a head!"

Boritt nodded. "Found one."

Dex rolled his eyes. "Wonderful. All right!" Dex turned his attention to the troop. "Bring those jugs over there," he said, pointing to the ground by the rear of the ship. Then addressing the supply frog, he ordered, "Follow me. Bring one."

The troop did as they were commanded, while Dex, Lacy, and the supply frog boarded the ship where Lacy could study the liquid… after she took a hot shower and had a proper meal — ration pills — of course.

Lacy worked all through the afternoon and into the evening running whatever tests she could on the Mok Tau's ceremonial drink to make sure it was compatible with the *Silent Horizon*'s engine, save for putting it directly into the thing. Right off the bat, the computer showed that it was a liquid very similar to their fuel, 92-96% similar. But that 4-8% could be all it needed to completely obliterate any chance of getting home. Figuring out what the different elements in it was the hardest part for her. But after some tampering with the liquid, adding in elements, and extracting others, Lacy was able to get a 99.5% similarity rating back from the computer, and that would have to do for a practical test. By the time she stood next to the filler inlet of the ship, Lacy's concerns returned. Part of her didn't want to fill the ship at all, or even more, hoped it wouldn't work. She was disappointed again in Dex for deciding for them that they would leave the Mok Tau to die with barely even a discussion about it. Holding the jug up to the inlet, Lacy had to remind herself, no, convince herself, *there's nothing we can do for them.* With a heavy heart, she poured the contents of the jug into the ship.

On board the ship, Dex had changed out of his jungle garb

and back into the clothes Korr had given him. As he packed the offerings into the overhead storage containers, Robbie tugged at his pants.

"What is it, buddy?" Dex asked.

"I have found this," Robbie said, holding a closed claw high.

Dex stared, confused. "That's great, Robbie… what is it?"

"The officer left it. We should bring it back to him. It's very small."

Dex knelt and on closer inspection, saw a thin, clear film. With his hand held out under Robbie's, the robot let the object drop. "Looks like a… like a contact."

Robbie shifted to one side.

"Huh," was all Dex could say.

The sound of Lacy's footsteps echoed from the hall. Dex stood back up and dropped the contacts into his jacket's breast pocket. He'd return to the contacts later, but for now, there were more pressing matters.

"Think we're all set?" Dex asked as Lacy walked into the cabin.

"Should be," she said quietly.

Dex rolled his eyes and they both took their seats at the console.

"You care to do the honors?" Dex asked.

Lacy shook her head with a blank expression on her face.

"Suit yourself." Dex crossed his fingers on his left hand and held his right index under the engine switch on the console. "If there's any justice or karma in the universe, please let this work." He flipped the switch.

Like a new model hot off the assembly line, the *Silent Horizon* roared to life. Dex howled a cheer and clapped his hands above his head. "Told ya it'd work, baby!" He leaned over to kiss her, but Lacy didn't reciprocate. Dex's lips landed on her cheek. His stomach dropped, but he wouldn't let show how he felt. They were going home after all, and if Lacy wasn't happy about that, there wasn't a damn thing he could do to change her mind.

"All right," he cleared his throat, trying to disperse the tension in the air he credited Lacy for creating. "Well. All looks good on the computer. I'd say we're ready to take off."

As his hand reached for the ignition, Lacy spoke up. "Just one more night!"

Dex froze. "What's that?"

Lacy sat up a little straighter in her seat. "One more night. Please."

Dex couldn't help but laugh. "One more night? For what? Ha ha! Lacy, we're good to go! We could be back on Earth in two hours, and you want to stay one. More. NIGHT?! *Jesus Christ*, Lacy!"

His criticism did nothing to break down her resolve. "Yes," she said flatly. "We're still safe here for now, and I'd like to at least try to accomplish our mission before we get home. We found plenty of terrible stuff out here, but I want to try to find something good. We've got the greenhouse in the back of the ship, your department. Maybe some of the plants around here have healing properties we could only dream of on Earth. How many pictures of the stuff around here have we gotten? None, probably, unless you did some sightseeing I didn't know about. If there's no immediate threat, I request we stay one more night." She paused, watching his face for a sign of a poor excuse of an argument, then added for emphasis of the importance of the mission, "Captain."

The lost look on Dex's face slowly broke into an inkling of a grin. "Okay, Lieutenant. One more night."

Before the last word was even out, Lacy stood and made her way to the rear of the ship with some pep in her step. "Good. I'll let the men know." She stopped halfway and added, "for security."

From then until nightfall, it was almost as if their ranks were reversed. Lacy continuously gave Dex taskings. The ship's green room quickly filled with small weeds, flowers, and ferns. Dex searched the ship for their camera, something he wished he'd remembered when they first stepped foot on Prullen-1, even if there had been the chance it'd be lost to the Empire. He took over a dozen quick-developing photographs of their clearing, and the surrounding plant life, as well as another dozen photos of Lacy with the Mok Tau.

Lacy's self-appointed taskings were much more humdrum and pointless, like counting the scratches on the ship's hull under the pretense of "ensuring it's still in good condition." Dex wouldn't argue, not when he was constantly toeing the line of keeping her in good spirits.

Only when night fell did Lacy let up on the menial tasks for Dex.

"Well, Captain. You've worked hard today. You're dismissed for chow," Lacy teased.

With a fake salute, Dex acknowledged the "command." They ate together quietly, the ration pills as well as another cracker each just so they could have something to chew on. With no need to do the dishes, when Dex was done, he stood and walked out of the ship. Lacy watched him leave but said nothing. It was Robbie who followed.

There were none of the yellow Mok Tau eyes watching him that night.

"Just a few more hours," he said to himself, looking up at the stars. The edge of the planet's moon peeked through the rim of the trees around the clearing.

"What'll it be like? For me, I mean." Robbie asked from where he stood on the steps of the airlock.

Dex spun around. "You? Huh, I hadn't thought about it, I guess." He turned and looked back at the moon. "Suppose you'll still be ours, but you can do whatever you'd like. You'll be the first of your kind back on Earth."

Robbie lowered himself onto his rear. His stubby feet dangled off the step like a child's. "First of what?"

"Uh… you. A truly sentient robot. You'll probably be a celebrity," Dex joked.

"I don't know what that means."

"Don't worry about it," Dex waved off the comment.

After a brief pause, Robbie asked, "What will you do?"

"Me? Retire. Wouldn't be ideal, retiring back on Earth, but at least I'll be away from this hell hole."

Robbie slid down one step, solidifying the childlike image. "What is wrong with Earth?"

Dex stepped back and sat next to Robbie. "Everything under the sun, little buddy. No matter how great life got for some people, all they wanted to do was break it down for others. And the ones that were already broken down only got broken down some more for good measure. They could send a man to the moon but couldn't spare the time to help the man come home."

"Oh… What happened to that man?"

"Huh?"

"The man that went to the moon. Is he still on your moon?"

Dex sighed deeply. "No. No, he's probably long gone now."

"Oh."

"Yeah. Oh."

The robot and the Earthling sat in silence together for a short while, listening to the sounds of the jungle. Eventually, Robbie spoke up again.

"I think that is what I will do on Earth."

"Huh?"

"Lacy helped me. I do not know what I can do for the man on the moon. But if there are other people on your planet like him, I can do for them what Lacy did for me."

"Oh yeah? How are you gonna do that?"

Robbie shrugged his thin arms. "I do not know. But I do not think Lacy knew she could help me either. But she attempted it anyway."

"Yeah… she has a tendency to do that. That's one of the things I love about her. You shoulda' seen her before the mission. We were competing against a hundred other candidates for this chance. She either didn't understand or chose to ignore the 'competitive' part, always helping the others do better in the ranking. I don't think she has a selfish bone in her body." Through the open airlock door, Dex could see Lacy hunched over the computer. He heard her listening to the logs he made on his flight from Reechi to the Heart of the Void. The sound of his own voice bothered him.

Dex dropped his head like he'd been stabbed in the chest, defeated in an epic duel.

"Are you okay?" Robbie asked.

"Nope. I'm the biggest idiot in the universe. Here's an important life lesson, Robbie. You listening?"

Robbie nodded his body.

"If you ever get married, just remember: your wife will *always* be right. Even if she's wrong." He stood up and walked back onto the ship to swallow his pride in front of Lacy.

Lacy heard him approach and gracefully rose from her seat at the console, turning to meet him.

"Pack your ruck and get out your finest loin cloth," he said. "It's time for adventure."

22. Land of 1000 Dances

"It's a quick run, got it?" Dex said sternly, pointing a finger at Lacy. He would compromise with her, but not feed any delusions of grandeur. It didn't matter to Lacy though. She couldn't contain herself. As soon as Dex hinted at going on Roak's quest she was prepping her gear.

"I mean it, Lacy. We're laying *LOW*. Killing a monster, not starting a revolution. Empire's behind this somehow and we are *NOT* taking risks."

She couldn't contain her glee. Every word sounded like a laugh or victory chant. "I know, I know. First sign and we're out. Just a monster." Lacy stuffed the camera and a med kit into her issued pack.

"Just a monster," Dex confirmed.

"And you don't want to fly there?"

"Too risky. Empire's been here before, and I don't think they've cleared out. I'll bet ya a million bucks we just got lucky not being seen when we landed."

"I don't need to take that bet."

"Can I come too?" Robbie interjected, bouncing lightly on his feet.

"Yes, of course!" Lacy said excitedly before Dex cut her off.

"No. You have to stay here with the ship. Call us if anything happens, and if things are real bad, you fly to our location. Got it?"

"Hold on, Dex. We can't leave him here," Lacy pleaded.

Quietly, not wanting to hurt Robbie's feelings, Dex told her, "He won't be able to walk through the jungle. And I am not carrying him god knows how far."

Lacy couldn't argue, but she still felt terrible leaving him behind. A robot with even minimum knowledge of Empire workings could be beneficial to their hunt, but not at the risk of slowing down or getting stuck in the labyrinths of roots and brush. "Okay, you're right. Go on, get packing!"

Robbie slunk over in defeat.

"I'm goin', I'm goin'." Dex found his own ruck and transferred over the contents from the one the Mok Tau gave him. Along with the food, he stored a canteen with water from the ship, a med kit, binoculars, and a set of skivvies.

Lacy tapped Dex on the shoulder and held something out for him. "Here, you should take this along."

Dex looked down at the book she was holding. "After all this business with the Emperor, you think I'm still gonna buy into that?" He took the pocket bible from her hand, the one his Dad had given him, and dropped it in the storage container above the starboard-side bed. "Besides, I don't think we'll have a ton of downtime for reading. I want to move as much as possible, and any time not moving is for sleeping."

Lacy pursed her lips but didn't argue. Instead, she moved on and went back to packing. "Who's going to wear this? You or me?" she asked, holding up the P.E.S.

"Neither of us. It'll stand out too much."

"I don't really have much else to wear then."

Dex flashed a grin.

"You were serious about the loin cloths?"

"Gotta blend in, darling." He grabbed the belt and holster that hung next to the bunk and said, "As best we can, anyway."

"What about shoes?"

"I've got a pair, don't worry."

She eyed him hard, waiting for him to realize what he was missing.

"Oh! Damn… huh…"

Lacy shifted to the right with a hand on her hip. "Plan on carrying me the whole way?"

Korr's boots wouldn't fit her, and none of the options they had were practical. Lacy had a pair of thin slippers for walking around the cabin, but those would fall apart too quickly out in the jungle. They had the PES and the space-walk suit, both with boots, but they were one-piece sets, and removing the boots would put the entire suit out of commission.

Dex sighed and took off the boots Korr had given him. "The things we do for love. Might not fit though."

Lacy accepted with a, 'who? Little old me? You shouldn't have!' kind of look. "I'm sure I can find something to stuff them with."

She gave Dex a kiss on the cheek then went back to looking for things to pack. "Are you going to record a log before we go?" Lacy asked.

Dex scoffed. "No way. I'm done with those."

Surprise flared on her face. "But that's your thing? What are you going to-"

"When we get back to Earth, I can tell them what happened to us. If we don't make it back to the ship, who's going to read the logs?"

Dex let her come to her own realization. If they failed, the Empire would most likely find the ship, then head straight to Earth with all the information Dex and Lacy served them.

"It'd be smarter to set this thing to self-destruct if we're not back soon enough." He ran a hand down the wall of the ship, thinking about what it'd be like if they did destroy it. If that would be enough to keep Earth safe.

Lacy closed the distance between them and wrapped her arms around Dex. She nuzzled her head against his chest.

"We'll make it back."

Dex took his hand off the wall and ran his fingers through her hair. *How does it still smell so wonderful?* He kissed her on the top of the head. "You're right," he said softly. "You're right, darling. We'll make it."

Dex felt her smile on his chest. Her arms tightened the littlest bit around him.

"Good," she said, almost in a whisper.

They held the embrace, letting it fill any dark corner of their spirits that were still looking for some of the light the Empire had stolen.

"All right now," Lacy said gently. "We'd better get back to

work."

Dex nodded in agreement, and they prepared for the journey ahead.

"Captain's log," Dex began. "For some reason, Lacy has convinced me to take on this… quest," he laughed at his choice of word, "to help these frogs."

He recounted for the log what Roak told him about the kron-kaal and Torro-Kaal, and the many Mok Tau that went to their deaths facing the creature. "We've agreed on a scouting run. No engagement. I believe the Empire is behind this and I'm hopeful it'll give us insight into their operations.

"We'll be leaving the ship behind. My guess is it would be safer on foot. We've still got a chance to make it home from here if we're walking under the tree's cover. If the Empire sees us, we'll have to throw them off our trail yet again. We got lucky landing here without the Empire seeing us, but I don't think we'll get that chance again.

"For some peace of mind while we're away from the ship, I'll be stationing a small squad of the Mok Tau, whatever the village can afford, to guard the ship. For some reason, I feel like it'd be better off with the Empire, but that's probably just because anything more than a slingshot is too complex for their primitive minds."

Dex paused the recording, and said to himself, "I should probably take that out. Lacy'll hate it." He scrubbed back the recording and erased the last line.

"I guess…" Dex sighed. "Until next time. Captain Dex Prullen of the *Silent Horizon*, signing off."

The words came out of his mouth, and he immediately detested the sense of finality that loomed over the *Silent Horizon*.

While Dex closed out the log and filed it away in the computer, Lacy was double-checking their rucksacks and the storage compartments to make sure nothing essential was left behind. In the over-bunk storage, she found Jaskek's data tablet buried under objects that shuffled around during their landing on the planet and pulled it out. When Jaskek used it, she saw something in his eyes, like reflections of a screen, but nothing appeared on the tablet to her. If only there were screws she could loosen, or a panel, she could access the motherboard inside of it (if it even had one) and try to re-program it like she did with Robbie.

"That the officer's?" Dex asked.

"Yeah. I just don't understand how it works." She sat down on their bunk. "Jaskek had like... implants or something that let him access it. Something in his eyes."

It clicked then for Dex. "Like contacts?" he asked, reaching into the breast pocket of his jacket.

"Maybe, I... hey, is that-" She stood and took the contacts out of Dex's outstretched hands and held them in front of her eyes.

Clear as day, she saw bright green words on the screen, like her ship's computer. In fact, she realized, it was the ship's computer. A complete backup of the *Silent Horizon*'s database from the day they were first captured, sorted in just the same way.

"What is it?"

"Hold on!" She insisted. "Just give me a few minutes!" Lacy radiated excitement again as she rushed from the cabin to the engine room, the place that was quickly becoming her private study.

When both the rucks were packed, and their clothes laid out for the journey ahead, Dex laid on their bunk. Lacy had been fidgeting with the data tablet for almost half an hour. For the entire time, Robbie waited outside the locked engine room door.

Inside the engine room, Lacy had become distracted by the wealth of knowledge on Jaskek's data tablet. There was no setting on it that let the true screen show anything without the contacts, but slowly, everything appeared anyway. It was as if once her mind knew what was truly there, it could no longer be hidden. The idea seemed so natural to Lacy, that she didn't even register it. Eventually, she put the contacts down on the worktable and never picked them back up.

A knock at the door broke Lacy out of her focus. It was Dex, asking her to come to bed. Only when it was mentioned did Lacy realize how tired she was, and sleep hit her like a freight train the moment her head hit the pillow.

* * *

Roak met the troop at the village gate with open arms and

through strained elderly breaths, demanded the Mok Tau prepare for a feast worthy of the gods. Lacy recoiled slightly at the sound of another "feast," recalling how the Emperor described the sacrifices brought to him.

Thankfully, the feast the Mok Tau held in the center of the village was far more joyous. And the food was slightly better.

The Mok Tau had built a roaring fire. The foundation alone was nearly ten feet high. The flames more than doubled that height. Villagers danced around the bonfire, banging drums and singing songs in their native tongue. Dex and Lacy sat with Roak on the sidelines, watching the festivities. Between taking photographs of the party, Lacy clapped along with the beat of the drums and mouthed the words of their songs to the best of her abilities, although she had no idea what they were saying.

Dex watched her lips move in joyful confusion. The flames danced in her eyes and lit up her already beaming face. Like every time he saw her, it was the most beautiful thing he'd seen in his entire life.

"We…" Roak coughed, wheezed, and coughed again. "We have not… had… cause… to…" he waved his hand around, looking for the right word.

"Celebrate?" Dex offered.

Roak nodded. "Cel-eh-brate… yes… celebrate, for long… time."

"Well, you'll be celebrating plenty more from now on, I'll tell you that," Lacy cut in, to Dex's chagrin. Another false hope for an already broken people.

"Yes," Roak coughed out a laugh. "Yes, I… I believe."

Platters of alien food were carried around by the temple women. The Mok Tau tried to be discreet about it, but they watched Lacy to see what she would and wouldn't eat. Anything she passed up, the Mok Tau would push away. Noticing this, Dex told her to at least pretend to eat it. With hesitation, she did, and in doing so, saved the Mok Tau from having an Old Testament-restrictive diet.

With their bellies full, Roak asked them if they would like to dance with the villagers. They would play any song sent to them in vision, which was every song they knew. Dex and Lacy gave each other a look of apprehension. Dancing to music composed by the Emperor? No thanks.

Smacking Dex's chest a little harder than she meant to, Lacy asked, "Did you grab that data pad?"

Dex coughed up his drink. "Jesus! Yes, darling, yeah. I grabbed all that stuff and put it in your ruck. It's back in the hut."

Lacy pushed herself to her feet and ran off without a thank you.

Dex and Roak exchanged a friendly side-eye. "Women," Dex laughed.

Though Roak didn't know what Dex meant by it, he laughed along.

When Lacy returned half a minute later, sprinting down the hill to the bonfire, she ran by Dex pulling him along with her, and announced to the tribe "I think I've got a new one for you!"

Roak's eyes, along with the rest of the tribes', widened in delight and intrigue. The entire village went silent.

"Everyone find a partner, and follow after us," she instructed the villagers. "Boys find a girl and hold them like this." She put Dex's hand on her waist and fit her left hand into his right. "Okay, great. Everyone see this?"

Lacy looked around the bonfire and saw a sight reminiscent of a high school dance.

With everything in order, she flipped through the data pad. Lacy found a song she thought would be perfect for the occasion. She turned up the volume and a light melody warmed the village better than any fire could do.

Heaven… I'm in heaven…

Dex swayed softly with Lacy, cheek to cheek.

Whether or not the villagers followed them didn't matter. All Lacy wanted was a moment between them where everything else could fade away.

For those short minutes, they were back on the ship. No running, no hiding, no fighting, no Emperor. It was the two of them wrapped in each other's arms with no worries in the universe except how long they would have this happiness together.

Dex sang quietly in her ear, "Heaven, I'm in… heaven."

He kissed her cheek.

She turned her head and kissed him back.

No 'I love you's' needed to be said, but it was a sweet sound to hear anyway.

They kissed again, and the soft piano melody transitioned into something soulful. Lacy began jumping around in dance and sang along with Ray Charles' newest hit, "Mess Around."

"Well, you can talk about the PIT!.. BAAARRBECUE!"

She danced alone for the first verse, with all the yellow eyes of the villagers on her. Dex shied away in secondhand embarrassment, but Lacy took him by the hand and pulled him back into the glow of the fire. His feet dragged at first but by the third time "Mess Around" was shouted, Dex spun Lacy under his arm. She swung back into him, with their hands interlocked, and from there they were really swinging.

When Ray announced that the band and people were "juicing," he may as well have been talking about the villagers too. Taking Lacy's lead, the Mok Tau picked up their feet and mimicked the swinging and jiving Lacy was showing off.

Off to the side, Roak was doing his best to clap in time with the rhythm. He laughed hard enough to have a heart attack when Dex slid Lacy low to the ground between his legs and pulled her back up into his arms for a spin.

Ray said "Stop" and they didn't move a peg. Ray said "Go" and they shook their legs. Ray told them to "mess around" and they got messy.

Everybody, in one way or another, sure was doing the mess around.

The instruments took center stage and all eyes were back on the dancing gods. There was no intention or sense to any of their moves, and it didn't matter. They danced like children without a care in the world, happy to be in good company, with good music, and half-decent food.

The music played from nine to one, and when the party ended, Dex and Lacy returned to their hut on the hill and continued… to mess around.

23. Into the Jungle

Lacy studied her figure in the low light of the humid hut. The feeling of weight loss persisted from the day before, stronger now. *I haven't been eating as much*, she told herself. While she did look the faintest bit skinnier, and more toned in the legs, it didn't look anywhere near ten pounds lost.

She shared her concerns with Dex, who only reassured her that she "looks great! So we've lost a little weight. It's been a rough week. I'll have those guys make you a nice cake when we get back, how about that?"

Lacy smirked and went back to studying herself. *Just need to eat better.*

The Mok Tau warriors waited just outside the hut for Dex and Lacy to join them. It came as no surprise to either of them how willing the Mok Tau were to join them on the quest. Dex, though, had no interest in taking half the village with them.

"Four! Give me four!" Dex commanded.

The Mok Tau stood fast in their zealous conviction. Could this be a test from the gods? Which of them would step out, showing off to the whole tribe that they were not worthy to serve the gods?

"I'm serious," Dex insisted. "Give me four! The rest of you stay behind and protect the village."

Lacy held on to Dex's arm, smiling at how determined the Mok Tau were to help them. She saw their resolve as a sign more of eagerness and hope than the religious fervor it was.

Dex scanned the line of warriors, watched them stare blankly back at him. Their hands were wrapped so tightly around their spears that dug into the ground next to their feet. Without explicit orders of who would stay with the village, and who would go on the hunt for Torro-Kaal, Dex and Lacy would always be no less than five feet away from the villagers. The Mok Tau might as well have packed up what belongings they had and moved their huts to Torro-Kaal's nest, hive, whatever it was.

"That's it. You, supply," he pointed to the supply-frog. "You're coming with us." *Always make friends with the supply sergeant,* Dex's Dad instructed him when he was commissioned. "Boritt, you're coming too. You're my Staff Sergeant now, got it? Now pick two more and meet us at the gate in five."

Boritt had almost no comprehension of half the things Dex said but understood the main points. Pick two, gate in five... minutes? Hours? It had to be *some* measure of time. Not wanting to disappoint or come off as incompetent, Boritt nodded and selected two, then dismissed the rest.

"Wonderful," Dex said when they were met at the gate two minutes later. "Now listen close, this is how it's going to work. From here on out, you'll address me as 'Captain.' Got it? Everyone repeat that."

"Cap-Tain," The Mok Tau, and Lacy, repeated.

"Wonderful. And you'll refer to Lacy as Lieutenant."

"Loo-tenent."

"Ya'll are doing great." Dex went down the line and put a hand on Boritt's shoulder. "Staff Sergeant. Okay? If myself, or Lacy, Lieutenant, that is, fall out or are not around, you take charge. Got it?"

Boritt nodded.

Dex moved down the line. "What's your name?" He asked the supply frog.

"Toork, Cap-Tain."

"Toork. You're my supply Sergeant. Do you know what that means?"

Toork the supply sergeant shook his head.

"It means keep doing the same thing you've been doing." He moved on to the other two. "Name."

"Burk," said one.

"Gurg," said the other.

"Private Burk and Private Gurg. You three report up to Sergeant Boritt, copy?" Dex made sure to make eye contact with each of them.

The newly enlisted Mok Tau all nodded, trying to comprehend the long list of new words Dex introduced to them.

"Now, if we were a real unit, Lieutenant Prullen here would be navigating us to Torro-Kaal. But in typical Army fashion, she would probably get us lost. Staff Sarnt', I'll leave that responsibility to you. Everybody ready?"

The squad nodded in unison. Lacy bounced on her toes, thrilled to go off on the adventure.

"Okay…" Dex took a deep breath. "Here we go. Open the gate!"

As the gate opened, the shape of a small black creature, covered in the thick morning dew greeted them.

The Mok Tau raised their spears in defense. "What is this? Strange rock?" Boritt asked.

Lacy laughed, and Dex sighed. "He's gonna wish he were just a rock. Squad, this is Robbie."

Robbie waved to his new companions.

* * *

Less than five minutes after Dex and Lacy left the *Silent Horizon*, leaving Robbie behind for the second time, boredom had overtaken him. He called Lacy over the comm device they'd left behind for him, but it wasn't the same as talking to them in person, and he didn't like that. Robbie could have powered down and let them wake him up when they returned, but doing that risked missing something important. Sitting there, though, doing nothing, seemed much worse.

Climbing up the brush wall was one of the hardest things he'd ever done, second only to flying the *Silent Horizon* over the Emperor's palace-city. The area of brush where he climbed was fickle. When he stepped too hard onto it, the branches broke and his foot would get caught. Step after step, he found himself caught in a tangle of vines and roots. It got bumped to third hardest when he tried to navigate through the dark, thick labyrinth of the jungle.

He followed their path all day and into the night. At least, it was the path he *hoped* they took, a straight line.

Jungle creatures heard his stubby feet pattering on the floor and would stalk him out. When one got close, Robbie locked up and tried to hide — falling face first on the ground in hopes they wouldn't see him and run off with a crunchy meal.

Robbie had less trouble overcoming the obstacles of the terrain. He refused to go in any direction other than a direct line, but couldn't climb over roots that were four times his height. After an hour of trying to pull himself up, Robbie looked for other options. He was very tempted to torch the entire place with his flamethrower hand, but something that had been growing in his programming, a conscience, Lacy might call it, told him that was a bad idea. Robbie had to adapt.

"What would Lacy do?" Robbie asked himself.

He sat and played back a recording he made of Lacy singing along to one of her songs while she worked the night before. He didn't understand what the point of it was, something like "anything goes" and "in olden days." Robbie thought if he put some music on, the problem would resolve itself.

It didn't.

A solution provided itself when a six-legged creature with sharp fangs and a shelled back entered Robbie's territory.

Robbie ran a few feet away and plopped face down.

The shelled creature cleared a spot at the base of the root, paced around it, and lay down to nap.

When Robbie felt safe enough to move, he looked at the creature and an idea popped into his head. If he was careful enough, Robbie could climb onto the back of the creature and reach a branch that extended from the root. With that little bit of a lift, he could easily climb over it.

Robbie would have to go for it or admit defeat and wait back with the ship as he'd been ordered. But Robbie was a free thinker now, and taking orders was for losers. Unless the orders came from Lacy, of course.

The creature stirred as Robbie climbed on its back, but as it slept it regarded whatever there was on its back as nothing more than an insignificant bug.

Pride and triumph overcame Robbie as he pulled himself over

the root. Standing tall on his hill, Robbie's brief moment of victory was killed when he saw all the other hurdles he still had to overcome before he would catch up to Lacy.

He reached the gate early the next morning. Just before he could knock, the gate opened, and there stood Lacy, laughing in joyful surprise. It didn't matter that four sharp spears were pointed at him.

"Robbie! What in the name of Sam Hill are you doing here?!" Dex shouted.

"I was very bored," Robbie replied plainly.

Before Dex could argue, Lacy chimed in, "And that's totally fine! We're glad to have you!"

If Robbie had a heart, it would have been warmed.

"Back to the ship, *NOW*," Dex demanded.

"Oh, Dex… *Captain*, I mean," Lacy corrected him and waved the Mok Tau to lower their spears. "You're not going to make him walk all the way back now, are you? Captain? He's already come so far, Cap-"

"I get it!" Dex rolled his eyes. "FINE. Robbie, you're coming along. But I'm not carrying you."

Like an invisible wall, the misty jungle air hit them the moment they stepped past through the gate. Although it would have been better to wear more protective clothes, cotton would have been too uncomfortable to walk in with the humidity so high, and clothes sticking annoyingly to their skin like they'd jumped into a pool fully dressed. The loincloths were the best outfit they could wear.

An hour later, Lacy assumed the contents of Dex's pack into her own so that Robbie could rest in it.

Now that Dex had officially taken the lead on his newly formed squad, he moved them as an actual unit. A minimum distance of ten feet was kept between each member of the squad at all times as they walked in a modified wedge formation. Boritt took point, leading them through the jungle. Lacy back and to his right, Toork back and to the left, and so on like that, with Dex in the center.

The further they walked from the village the more creatures crossed their path. Dex was apprehensive of every strange plant or animal that they came in contact with, while Lacy looked at them as cute little things that were just looking for something to eat.

"Yeah, it's looking to eat *you*," Dex said, holding his spear ready to stab a bulbous cloudy yellow thing that hung from a tree branch.

The creature wobbled like Jello. There were no discernible features like eyes or a mouth, and in passing, it could have easily been mistaken for a large collection of tree sap. But when Dex's squad passed it, it leaned into their direction and caught their eye.

"Careful," Boritt warned. "Good for burn. Bad for eat."

The earthlings watched as a bug flew into the gelatinous thing and instantly dissolved. A pure acidic creature.

"Keep moving," Dex ordered.

According to Boritt, their journey would take them well over a week to reach the dwelling of Torro-Kaal. By Dex and Lacy's Earth standards, that would be closer to a week and a half to two weeks.

They stopped briefly for lunch, but Dex ensured they were back on their feet as soon as possible. "If this is more than a week-long mission there and back, I want to be at the mountain in five days, maximum. You all got that?"

Robbie was the most compliant with Dex's terms. He even helped to motivate the squad, asking them every so often if they wanted a song to motivate them. Lacy was all for it, but Dex shot the idea down, not wanting to draw attention to themselves.

That didn't stop Lacy. She hummed a song she and Robbie had become familiar with until they were both singing to it; Lacy under her breath, Robbie with his speakers turned down low.

Dex couldn't help but smile and exhale a soft laugh. For a moment he was tempted to join in, until something large crashed at their three o'clock.

"Down! Everyone down!" Dex whisper-shouted.

The squad did as commanded. Lacy reverted back to Soldier mode and from there, it could never be guessed she'd be able to break out in song.

Boritt jumped into a tree. His green skin shifted into a light brown to blend in with the bark.

It was then that Dex wished they'd established hand signals. He whistled to get Boritt's attention, then pointed at his eyes to ask,

"What do you see?"

Boritt gave Dex a blank stare.

"SEE! What do you SEE!?"

Boritt signaled with his fingers a walking motion.

Dex peaked up above the log he hid behind. "There's no… way…" He softly exclaimed.

A creature like a dinosaur, walking on four thick legs, with two rows of ivory spikes along its back and a tail twice its length, with a blunt hammer of a tip, wadded through the jungle. It had a turtle-like head with a single eye in the center of its face. The creature's skin was leathery and tough.

Boritt dropped down from the tree but was careful not to make too much noise.

"I do not know what name it is in the god tongue, but we are safe. Beast is not bad." Boritt told Dex and Lacy.

Dex looked again at the beast. "Looks like what we call a dinosaur. And the spikes on the back…"

"Like a razorback," Lacy finished.

"Good a name as any." Dex.

"We wait," Boritt offered. "Razor pass."

The squad remained still, quiet, and the razorback passed them. Its tail slunk behind, swaying from left to right, knocking into trees and roots leaving huge dents. The thing looked too top-heavy on its stubby legs to be practical from an evolutionary standpoint.

Lacy carefully retrieved the camera from her pack. "The team back home will never believe this," she said to herself.

Dex replied jokingly, "This is where you think they'll draw the line?"

Lacy laughed quietly and shrugged. "Just like those cheesy movies you like." She pointed the camera, and just before releasing the shutter, stopped herself to make sure the flash wasn't on.

The camera clicked. The razorback turned at the sound but didn't change its direction.

"Let's see if we can get that in the National Geographic," Dex teased.

The razorback cleared out of their path. As Dex began to stand, Boritt put a hand on his shoulder. "Haahhh…" Quiet.

Rattling in the bushes to their right.

Dex, Lacy, and Boritt shot their heads toward the sound. Out of the foliage jumped a biped creature, its mouth open with layers upon layers of teeth. In a blur, it shot up along the razorback's trail, intent on taking a bite of delicious dinosaur meat. A *hyper-raptor* was Dex's first thought.

The razorback sauntered unbothered by the entrance of the foe, even at its screeching that tore through the jungle like nails on a chalkboard.

Lacy's eyes widened in worry for the razorback. She nearly jumped from her place behind a log, until the hammerhead tail of the dinosaur swung back, and whacked into the side of the hyper-raptor.

The raptor was thrown into the side of a mossy boulder but was quick to get back on its feet. The beast lunged at the razorback, its mouth wide with ferocity.

The razorback was slow to move. Its leathery skin shielded it from the bites of the hyper-raptor.

Dex saw Lacy's concern and grabbed her by the back of her chest cloth to hold her back. There was no need to get involved. As long as they could stay out of the way, they'd be safe. Lacy knew this, but her want to help threatened to overtake her.

The razorback swung its tail around to knock over the hyper-raptor. The raptor leapt, avoiding its tail, and lunged into the razorback's side, tearing a chunk away with its teeth. The razorback roared and thrust its weight into the smaller creature.

The hyper-raptor crumbled but was back on its feet before anyone could register that it had fallen. The thing was fast. Too fast for the razorback. Too fast for the squad as well.

Dex threw up a knifehand, spun it around, then pointed to a tree fifty meters to their right. *Regroup on that spot.*

The Mok Tau required little guidance, associating the movement and direction with commands. Dex and Lacy kept low to the ground in a high crawl to avoid detection, while the Mok Tau jumped through the trees.

The slightest electronic sound escaped Robbie's speakers.

"Haaahh!" Dex whisper-shouted, and Robbie shut up.

He and Lacy low crawled through the jungle and the razorback and hyper-raptor tore into each other.

The razorback stomped its stubby legs, trying to crush the smaller but more nimble hyper-raptor. The powerful defensive maneuvers were barely enough to keep the hyper-raptor at bay, but it gave the beast a few extra seconds of safety. Its tail rose high, and when the hyper-raptor ran to attack, the tail swung down and threw the beast across the jungle.

It crashed into a small hill, bounced off, and fell into the tangling of brush around a tree mere feet from Dex's squad.

They all froze as the hyper-razor thrashed its way out of its earthen shackles. The Mok Tau dropped down to protect their gods, then readied their spears, holding them high to skewer the beast. Dex raised his own, but the sound of the razorback charging toward their location halted them all.

The beast had taken to offense.

The razorback crested over the hill at full speed. Though it bled profusely from the side, it refused to fall to such a small adversary.

"Move! NOW!" Dex commanded, and the squad dispersed to make way for the charging razorback.

The Hyper-raptor, unable to detangle itself, gnawed away at the vines and roots, unintentionally biting itself, and escaped just in time for the Razor-back to ram into the base of the tree. The razorback stood on its hind legs, ready to pummel its foe into a paste.

Using hand signals, Dex ordered the squad to move while the creatures were distracted. Lacy, leading the pack, took three soft and quick steps and came face-to-face with a second hyper-raptor.

She raised her spear and almost fell into Boritt.

The hyper-raptor screeched. Its layers upon layers of teeth shined, eager for a taste of Lacy.

A laser bolt shot past Lacy and Boritt, skimming against the side of the hyper-raptor's face.

At the screech, the first hyper-raptor bailed on the razorback. The squad had stolen its attention. No more time for stealth, and there was no outrunning the raptors.

"Fall in! Back to back! Spears up!" Dex ordered.

They all bunched up, back-to-back with their spears raised.

Dex held his high in his left hand and shot off laser bolts as fast as each shot would charge.

The two hyper-raptors ran sprints around the porcupine formation, looking for a way in. They snapped the Mok Tau, mostly to intimidate and catch them off guard before tearing into them. Spears jabbed at the raptors, but they were too fast. With each threatening bite, the formatting fell in closer together.

Boritt gritted his teeth. With each pass, he thrust out a killing stab of his spear, always just missing it. Even as the hyper-raptors pushed in, he remained sturdy, and resolute in his fight for survival, demonstrating why he was a leader among the Mok Tau.

"Dex! Dex I can't breathe!" Lacy shouted.

They were suffocating on each other. At some point, they would let their guard down and the raptors would pounce.

The razorback had all but forgotten about the skirmish and was now fleeing the scene. Dex knew the beast was their only chance at survival. Shifting his sights from the hyper-raptors to the razorback, he fired two shots at its leathery skin. It didn't penetrate, but it was enough to anger him.

The razorback turned, its long tail sliding across the jungle floor.

"Everyone run! Now!"

Their defenses dropped and their feet picked up.

A hyper-raptor bit at one of the privates. The two of them were tripped up as the razorback's tail swept under them.

Both hyper-raptors were focused on the razorback again. They screeched and charged for the razorback.

Wait! Back! Dex!

The squad took full advantage of the precious moments of distraction and fled deeper into the jungle.

The sounds of violence and bloodshed followed them until one of the creatures let out a dying scream. From then, the only sound from the battlefield was faintly reminiscent of someone having a very large, and well-earned meal.

The squad came to a halt by a stream next to a large hollow log. They hid inside of it to regroup and collect themselves.

"We have to go back," Lacy stated. There was no hint in her

voice that it was a suggestion, but a mere fact that going back was the only thing that *would* happen next.

For all the conviction in her voice, Dex still argued. "That's ridiculous. We can find the right path from here." To Boritt he asked, "Sarnt', you can still get us to Torro-Kaal from here, right?"

"This isn't about the path, Dex. Burk's back there."

Dex looked from her to the rest of the group. It was true, one of the privates wasn't with them.

"Sergeant Boritt, why aren't all your men with us?"

Boritt began to speak, but Lacy stepped up again. "This isn't on him, Dex. You wanted to be in charge of this. We have to go back and find him."

"No way, Lieutenant."

"Drop the 'lieutenant' crap, Dex! I'm your wife, not your subordinate."

Dex's voice dropped low, "Not here, Lacy. Don't argue here or we'll never make it to the mountain." He looked over his shoulder. "Sergeant, take the others and make sure this place is safe. We'll camp here tonight."

"Yes, Cap-tain." Boritt nodded and the three Mok Tau left the log.

Once out of sight, Dex returned to Lacy. "I know, Lacy. I know this rank stuff doesn't matter now. But we're moving as a team in a hostile area. If we *don't* have some form of chain of command and adherence to that, then we're *dead*. Okay?"

"Then don't just talk about it. One of us already is dead. We left a man behind and you didn't even notice."

"What do you want from me, Lacy? We're out here, aren't we? We're on their damned quest! What more do you want?!"

"What good is all this if we're just leading these people to a faster death?"

The fact he was arguing with Lacy, not that she was arguing, made him want to pull out his hair. Instead, he tightened his grip on the spear. Dex almost snapped the thing in his strained hands.

"If you're being as careful as you say you are, just remember," Lacy warned. "One prayer to the wrong god and we're dead. Empire forces all over us. You want to make it through this one, take better care of your men. And listen to them." She pointed to Robbie. In the heat of the escape and ensuing argument, Dex had completely forgotten he was carrying the little robot.

Dex craned his head and saw Robbie holding up a hand. After a deep breath, knowing what was coming, Dex asked, "What is it… buddy?"

Robbie's claw opened and a short flame, no larger than necessary to light a cigarette, blew out.

One strong blast out of the porcupine formation may have been enough to scare or ward off the hyper-raptor. At least enough to give them a few extra seconds head start to escape. Enough to give Burk a chance.

It didn't take anything more for Dex to drop the officer act, "I'm sorry."

24. Histories

The five-man squad camped by the log that night. Robbie did the honors of lighting a small fire.

Although he wasn't asked to by Boritt or the other Mok Tau, Dex searched around their immediate area for the right leaf to tie to his spear. Fifteen on the count now.

Toork rationed out their meals. Dex and the Mok Tau ate the leaf-wrapped beetles, with the crunchy little bugs for the extra flare. Lacy, to her credit, gave the jungle food another chance but was also quicker this time around to reject it. She settled on crackers and a meal pill.

The fire was warm, but a cold air consumed the night. As close as she sat, Lacy couldn't keep warm.

"Here," Dex said, pulling Korr's jacket out of one of the rucks. "You look like you're gonna freeze to death."

Lacy took the jacket greedily and threw her arms into it. "What happened to blending in? Or was that just an excuse to see more of me?" She teased, her eyes flashing down to her hips.

Dex didn't have an answer that wouldn't get him in trouble. Though even with the light flirting, the weight of the day still hung over them.

They made small talk, but no one mentioned Burk until Lacy asked, "Okay, who's got a story about Burk? A good one, nothing too embarrassing."

Uncomfortable glances and side-eyes overcame their faces.

"Well come on," Lacy insisted. "Someone's gotta have one good story."

"Not right, we thought." Boritt offered up apprehensively.

"What do you mean it's not right?" Dex pried.

"When Mok Tau die, spirit go with you. Memory go with you.

we learn, to speak of dead, is to take what is god's."

"Listen, Sergeant, you can talk about whoever the hell ya like. Tell that to Roak when we get back. In fact, I'll tell him myself. Come on, he was your friend, right? Can't treat him like he never existed. Private… uh… Greg…"

"Gurg," Lacy corrected.

"Gurg, yeah. Tell me something about him."

Possible centuries worth of dogma came to a clash with the sudden change in mourning practices. The 'gods' gave them a command, but it still felt wrong.

"Did I ever tell you about my great grandma?" Lacy planted her arms on her legs and sat forward in a perfect impression of a grade schoolteacher addressing her class. "She died a long, long time ago, but she was a swell lady," Lacy laughed. "I don't think she was technically my great-grandma, but we remembered her as much."

Dex leaned in. Now that he thought about it, he didn't think he'd heard this story either. Whether or not whatever Lacy was about to say was true, he was curious to see where it was going.

"Where we're from, there's a place called the 'old west.'"

Dex tensed at the notion that they weren't gods, just people, but the Mok Tau didn't seem to mind. They were enthralled with every word that came from Lacy's mouth, taking it in as gospel.

"She was a bit of a legend if I do say so myself. Folks called her one of the last true gunslingers or the true West, and for a while, I thought it was just a fun story my dad told me. But this woman wasn't afraid of nothin'. She went for bounty after bounty, not giving a care who they were, how tough they were, or how terrible their crime."

Dex almost picked up a hint of an Old West dialect as she spoke.

Lacy continued, "Great-Grandma Maddy really earned her legendary status for the capture of this terrible monster, 'The Cannibal of Roldston Valley' they called him." The fire blazed and illuminated her starry eyes. There was no breaking the squad's attention on her. "Not even the toughest lawman in the whole west of the Mississippi could take him down, but Great-Grandma Maddy wasn't no lawman. She used her womanly charm to trap the monster and bring him to justice. That's how she was. Brought peace to the land through nothing more than what God gave 'er."

Dex froze. Had the Mok Tau noticed what she said? Was there a chance they would see through the facade they'd created for themselves and turn, spearing Dex and Lacy where they sat?

"I do not understand much of what is said," Boritt admitted.

Relief swept over Dex.

Lacy, on the other hand, felt a twinge of disheartening.

"Your words, we must learn. But from what we do speak… your blood, there sounds honor."

Dex relaxed. The acknowledgment of a god other than themselves didn't register with the Mok Tau. All they heard were strange new words from a strange new world.

"It's good to remember the dead," Lacy told them, with her eyes on Dex. "They remind us what to live for."

Her words hit Dex like a wrecking ball, but Dex's walls were made of the strongest steel. It was undeniable though, that a dent was made.

"He was a brave man, Private Burk," Dex said. Once he began speaking, he realized he had really nothing to say about their fallen comrade. Dex stood awkwardly with his canteen held high.

Lacy looked from him to the rest of the group. They all watched Dex with anticipation. How would one of the gods honor Burk?

"He was… very brave." Dex reiterated.

Lacy stood, trying to save Dex from embarrassment. "Burk will always be remembered. Burk was there when you found our star, and he'll be in our memory when we return to the village. His sacrifice will be recorded, and your children and children's children will know of him."

The fire crackled between the two races. Lacy prayed for a round of applause, any sign of validation.

Toork raised a fist to his chest. The others watched him.

With his eyes locked on Lacy, Toork beat his chest. The thud silenced the rest of the jungle. He beat again with his other hand, then continued two, four, six more times. Six more beats.

Tarzan, Dex thought with a smile breaking through his lips.

The others stood and beat their chests.

Metal clanged and drowned out the rest of them as Robbie got in on the action.

Lacy laughed, and even she beat her chest.

Dex put his hands on his hips, bewildered at how they assumed his joke and turned it into something reverent.

They continued to beat, waiting for Dex to join. Even Lacy egged him on.

"All right, all right! Ooh! Ooh! OOH!" He laughed and beat like Tarzan.

Cheers rang out, and they all took a drink in memory of Burk.

When they took their seats again, Gurg said, "Burk Mok Tau Hruur."

Boritt and Toork gave Gurg an almost comically quizzical look.

"Poor Hruur," Gurg clarified and the three of them laughed.

Lacy laughed too, but only to be polite. "What is Hrar?"

"Hruur," Boritt corrected through a smile. "Keeper of beast."

Dex and Lacy recalled the village. "I don't remember seeing any animals."

"*Very* poor Hruur," Gurg laughed.

"Mok Tau need beast for strength. Burk like beast for home."

Like having a dog? Lacy thought.

"Where we're from, we would call him a shepherd."

"Shep-herd," Gurk repeated, rolling the word in his mouth, testing it out. Toork and Boritt did the same. Another word to share with the village.

"Burk keep little tuk," Gurg held up his hands like he was displaying something in them. "Small beast, no strength. But children," Gurg shrugged. "Children and women think fun. Look like something from children story."

Lacy's eyes beamed. "Children's stories? Like make-believe? Fairy tales?"

"Make believe," Gurg confirmed, and they all looked for a follow-up from Lacy, confused as to why that meant so much to her.

"Something up?" Dex asked.

"We'll talk about it later." Then to the Mok Tau, she asked,

"What are these stories like? Tell me one!" Her voice was filled with excitement.

Gurg almost spoke, but Boritt held out a hand to stop the private and shook his head. "Stories fading."

Lacy's smile fell.

Boritt continued, "Some live. Most gone. False truth, take away from gods."

Even without looking, Dex could feel how hard Lacy rolled her eyes. He was dying to know what was going on in her head. But if there was something Boritt was hiding, or Lacy wasn't ready to tell, he'd figure it out later. For now, he wanted to keep some reverence on Burk.

"Tell me more about Burk. If he was such a bad shepherd, why didn't the village find a better one? Why'd you pick a shepherd anyway for this mission?" When the question came out, a spark of anger lit in Dex. Taking someone with such little experience could get them all killed.

"Burk blood all… shep-*hard*," Gurg said.

Boritt picked up the answer. "Burk poor at shep-herd, but good heart. Mok Tau look for good heart. Burk serve true, never…" he searched for the right phrase. "Never lose heart in other Mok Tau. Only want to serve. Good heart… is good warrior."

Lacy put a hand on Dex's leg.

It was an honorable thing, Dex knew, but he was still disappointed in Boritt's judgment. "Sergeant, next time you put men's lives in danger, pick ones that can handle it." *I don't want more blood on my hands.*

Boritt nodded, accepting the condemnation from his god.

This time, it was Robbie who revitalized the atmosphere of the camp. As if Dex's previous remark was never said, Robbie stated, "I have no blood. But I have an assembly line. I guess that means I have brothers. Many, many brothers. But they are all boring. They do not have free will. I do. That is why they work in kitchens and in cleaning, and I am covered in mud. I am doing better than they are."

They all stared at Robbie, unsure how to respond, but also, on the part of the Mok Tau, still unsure what Robbie even was. But he had arrived with the gods, and the Mok Tau would not question that.

Robbie was as mystical to them as Dex and Lacy.

"Okay... who's next?" Lacy asked.

"I have story." Toork chimed in. "I had enemy. His name, I do not know. Mok Rork, Far away tribe near Hidden Swap. I assist Scared Speaker Roak in making truce." Toork interlocked his fingers to emphasize. "But Mok Rork set trap. They try to drown Mok Tau in swamp. We escape, and send spirit of one Mok Rork to Maoul."

Maoul, the Emperor's Hell.

Toork laughed at the happy memory. "Mok Tau not as strong as Mok Rork, but we smarter. And gods smile on us." Toork said it with an invisible *wink wink, nudge nudge* look.

The other Mok Tau in the group grunted in agreement.

"Rogar, mine brother," Boritt said. There was melancholy in his voice. Memories buried too deep struggling to resurface "Two years it has been since journey to defeat Torro-Kaal. We were to journey as one. But Rogar go alone in night. Said I was still a tail."

Lacy wanted to ask what Boritt meant by 'tail,' but didn't want to interrupt.

Boritt continued, "Rogar always make fun. I follow him in quiet to Great Break, but moon not right. I could not keep up. Watch Rogar cross. I stay behind two weeks to wait. Torro-Kaal take Rogar."

Lacy crossed their small camp to sit next to Boritt and put a hand on his shoulder. "I'm sorry for your loss."

"Rogar in good place. But, I still defeat Torro-Kaal for him. Moon right this time." He pointed up to the sky.

They all looked up and saw, next to the bright teal blue moon they'd become familiar with, another larger one was catching up to it.

"Big brother. When he catches Little Sister, world filled with joy. All become light."

"What do you mean, light?" Lacy asked. "Like, night becomes day?"

Dex answered for the Mok Tau. "Light. Like weight. We've got the gravitational pull of two moons. That's what we've been feeling since we got here."

As if he never stopped talking, Boritt went on, "With Big Brother in place, we cross Great Break. Torro-Kaal screams will shatter all evil. Bring back peace."

"Cheers to that," Dex toasted, holding up his canteen.

The others gave a quick Tarzan beat of their chests. Dex and Lacy laughed.

Before anyone had the chance to speak again, Lacy said, "Dex, your turn."

He was caught off guard and chuckled when he thought she was joking. But Lacy continued to eye him enthusiastically.

They need this, she told him mentally.

They don't need anything from me, he shot back.

Want to be a leader? Open up to them. Be human for them.

Dex sighed and strained to address the Mok Tau.

What did Lacy want him to say? Who would he talk about?

The Mok Tau waited patiently, intently.

Lacy nudged him, and whispered, "Well come on."

Dex stood on the center of the tightrope.

"My... my dad. He's probably gone by now, but he was a warrior too."

Dex paused, wondering if the mention of a father would sound any alarms for the Mok Tau. But if Lacy talking about her great-grandmother didn't do anything for them, then neither should this. Either way, who knew what the Mok Tau thought of their godly world?

"When he was younger, he fought in this Great War, where we're from. The mightiest of armies, all clashing in every corner of the world. In one way or another, everyone did their part. It was good versus evil. Millions of lives were lost, and those who survived were never the same. But my dad... he always seemed to know what was coming, and he went anyway, even if it cost him his legs. I don't remember much of him before the war, but he always had hope. Even when he came home and the night terrors got to him, the screaming no one but him could hear, he believed there was something coming just around the corner to help him, and those like him. When his body started failing him, when the uh... when his heart started to give, he never complained. He still believed something would come and make it all go away. I guess it did... in a way. He told me before I left, I'd find what I was looking for out here. He believed it too, as certain as the sun coming up in the morning. That was him though. Always looking up at the stars, waiting for something great to happen, and if it wasn't coming down to him, I'd go up and find it for him. My dad was the happiest guy I knew, even with the whole world against him. Always had faith."

Your ruck... Lacy told him.

Dex's eyes drifted toward her and saw a nod of approval.

After a few minutes of silent reflection, Dex closed out the evening. He ordered a security rotation throughout the night. All would take turns, including Dex and Lacy. Robbie offered to cover all the shifts, which Dex was all for, but Lacy wanted him treated just the same as the rest of the squad.

Dex took the first watch. The others slept in the log.

As they bed down, Lacy looked up one last time at the sky.

"Look," she said with wonder in her voice. "Falling star?"

Dex saw where she pointed and caught a glimpse of something large and bright through the trees, trailing across the sky. "Definitely falling. Let's hope it's a star," though as he said it, they both knew better. Tension threatened to poison the air, but Dex added a soft, "Come on, get some rest."

Lacy kissed him on the cheek and took one more anxious look at the sky before leaving the day behind her.

Beside the blow of the fire, Dex looked in his rucksack for whatever it was Lacy wanted him to find. He pushed aside his tools, clothes, and rations, and found nothing. But he didn't need Lacy's voice in his head again to tell him there was something waiting for him in there. Dex dug a little deeper, and there, somehow stuffed in a spare skivvy top was his father's pocket bible.

Dex rolled his eyes but took the little book out and flipped through it.

He skimmed over the familiar verses from Sunday school, the chapters he'd used to criticize, the prayers he'd heard a million and a half times. He turned it over, then flipped it back to the front. *What could be so important here?*

Toward the back of the book, Dex saw a small tab and opened to it.

Romans chapter eight, verses twenty-four and five:

> *For in this hope we were saved. Now hope that is seen is not hope. For who hopes for what he sees? But if we hope for what we do not see, we wait for it with patience.*

He shut the book and shoved it back into his rucksack.

Coincidence, he told himself. But in his heart, he knew it was much more than that.

25. Predators and Prey

Robbie woke them one by one with gentle nudges. They were all drenched in the morning dew.

As the group evacuated the log, Boritt pointed out the intensity of the light streaming through the treetops.

"Robbie, what time is it?" Dex asked, already guessing the answer and getting ready to fume.

Robbie shrugged.

"How long has the sun been up?" More intensity in his voice.

"I think a few hours. I am very wet. I feel very slow. Cannot process." Robbie sat down by the log as if he'd just got off the longest shift at the office. All he needed was a tie to loosen and a cold bottle of beer and he'd be the perfect picture.

Daylight was lost. Even though the days were longer, it was wasted time by Dex's count, and time they would have to make up in the nights. This also meant less time to stop and eat.

"I want everybody moving, time now," Dex ordered and hand signaled Boritt to begin leading them. "Eat while you walk. And don't choke. Shouldn't have to say that but I'm sure if Robbie needed to eat then he *would*."

From the very first step they took, Dex and Lacy felt like they could jump ten feet into the air. The Mok Tau on the other hand, barely noticed, but knew it was a good sign. The gods had come to them to fulfill their promise, and the moons were in the right place to safely cross the Great Break for their quest. Just as long as Robbie didn't hold them up anymore, everything would go smoothly.

"Dex, do you have the rations?" Lacy asked, scouring her pack as they walked.

"Yeah, just a second." He unslung his pack and tried not to lose his footing as he got her food. "Hold on, I know I was the one to pack it." He pushed the tools to the side, the clothes, the book, but no sign of rations.

"Sergeant Toork."

Do you really still need to do that? Lacy shot him a thought.

Yes, Dex let her read. "Did we assign you responsibility of rations?"

"Yes, Cap-tain," Toork responded promptly.

"MY rations, Sergeant. Mine and the Lieutenant's." Dex clarified, dreading the answer and what it meant.

"No, Cap-tain. You keep you own rash-ons."

Five minutes into the morning and two bad holdups.

Dex stopped where he was and planted his hands on his sides. He groaned to the sky then asked Robbie, with his head still up, unable to look at the little robot, "Robbie, did any animals get into our packs last night while you were on guard?"

No answer.

"Robbie!" Dex spun around and saw the robot bouncing on a rubbery plant.

Robbie glided nearly four feet high and gently fell back down to a halt on solid ground. Once landed, the little robot shied away a few inches.

"Dex, don't shout at him. He's just a little guy."

Too much. It was too much for the morning and he was in no mood to argue. Lacy assumed responsibility and knelt beside Robbie.

"Robbie, can you tell me what happened?"

"Will Dex shut me down?" Robbie asked, his voice trembling.

Lacy tried not to laugh, but a small giggle escaped her. "No, of course not. No one's shutting you down. Just tell me what happened."

Robbie leaned to look over Lacy's shoulder at Dex, then whispered to Lacy, "Little people walked into the log this morning. They walked out with the rations. The water in the air made me slow, and I could not catch them. I think I have to dry. I am very slow. There is a high volume of water still in my system."

"Are you going to be okay?" Lacy put her gentle hand on Robbie's head. "Do you need me to carry you?"

"No. Planet gravity has decreased by eight percent. I can walk easy, even with minor system delay."

"Okay. You can take a different shift at night so this doesn't happen again. And if you need to be carried in the morning, I can carry you. Does that sound okay?"

Robbie sank in his little feet. He whispered, "Is Dex mad at me?"

"YES," Dex stated.

"No," Lacy corrected. "He's not mad, just a little disappointed."

Robbie "boooooo"-ed and fell on his rear.

"Come on, we'll get this fixed." Even though Robbie said he could walk on his own for the morning, Lacy took him by the hand and carried him in her arms against her chest. He was light enough then that she carried him comfortably for the first mile. It was his blocky shape more than anything that gave her discomfort and when they came on rough terrain he offered to talk again.

That late morning, all eyes were kept open and alert for possible food. Dex and Lacy did their best to be useful in the hunt, but they were told that most plants they found were inedible, whether indigestible or poisonous.

Dex instructed that animals were off-limits for the morning. He wanted nothing that would hold them back longer from reaching Torro-Kaal. It was nuts, fruits, or bugs that wouldn't give them some terrifying alien parasite.

Lacy's protests of their new diet ended that morning. When she was hungry enough, she told herself she didn't care if she had to eat another giant beetle, as long as she ate. She tried to distract herself from the mounting hunger, but memories came to her of camping with her family as a kid. The Carradine's annual trips to Bear Mountain were always the best summer vacations. Her brothers always threatened to lose her in the woods, and she'd tell them 'I hope you do. It'll be more fun finding my way home that way,' then stick her tongue out at them. *And look at me now*, she laughed to herself.

On the other side of their wedge formation, Gurg jumped out into the brush, spear first.

Everyone turned, ready to attack whatever it was. Dex wanted to shout at him, order Gurg to report his sightings, but Gurg had already returned, with a new breed of disgusting bug on his spear.

It was the thickest, longest, deep blue-brown centipede Lacy had ever seen with massive lobster claws just behind the front of its body. The bug was almost as large as a wiener dog.

"Nothing we have to cook, Gurg," Dex reminded him.

At the thought of eating that bug, all the work Lacy had done to convince herself the beetle wasn't *that* bad went away. *But thank god Dex is being so hooah.*

"No cooking," Gurg said, and took a hearty bite out of the centipede. Juices splashed out of the bug like a tomato.

We should have gone back to Earth, she told Dex.

You tell me now?

When they were in it though, even Lacy had to admit, the bug didn't taste that bad. The worst part was the idea of it. It went down easy enough but didn't sit great. When Lacy told Dex she felt like throwing up, he didn't argue. The bug was good for one meal, but it wouldn't become a regular on their menu.

Noon came and went without conflict.

A pack of squat, scaly creatures roamed alongside them for a brief while. The creatures were shaped like evolution put legs on a turtle shell and forgot to add anything else. No head or other appendages, not even eyes. But the creatures navigated the thick jungle without hindrance. Their young walked between their parent's legs.

Boritt explained to Dex and Lacy that the creatures saw through a hidden sense, not quite hearing, as they had no ears, but through vibrations. And they did in fact have mouths, as Robbie almost learned the hard way.

In his curiosity, Robbie tried to approach the hatchlings. They were about his size and the closest thing he'd seen since the transport ship he was assigned to that looked remotely similar to him.

Boritt and Toork jumped after him and pulled Robbie away just in time for a two-meter-long tongue to shoot out of the stomach and try to ensnare him.

Lacy threw herself in front of Robbie and the two Mok Tau, just in case, while Dex remained in the center of where his formation should have been.

"Are we moving or what?" he asked, appearing unfazed by Robbie's near-lunch experience.

Even so, Robbie stayed a few short arm's length away from the creatures, studying them as they walked. Except for when they got too close, the Bottom Feeders, as Boritt translated to Dex, didn't seem to mind the company.

"Think we can ride them to Torro-Kaal?" Dex asked.

"No," Boritt was quick to reply. "Bottom Feeder not like rider."

"Shame. You know, ya'll need a better name for these guys. To us," he gestured from himself to Lacy, "a bottom feeder is a bad thing. An insult for something worthless."

"Still not bad name. Bottom Feeder waste of space. Only roam and eat. Hard to kill, but can not fight. Only defend."

"Is that such a bad thing?" Lacy chimed in.

"Yes," Dex and Boritt agreed, and that was that.

Every so often, a tongue would shoot out from their bellies to grab some vegetation and they would feed it to their young or keep it for themselves. It was a peaceful sight until all at once, the adult Bottom Feeders ate their young!

Lacy screamed in shock, and Dex raised his blaster, but the others crouched low in the foliage.

"Down, Cap-Tain!" Boritt whisper-shouted. "Children are okay. Down… Haaahhh."

Dex and Lacy did as he said, and Dex high-crawled over to Boritt. The foliage just barely covered him.

"What is it, Sergeant?"

"They are protecting the young. They are safe. But they sense something. Danger."

Dex peaked his head above the bushes. The Bottom Feeder had quickened their pace and fled the area. They were alone.

Using hand signals, Dex ordered Gurg to get in one of the trees to get a better look of their surroundings.

In two quick hops, Gurg was fifty feet up in the nearest tree. His skin color shifted to that of the tree, and he scanned the area.

Silence.

"Sergeant," Dex whispered. "How strong are those things'

senses?"

"Very strong. But they would not flee if not needed. We may be okay for now, but I say we keep move if Gurg see nothing."

Gurg signaled down to the rest of the squad. The coast was clear.

Dex threw his hand in a circle above his head. *Everyone on me.*

They returned to their trail, quietly. Dex ordered hand signals only from there on out unless it was an emergency.

The trek that day, even with the low gravity, eagerly threw hurdles in their way. They pushed through tight corners of tangled trees and roots, crossed violently rushing streams, and scaled alongside sharp rock walls over a pit of something that smelled toxic. For all the obstacles, Robbie requested to be carried.

The low gravity helped them keep their strength, but by the time they made camp that night, all of their bodies ached.

Except Robbie's.

There were no stories that night, and the fire was kept small. They found a small cave underneath a large tree. Easy access in and out, but low visibility.

Dex took the first watch again.

Beside the faint glow of the fire, he fingered through the pocket bible. Dex flipped through the pages, skimming the words without reading until he was fanning the pages out of boredom.

It was all ridiculous. A thousand years before space travel? *Sure,* Dex thought, *big man in the sky watches over everything.* Now the idea felt more true than ever but tainted. It wasn't some benevolent god running the show, just another dictator. A dictator god that could reach into the minds of his people and cause pain from across the galaxy. And where were the other gods stepping in to do anything about it? All the gods that ruled earth with complete omnipotence, and not a word of the Emperor?

But…

But there was the voice… and the Valley.

Someone had reached out. Someone called his name.

No, it was just my imagination. Caused by the jump to hyperspace.

Dex gave the book one more fan and shoved it back into his pack.

Just my imagination.

He told himself he had better things to think about anyway. The book was a distraction when he should be watching for dangerous animals, or worse, the Empire. Dex tried to keep in the back of his mind that at any moment it was entirely possible for Zar-Mecks to swarm the place. All it took was one look by the Emperor into the minds of the tribe. If he was looking, it was only a matter of process of elimination until he got to the Mok Tau and whatever planet this was.

How quickly would the Mok Tau turn on them then? Hwaq the mechanic had no problem with it.

Not worth thinking about, Dex told himself. Just *stay focused on the mission.*

He toiled for his entire shift, going back and forth between scanning their surroundings and looking for ways everything could go sideways.

Small nocturnal creatures teased the idea of infiltrating the squad's campsite.

Though he was hungry, Dex didn't risk trying to eat the ones that got close enough to spear. He did his best to just scare them off. A dead animal or bug would only attract more of them looking for something to eat.

After two hours, Dex was relieved by Gurg.

As he tried to fall asleep, the voice of the vision permeated in his mind.

The voice. The Valley.

* * *

Robbie woke them at dawn with a siren.

The squad all jumped up and grabbed their spears ready for a fight and took prone positions around the egress points of the under-tree. Lacy doused the fire.

Dex jumped to Robbie and silenced him. All was still dark outside, not far past midnight if it was Robbie's shift.

"What the hell is it, Robbie?!" Dex shook the robot. If it was something hostile, he was ready to tear Robbie apart for giving away their location.

Robbie whispered back, "The monster is back."

Chills ran down Dex and Lacy's spines. The monster from the clearing, missing when they had returned to their ship.

"It can't be," Lacy demanded. "We blew its head off!"

"It... it found another," Dex slowly repeated Boritt's words.

Far off in the jungle, a deep rumbling was heard. Thudding with no rhythm. The sound of mangled, uneven arms and legs, moving without proper coordination, but with terrible strength.

It was too dark to give hand signals, so Dex slowly crawled over to Boritt.

"Sergeant, are we safe here?" Dex whispered so low he wasn't even sure words came out.

"Kron-kaal nose is mystery. Sometimes stronger than Tuk, sometimes weaker than rock. Eyes too. Only thing for certain, kron-kaal strong." Though he tried to hide it, there was fear in Boritt's voice.

"Let's hope its hearing isn't too good. We're moving out." Dex crawled back to Robbie and helped the robot back into his rucksack. "If the monster gets too close, what are you going to do?"

Robbie answered with an opening of his claw. Torch the monster.

Dex nodded and put a finger to his lips.

One by one, with Boritt in the lead, the squad crawled out of the under-tree. They stayed close together, relying upon the Mok Tau's night vision to guide them through the pitch black of night. Dex held onto Lacy's spear, and Lacy held onto Boritt's. Dex kept his other hand on the holstered blaster. Toork and Gurg followed behind them. Gurg, pulling up the rear, kept a watch at all times on their six 'o'clock.

The kron-kaal was invisible in the dark of the night, but the sound of its fists pounding into the ground told them it wasn't gaining on them or falling behind. For certain though, it was too close.

The rest of the jungle knew it too. All other creatures had fled the area, leaving no ambiance to mask the squad's slow crawl through the jungle. There was only the sound of vegetation being brushed against, and the deep *Thump... ThumpThump... Thump Thump...*

Thump...

Behind them, unclear how far behind, a tree cracked and fell. No birds flew from it. A crash and the thumping continued.

Dex had adapted well enough to walk without proper footwear. The calluses on his feet were hard and protective, though he envied Lacy with the boots. But now the branches, rocks, and twigs scraped against their thighs and knees.

Lacy slid her leg against the jungle floor, and her knee tore open as she dragged it against a sharp rock.

A voracious scream begged to be let loose on the night. Letting go of Borrit's spear, Lacy clapped both hands over her mouth. The tiniest squeak escaped through her fingers.

The thumping stopped.

The squad froze, in movement and in their hearts.

Lacy's heart pounded in her chest. So hard it beat, she felt it would be enough to push her off the ground.

Somewhere not far behind them; BOOM!.. BOOM!.. BOOM BOOM!

The kron-kaal beat against a tree in fury, then uprooted it completely.

Gurg saw it happen. Their tree, the one they'd made camp under. If it hadn't smelled them before, there was no way it couldn't pick up their trail now, even if its sense was worse than a rock.

Lacy's breathing had picked up, in and out with the beat of her heart. Any faster and she would start hyperventilating. She needed to find a way to calm herself and block out the pain.

She pictured herself in the first place which gave her comfort; back on the *Silent Horizon*. Back on their port-side bunk, curled up in Dex's arms, with a slow song played over the computer. Lacy told herself they were there now. In her mind, she *was* there.

Back at their upturned campsite, the kron-kaal threw around the vegetation in search of its prey, and as if called by someone, paused, then jumped into action after something in the opposite direction.

The uneven beat of its movement slowly faded, but never quite left.

Dex crawled ahead to Boritt and did his best to signal in the dark that it was time to move. He wouldn't take any chances just laying there, waiting to die.

Boritt did as he was ordered and began to crawl again.

They stayed low to the ground until sunrise. They hadn't traveled far, but they were safe.

Even after all that time, Lacy still thought she could hear the thumping of the kron-kaal.

26. The Swamp

The slowness of their travel in the night carried into the day. The kron-kaal may have been gone, but Dex wanted to take no risks. They paused only once for breakfast, and to get their bearings. Two more days, Boritt told them, until they would reach the Great Break. It would be the perfect time to cross with Big Brother passing over them.

"Why do you call it 'Big Brother?'" Lacy asked, wiping the morning dew off her face. She looked at the back of her wet hand and saw how filthy it was. For as drenched as they were each morning, it did nothing to clean the dirt and grime off of them. A nice hot shower was in order very soon.

"It has been long time since we shared story of the moons," Boritt sighed. They all noticed how his shoulders hung when he spoke. Gurg and Toork understood but didn't feel it was their place to say anything.

"Why's that?" Lacy asked, wanting to put a hand on Boritt's shoulder for comfort.

"Do you not know?"

Lacy shook her head.

Boritt took a deep breath in, almost mentally preparing himself for what was to be said. "When Torro-Kaal came, and god gave us promise, we say 'no' to old way. Our story, give up for god. God tell us new truth, and that becomes ours."

Jaskek came into Lacy's mind; their discussion on the transport. The Empire shared no stories except Imperial history. Everything came back to the Emperor and his glory. She wouldn't have to fill Dex in after all. Instead, she shot him a knowing eye, and he acknowledged.

Stepping back into her god-shoes, Lacy said, "I request you

share the story now." A bug zipped by her neck and she swatted it away.

"Mok Tau… we do not remember much. Anymore." Toork chimed in.

Lacy turned around and walked backward. She limped from the gash the rock tore in her knee, but cared more to hear what Toork had to say than to give the pain any attention. "You've gotta remember something right?"

"Lacy, ugh…" Dex grunted as jumped to grab the top of a ten-foot-tall cliff blocking their path. Boritt, standing at the top, pulled him the rest of the way up and he continued, "Lacy, I wouldn't bet on it. Those myths would have died a long time ago."

Not wanting to admit he was right, Lacy protested, "There's gotta be something. Come on!" She looked up at Dex and saw him waiting with an arm outstretched to help her up. Lacy made the leap eight feet into the air and grabbed onto a cleft to hold herself. Her leg burned with pain on the jump.

Dex reached down for her, and as he pulled her up, she said, "If you all don't remember the story, make something up. Take it back to the village and tell 'em the gods told you."

Dex gave her a warning look, to which she shot back a playful one saying, *it'll be fine!*

From beside the two humans on the top of the cliff, Boritt said, "You are strange gods."

Toork and Gurg halted in their tracks, shocked and terrified of Boritt's heresy. Even Dex became worried as to what was going on in his Sergeant's mind.

Lacy though, couldn't seem to care less. She only asked, "How so?" Like they were all good friends and Boritt had given an inkling of some interesting trivia.

"You are not what Mok Tau expected," Boritt continued with his boldness.

Toork and Gurg jumped to the top of the cliff without hindrance and listened to what Boritt had to say.

"We are told to forget our dead. You say otherwise. We are told to forget our tradition. You tell us make our own."

A bug landed on Dex's hand, but he ignored it. He was ready

to reach for his blaster if Boritt made any sudden moves. *Just like the mechanic.*

But Lacy's voice in his head, *trust, Dex. Trust me.*

Dex's hand steadied, but his mind stayed ready for an attack. *Alright, Lacy. As you wish.*

After his brief pause, Boritt said, "Times do seem to be changing. And who am I…" he nodded at Dex, "but a simple Staaf Sar-gent."

Something changed in the air at that moment. It wasn't the smell, or the humidity. It was something they couldn't measure or see, but without a doubt, something changed.

"It is for the story of the shaping of Taranok, and the Great Break," Boritt spoke proudly, like he'd been waiting his entire life for the chance to share the story. He started walking again, not waiting for a command from Dex or Lacy.

"Long before Mok Tau grew from tails, and Torro-Kaal had come from stars, planet was whole. Birth of planet came with birth of moons, and they were twins. The Brother and Sister were in a race to be born. They push and fight each other to escape the belly of Taranok. It so violent that it break the womb, and mother break in half. Brother came first, and then sister.

"Little Sister challenged Big Brother to another race, one around the mother. But Big Brother happy with one victory, and he let little sister run around mother. Big Brother good.

"Because of harm Big Brother did, he give back now. Big Brother watch over whole world, and where he goes a weight is lifted on world, while Little Sister run around, Big Brother travel slow, watch closely. Keep us safe."

They carried on a few steps quietly before Dex asked, "That's the best you got?" Then swatted a bug that flew by his ear.

Lacy was quick to scold him with a *TSSsss!*

"It is my story," Boritt replied plainly.

Dex shrugged with a laugh and said, "Fair enough." He swatted another bug that flew too close to his face.

"You do better, Cap-tain." Toork teased and got a laugh from the other two Mok Tau.

Lacy was still mildly annoyed at Dex's comment, but they

were laughing. How upset could she be?

"No, I'm alright. I'd rather watch… or listen to stories than tell my own."

The bugs were becoming insistent and bothering not just Dex or Lacy now.

"I got one go ya," Lacy said to no one in particular. She smacked a bug against her leg, a big, green juicy one, and began, "There was a woman once. An old woman, who had just lost his husband. Shortly after he passed, this woman took to drinking. Two to three bottles every night. OOF!" Lacy caught herself as she almost tripped, distracted by all the bugs flying around her.

Boritt extended a hand to catch her, but Lacy waved him off.

"Just missed a step. *Anyway,* the drinking got so intense that she had to be hospitalized. She… went to the witch doctor I guess."

All the Mok Tau gave her a quizzical look but didn't stop walking.

"Medicine man? Healer? Whatever. So she went to the healer, or, had to be brought it."

Dex interjected, "You're losing the crowd, darling."

"She was brought in and the doctor said, 'you have to cut back on the drinking. I know you're upset about the loss of your husband, but if you don't stop you'll be meeting him soon.'" Lacy paused for dramatic effect. "The next week she goes back in. The healer runs all these tests and says, 'wow, I've never seen someone recover so well! How'd you do it?' And the old woman says, 'well, you told me if I kept it up I'd meet my husband again. Why do you think I started in the first place? It was to celebrate!'"

Lacy stopped and turned to face her audience like she'd just wrapped on a Broadway show.

The consensus from the crowd was that the kron-kaal episode had been more entertaining.

Lacy dropped her hands to her hips. "You all just don't have a sense of humor. *swat*

Dex drew close to her and put a hand on her cheek. "Lacy, I love you. I love everything about you…except your stand-up." And with that, he kissed her on the forehead and they walked on.

"YOU tell one!" Lacy demanded, trying to hold back a smile.

"I don't know any not from a movie, and I won't tell them half as good as the original."

"What is movie?" Toork asked.

"What is doctor? Or Witch? Is it Mok Rork woman?" Gurg asked, then choked, accidentally inhaling a bug.

Dex threw over his shoulder jokingly, "Private Gurg you are way behind on the conversation."

Neither Toork nor Gurg got an answer to their questions. The contestation was interrupted by a bubbly *Plop*, and Boritt jumped back, almost bumping into Lacy.

"Hold," he called to the rest of the team.

"What is it, Boritt?" Dex asked, moving to the front of their formation.

"We are at swamp. Must be very careful."

"Swamp? What swamp?" Dex looked out into the jungle, the same view, more-or-less, they'd seen the last few days. Everything looked normal; thick trees, twisting roots, solid ground. A little less vegetation on the ground, but still moss and grass and the trees were spread out further. In fact, it looked like the easiest part of the jungle they'd be traveling in.

"Down. Look." Boritt picked up a rock and tossed it. The rock landed with a thunk, throwing up bits of dirt, grass... and water.

"Very thick," Boritt warned. "Do not get pulled in. Many creatures. We stay close to root and rock."

Taking another scan of their environment, Dex and Lacy wished this part of the jungle was as dense as where they landed the *Silent Horizon*.

Birds hung from branches high in the trees, sleeping like bats. One stretched out is membranous wings. The front edge was trimmed with something resembling a dull copper.

"Is there a way around this?" Dex asked.

"No telling. Swamp travels, same as us. I hoped it would be out of our way." Without instructions to do so, Boritt climbed onto the nearest tree and hopped from that to the next, then waited.

In the rear of their formation, Gurg and Toork removed thin sacks from their rucks. The sacks looked like pale balloons, which they used to catch the nearby bugs with. "Stink bombs," Toork informed Dex. "If we get trouble, distract beasts. Make them think there dead animal nearby to eat that is not us."

Dex only nodded, hoping that the four bombs they made up would be enough.

Lacy looked back the way they came. The kron-kaal had left them in the night, but they all knew it was only a matter of time until it closed in on them again. They would have to push through and tread carefully.

She sidestepped to a spot of solid root bending up out of the swamp. "Just like 'The Floor is Lava'," she joked.

Lacy broke a branch off the nearest tree and stuck it into the ground. It went in easy enough, but pulling it back was like pulling a ten-ton dumbbell out of quicksand. She jumped to the next rock, and Dex took her place on the root.

The Mok Tau kept to the trees, hopping from one to the next but staying close to the base. The birds above paid no mind to them but stirred more with every sound the squad made.

As they traversed the swamp, the birds awoke and traveled with them. The bugs had become more than a nuisance, biting at every inch of the travelers they could without being swatted away. Patches here and there of mud showed themselves, but it was near impossible to tell where the swamp ended and solid ground began.

Dex picked up another rock to toss into the water. It landed with a solid Plunk. The land rippled the entire area around them. And next to where the rock landed, something scaly crested over the water and dove back in.

"What was that?" Lacy questioned any of the Mok Tau who knew.

They all looked and saw the creature slither through the swamp.

"Do not disturb creatures of swamp. They are not nice like Bottom Feeder."

Neither Dex nor Lacy had to be told twice not to mess with it.

The scaly creature slithered away back under the water but stayed close to the surface. Ripples of its movements circled around the trees and boulders they climbed on.

Jumping as cautiously as he could from rock to root to rock, Dex kept glancing up at the birds. Their following, though without signs of aggression, filled him with discomfort. A closer look at their wings showed the copper trim had some bite to it. Fully extended, they looked like the birds were just as powerful as swords with jet engines on them, cutting through anything that got in their way.

He lunged for a knot in the tree, trying to gain some height and join the Mok Tau. The low gravity gave him the boost he needed to reach the knot, but the tree itself was too thick. He couldn't get a proper grip around it and began to slip.

Lacy saw and bounded to the base of the tree to catch him.

Dex shooed her out of the way and lost his footing as he hit the ground, falling backward.

Lacy dropped down and grabbed his arm, his head just inches from the water.

He saw the look in her eyes and agreed, "rocks and roots."

Lacy almost let his arm go, when from far behind, they heard the familiar uneven rhythm of something large crashing through the jungle, and a loud splash.

Dex didn't hear it, just shouted, "Lacy! Hey! Pull me up!"

She did and shushed him. Voice trembling, she whispered, "Dex, it's back."

Dex got to his knees and looked out to their rear. The kron-kaal was too far away to see, hidden behind the trees, but she was right. He too heard the un-rhythmic thumping.

He whistled to the others and pointed. They noticed the sound right away, and Boritt shouted, "We must move faster! We will get trapped here!" Then to Gurg and Toork, "Stay in rear. High. Keep them safe."

Toork and Gurg nodded and beat their chests. It was the one reassuring sound Dex heard before all hell broke loose.

No more lightly hopping from rock to root, Dex, aided by the low gravity, assisted Lacy's jump to the next safe spot by throwing her. She landed hard on a boulder but was quick to rise and ready to catch Dex.

The kron-kaal closed in. Rushing through the swamp and

tearing down trees. It was still out of sight, but the thrashing and thumping was louder. The birds above heard it too, and sensed what was coming. They began flapping their wings and screeching a high pitch screech, like nails on a chalkboard.

"Go! Go! We protect!" Boritt shouted mid hop.

One of the birds swung down by his right side. Its wing clipped the side of the tree and splinters shot out, slicing tiny cuts into Dex's back. The bird seemed unfazed by the nick. It screeched again, revealing a tiny row of dozens of teeth lining its beak.

Adrenaline was building in the earthlings. Danger from above, danger from below, and danger on their tail.

Thump-Thumpthumpththump-Thump

Please, God, get us out of this! Lacy prayed, struggling to pull herself over a root.

Sweat poured from every inch of her body like it was still early morning.

Dex stayed as close as he could behind her, instinctively boosting her up over obstacles, forgetting the aid the low gravity gave them. He nearly pushed her hard enough to go flying an extra foot in the air.

When Dex climbed to join her, his foot slipped. It was enough for him to temporarily lose focus and let go of the branch he held onto. Again, Lacy reached out for him but missed by an inch.

His foot fell into the water.

ThumpThump-Thump-Th-Thump

Lacy threw herself down and grabbed him by the fingers in her second attempt.

"Give me your other hand!" she demanded.

Dex felt the strong pull of the swamp on his right foot. His left was planted sturdy on a small patch of solid ground, but he was leaning back, and unable to straighten.

ThumpTHu-Thump-ThThTHTHUMP-THUMP THUMP

Robbie tried to reach out too, but to no avail. His arms were too short, and his weight was pulling Dex down.

"PLEASE HELP!" He shouted at Lacy.

Lacy's sweating hands were losing their grip on his fingers.

"Lacy! Give me your spear!"

She didn't hesitate. Risking letting him go, he tightened one hand as much as she could on Dex's fingers, and grabbed her spear as it was tied to the side of the ruck, with the other.

Dex grabbed on-
THUMP THUMP, CRASH!

If only by a miracle was Lacy able to pull Dex up, as a tree crashed just west of them. They both looked and saw it in the light.

The oily black skin of the monster from the clearing, its legs, and fists, all familiar, but the head and torso… It had merged. The kron-kaal that attacked them near the village, had merged. By the midsection, the weak lower body of the second attacker slunk out to the side like an unwanted appendage, but now it had strong legs to complement its ape-like arms. Its many, ape-like arms. More on the right than it had on the left, and a clear missing spot for the arm torn off at the village border. It was the most abhorrent, terrible thing they'd ever seen. Blasphemy against all of nature. A mangled mess of anatomy that made no evolutionary sense, and only lived to destroy.

The kron-kaal let out a roar, satisfied it had their attention, and charged again.

Darkness descended upon them as the birds were all at once scared away from their perches. From two fronts, hostiles came at Dex and Lacy.

Up above, the Mok Tau maneuvered around the trees to be out of the birds' way and jabbed at them as they flew by.

Toork struck one, skewering it through a wing. The membranous tissue tore away and the bird collapsed, falling to the ground where it was caught by the kron-kaal and ripped in half. A terrible display of its brute strength.

If not for the low gravity, Dex and Lacy wouldn't have made it another twenty feet before meeting their doom. But they jumped and nearly soared through the air from safe spot to safe spot. With their blood pumping and adrenaline flowing, they rushed through the swamp, but the kron-kaal gained and almost took them over.

Boritt jumped from his vantage point, spear at the ready, and plunged into the back of the kron-kaal. The spear penetrated and held tight as the kron-kaal thrashed its body to rid itself of its unwanted rider. But Boritt held true, giving Dex and Lacy the distraction they needed, if only for a few more moments of life together.

One of the kron-kaal arms reached back, attempting to grab Boritt. The other half dozen arms shielded the beast from the birds swooping down.

Boritt dodged each swipe, just barely getting caught by the serrated talons of the kron-kaal, but the beast refused to be mocked. Unaffected by the pain it caused, the kron-kaal's arm snapped back, breaking the bone, and grabbed Boritt!

Lacy screamed for her friend. The birds flew by her, one nicked her arm, but she cared none.

Boritt's eyes felt as if they were going to pop out of his skull. The kron-kaal tightened its grip and reared the Mok Tau around to meet him face to face.

Dex saw where the monster stood, an unsteady bridge of roots and weeds, just above a plot of open swamp water. He picked up a rock and threw it, hoping his aim was true, but not at the kron-kaal.

The rock sunk in the water, and the swamp serpent shot up, smashing through the bridge.

Boritt was released from the kron-kaal's grip and flew across the swamp.

For a moment, Dex saw the troop leader from their flight to the village. He saw his body splatter against the tree, and the green blood still trickling down the wood the next morning.

A minute was an hour of the terrible fate replaying in his mind. Dex looked into Lacy's star-filled eyes, saw her heart, and turned back to Boritt. Dex couldn't look away, but wouldn't let himself freeze when Boritt's body bounced from a rock, and landed at the base of a tree, with his legs dipping into the water.

"Go on!" Dex ordered Lacy, almost shoving her away, then took off to help their companion.

Lacy's arm twitched in his direction, but Dex was already gone.

Dex raced to aid their fallen while the kron-kaal was caught in battle with the serpent.

Muddy water splashed against his back, as Dex knelt in front of the Mok Tau. Dex smacked his cheek shouting, "Boritt! Hey, come on, man! We're not out of this yet!"

Dex shuddered at the sound of the kron-kaal beating the serpent back into the water. Try as he might to pull Boritt from the swamp, with every tug out, the water pulled him in deeper until it was up to his knees.

Two thoughts battled in his mind, neither of which he wanted to live with; accept Boritt's fate in the swamp or leave his legs behind.

"Gurg! Toork! Cover me!" He knew it was a risk shouting, but if it could afford him only a minute more, he'd take it. They threw their bug sacks down, exploding like airstrikes around the kron-kaal. The birds found a new direction and dove at the scent of their next meal.

As the kron-kaal fought on two fronts, Dex ripped two vines from their surroundings and tied them tight halfway up Boritt's thigh. Then, with a crudely made stone knife from Boritt's belt, Dex freed the Mok Tau from the swamp.

Sensing the battle was lost for the moment, the serpent slithered away, leaving the kron-kaal free to tear Dex apart. The contorted face of the beast had the air of an evil grin.

Green blood covered Dex's hands, but it was better than being splattered across the jungle floor. He pulled Boritt from the straps of his pack and threw his unconscious body over his shoulder, then turned to flee the scene. But the kron-kaal was on his tail.

Dex drew his blaster, and on the pull of the trigger, flames roared across his vision, shielding him from the beast.

"Wh- Robbie! Ha! I forgot you were there..." Dex breathed but didn't hesitate to flee back toward Lacy.

"I have been in low power. There is too much water around, and you keep falling."

The kron-aal withdrew, along with the birds circling its head. Now they flew back to the Mok Tau in the trees holding back their brothers.

Lacy ordered Toork and Gurg to leave. "Just lead us out of here!"

Dex hurdled over the foliage, weighed down so by Robbie and Boritt, that the low gravity no longer mattered.

Coming up behind him, the insistent

27. Missionary Work

An image played in Dex's head; hands and feet tied to a stick that the natives carried on their shoulders, like in some western cartoon about cowboys and indians.

If only they were that lucky.

Their hands were tied, yes, but on a long string connected to the tail of the razorbacks. With every step the alien dinosaur took, its tail swung hard one way, jerking the captives to one side and then the other. Adding insult and shame to their already terrible situation, Mok Rork riders tossed pebbles at them, laughing and antagonizing them in their own language.

Their one solace was that Boritt didn't have to endure the humiliation.

"Help him!" Lacy demanded, tears streaming down her face as their captors pulled them away from the swamp, leaving Boritt to slowly bleed out on the edge of the swamp.

"Please! Help that man!" She begged and begged, wishing, willing the power she shared with Dex to extend to the beings of this planet.

One of the Mok Rork slapped her with a thick "HAAHH!"

Fury roared from every inch of Dex's being. He lunged at the Mok Rork, held back by only inches by his bindings.

The Mok Rork laughed at the futile attempt, but if only he'd seen how deep the bindings cut into Dex's wrist, and how little Dex cared, he never would have laid a hand on any enemy, ever again. He was lucky, really, the Mok Rork. If whoever tied Dex's bonds were just the littlest bit careless, the Mok Rork's head would have been torn from his shoulders faster than another frog could say "Haahh" again.

"Gur rubba," the Mok Rork said, and gurgle-ribbitted the rest of his words.

"He say 'you be tossed into the swamp if you act like that,' Cap-tain," Gurg translated.

"To hell with what he said! Pick that man up, you goddamn frog!" Dex tried to swing his fists to hit the Mok Rork, but was again pulled back by his bindings. "Pick him up!"

The Mok Rork scoffed, and eyed Boritt's unconscious body.

From the trees, the rest of the Mok Rork began to chant, an encouraging sound if Dex heard one.

He strode over to Boritt, and taking him by the forearm, dragged the body across the jungle floor back to Dex.

The trees erupted with laughter.

"Stop that! Please stop! Just help him!" Lacy's pleas could have been as loud as a hurricane, but they still fell on deaf ears.

The Mok Rork gurgle-ribbitted again and bound Boritt's hands to a razorback tail just like the other captives, doomed to be dragged across the jungle.

Their rucks were confiscated and thrown onto the backs of the razorbacks. Robbie stayed quiet, as per Dex's quiet instruction when captured, but was ready to light the place up again if only asked.

Through their protests, Toork's most violent of all of them, the Mok Rork pulled them through the jungle.

"Brup piit!" Took's guard shouted and brandished his spear.

Toork cured in his native tongue then said "My Cap-tain crush Mok Rork village! My Cap-tain destroy all Mok Rork!"

His threats were met with a shower of rocks and sticks.

"Cool it, Sergeant," Dex ordered. "Won't do us any good. Lacy, how are you holding up?"

Lacy looked only half conscious. She walked just fine, but her eyes hung low like she was sleepwalking.

"Lacy! *LACY!*"

Her eyes shot open and she looked around for Dex like she had no idea where she was.

"Still with us?" Dex asked, trying to maintain some assurance in his voice. Through everything he did, body language and voice, he had to tell them, and himself, they would all be okay.

Lacy only nodded.

"Stay with me, darling," Dex soothed.

The bindings tore at their wrists. Soon enough, the soles of their feet were caked in their own blood. For Toork, the blood loss only fueled his rage. He threw his arms at the Mok Rork riders. Few and far between, droplets of blood landed on the razorback and the faces of their captors. Every curse he bellowed at them only fed their laughter, in turn adding to Toork's fury.

At any moment, Dex anticipated Gurg's — and Toork's especially — rage to turn from the Mok Rork to him and Lacy. What pitiful gods they were. One man dead, one without legs, and them all now hostages. What a mighty god Dex was. And then there was Lacy; all the powers of the Emperor, theoretically, but only in regard to one of the uncounted species on the planet.

The pain would have to endure. And when the blows came, from the Mok Tau or the Mok Rork, Dex and Lacy would have to accept their fate. In Dex's eye, their journey was coming to an end.

Drums. Drums echoing through the jungle. And through the beating of the drums, a horn blew once, announcing their arrival.

A messenger must have been sent ahead to tell the Mok Rork village of their warriors' capture. Dex could see it now; a blazing fire, and knives at the ready to sacrifice them to the gods. No, not *gods*, god. The Emperor. They would pray and the legions of the Empire would know their location. Maybe this would be easier, better. No matter how they were tortured or slow roasted, they wouldn't have to suffer the eternal damnation Lacy knew was awaiting one of them in the Emperor's court. Just a relatively quick death. It was a thought, a hope, really. But everything about the Mok Rork village when it came into view, laughed in the face of their hopes.

Bones littered the grounds surrounding the village, like a graveyard that rejected its occupants on blasphemous integrity. The village wall spoke no intention of disguise as the Mok Tau's had. No, this only warned others, beast and man alike, that the Mok Rork were to be feared. Hyper-raptors were kept on leash, tied tight against a wall of jagged rock, topped with skulls of some beast too gruesome to imagine alive. They were all kept only inches away from each other. Claws could graze their neighbors and spill blood, and their teeth could catch a bit of tail, but all at a safe enough distance only to antagonize each other. They were being starved, and by the looks of the guards tossing them morsels of food here and there, starved just enough to set loose on enemies in the most brutal fashion. If only the hyper-raptors had an infinite supply of blood, a scarlet moat would have encircled their village.

The village gate opened like a great maw, ready to swallow them whole. The prisoners were loosened of their dinosaur escorts, the razorbacks taken away to be tended to elsewhere, and Dex, Lacy, and crew were brought into the fire.

Stones were hurled. Vines of thorns and barbs were whipped at them as the gods and their Mok Tau warriors passed through the gauntlet. Gurg collapsed with a howl, his knee bent inward when a villager ran up with a club and rushed off with a laugh. Dex turned at the sound of pain and was met with a swift *snap-CRACK* of a whip, ripping his cheek open.

"Gu Praa!" A blue-spotted Mok Rork demanded of Dex.

Whether or not it was meant that way, Dex interpreted it as 'eyes front,' and received no further reprimand. But the spitting and foreign-tongued curses persisted until they were brought to the center of the village, where there was no humble temple like the Mok Tau's, but a terrible alter, presided over by a Mok Rork woman dressed in a scarlet robe and pierced almost entirely from head to toe with fine metals and jewels. And upon her head, a sight Lacy knew all too well.

A crown of bone ejaculated out of her head like her skull was too power-filled to fit inside under her skin.

Lacy's eyes widened in terror. She had been brought back as a prisoner to the Emperor's court. Pillars of fire ensnared her, and before her was the black pit where the mangled carcasses of the Emperor's victims were lost forever. Soon she would be placed on the platform to have her soul sucked from her body to become an eternal prisoner in His world. She fought hard, beating her feet against the ground, pulling her arms this way and that, screaming at the top of her lungs to be let free. Dex's pleas for her to remain calm were drowned out by the cheering and chanting of the Mok Rork as she was pushed closer to the Priestess in Red.

With a swift smack in the back of their knees, the captives were forced to kneel before the altar.

The priestess slowly lowered her head to face the crowd, who all quieted their chanting in anticipation of what was to come.

From the way she'd been standing and chanting, with her head held high, she looked to Dex and Lacy like her eyes were rolled to the back of her head, as if in some spiritually bound trance. But the Mok Tau knew better. From the jungle legend of the Mok Rork High Priestess, they knew the horrible face of the woman who held their lives in her hand.

Her eyes did not roll forward to look upon the prisoners. They did not reside in her head at all. From behind the hollow sockets in her face, the High Priestess felt the presence of five outliers kneeling before her. Five, that would make adequate offerings to…

"What… tribe… do you come from?" Her voice was raspy but clearer than the gurgling that the others spoke with. It was the most human voice Dex and Lacy had yet heard on this planet.

Lacy couldn't answer. The garb the priestess wore had her in a paralyzing hold.

It's over! Oh God! It's all over! The dread rang in her head, echoing in the grand and horrible temple of the Emperor, and a voice taunted back, 'There was never any hiding.'

Toork cursed again, the only sound in the jungle except for the torches burning by the altar.

The blue-spotted Mok Rork held up a hatchet to bring down on Toork's head, but the Priestess demanded he halt. She stepped down from behind the altar, walking gracefully like the lack of eyes was no hindrance at all to her vision, and took the hatchet from the eager Mok Rork.

The High Priestess brought the hatchet down into his side, turning Toork's curses into cries of pain.

Addressing the village, she bellowed, "They serve none if dead before offering. But… the suffering holds its own strength for me." Then to Toork, whose skin was already going pale, she asked "What tribe is it do you come from?"

Toork threw back his head, struggling to control his breathing and hold back the pain. Blood gushed like an overflown river from the flab of skin that hung off his side.

"Mok Tau!" Dex answered in Toork's place. "We're Mok Tau. We meant no harm. We just need to pass the Great Break."

The Priestess shot her head toward Dex. Her hollow eye sockets glared intently into him. She stepped forward slowly, but not with hesitation.

"*They* are Mok Tau. Where are you from?"

Dex looked to Lacy for an answer.

Lacy! Get in her head! Tell her to let us go!

The Priestess repeated herself. "Where… are you from?"

Her fingers wrapped around Dex's chin, forcing him to look back into her sockets.

If only he had his rucksack he could pull out the scarlet P.E.S. Maybe, he thought, it would work on the Mok Rork the same way it convinced the Mok Tau. But no, this was different! The others had seen the ship fly over them, and something about this Priestess told him she wouldn't buy into the lie easily. Either way, it was worth a shot convincing them.

With all the fortitude Dex could muster, he claimed "We come from the stars to pass judgment on the Mok Rork."

There was a collective gasp among the crowd, but the Priestess held firm.

"Hm. Judge then," she invited Dex, and backed away, up to the alter. "How would you judge? What do you see here, star man?" She waved her arms around the village, holding an air of pride in her chest.

Dex looked around at his captors and the village. It was fuller than the Mok Tau village. Sturdier huts made with more stone than wood, and primitive roadways under their feet. Even the population was larger. Where the Mok Tau had maybe one company of warriors, the Mok Tau had a battalion.

"Did I not say I would come to defeat Torro-Kaal? I judge that you have all failed at protecting this world, and have lost sight of your purpose," Dex said. "You've abandoned your brothers and your god."

His words snapped Lacy out of her shock.

"Dex…" she began but caught herself and sent him a message between their minds. *What are you saying?*

Trust me. But I could use some help if you can get in her head.

"My people have no duty to the other tribes. Mok Tau can die fighting Torro-Kaal, but Mok Rork stay strong, keep kron-kaal away."

"And what happens when you're the only tribe left? You can't defeat the beasts on your own, no matter how strong your tribe is."

Lacy, push her!

I'm trying!

The Priestess shuddered and brushed her hands down her throat and chest. "I see…"

Hope came to Dex and Lacy. Were they in her head? Had it been that simple?

"I see the demon in my presence. Did you tell these people that you were their god?"

Dex and Lacy looked at the Mok Tau. Toork was only half conscious, and Boritt was still out cold, but Gurg was aware of everything being said and his head drifted to meet his gods.

"It looks like the Mok Tau have put their faith in the wrong god!" The Priestess proclaimed with delight, and the Mok Rork laughed with her. "How many were there when you left the village? And now what is left?"

"It's more than you've done for this world!" Lacy snapped at the Priestess.

"Silence, demon! I see your mind. You would turn my people away from me, but they are not Mok Tau. Mok Rork know their true god."

The Mok Rork began their chant again, a name that neither the humans nor Mok Tau could decipher, all directed not at the sky, but at the Priestess.

No mental communication was needed between Dex and Lacy.

"I have been chosen by He to lead the people of this world. I am the one to whom he gives sight. I have seen his face and it is not yours!"

The village turned mad with walloping, croaking, and chanting, like caged animals in a zoo ready for their next meal.

Dex fought to be free of his bonds, delusionally hoping he could fight off the Mok Rork and get Lacy to freedom, but someone kicked him from behind and knocked him to the ground. Dirt puffed up into his nose and eyes, then hung in the air just above the ground.

"You all reek of evil," the Priestess sneered, then to her people, shouted, "They will be offered up! Tonight! Prepare them," she pointed to the blue-spotted Mok Rork. "I want them ripe for sacrifice."

Of all of them, save Boritt, Gurg was the most calm, maintaining his dignity as he was carried to his death. Toork, though fading in and out of consciousness, kept trying to resist the Mok Rork. Dex and Lacy, fought hard as they were dragged like pigs over to the village wall, where there stood a series of stone archways that loomed high over the prisoners like gallows.

Dex saw as they approached, the ground around the arches was strewn with sharp crystalline rocks no amount of callus could protect his feet from.

But there was no stopping the Mok Rork. The long ropes of their bindings were tossed up through hooks at the top of the archway and pulled down on the other side. Mok Rork laughed and taunted as they pulled on the ropes, bringing the band closer to the rock pit.

A Mok Rork child laughed as they removed the boots from Lacy's feet, curious as to what the stranger was wearing.

Lacy screamed as the tips of her toes dragged over the sharp rocks. It distracted Dex until he too was forced to step onto them, the bottom of his feet tearing open as he did. Toork had lost all energy by the time they reached the pit. The hatchet in his side had fallen out somewhere along their drag to the arches, and the last of his ability to fight with it. Gurg did all he could to hold it in and calm the others.

"Do not scream," he said through gritted teeth. "Do not show them pain." Sweat dripped from his brow and with every word he spoke, Gurg shivered, looking ready to explode. "Up! Pull yourself up!"

They saw as Gurg tried to grip the rope that held him and lift off a few inches from the ground, finding relief from the sharp rocks.

Dex could almost laugh at the flaw in the Mok Rork torture "device." It gave him and Lacy a short burst of energy to pull themselves up. But Toork only tried to kick at anyone who came close to him with a club or spear.

"Come on Lacy, just to the top," he tried to encourage her, but Gurg shouted, "NO! Not top!"

Lacy didn't register his demand. As her hand wrapped around the top of the arch, something sliced through her back. She lost her grip, fell, and couldn't tell what hurt worse; the rocks like glass stabbing into her feet, the torn muscles and tendons in her arms when the rope ran out of tension, or the whip across her back.

"Only little bit! They will not let you climb up!" Gurg told them.

So that was it, Dex realized. It was only torture now. Not for information or allegiance. Torture for the sake of torture, physically and mentally to make some insane sacrifice that much more satisfying to some blind lunatic.

"She's going to pray," Dex admitted to himself. "She'll call to the Emperor and he'll send in the troops."

Lacy breathed out a weak, "No…"

"Probably better this way. At least we won't become like those ghosts in his palace."

"No, Dex. That's not it at all."

Dex shot a side-eye at Lacy, all he could manage.

A mental image appeared in his head of the Emperor's court, and the frog-man phantasm amongst the rest of them.

You heard her, Lacy said, then swooned. The mental efforts she made were quickly wearing her down. But she kept going. *She… she sees herself as their guide… to his court. She's… they're not praying to anyone… other than her.*

It was a wild theory, but Dex found it hard to argue, whether out of lack of energy to do so or want to believe. The High Priestess assumed the role of their god, in the image of their race's emissary in the Emperor's court. And the power had gone to her head, right through her eyeless sockets.

Sour water was brought to them by two women, who walked

with the rigidness of Roak's assistants. Their hands and forearms were tattooed with red lines much like the High Priestesses' were and Lacy's had been when prepared for sacrifice before the Emperor. Lacy hadn't noticed, but the image stuck with Dex. Toork and Gurg drank what they could, just enough to keep their hearts beating. Even Lacy drank without arguing. Greedily, even. When it came to Dex, the water bearer took one look at him and moved on. The Mok Rork wanted to keep them just alive enough, and he was keeping up an image of strength too well.

There's... out...th-...

Lacy's voice drifted in and out of his head like a bad radio signal.

"Hey! Lacy! Talk to me! I can't keep this up if you're not with me. Come on, Darling! You're stronger than this!" And she was, he knew, but she was losing strength faster than the others.

Lacy's face was paler than Toork's, but her wounds weren't as bad as his. It was just like when she'd passed out in the village. She had the same look when she woke up and was just as dehydrated.

"Lacy," he whispered, pulling himself up an inch from the rocks until his arms gave out again. "What are you doing?"

"Where's Boritt?" She asked.

"I... I don't know. I don't know where they brought him. Stop thinking about him!"

"He'll die, Dex. We need to help him."

"*You're* dying Lacy. Whatever you're doing, stop. Get it together, he'll be okay. Just keep yourself alive."

She tried to lift her head to show she was okay, that she could handle everything being thrown at them, but the slightest movement dug her feet deeper into the sharp rocks. Tears would have trailed down her cheeks if only there was water in her to spare.

The invisible tears broke something in Dex and hardened his resolve.

The Mok Rork had mostly dispersed by then. Some of the younger ones, tails, if that was what Boritt had meant, still hung around but were mostly focused on each other. Warriors paced atop the village walls, vigilantly watching the jungle. Dex looked around, being cautious not to turn his head too much.

Through the densely packed village, Dex could just barely see the altar. Their rucksacks, at least one of them anyway, though he couldn't tell whose it was, rested at the bottom. Robbie lay next to them, under the altar, presumably having fallen out when they were tossed on the ground. Just as Dex had instructed him in the jungle, Robbie wasn't moving, wasn't speaking. If the Mok Rork hadn't noticed him yet, they'd Dex thought it was a safe bet to assume they looked over him as nothing more than a large rock.

If only he could get Robbie's attention, the ash-black robot could sneak over to them in the night-

No, we don't have that much time!

The one ruck he could see was picked up by a red hand and moved out of his line of sight. Shortly after that, candles were lit around the altar.

The next hour was filled with prodding and beating by the Mok Rork children. Gurg had held himself above the rocks well enough, but whenever their guard got bored of seeing the lack of struggle, he promptly whipped the Mok Tau back down.

Toork was all but lost. The wound in his side stopped bleeding, and his skin had turned almost totally grey.

Dex did all he could to block out the thought of losing another soldier. This one wouldn't be his fault, not like... *what was his name? Jesus Christ, I can't even remember his name!* But Toork wasn't the same. Dex was stuck too. *It wouldn't be my fault!*

The High Priestess' assistants came around again with the sour water. They approached Toork first but Dex shouted at them, "She needs help! Look! She's dying!"

The two women stopped just before Toork and eyed Dex cautiously. The first one jerked her head to the side, commanding the other to attend to Toork, then walked over to Lacy.

She studied Lacy carefully, then put a hand on her cheek. The moment her fingers made contact with Lacy's flesh, something changed in both of them.

Lacy became alert as ever.

The Mok Rork priestess' eyes opened wide and her mouth dropped open, sucking in air. Everyone in the area turned and saw the life draining from the woman, and shied away, screaming terrified of whatever dark magic this strange-looking prisoner was using.

One of the guards was quick to intervene, pulling the priestess away from Lacy before she withered away to nothing but bone, then threatened to whip Lacy again, but a haunting raspy voice held him back.

"Stop! She is ready," The High Priestess said to the guard. "Bring her to my table."

Lacy's bonds were cut and she fell onto the sharp rocks. Dex instinctively tried to catch her fall even though he was still stuck. But Lacy needed no help. She showed no sign of pain when her hands and knees hit the rock. In fact, she fell with the grace of jumping on a soft mattress, and Dex was the only one to notice.

"Come. Do not touch her," The High Priestess instructed.

The guard cautiously picked up the rope tied to Lacy's wrists and ordered she follow.

Lacy rose to her feet in a ghostly way, like she weighed nothing. Her skin radiated again, and she had a look in her starry eyes like she'd not a care in the world.

I trust you Dex. Make me look good.

He had no idea what she meant. *Look good how? What's your plan?* But all he heard in return was a playful laugh.

Dex almost shouted at her for a straight answer but held himself back. There was a reason she didn't say it out loud. He'd have to trust in her.

One of the Mok Rork children helped the priestess up. She shivered and had a glassy look about her, staring straight ahead, unaware that the child was next to her. The child said something in their native tongue, possibly asking the priestess if she was okay, but to no response. Slowly, the priestess turned and walked gingerly back to wherever it was she came from.

Once out of sight, the remaining Mok Rork took one last look at Dex and the other prisoners and fled the scene, not wanting to be the next victim of dark magic.

Even Toork and Gurg watched Dex with some apprehension.

But Dex was focused on a sign of what was to come next.

The horn blew high above them. From all around, villagers made their way to the village center, the altar. One guard stayed behind to watch the prisoners.

Whatever it is you're planning, Lacy, let me know now, Dex thought, not knowing if Lacy was reading him.

Going against the crowds, the priestess returned once again. Her walk was a bit more normal than when she left, but the glassy look remained, like there wasn't much going on in her head. But it was what was in her hand that caught Dex's attention.

With a hollowness in her voice, she told the guard, "Let him down."

The guard didn't hesitate.

Dex dropped to the ground, opening fresh wounds on the rocks. He could barely hold back screaming through the pain. But one wrong move, one shout could throw off Lacy's unshared plan. He gritted his teeth and pulled himself out of the rock pit.

The guard asked something in their language and gestured at Toork and Gurg.

The priestess shook her head. "They stay. For now."

Dex took a moment to breathe before standing, thanking whoever was listening for the softness of the dirt below him. He could almost rub his wound in it like a pillow if only he wouldn't get a deadly infection. But there was no time to relax. Lacy had a job for him, and it looked like she'd sent him the tools to do it.

* * *

A thousand glowing eyes watched Lacy kneel atop the altar. She swayed like a gentle breeze from left to right, lit by the glow of torches. When it came to being a sacrificial offering, she ranked this experience above the previous, because here at least, she was looking down on her audience. The idea was humorous even, how fast she'd gone from sacrifice to god, to sacrifice again.

What a wild universe this is... she giggled.

Her laughter stirred the audience. What power did this woman hold that she could laugh in the face of death?

"Enough of this," the High Priestess admonished Lacy. "My people!" She threw her arms wide and stepped in front of the altar. "This creature has claimed to be your god. But you saw how she tried to kill our Burrgip! Have you anything to say for yourself?"

Lacy lifted her head toward the sky, with her eyes closed and a soft smile on her face. She slowly raised her hands, palms upward, and said, "I have come to free you all from the evil of this world." Her voice carried across the crowd like a summer wind. There was tenderness in it, that quickly turned to steel when she opened her eyes and glared at the Mok Rork. "You saw how I nearly killed your priestess. I could with no more difficulty do that to *each* and *every* one of you this very moment!" She traced a sharp finger across the crowd.

Then, underneath the sound boom of her voice, an eerie melody crept into their ears...

* * *

Dex could only faintly hear what was being said down below at the altar.

"Don't start too soon, Lacy," he whispered to himself, data tablet in hand. He tapped on it vigorously, trying to figure out how to operate the thing.

It was a miracle that the priestess had managed to lead him to the perch unquestioned by other villagers. She left him with Lacy's ruck and returned without a word to rejoin the rest of the village.

From the moment he felt the data tablet in the ruck, he knew exactly what she wanted of him. But now came the moment of truth, and he still had no idea how to use it.

Down below, Lacy was instructed to step onto the altar surrounded by torches.

The glow of the fire looked so warm compared to the chill wind that blew against him up in the trees.

The wind. Cold. The jacket!

Dex berated himself for not thinking of it sooner. He scrounged through the ruck to find his jacket, then pulled two small transparent items out. Jaskek's contact lenses.

He couldn't think about how unsanitary the act was and slid them under his eyelids. Visuals appeared instantly on the data tablet, the *Silent Horizon*'s complete musical library, just as Lacy had left it, and the perfect song for the occasion wasn't hard to find.

Everything was coming together in pure Lacy fashion.

Dex held the tablet up to the mouthpiece of the horn. Though low to the jungle floor, the Mok Rork were about to experience… "A Night on Bald Mountain."

* * *

The blood of the Mok Rork ran cold. When retelling their children of that night, some would say the ghosts of their enemies reached through the ground to pull them into an early grave. They all jittered around anxiously, feeling that at any moment their neighbor would become possessed, or be drained like Burrgip, the priestess. The distance between the front row of the crowd and the altar grew a meter.

"Stop this," The High Priestess demanded. "Stop this dark magic."

Lacy ignored the woman. "Even if you killed me now, I would only return to haunt this village until the end of days. You will never know peace, your crops will die, and your hunters will never return from the jungle! Prey for the Kron-Kaal!"

"Stop this, demon!"

"See now, the power I have over nature, as I give life to this rock!"

Burrgip the priestess approached the altar, looking from Lacy to the High Priestess. The glassy non-present visage had been replaced by a fear driven by self-preservation. Both of the women could easily kill her, but one of them had true power. One of them had been in her head and made her do things. The other had hurt her plenty, mutilated even, at times, but it was nothing like what was done by this demon… witch… god?

The High Priestess pulled out a knife from a hidden sheath beneath her gown. "Stay back, Burrgip. Don't listen to this demon."

Burrgip turned to the crowd for an answer, but they were as terrified as she was. Could this woman really give life to a rock?

If it was a trick, that would be that, and the High Priestess' knife would find its way into both her neck and the demon's. But if she did nothing, and the woman on the altar was a demon, all of their fates would be worse, on an eternal level.

Burrgip slowly stepped closer to the altar and picked up the rock.

Robbie was powered low, with his arms and legs locked in place as close to his small body as they could be.

The music lulled as Burrgip placed Robbie on the altar.

"Thank you, sweetie," Lacy said to Burrgip with a wink.

The eerie strings teased a magical air.

Lacy swished her hands over the robot in rhythm with the music.

"Time to wake up buddy," Lacy whispered. "Slowly."

Robbie's eye turned on. He saw how Lacy's hands moved, and as she told him, slowly began to sway with them.

The Mok Rork villagers gasped.

Lacy had to hold back a laugh.

The High Priestess had had enough. With a tight grip on the knife, she lunged for Lacy.

From the corner of her eye, she saw the attack come and held out a hand. "You know my power, Morgup! Keep that knife far from me."

How she knew the High Priestess' name shocked all who heard it, even Lacy.

Morgup the High Priestess dropped the knife. Her jaw hung open in terror. How... what else did the demon know about her? The things she'd done in secret, the blasphemes she'd spoken in her dark prayers to herself... how she'd stolen glory from... Him... the God in Red. Morgup saw then the colors in the demon's bag. Could she really have been sent for judgment?

"See now! I give you..." Lacy, with one hand holding back the High Priestess, put her other on Robbie's chest.

"LIFE!"

The crowd gasped as Robbie raised his arms and sat up like a monster from an evil scientist's lab.

"Life!" Lacy repeated!

Morgup fell back, into the crowd.

"It cannot be! This is a trick! A trick!" Morgup shouted, trying to convince herself. Although she knew better, she screamed hysterically, shaking the villagers around her, "It is as I said! A demon! Come to curse us!"

The Mok Rork backed away from her, fearful of her touch. They could all feel the wrath of the woman on the altar directed solely at Morgup, and none wanted to be caught in it.

"If you are so powerful, Morgup, show us!" Lacy taunted.

"I... I... I..."

"Yes, *you*. You have poisoned this place for too long. And I have come for the people, to free them from the evil of this world. Evil... like... *you*..."

Lacy pointed at Morgup, and the High Priestess dropped dead.

Through her mind's eye, Morgup saw a bright red light, the wrath of god, blazing before her. Her head burned, and all went black.

The music stopped. All went silent in the village.

Lacy knelt, frozen for a moment, then turned to look at the trees behind her. High above the border wall of the village, Dex was perched by the horn, blaster in hand.

28. The Great Break

The jubilations the Mok Rork held for the arrival of their gods were too macabre for Dex and Lacy to handle. Unlike the Mok Tau's quiet and pensive offering of gifts, this new tribe which was keen on exaggerated displays of power and willingness to torture prisoners, threw a raucous party, abundant with…offerings.

Lacy dismissed herself from the sight of an animal calf being slaughtered in her honor to attend to their wounded Mok Tau companions.

Dex sat back a little while. There was no tribal or spiritual leader to teach him about the tribe's traditions, though, what traditions does one even have for a god's arrival? For all it counted, Dex thought he could say whatever he wanted and it would become a tradition. But Lacy wouldn't have gone with it, and he had no need to assert himself any more than their journey to Torro-Kaal demanded.

So, he sat through a series of blood offerings, waiting until it died down and he could retreat to join Lacy and the others.

Robbie stayed behind. Being worshiped as a miracle from the gods and served platter after platter of exotic food was too good to turn down, even if he couldn't eat them.

Lacy knelt at Boritt's bedside. Toork and Gurg lay in cots next to him. Their feet were wrapped, along with Toork's side. The priestesses attended to them in the low candlelight of the hut. When Dex pulled the portiere to the side and entered the hut, his first thought was a field hospital from war films, a sight he'd always considered himself lucky to not have seen in person, until now.

The color was finally returning to Boritt's skin. His chest rose and fell at a steady pace. It lightened the load that had been weighing Dex's spirit down, but the rest of the room didn't reciprocate his optimism.

Lacy caught a glimpse of Dex and held a finger to her lips.

He nodded, sidling toward Lacy, then knelt beside her and put a hand on Boritt's arm. The amputee jerked unconsciously.

"Tired of being a god?" Dex whispered.

She raised her eyes to the priestesses, conscious of Dex's hazardous words. The women showed either no concern for the statement or ignorance of it. Lacy then stood and walked over to the women. "You've done enough for them tonight," she said. "Enjoy the celebration. Please," she smiled earnestly.

The priestesses nodded and left the hut.

For a full minute, the only sound in the room was the faint flicker and crackle of the candles. The revelry outside came through in muted hums. Lacy stood over Toork with her hands on her hips.

Dex knew better than to be the first to speak.

"I don't want to argue about what happened tonight." Reluctant resolve held her voice captive.

Another long moment passed before Dex navigated those treacherous waters.

"I'm sorry, Lacy," he paused. "But, I'm going to keep us safe. At all costs."

She turned and met his bold eyes. "At all costs?"

He nodded.

"I know she hurt us. What you did was…"

Dex stood, waiting for her to finish.

"I want to help this world. I know we have to do what we can to survive. I just don't want to lose control."

"Lose control of what? This show can only last for so long, and that time's comin' up soon."

"Not that, Dex." She brushed a strand of hair out of her face. The stars in her eyes shined bright, drawing Dex closer. "I know all you've done for us. I know the choices you've made haven't been easy. And I… I just don't want them to become you." She put a hand on his cheek. Stubble scratched her hand.

"What do you think's going to happen to me?"

She dropped her head, shielding herself from the hurt behind his eyes.

"Lacy," he said with a finger and thumb under her chin. "It's still me. It will always be me. The world's changing beyond our control, but I promise you, there will always be one constant. That's us." He lifted her chin. "No matter what happens, I will never let you down."

'At all costs' replayed in her mind. They wouldn't be in this village, Boritt would still have his legs, and Dex wouldn't have taken the life of a defenseless woman if she hadn't pushed them to help the Mok Tau… if she'd let them go home.

"We'll be there soon." he said, reading her face.

"We'll never be able to leave this behind us." Tears welled up in her eyes.

"Yes, we will. Once we're home and tell everyone what's out here, someone else can deal with it. Earth will be ready. We'll've earned that retirement," he tried joking, but Lacy's expression remained the same.

When she said nothing, he pulled her tightly into his arms. Lacy's head pressed against his chest. His heartbeat resounded in her ears.

"I just want to go home…"

The planet would have flooded with her tears if Dex weren't there to wipe them away.

* * *

The razorbacks were near impossible to mount, slick with the heavy pre-dawn dew.

"Are you sure you do not wish us to wake Mok Tau?" Juruuk the priestess posed.

"No," Dex grunted and hoisted himself onto the alien dinosaur then continued with Juruuk, "They've been through enough. Tend to their wounds until we return."

The blue-spotted Mok Rork rode his razorback up to the side of Dex's. "We leave now if you are to make it across Great Break. You are losing moon."

Gravity hadn't felt lighter that morning, but it didn't feel heavier either.

"We leave when the lady's ready. Everything still in the packs, darling?"

Lacy sat on a stump going through her pack. Dew streamed down her face and arms, dripping into the pack. Robbie sat beside her, looking through Dex's, making sure there was still enough room for himself in there.

"Everything and more," Lacy confirmed, holding up freshly added Mok Rork MREs.

"Beetles?"

Lacy sniffed and recoiled.

"Wonderful. All right, if that's everything, let's get going."

"Come on little buddy." Lacy picked up Robbie in her arms and joined Dex, after a few failed mounting attempts, on the razorback. One large ivory spike separated them, but it was something to hold onto.

Lacy looked back at the village one last time as the small party resumed their journey to Torro-Kaal.

"They'll be *fine*," Dex reassured her. "Better here at least than if they came any further."

Lacy still worried.

"They'll be fine. We can make our own way once we cross the Break. Blue guy told me the way."

"You didn't get his name?"

Dex shrugged with the trudging of the razorback. "This wet rag? No," he laughed. "The gods will not remember this one."

Lacy half playfully, half annoyedly smacked Dex's back. He grabbed her hand as she did and pulled it close to kiss her fingers.

The distance between her and the Mok Tau they left behind pulled on Lacy's heart like elastic being stretched beyond its limit. In a way, she felt a parental responsibility to them. They had trusted her and Dex as higher powers anyway. And now all that was left was their original three. At the very least, Boritt, Toork, and Gurg still had a chance to go home.

The new party of travelers rode their razorbacks in silence for the long journey to the Great Break, where Boritt said it would have taken two, maybe three days if they were held up, to reach, they'd make it just before nightfall.

As they stepped out of the tree line, the open air overcame

their senses like a tidal wave of clarity. The humidity of the jungle vanished, and a warm breeze rustled their hair. After over a week in the jungle, the sight of the open sky with the sun beginning to set far to their left, felt like they stepped into another world. But when Dex looked out across the Great Break, his spirits returned to the jungle.

Seeing the Great Break from space, the thick system of roots and vines that held the two halves of the planet together, was awe-inspiring, something he hadn't even fathomed seeing in the pictures. Having to cross it now though, one wrong step and he would never see the light of day again. Up at ground level, thin strips of vine ran out and down into the break, guiding toward the thicker roots that took the brunt of the planet's weight. That, Dex saw, fifty to one hundred feet below ground level, would be safest to walk. And it was clear now why the Mok Tau waited for the moons to be in the right position for the journey. From the top of the Break, it looked dense enough to traverse like any other part of the jungle. But tilt your head and squint your eyes just enough this way, and the gaps between each planetary root, another hundred or so feet.

Hope in the journey could have still been had if they couldn't see the other side. But no, instead, rising above the horizon was the peak of Torro-Kaal's mountain, mocking them. *Look how far you'll go, just to walk back into my hands.*

"Almost there," Dex said, half to himself, and dismounted the razorback.

The blue-spotted Mok Rork began to dismount as well but Dex stopped him and waved to go back to the village.

"What are you doing?" Lacy asked as she, too, dismounted the beast.

"He was right. Mountain's right there. We don't need a guide anymore." He took the packs off of the beast's back and gave it a gentle smack.

The razorback sauntered off to join the rest of the pack.

"Come on," Dex continued. "We've still got a little bit of light. Let's get a feel for this thing before we bed down."

Dex looked over the edge of the Break, planning a route.

"Here, might wanna put Robbie back in the ruck." He opened up his sack.

"Let's wait until tomorrow," Lacy pleaded. "We've only got another hour or so of light anyway.

Dex shook his head. "Trust me, Darling, gotta count our blessings."

Lacy smirked at the comment.

"We got off easy with that ride, and I don't want it going to waste. When that moon passes by, we'll have a much harder time coming back over."

"And you expect we'll be sleeping down there tonight?"

"Either tonight or tomorrow." Dex helped Robbie into the pack.

"Do I have a say in this?" Robbie asked politely.

"Luggage doesn't get a vote. If you want to walk, speak your peace. Otherwise, get comfy," Dex joked. With Robbie in tow, Dex tested the vines that hung over the cliff, looking for one sturdy enough to hold their weight.

"Yes you do, Robbie. You have just as much say as the rest of us," Lacy shot back, in a playful challenge of Dex's decree.

He paused with one foot on the edge, waiting for Robbie to give his input.

"I think…" Robbie began.

"You've got ten seconds to make up your mind or I'm leaving you up here," Dex threatened like he was telling a child to finish their chores.

Robbie said to Lacy as if Dex couldn't hear, "I think Dex will go with or without us. I say we go with him."

Lacy rolled her eyes. "He would never leave us behind," she said, grabbing an uncomfortably squishy, yet coarse vine. The vine molded in her hand like a pillow, and when she pulled on it, her hand was firmly held in place. Not an inch gave to slipping or sliding.

She looked down over the ledge. Dex had already begun his descent and had a good fifteen feet on her, making his way down to the nearest planetary root. The distance from where she scaled the ledge to the root wasn't bad at all, just a couple dozen feet, but past that if she slipped? Anxiety inducing.

Lacy focused strictly on the wall in front of her, trying to ignore the drop.

"You'll be fine, Lacy," Dex called. "Plenty of room to walk around down here."

She peeked down again and saw Dex taking his first step onto the root. Inch by careful inch, Lacy lowered herself down the vine. "Should have taken the ship! Should have taken the ship!" She whisper-shouted to herself.

"Empire'd get us, baby," Dex shouted up at her.

"Yeah well, I haven't seen a whole lot of them patrolling the jungle. Have you?"

Dex laughed.

"Quit it! I can't focus with you laughing at me. Ah!" Out of the cliffside, a crablike insect crawled, pinching its claws in front of her face. Lacy reflexively pushed off the wall, swinging out, and back it.

"Watch it, Lacy!" Dex shouted as if his words could stop her from crashing into the cliff.

She saved herself, stamping her feet hard into the wall, but on her impact, dirt shook off the wall, and the crab's neighbors came out.

They skittered every which way, in a frenzy over the disturbance, and snipped at Lacy's feet as she tried to stomp them.

"Ignore them!" Dex called. "Just get down here."

Lacy didn't hear him. With every stomp, another crab snipped at her boots or latched on to them. They were quickly shredded to ribbons, and the more that climbed onto her, the more Lacy tried to fight them off. One crawled up her leg, and Lacy swatted the bug. The thing splattered against her leg, spraying searing bug guts on her skin. In shock at the pain, Lacy let her grip loose from the vine.

She screamed. And fell.

"DEX! HELP!"

"Lacy," Dex said bluntly, already holding her in his arms. "You're fine."

Lacy opened her eyes. It'd only been a few feet to fall. The crabs were already ignoring her and burrowing back into the cliffside.

"Ugh. I hate heights. I didn't think I did, but I do now."

Dex put her back on her feet. "You'll be fine. I'll always be here to catch you," he said, planting a kiss on her forehead. Then, taking her hand, he led her across the Great Break.

"OOH!" Lacy almost jumped at the feel of nature on her exposed feet.

"You'll get used to it. But you owe me a new pair of boots."

They walked for an hour before it became too dark to walk safely across the planetary root. Scattered across the root were dells that Dex determined were safe enough to sleep in without rolling off in their sleep.

"What a way to go that would be," Dex pondered, looking again over the side, wondering if he'd wake up before he met his death, splattered against some other massive root, or if he'd sleep peacefully through it.

"I'm trying not to think about it," Lacy said. She took the jacket out of her ruck to use as a blanket and molded the sack to lay comfortably on as a pillow. "Are we pulling security tonight?"

Dex exhaled slowly. "We should. Don't know what lives down here. But with just three of us taking shifts…"

Lacy pursed her lips. Their old rotation gave everyone plenty of time to sleep, but now, a six-hour shift would drive her insane.

With the sweetest voice possible, Lacy asked, "Robbie? Do you mind watching out for us tonight?"

Robbie lay in the ruck, pulling himself deeper in like he was hiding under a blanket. "Do I still have free will?" he asked sincerely.

"Yes, buddy," Lacy giggled.

The laugh caught Dex's full attention. The night before and well into the morning, she'd been torn up over everything that happened in the Mok Rork village. It amazed him how she could so easily find happiness again with tragedy looming so close behind them.

God, I love you, he thought, hoping she was hearing him.

Lacy's eyes met his. Her lips curved into a cheesy smile, and her cheeks flushed. She puffed for a silent guppie kiss, and Dex returned the favor.

"Since I have a choice, I will take watch over you for the night and wake you up very early."

"Not until there's light," Dex instructed as he lay down next to Lacy. "I want to sleep in for once."

"Ha, like these nights aren't long enough already," Lacy chid-

"They never are when I'm next to you." Dex kissed her and they said their goodnights.

Lacy closed her eyes and slept, nestled in Dex's arms.

He looked up at the open sky, the stars and the two moons of the jungle planet. *What had Boritt called it? Taka... Tora...* The name felt so familiar, right on the tip of his tongue. In fact, so much about this place had been familiar, and rightfully so. Even the moon above them, he felt it watching him, looking for him.

Dex rolled into Lacy to avoid the moon's glare. He closed his eyes tight, willing himself to fall asleep.

Somewhere far off, creatures were gibbering like apes. They hadn't started making themselves known until the sun was gone. It made Dex wish his dad could have taught him to hunt when he was younger.

Lacy slept undisturbed by the gibbering. Dex bided his time, reading the pocket bible until sleep forced its way into him, and he once again saw the Valley.

* * *

"I miss the boys," Lacy sighed.

Ahead of her, Dex harrumphed. "They're doing all right." He kept his attention on Robbie, who had decided that morning he could walk on his own. The planetary root they traversed was wide, but both he and Lacy were cautious of Robbie's ability to keep his balance.

"I'm sure they're fine, that's not what I said. I said I miss them."

"Yeah..."

They took a few more steps before Lacy prodded him. "What about you?"

"Huh?"

"Don't you miss them at all?"

"Darling, they're fine-"

"-I know they're fine-"

"- and they're better off back there than they are here with us, so no. For the sake of their safety, no, I don't miss them. It's been a day," he tried to sound light-hearted saying it. "I'm not going to miss someone after just one day." Dex brushed aside a vine that hung in his way.

"What about you Robbie?" Lacy asked, hoping at least the robot would be on her side.

Robbie shrugged. "I do not think they liked me."

"What? Why would you ever think that?"

Dex cut in. "Probably because their primitive minds can't comprehend him. Just another mystery of the gods."

"Rude," Lacy teased, forcing a smile on Dex's face she couldn't see but could feel.

"It may have been that," Robbie said. "They didn't talk to me."

"You were also in my ruck for so long, they probably forgot you were there. I did a few times." Thinking again of the ruck, Dex readjusted the one on his back. He'd swapped with Lacy to give her a reprieve from the slowly increasing weight.

"Think we'll make it back on time? You know, for the moon."

"I hope so- Hey! Robbie! Away from the ledge," Dex scolded.

Robbie stopped where he was, inching close to the ledge. "How far down do you think it goes?"

Dex jumped forward and took the robot's claw. "Too far," he said quickly. "Do I have to put you back in the ruck?"

Behind them Lacy giggled, picturing Dex and Robbie as a parent and child.

"Away from there," Dex pulled.

"Or you're grounded!" Lacy added.

"Yeah, you're- what?"

Lacy gave a cute smirk-and-shrug.

"I just thought an alternate route would be optimal." Robbie offered.

"Yeah? Why's that?" Dex asked. Taking navigation advice from a robot somehow sounded like a worse idea than taking it from a lieutenant.

But it wasn't Robbie who had to answer.

"He's right," Lacy said, putting a hand on Dex's shoulder.

"Something's blocking the path. Look." Up ahead something dark and fluid wrapped around the planetary root.

Dex slowly reached for his blaster and asked in a hushed voice, "Another kron-kaal?"

"Maybe. Don't really care to find out." She looked back the way they came, letting the possibility of doubling back to find another route settle in her mind.

"Me neither," Dex agreed. He looked about, partially on Lacy's same train of thought, but going back now would lose them too much time. "Here, let me try something. I think I see why they wait for the moon to cross this," Dex said kneeling down and instructing Lacy to do the same.

"Why? What are you thinking?"

"Give me your ruck." Before she could acknowledge him, Dex was helping her take the rucksack off her back and traded with her. He then put Robbie back in his place. "We're not supposed to ride this trail the whole way. Come on, you wanted an adventure, right?" He flashed her a smile.

"Dex..." She pushed sternly.

He slung the rucksack with Robbie onto his back and gave Lacy a quick kiss on the cheek.

"Dex!" Lacy shouted this time as Dex terrified her with a running jump off the root.

He lunged out as far as he could, the low gravity helping him glide farther than the greatest Olympic athlete on Earth, and caught a vine.

Lacy clapped her hands over her face, leaving just the smallest crack between her fingers to see the insanity before her. Even if she shouted again for him, Dex wouldn't hear. His own shouts of excitement were too loud.

Dex swung on the vine, and as it came to the height of its swing, he leapt to another and leapt a final time to reach another thick planetary root. He hit the ground with a fall that would have shattered his bones back on Earth, but here, he felt like a comic book hero. Adrenaline pumped through his veins. It was like their escape from the palace-city, swinging over the collapsed bridge, but here there was no one shooting at them. It was, against all reason, fun.

In less than ten seconds, he'd crossed a two-hundred-foot chasm and dropped fifty feet. *And God, do I want to do that again!*

Lacy, still on the first root, didn't feel the same. "What in the hell is wrong with you?!" She shouted.

"It's fun! Try it! Look, even Robbie liked it!" Over his shoulder, Dex asked Robbie, "How ya feeling little buddy?"

"If I still have a vote, I would not like to do that again."

"Yeah well, you don't get a vote unless Lacy's around," Dex teased.

Robbie raised his speaker volume, "IT IS A VERY GOOD TIME. NOT AT ALL TERRIFYING. PLEASE COME HERE AND SAVE ME!"

Lacy dropped her shoulders. Fear left her, and annoyance took over. "That's manipulative, Dex!"

Dex laughed. "It's the swing or that!" Dex pointed his blaster at the black mass that slithered around Lacy's root.

She considered for a moment. *It's probably not one of the kron-kaal anyway. Just weird alien moss. Dex is just being rash.* Lacy bent down and broke off a branch from the root.

At that distance, it was tough to see for certain what she was doing, but Dex knew her well enough. "Don't try it! Just-"

She threw the branch, hitting her mark on the mass.

The thing rose up in a wave, and dropped down a dozen feet closer, moving toward her like something from the creature features Lacy detested. *The Attack of the Killer Moss!*

Shit! She mentally shouted, unknowingly sending it to Dex.

"Swing, baby!"

Lacy looked back once, the way they came, then to Dex. She gritted her teeth and clenched her fists.

The creature wove closer, rising slowly, then crashing down hard and fast, shaking the whole root.

"COME ON!" Dex shouted again!

"Oh, goddamn it!" Lacy muttered and ran to the side of the root, leapt off, and soared over through the Great Break. The vine swung to its height, and Dex shouted at her to jump, but she held on tight and let the vine carry her back.

"Lacy! You have to jump!"

The wind whipped her back, throwing her hair into her face. She couldn't hear anything Dex was shouting at her. On the forward swing, her vision was cleared and she saw Dex and Robbie, waving her over. The vine crested again, and she let fate decide what happened next.

She let go, letting her momentum throw her toward the next vine. It swung to meet her, still moving from Dex's swing.

"I'll tell you when to let go! Ready... now!"

Lacy jumped when Dex told her to and flew right into his arms.

She shook violently with adrenaline.

"Look who's Tarzan now," Dex joked, knowing it would earn him a smack on the chest or shoulder but not caring.

"I am NOT Tarzan!" she said, lightly hitting his breast.

There it is, Dex thought.

"You Tarzan..."

Dex looked down, pleasantly surprised at her comment.

"You Tarzan. Me Jane," her laugh shook.

"All right, Jane... how's about we get through this jungle?" He looked up, searching for the next vine to swing from.

"How's about we *walk* a little more?" She gestured along the path the planetary root provided. It was thinner than the last one they walked, and sleep didn't look like it would be an option here, as it thinned out down the line. If they were lucky, as Lacy hoped, they wouldn't have to spend another night worrying if they would plummet to their deaths.

"For now," Dex agreed, almost reluctantly. He'd discovered the thrill of a childhood dream, swinging like an ape-man through the jungle, and was already eager for more.

Lacy walked cautiously along the root. From where they landed, it looked like they'd cross plenty of ground before it became too thin to cross, but that was only an illusion. Before they knew it, they were both walking with their arms out wide for balance. Each step quickly became a gamble. Was that patch of green slippery moss or the color of the root's surface? Lacy walked ahead, Dex only two feet behind her at most to catch her if she slipped.

Rescue came in the form of a withering and winding branch

above them, an offshoot of a stronger vein. Dex boosted Lacy's jump, giving her the extra foot she needed to reach the twelve-foot-high branch. She clung to the branch like a pull-up bar, testing its strength before shimmying to the body of the root.

Dex followed only after she'd pulled herself to a safe spot.

It carried on like that for the next few hours. The black gooey moss, or the orange blobs Boritt had warned them not to eat, would be in their way and they'd swing or jump to another root. Their path would thin out or be too rotted away to cross, swing or jump to the next.

It drained them fast, but Dex ensured they pushed on. "Don't wanna lose the moon," he'd constantly remind her. The mantra would give her back a little extra energy. He was right, trying to trek through all this without the low gravity would be near impossible. And the further they got into it, she thought even the Mok Tau with their incredible agility and strong legs would have trouble getting through. That's why Boritt wanted to, no, *needed* to come on the mission.

Boritt, who would never cross the Great Break now.

"Dex... Dex hold on." Lacy was breathing heavily, totally worn out.

"Just a little further, Lacy. Don't wanna lose the moon."

Lacy stopped where she was. "Dex. We need to eat."

He kept on, not noticing she wasn't following. "We'll eat in a bit. Just a li-"

"Now, Dex. Come here, sit."

He looked over his shoulder, still walking, and saw her taking a seat. Her legs hung over the side of the root. At the pat of her hand on the ground, he reluctantly stopped.

"All right, but let's eat fast. I think I can see the other side."

Lacy offered him a smile that said, 'I know you're lying.' "Eat," she repeated, already taking their rations out of her ruck.

"Fine," Dex sighed. "Let's not take too long though, okay?"

Lacy ignored the request. For how hard they'd been pushing that day, she had no problem taking her sweet time to "enjoy" their lunch.

After nearly a week of the Mok Tau MREs, Lacy had given up complaining about having to eat the alien bugs. She still would have gladly stuck to the horribly dry crackers, but these would do.

"Shame they don't put cigarettes in these things anymore," Dex said, thinking about being in the Army back on Earth. Just before the start of the Eurasian War, there'd been a push to ban them from all military use. Gotta keep that top-notch fighting force. It hadn't gone well with the troops and retention. For many, it was equal to banning coffee from MREs. Probably would have lost the war too if there hadn't been such extreme push-back on that one.

"Thinking of picking up the habit now?" Lacy asked, taking a scoop of bug meat in her fingers.

"Eh, wouldn't say no to a cigar when we're done with this. Nice tall bottle of Irish Whiskey."

"And a beach somewhere warm?"

Beside her, a small blue and orange creature tiptoed toward her, walking on two legs. The thing was only three or four inches tall with a bulbous head. A tuk, by the way the Mok Tau had described the little food-stealing creatures. It was so cute with its big eyes, Lacy felt she just had to sneak it a piece of food before Dex noticed. "Here you go," she whispered.

Dex swallowed his next bite, then said, "No. I need a break from the heat. I'm thinking somewhere cold next."

Lacy laughed, wiping her mouth. "How about a snow planet then? We can bundle up close and never leave the house."

"Uh uh, that's a little much. Not the bundling up close part," he winked. "But no ice planets, no desert planets…"

The Valley…

"Maybe… we could go somewhere just…" the right word eluded him. The Valley from the vision wasn't something he could describe physically; it was an emotion.

But Lacy, he realized, wasn't listening anymore. He turned and looked her way, and saw her giggling as the tiny creature nibbled at their rations.

"What the hell is this?" he asked, wanting to be mad or annoyed, but unable to with Lacy smiling as she did.

"He's just a cute little guy!" She laughed.

"He's not 'just a little guy,' he's the reason we ran out of rations the other day. Skat!" He waved away the little tuk, but the creature looked up at him with its big beady eyes, holding a piece of meat close to its mouth.

"Go on, get!"

The beady eyes stared.

"He's like a little puppy. We should keep him," Lacy said.

"Nope. Vetoing that right now," Dex stood. "We've already taken on too many strays," he thumbed Robbie. "But at least this one won't steal all our food."

"That is true," Robbie agreed. "I do not require food."

Lacy wrapped up her leftovers in the leaf they came in and stuck them back in her ruck. She then carefully stood and followed behind Dex.

The tuk followed the three of them.

"What do you require anyway?" Lacy asked, realizing they had never discussed Robbie's power system.

"My units run on a miniature nuclear cell. It has a very long span. Many months."

"And how do we fuel it?" Concern grew in Lacy. They didn't have anything on the ship except for the ship itself that could fuel a nuclear reactor.

"It is only a single-use cell," Robbie said plainly.

"Hold on, single-use? You mean that's-"

"Lacy," Dex interrupted. "Don't give him an existential crisis. No one needs that right now."

But questions swirled in her head. How old was Robbie? How many months did they have left with him? How could they extend his battery life? She could probably find a way to replace it, right? What if he shut down now? Right there in the middle of the planetary root?

"Lacy!"

Dex's exclamation brought her back to reality.

"I can hear you. Don't think about it. He'll be fine."

"I'll be fine." Robbie agreed. Both Dex and Lacy had noted how he spoke, more casually than his, for lack of better words, robotic manner, using "I'll" instead of "I will."

Their short break was far from what Lacy, and Dex (although he wouldn't admit it), needed to properly recover. With every root they crossed over to, they seemed to descend a little further into the chasm, until it was like they were back in the jungle. Goodbye, blue sky.

Dex eventually blocked out Lacy's not-so-subtle attempts at dropping their pick-up little bits of cracker.

When they came upon another blocked path and had to swing again, Dex was thankful for the universe telling Lacy it was time to leave the tuk behind. She didn't put up a fight or ask to let their fellow traveler in her ruck, just gave the little guy a pat on the head and a soft goodbye.

Dex promised he'd get her one on the way back as if there were a tuk adoption center on the road to the Mok Tau village. But the adoption center wouldn't be necessary. Just ten minutes after abandoning the creature, they heard loud rustling and thumping behind them, and when Lacy turned around to investigate, she saw the tuk right there, looking up at her with hungry, beady eyes.

"How'd you get here?" she asked, talking like the tuk was a child or a dog, but seriously confused. There was no way it could have made the leaps onto and off the vine.

Dex, on the other hand, questioned how it made so much noise.

Their answer came to them in the form of a familiar voice. "We do not question tuk. Where there is food, tuk will appear."

"Toork!" Lacy exclaimed. "Gurg! What- what are you doing here?"

The two Mok Tau dropped down onto the root from another, not far above Dex and Lacy. Toork strained when he landed, gripping his side. Purple leaves wrapped around his body and covered his wound.

"We sorry. Missed move out. Overslept," Gurg answered for the both of them.

Dex stepped forward. "No, no you guys didn't have to- you weren't supposed to come!"

"But we are. We come, all the way to Torro-Kaal. We can not let down our-"

"Don't say it," Dex cut him off, then looked at Lacy. The loyalty the Mok Tau showed was far too much for the lie he and Lacy had let go on for too long.

She nodded, seeing in his eyes where his intentions lay.

Dex took a deep breath. "Listen… Toork… Gurg…" He took his time saying their names, looking them directly in the eye as he did. "Lacy and I need to tell you something." The admission stuck like a frog in his throat. "We… we lied to you. See, we're not… gods."

He waited for their spear to jab forward and stick them, but the Mok Tau seemed unaffected.

"We came from the stars, yes, but we didn't know about this place until we got here. We never promised your people anything or sent you visions. That wasn't us. We just got lost… stuck. There's no divine reason for any of this. I'm sorry, but we're only here so that we can get home too."

Toork and Gurg exchanged a look, one neither Dex nor Lacy could discern through their alien features. Then, Toork stepped closer to Dex, and took the spear from him. He held it up, inspecting the leaves tied to it, one more than it had when he'd given it to the man from the stars. Leaves, that remembered the dead.

"We know. You are not gods. But when you come to us, some thing change in Mok Tau village. I saw in you… when you take this… you would not forget, like Mok Tau must. I knew I was right, when you return again to village. I know now, you are not gods. But I do believe, one has sent you." He held out the spear for Dex to take back. "We come now, to defeat Torro-Kaal, with our Cap-tain from the stars."

29. Starlight

The Mok Tau's arrival marked the end of the journey across the Great Break. No more than an hour later, they reached the other side and saw just how far they had descended. Their road shifted from swinging the vines to scaling a nearly three-hundred-foot cliffside.

"How the hell are we supposed to get up there?" Dex questioned his newly promoted Staff Sergeant Toork. An Army Commendation Medal unfortunately wasn't available for the ceremony.

"We climb," Toork said. "Fast. Rain coming."

Dex and Lacy looked up at the slivers of the sky they could still see through all the intertwined roots. It was just as bright as always.

"How can you tell?" Lacy asked.

"Can smell. Fast. We move." He and Gurg jumped and scaled the wall, sticking to it like... *well, frogs, I guess,* Dex realized it wasn't that odd.

For he and Lacy though, they had to be more cautious. They set small goals, not looking at the climb like a straight three-hundred-foot shot. Find the closest platform, make it to there, and call it a win. But acting against them, gravity was slowly returning to normal. From the time they woke up that morning to when they reached the cliff, the world felt noticeably heavier. The rucksacks weighed down their shoulders more, and the ache in their backs persisted stronger than ever.

Lacy went up first, grabbing onto a branch that shot out of a crack in the rock cliffside. She found a solid foothold and used that to jump up to a thin ledge three feet above her head. Lacy caught her balance, getting a new foothold on a rigid jut of the rock wall. It grazed against the bottom of her foot as she landed, and the short bust of pain fueled her to throw herself off and latch onto a low-hanging vine.

From below, Dex saw the redness under her foot, and how her face contorted trying to ignore the hurt.

"How ya' doin' baby?"

"Dandy!" She lied. "I miss my boots!"

"Yeah, you'll get used to it. I'm comin' up!" Dex followed, taking the same trail as Lacy until they reached their first milestone.

Lacy breathed heavily. After a long day of almost slipping and falling to her death fifty times, rock climbing was the last thing on her relaxation to-do list.

"You wanna go first this time?" She asked. "I'll hang back-"

"No!" Toork exclaimed. "We keep move. Feel rain."

"We're coming, don't worry," Dex called to the Mok Tau who had a good thirty feet on them. Then to Lacy, he said, "You first. I'll be here to catch you."

Lacy smirked and kissed him on the cheek before collecting herself and returning to the cliffside. "And who'll catch you?"

"I'll be fine. Go on!"

Something shined for the briefest moment in the corner of Dex's eye. He shot his head to the side, looking out for any predators, but saw nothing.

"Where'd my safety go?" Lacy teased. "Come on, Captain. Don't wanna look bad in front of the men, do we?"

Dex returned to the wall. Must have been a trick of the eye.

But after the first ten feet of the climb, he saw it again. And this time, Lacy took notice too. A bright light, like a diamond held up to the sun, fell between them.

"Did you see that?" Lacy asked.

"Was that-"

"Rain," Gurg told them. "We not have time for talk."

"It looks like stars," Lacy whispered to herself.

The race began to make it to the top of the cliff before it was too slick and dangerous to climb. Dex stayed close behind Lacy, and watched her intently for the slightest misstep, even as he lost focus on his own footing.

Lacy took one wrong step, her foot slipping on wet moss, and

Dex threw out a hand to let her stand on.

She laughed out of fear and relief, gave a quick 'thank you,' and pushed on.

As Dex pushed her up, the small root he held to gave an inch. The slight but sudden movement forced his heartbeat into overdrive. It was a long way down if it did break. He wasted no time then, climbing to the next rock ledge.

Toork and Gurg reached the top, beating them by a hundred feet, and disappeared from sight. Moments later, a long vine was thrown down to Dex and Lacy, accompanied by Toork's demands for them to "Grab on!"

Lacy reached for the vine. The tips of her fingers just barely grazed it even as she leaned as far as she could while clinging to a thin root.

"Jump for it, Lacy!" The starlight rain beat down on Dex's face.

She threw her full weight into the vine. Lacy's fingers wrapped around it, but as her momentum carried her forward, her foot found itself caught in a tangle of roots.

Dex could already see her losing grip on the vine, and falling deep into the Great Break. He'd reach out but be unable to grab her rain-soaked hand.

Her voice brought him back to reality. "You coming or what?" There she was, the starlight dripping down her hair, matching her shining eyes.

Dex laughed and mounted the vine. "Thought I'd have to catch ya again." He climbed up to meet her and wrapped an arm around her waist.

From above, Toork and Gurg began to pull them up to safety.

"Dex… you don't always have to save me."

He didn't know how to respond.

She went on. "I can handle myself once in a while," she said through a smile. "Let someone else in on it for once."

"And what about when you do need saving?"

Lacy shrugged and bit her lip, "I'm not saying I don't like when you're there to catch me."

* * *

Within the hour, the rain turned the jungle floor to glistening mud. Toork thought they could have made it to Torro-Kaal by nightfall, but every step was a fight to free their feet from the ground, like being back in the swamp. They were desperate to find reprieve from the beautiful yet retarding rain. And with the sun beginning to set, they would need somewhere warm to bed down for the night.

It was Robbie who noticed the cave. He was well covered in Dex's ruck, but the rain threatened to seep in. It was proper motivation to keep alert for any source of better cover.

The group trudged toward the cave, buried in a hillside. The opening was small, but just a few feet in, it opened into a room almost as big as the *Silent Horizon*.

Toork and Gurg grabbed sticks on their way in to make a fire. The only source of light was a stream of starry rainwater flowing into the cave, but the light it gave off was faint. They fumbled about blindly for a moment in the dark cave, until Lacy grabbed a flashlight from her pack, and further blew their primitive minds.

"You are true that is not tool of gods?" Gurg asked humorously.

"Is that a joke?" Dex asked. "I'm pretty sure that would be blasphemy, haha."

Toork began, "We would like to hear more of your world." He struck a starter stone above the kindling they'd gathered, and a fire roared to life. "If not gods, what we call you?"

Dex sat by the warmth of the fire next to the two of them and took Robbie out of the rucksack. "Humans. And we come from a world called Earth."

"Where this Earth?" Gurg.

"Far away. Millions upon millions of miles away."

"And you travel on stars?" Toork.

"No," Dex laughed. "We travel on boats. Big boats that take us up into the sky."

Toork and Gurg both laughed. Took chided Dex, "You lie. Make us fools. Boats can not fly. It is magic, yes?"

"What are you talking about? You saw the boat with your own

eyes! After all we've been through you think I'd lie to you?"

"Yes," the Mok Tau said in unison. Then Toork clarified, "Yes, great holy god Cap-tain Dex." They laughed again.

Dex threw his hands up in defeat, "All right, all right… ya got me there."

"So how hoo-mans ride in star?" Toork asked again.

Seeing there was no other answer they would accept, Dex simply said, "magic."

The eyes of the Mok Tau showed that was what they wanted to hear, but the questions didn't stop.

"How magic?" Gurg asked. "How make magic star?"

Dex dropped his head into his hands. "I don't know, guys! I just flew the damn thing," he chuckled in light-hearted frustration. "Lacy know's better. She can explain it. Hey, Lacy! Wanna help me out here?"

They all turned to where Lacy was last seen, but only saw a stream of rainwater.

"Lacy?" Dex called.

A sliver of light shone on the back of the cave wall where the stream stopped, and from that spot, Lacy's voice echoed, "Dex, come back here!" Then an excited laugh, "You gotta see this!"

Dex picked up the blaster and told the others to stay there while he checked on Lacy.

The back wall was an optical illusion. At first glance it looked like a flat surface, but only when up against it, when he was touching the wall where the glare of Lacy's flashlight shone, did he see the lip of a secondary tunnel system.

Dex disappeared behind the wall. Toork and Gurg held their spears tight. Neither of them had crossed the Great Break before, and all they knew of the other side were myth. Horror stories of other tribes and monsters.

It was a relief when Dex popped his head out a moment later and told them it was "Okay, but stand guard. Make sure nothing comes in here," and he hurried away again.

Meeting Dex on the other side of the tunnel was a marvelous sight.

Rainwater flowed through the tunnel, into a larger cave room, and fed into a pool. The starlight illuminated the pool and shined back onto the roof of the cave like they were back on the ship. Dex and Lacy were sailing again through space on those early days of their voyage. And by the water's edge, Lacy waited for Dex to join her.

The water breathed new life into their aching muscles. The dirt and sweat of a week in the jungle were cleaned off, and the two of them felt like human beings again. More than that, splashing around in the water, holding each other close in its warm embrace, they could put everything outside of the cave, outside of their minds.

There were no monsters in that cave. No quest. No Empire.

Just the two of them, and their lips pressed together.

"Heaven…" Lacy sang and she floated on her back. "I'm in heaven…"

Dex tread the water, watching her, listening to her. Lacy caught his look and swam to him. Just before him, she tilted her head down and lifted her eyes to look into Dex's, a look that could melt him. "Is this what it'll be like?" She asked.

"What what'll be like?"

"The world you've been thinking of. In your sleep."

Dex was caught between confusion and intrigue. "I don't know what you mean."

Lacy rolled her eyes with a smile. "Don't kid, Dex. I do pay attention you know. You spend your whole watch reading, and when you sleep your mind goes off to… somewhere. I hear it all the time. You call it the Valley." She saw the recognition in his eyes and understood he didn't quite comprehend it either.

"I… I don't remember."

"What is it?"

They found themselves slowly drifting back to shore.

"I don't know. It's… it's like a dream. It's there in the back of my mind, but whenever I try to bring it forward, it escapes me. That's all I remember, a valley. And…"

"And what?" Lacy pressed, almost on top of him as he lay in the shallows.

"And a voice, I think." The memory slowly came back to him, but everything was still cloudy, although through Lacy's insistence, her energy pushing for an answer, things began to clear up.

She felt it in him, something hidden, and searching for a way out.

"I want to try something," she said, sitting up on him. She placed her fingers on the sides of his head. When she touched the officer on the docks, there was a brief moment where she could influence his thoughts. Then, in the Mok Rork village, when she touched Borrgip the priestess's hand, she caught a glimpse into her mind. With Dex, maybe she could help him remember.

Lacy closed her eyes and concentrated on the idea of the valley.

Dex cleared a path in his mind for her to traverse.

For a moment there was nothing but the small waves of the water running up his sides. But then the room dimmed. The stars in the water lost their vibrance, and Lacy breathed deep and saw… everything.

Moments flashed like a sped-up film reel with missing frames. There was Earth and happiness; birthdays, school, friends, graduation, parties, racing cars through the Brooklyn streets, lectures from parents, college and commission, a man, Steven. Emotions changing. Death, war, the soldiers, letters, the reports, his father returning a changed man, half the man as the neighbors whispered, anger. There were the screams at night, echoing through the halls of the Prullen home, keeping Dex awake in fear and bitterness. The day Dex met Steven's commander and the fistfight that ensued. Demotions and a near discharge, and then, an opportunity. There was an exam, a psych eval, and a board. Six officers and six scientists. A mission beyond the stars, and an escape. And then, a woman. Herself. Lacy looked into her old eyes, and everything changed again. The bitterness remained, but there was something new. She saw how Dex snuck looks at her during training. She heard his conversations with other applicants, asking about her. She saw his attempts to talk that she hadn't noticed before, and the first time he formally introduced himself. There were the one-on-one field exercises, the test flight when he'd almost crashed because he couldn't take his eyes off of her. Through his eyes, she saw the attempts she'd made herself to spend time off hours with him that he didn't recognize, and their first date in the observatory, when everything was right in the world. Then the voyage came into view, and their crash landing on the outpost. Prullen-1, a name they would change unless "we find Prullen-2." And from there, Dex was on his own and she saw firsthand all he'd done to get her back. The violence and the loss. She felt how his heart was caught in death repeating, minute after minute until she was back in his arms and… the Valley.

Lacy saw the streams cutting through the hills, separating squares of the valley into elevated chunks. She saw the trees of green and orange.

Lacy heard the voice, but not as Dex had. This time, it called her name.

She pulled out of his mind and stiffened. Her heart beat hard against her chest, and she knew she'd left just in time.

The Emperor's power loomed near the cave. Just outside, she knew, it almost found her.

"What'd you see?" Dex asked.

Lacy processed the memories. The Valley she didn't understand, and the memories she did. "Everything," she said, and kissed him with all the joy of their time together since he first saw her.

30. Torro-Kaal

"Do not step there." Toork held out an arm to halt Dex.

Everyone stopped and scanned their immediate surrounding. They had stepped into a small clearing. The ground was laid with twigs and brush beat down as if intently. Off to the side of the clearing was a mound supported by a rock foundation and lined with leaves.

"What's wrong?" Lacy asked. She kept her voice low.

"Nest," Toork told them. "See there?" He pointed toward the mount. "Egg."

"And the parents?" Dex.

"On hunt. We safe now, but not stay. We are almost to Torro-Kaal."

The mountain came into view when the sky had cleared up that morning. Through the jungle ceiling, they could just barely make out the mountain's frame. It loomed over the trees, loomed over them like it was watching them. Like a statue that awaited their arrival into another world. The Emperor's world. And just like that, they were back on the Heart of the Void, staring down the Emperor's grand shrine.

"Let's move," Dex ordered. The sooner they could scout out Torro-Kaal and return home, the better.

Every step closer felt both magnetic and repulsive, like they were being pulled toward the mountain by a tractor beam. They knew evil lay there, an evil no other Mok Tau could escape from, yet they continued on. Step by step through the jungle.

Dex held on tightly to his spear as if at any moment Zar-Mecks would ambush them from the trees. Those black-suited machine-like men who fought with such intensity for the Empire. After so long in the jungle, it was easy for Dex and Lacy to leave them behind in their memories, but no longer. The mountain reminded them that no matter where they were, or what planet they found themselves on, the Emperor would always be there.

Lacy felt herself again on the procession to the Emperor's temple. She could almost hear the chanting of the Children of the Void, praying for her death.

I will not fear him. The Emperor. Torro-Kaal. I will not fear him.

Toork and Gurg would soon face the terror that had taken so many of their fathers and brothers. They made it through the hidden swamp, survived the Mok Rork village, and crossed the Great Break. There was nothing, they believed, they couldn't face now. Toork and Gurg held their heads high as they approached the mountain.

Robbie...

Robbie was happy he wasn't left back at the ship and missing all the fun.

The Empire too, welcomed their arrival.

Dex pulled aside a thick tangle of brush and stepped through, falling a foot onto a path. He knelt down to examine the path. It was wide enough for the *Silent Horizon* to fly through. Maybe a path some herd of jungle creature often trod. But there was something off about the path. Spread out at even intervals in the dirt were thick straight lines, with the dirt piled up heavier on one side like it was being pushed away. Tread marks. Recognizing what it meant, he quickly jumped back into the jungle and ordered the rest of the group to drop.

Whispering, he told them, "We're here. Lacy, take this," he handed her the blaster.

She shook her head. "You're a better shot. Besides, it's about time I put this to use," she fingered her spear.

"Very non-violent," Dex teased.

Lacy hardened her face with a smile, "Empire squares don't count."

Dex reholstered the blaster. "All right, listen up everyone. Chances are, *Torro-Kaal* will know we're there the moment we arrive on their doorstep. So, we need to find a back door. Toork, Gurg, either of you know how to get in?"

Gurg answered him. "They speak of the mouth of Torro-"

"I don't want a mouth. Back door. Think, private. Do they speak of any other ways in?"

Toork and Gurg exchanged a look of apprehension. "I… backside?"

Dex rolled his eyes, and Lacy laughed at the misunderstanding.

"All right, listen, we're not going in through Torro-Kaal's mouth. I guess it's time… look you two are smart enough to understand. It isn't a big monster in there giving birth to those things in the jungle. There are warriors. People like the Lieutenant and I that came down from the stars. Except these people are evil. They're the reason your people are dying. If we can get in there, as quietly as possible and not get caught, we can find out how they work. You two take that information back to the village, use it to free yourselves of the emp-… Torro-Kaal. You got that?"

"We…" Toork looked back and forth between Dex and Lacy. "We not fight?"

"No." Dex shot him down. "What we do now will do more for your people, for this planet, than any attack you've sent in the past. We told you we would help you, and this is how we're going to do it."

Toork and Gurg shifted where they crouched.

"Listen, guys. This is how it works. Your people have been running in blind, fighting an enemy you didn't understand. I'm sorry this isn't what you expected, but this is how we win. You have to trust me."

"I trust you," Robbie whispered from the rucksack.

Lacy patted him on the head.

Dex held out his hand for the two Mok Tau. "We're in the home stretch. Trust me."

Neither Toork nor Gurg knew what 'home stretch' meant, or what Cap-tain Dex was doing with his hand, but they'd come this far.

"I trust my cap-tain," Gurg affirmed.

"I." Toork agreed with a nod.

Neither of them took Dex's hand, but it didn't matter. Their words were enough.

And with that, it was time to find the entrance to Torro-Kaal.

They walked along the path, cautious of any sounds that weren't natural to the jungle. The tracks in the dirt implied ground transportation. An odd choice, when all the other transports Dex and Lacy had seen on this side of the Empire were hover-vehicles. The likely reasoning, Dex thought, was that it was easier to blend in with the environment. A shuttle flying above the trees could easily disguise as a bird, and a crawler could easily be an animal with the right cover. But something that levitated just above the ground might tip off some of the locals.

But that brought the question back to, what was the point of it all? If the Empire was already on this planet, why hide? When would be the right time for the Emperor to make his grand appearance? What were they hiding in Torro-Kaal's mountain?

All along the trail, a queasy feeling haunted Lacy. It could have easily been chalked up to nerves, but no, her nerves only further upset the sick feeling already in her stomach. As far as their journey went though, there was no reason to bring it up to the group. What was an upset stomach in the face of danger?

As they approached, a soft rumble emanated from the mountain.

"Torro-Kaal is busy in there, ain't she?" Dex joked, seeing the tension spread across the Mok Tau's faces.

Slowly they realized that for the last mile or so, they hadn't seen any small jungle creatures, or heard any birds. It was like the night of the kron-kaal attack all over again. Torro-Kaal had a wide circle of influence over the land.

"Mouth ahead," Toork whispered, returning from a quick scouting run. "Just past hill. We made it." Timid relief carried his voice.

"Wonderful. Did you see anyone?" Dex asked.

Toork shook his head.

"All right, that doesn't mean no one is out there. Toork, what's the area like around the mountain?"

"Open. No trees. Mountain bare. All rock."

Dex pursed his lips. "Damn. We'll be out in the open any way we try to get it." He looked around the small group. "Anyone got any ideas for cover?"

After a moment of thoughtful silence, Lacy offered, "Pray it works out for the best."

Toork and Gurg nodded naively in agreement.

"I don't think that's our best option right now, Darling. We need camouflage. Someone has to get closer and scout out another entrance."

Gurg perked up. "We wait," he said like it was a solution in and of itself.

"Private, I don't know what good that's going to do us to just wait for the answer to show itself," Dex said.

"No, no, cap-tain. We are at mouth of Torro-Kaal. Nest, yes?"

Dex went along with it to humor the frog. "Sure. What of it?"

"If nest, and tracks in dirt, kron-kaal must be come back. We sneak behind. It risk, but way in."

It was an option. Not a great option, and Gurg's presumptions were a little off, but he was onto something. Eventually — hopefully, at least — a transport would enter or exit the mountain. On its way in, if they were lucky, they could sneak in behind the vehicle. If they searched for a back door as Dex had wanted, they would undoubtedly be caught by sensors or security teams patrolling the area unseen.

Above them, thunder rocked the skies, and a dark energy shrouded Lacy.

They all looked up.

"Hey, Toork?" Lacy asked. A horrible darkness swelled in her mind and gut.

"Yes, Loo-tent?"

"Do you smell rain?"

"No."

Dex turned his attention to Gurg. "Pop out, go check what that was." The Mok Tau's ability to blend their skin tones in with the environment would prove valuable yet. But Dex, Robbie, and Lacy had a feeling they already knew what the sound meant. A ship must be coming in.

Gurg rushed high into the trees and crawled out along a branch that hung over the clearing. Far above the peak of Torro-Kaal, a silver saucer hovered for a moment, then descended until

It disappeared into the mountain.

He rushed back down, careful not to shake any branches or rustle the leaves.

"What'd you see?" Lacy asked.

Gurg shook his head. "Not know. Big..." he traced his finger in a circle. "Not know word. Can not know. Big circle fly, and fall slow into Torro-Kaal."

Dex and Lacy exchanged a look of awareness. An Empire transport ship. Lacy and Robbie were all too familiar with them.

"All right, so we've got two ways in. Wait for an opportunity to sneak in the front door or scale the mountain." Neither option was good, but at that moment, Dex thought he'd try something new. Taking a page from Lacy's book, he tried being optimistic. They couldn't have come all this way just to admit defeat at the finish line. "Either way, we're getting in. I'm willing to hear what the team thinks."

Lacy offered her thoughts first. "I say we wait. I think our chances are best if we sneak in behind a transport."

Dex nodded acknowledgment of her vote.

Gurg spoke next. "Many Mok Tau enter through mouth. None come back to village. I say we go to top."

"I like where your head's at," Dex told him with a grin. "Sergeant?"

"I say top. Agree with Private Gurg."

"It's settled. We scale the mountain." Dex slapped his thighs as he stood up, ready to conquer the next step of their journey.

But another voice spoke up. "I can go in through the front."

They all turned and saw Robbie sitting just outside their circle.

"No, Robbie, we couldn't-"

Dex interrupted Lacy, "Yes! We c — sorry, darling (he kissed her cheek) — we could! No one would think twice about him. He's one of who-knows-how-many identical robots. Robbie could just walk in the front door and walk back out, saying he was on an assignment. All he's gotta do is pop in quick, scout out a safe way in, and report back."

Lacy tried to protest but found no argument past one based on emotion. It was a risk like all their other options, but unlike the first two, this one had a chance at working.

As if he hadn't already convinced her, Dex added, "Just a quick scouting run."

Robbie felt his gears freeze when he stepped into the clearing. The feeling he got standing in front of the mountain, the base of the Empire he'd so readily abandoned, was one both alien and familiar. The thought of the transport ship hidden deep in the mountain was like a trap, waiting for him to make the wrong step and he'd be brought back on board, forced to spend the rest of his life serving Imperial officers. No more, "thank you's" or "could you please's." No more "Robbie."

Every chip in his processing units told him not to approach the mountain. But that was just programming.

If he had lungs, Robbie would have taken a deep breath and walked with his chest puffed toward the entrance of the mountain. But without lungs or a chest, he could only mimic the actions.

Slowly, the robot disappeared into the blackness of the mouth of Torro-Kaal.

"Do you think he'll be all right?" Lacy asked, her hand placed firmly on Dex's chest.

"He'll be fine. Robbie's a good kid."

They held their position in silence from that point forward, attentive to any sounds escaping the mountain, or approaching from behind. Toork and Gurg ate up in the trees where they had a good vantage point of the mouth of Torro-Kaal.

Everything around the mountain was dead quiet. The Empire ship never came back out of the mountain, and no ground cars came in or out. There wasn't even a single patrol. Just hums and rumbles from inside the mountain.

Lacy took that time to sneak a quick photo of the mountain. The click of the shutter was no louder than a branch snapping but in the eerie silence, they all noticed it. But no response came from the mountain.

"What if he doesn't come back?" Lacy whispered to Dex, asking mainly out of her own concern than to form a backup plan.

"He'll be back," Dex reassured, rubbing her back gently.

Another twenty minutes went by with no sign of the robot.

And still, no movement around the mountain. Was this even the right spot? Toork and Gurg had never actually been there before, it was all just legend. But no, the ship flew into the mountain, of course it was the right spot. Unless it was just a scouting ship. But what if they had the wrong mountain too?

Dex picked up a stone and threw it up toward Toork. It hit just below the branch he was perched on with a soft *thump*.

Toork took a final look at the mouth of Torro-Kaal, then dropped from the tree to meet Dex.

"You sure this is the right place?" Dex prodded him. Impatience was beginning to seep into his voice.

"Yes Cap-tain. I feel in heart."

"Feelings aren't good enough, Sergeant. Are there any other mountains in this area?"

"I not know."

Dex rolled his eyes so hard they nearly fell out of his head and all the way back to the *Silent Horizon*.

But Toork added, "But there are many ghost. I hear they cry."

Not one for ghosts or superstition, Dex was about to dismiss him when Gurg rejoined the group. "The Robbie is return."

They all rushed to the tree line, where Gurg pointed to the road to the left of them. Strutting casually toward them was Robbie, like he was on an evening stroll. Dex's idea that they had the wrong mountain persisted even more. He wanted to rush out into the field and grab Robbie's arm like a disobedient kid and bring them all back to the ship. *That's it, I'm turning this car around.*

Robbie joined them again and, reading the look of anticipation on all of their faces, promptly said, "I'm sorry I got lost. Many caves in there. And there are a lot of Zar-Mecks."

The Mok Tau didn't understand, and though it didn't brighten Dex or Lacy's day, they were at least satisfied they'd made it, and Robbie had found a safe way in and out.

"You did great, buddy," Lacy was quick to tell him before Dex brought them all back into army mode, and he did so almost immediately.

"Where are the caves? How big is the place? Were there any guards? How many-"

"Dex, please." Lacy interrupted. "One at a time." Then privately, "He could've died in there, I'm sure he's terrified."

"Okay, sorry. Robbie, how did you get out of there? You said there's a cave system?"

Robbie nodded his little head. "There are a lot of them in the walls of the mountain. I got lost trying to find my way out and ended up at the top of the mountain. It was very hard getting down."

The newly acquired dents and scratches on his body became more apparent.

Lacy put a hand on his head. "Oh, you poor thing."

"What of Torro-Kaal? Did you see beast?" Toork cut in. In the entire history of the Mok Tau, the little robot was the first to enter the mountain and make it back out alive. Make it out in any condition for that matter.

"Sergeant, we told you. There's no monster in there," Dex reminded him. It wouldn't be easy to break hundreds of years of myth, but Dex also needed to be sure they were listening to him to begin with.

Robbie responded to both of them. "There might be. I heard a lot of screaming."

They all looked at him, stunned.

"Screaming?" Lacy asked.

Looking at her, Robbie said, "I did not see who was screaming. I didn't want the monster to get me."

Lacy shifted her apprehensive look to Dex. Could there really be a monster in there creating the kron-kaal?

"Probably some machine," Dex blew it off, but Lacy wasn't entirely convinced. "Either way, we're not going to figure it out by sitting on our butts down here." He was on his feet, pushing himself up with the help of his spear. With gravity slowly returning to normal, and how exhausted they already were, every pound felt like ten. And the way home soon would be no easier.

Robbie stepped back into the clearing, leading the pack just in case now was when the Empire forces in the mountain collectively decided it was time for a smoke break. But no Zar-Mecks, and no alarms. The Empire was making it too easy.

They filed out one by one, crossing the twenty-foot-wide road and hiding in a ditch on the mountainside. Lacy went first, kicking off with a jump to cover as much distance as she could, and taking advantage of the lower gravity while she still could. She met Robbie in a ditch next to a boulder, cover from the mountain's entrance. Once down, she signaled for Gurg.

Like Lacy, Gurg jumped from the wood line but made it all the way across the road. When he landed on the rocky slope of the mountain, his skin took on a darker tone. It wasn't a perfect camouflage of the mountainside, but enemies would be hard-pressed to spot him if they weren't already aware of his presence.

Toork jumped the same as Gurg, but with a heavier pack, he barely made it to the edge of the road.

Last came Dex. His first thought was to give the road the old 'I'm up, they see me, I'm down.' But with no cover, it was quickly dismissed for a full-on sprint.

Now, if there weren't any regular patrols on the road around the mountain, all they had to worry about were ships flying in and out of the mountain, and hidden security measures on the trail Robbie led them.

After the first fifty meters of shifty rocks, the incline of the mountain sharply increased. They'd gone from crawling on all fours for safety against the loose rocks and gravel, to rock climbing again at nearly seventy degrees. All the while, they kept their eyes peeled for the easier paths Robbie promised them he'd taken to get down in one piece.

Dex stayed on the rear, looking back regularly for signs of the Empire. His caution grew to the point where he wanted the Empire to show up. Robbie claimed he saw them, but he couldn't remember the path he was on just five minutes prior and believed in the monster in the mountain. *Maybe he is coming up on the end of his battery life.*

Don't even joke about that! Lacy's voice shot into his head.

Dex nearly lost his footing in surprise and grunted as he tried to steady himself. *You know when I married you, sharing everything and all that, I'll admit I didn't think it included all this.*

When Robbie did find the right path, they'd already climbed half the mountain and it was well past noon. Without the protection of the trees, the sun beat down on them hard. They stopped once to hydrate, but only briefly, and were on their feet again. Robbie was sure they were almost at the cave he'd come out of. What eventually led them to a cave entrance, whether it was the one Robbie was trying to find or not, were the screams.

They were faint at first. Dex could still excuse them as machinery, but as they got closer to the source of the sound, it was harder for Dex to ignore the truth. Still, though, there was no way it was a monster.

Right?

"Here," Robbie exclaimed, "This is where I came out. But it looks a lot bigger than it did before."

The entrance to the tunnel was only about four feet tall, and two feet wide in length. A tight squeeze for all except Robbie.

"That's probably because it's a different cave," Dex reprimanded. It took the robot a little over an hour to get back to them on his first trip but way longer than that just to get back inside? No, they got lost along the way.

Lacy gave Dex a disapproving look then consoled Robbie, "Don't listen to him. You did great."

A nice moment, cut short by the hushed cry of someone deep in the mountain.

They all stared down the tunnel.

"This is it," Dex quietly announced.

Lacy pulled her camera from the rucksack. "Quick in and out?"

"As quick as possible. Get whatever we can record and get out."

Lacy had come to accept the mission for what it was. This wouldn't be humanity's defining moment against the Empire. But if they were smart, and moved fast, it'd go far to give Earth a head-start in the fight against them. The Mok Tau would just have to be patient. One day, hopefully, their real salvation would come.

She took a deep breath.

They took another step closer to Torro-Kaal.

* * *

Robbie used a tiny flame from his claw to light their way. Every few seconds, another scream would come from the bowels of Torro-Kaal, echoing down the halls of the tunnel. Lacy's blood went cold, while Toork and Gurg's froze. The ghosts of their fallen brothers cried for them, begging them to stay away.

The further they went, the tighter the cave became. The air around them was growing scarce. Robbie's flame ate up all it could to stay bright. But just as it began to dim, a light showed itself in the distance.

Through tough, slow maneuvering, Dex took the lead.

No longer was it just screams of pain they heard. There was the clinking and banging of tools and the whirring of machines. The soft hum of engines.

Dex approached the crack in the wall, motioning the rest of the group to hold back, by the faint glow of Robbie's torch.

When he peered through, the first thing he saw... was a floor.

Not dirt, not gravel, not even wood. Grating. And just above that, a railing. Past the railing, he couldn't see. He was entering a large room, and all the sounds he heard came from far below. Pushing through the tight crack, he saw the cavern was illuminated by harsh white lights, crudely bolted to a half-boarded wall. A solid grey material covered the first five feet up from the grate, and the rest of the way up was natural rock.

The screams stole his attention again.

Dex took slow steps to the railing, careful not to come down on the metal too hard and let the echoes announce his arrival.

Peering over the ledge, Dex finally saw Torro-Kaal, and his horror made him wish the monster was real.

For generations, warriors had been coming to this place to defeat the beast and bring peace to their world. For generations, they had entered the mountain and never saw home again. They were believed dead, and their tribes told themselves they'd moved on, in the name of a false god. For generations, no one had told them the truth, that Torro-Kaal did live in the mountain, and it kept its prey alive, in the service of the false god.

Whips cracked. Stun batons shocked fallen bodies. Zar-Meck soldiers watched over the hundreds of captured warriors from tribes across the planet who were chained together, digging out the mountain, and laying down the foundations of something stronger.

Semi-electronic voices shouted, "YOU THERE! ON YOUR FEET!" And the crack of a whip and a scream would follow.

But this was just one room in a massive mountain.

Another cry of pain and sorrow, and Dex fell back to the crack in the wall.

"Lacy," he whispered. "Hand me the camera."

She did as she was ordered.

Dex primed the shutter. He kept low to the floor and aimed the lens through the holes in the grates. The click of the shutter was muted by the sounds of suffering below. One photo was good, but there was more to the mountain than just one room.

"Stay here. I'll be right back."

Lacy reached out to stop him, but he was already off.

Dex stayed low and close to the wall of the thin walkway that wrapped around the room until he made his way to a hallway of curved grey walls, reminiscent of the outpost he and Lacy first landed on.

With every turn, he snapped a photo. The deeper he walked into the base though, the more patrols threatened to catch him. He just wanted to get one solid shot of a Zar-Meck to show the boys back home. And if he caught one without the helmet on, the pale face and dead eyes, that'd be the prize-winning photo.

Like the pictures he took, the full extent of the Empire's operation was coming into focus.

The one thing he wasn't seeing was officers. He wanted to catch a shot of a humanoid face. A species so close to humans on the far side of the universe would overload their brains with questions, both theological and evolutionary.

Dex had made his way down to the level just above the work floor. Hiding behind a loud machine, he was able to get an up-close and in-focus shot of one of the Zar-Mecks beating one of the warriors with a baton.

The Zar-Meck shouted at the captive to "GET BACK ON YOUR FEET!" But every time the captive tried to get back up, the Zar-Meck would bring the baton down again on his back.

Dex snapped a picture of the abuse, focusing on the weaponry the Zar-Meck used. The baton could easily morph into a bladed weapon or a blaster. At times, Dex was sure, these prisoners wished they would, and their misery would end.

On the snap of the shutter, the Zar-Meck darted around. Their reflexes were just as terrifying as Dex remembered from his first encounter at the Royal Void Outpost.

He ducked low behind the machine and looked up at the rafters he'd entered the base from. Faintly, he thought he could see Lacy's head popping out of the crack in the wall. She looked so far away.

Shit! How did I end up down here?

Through the trudging of workers and machinery, the approaching Zar-Meck's footsteps echoed the loudest, and Dex was more than ready to sound retreat. He'd gotten more than enough evidence of the Empire's brutality.

Darting quickly from his hiding spot to a crack in the unfinished wall, he evaded the purple gaze of the Zar-Meck's visor just barely spotting him.

He took his time catching his breath. His heart beat at a million miles a second. Even though he'd worn the suit before, he had no idea what its full capabilities were. How good was it in the dark? Could it see him in that tunnel? Dex moved a little further deeper.

Outside, the Zar-Meck scoped out the area Dex had been hiding, then promptly went back to his post, beating the helpless frog.

It was a close call. He was safe though, he could still get back to Lacy.

Obviously, there was no going back out the way he'd gotten into the tunnel. He'd have to push through and hope there was safety on the other side.

Taking one last look out at the Zar-Meck, and the machine he'd used for cover, another piece of the puzzle clicked into place.

The tunnel he'd found himself in was just as dark as the last. He crawled along slowly through its sharp turns and steep inclines until an exit presented itself. The sounds that came through the exit held fewer sounds of pain and beatings, a hopeful sign.

Light seeped into the tunnel in a series of thin lines. As he approached it, the walls around him smoothed out, replaced by metal. Before long, he'd realized he'd stumbled into an unfinished ventilation system. If he was careful, he thought he could easily ride it all the way back up to Lacy. Or better yet, he could make it out of the mountain, and double back to pick them up so he didn't get caught wandering the place. Either way, he'd found his ticket out. All he had to do was orient himself.

Okay, I started by going to the other side of the construction room, went down a few flights, took a left... or... yeah left for about twenty feet, then, wait... no, double back a flight first, then I went down the hall... no, wait...

He was lost. The only direction he knew was up, but not left, right, forwards, backward, or any manner of horizontal. He'd have to go with his gut and pick one direction until it bought him out of the mountain, and where he lay, he had three options. Left, right, or bail and run out in the open through the vent directly ahead of him.

Bailing was out of the question so he turned left until Lacy's voice stopped him.

No. You're getting further away. Turn right!

Lacy? How do you know which way to go?

I just feel you getting further away. Turn right, you feel closer. Trust me!

A lieutenant's gut feeling when it came to land navigation was never a good thing. Regardless, it was better than nothing.

He turned right instead, until on the other side of the grille he heard people talking. Real people, with real voices. Not the semi-electric synthetic Zar-Meck voices, nor the broken English of the Mok Tau and other tribes. This was real, clear dialogue.

"Careful now, careful. That's it. Who- Who's got that dammed key? Here now. Careful!"

A roar erupted from the room. Dex edged closer to the grille and peaked through. It was a hanger bay, he realized, and there was the Imperial ship that had just flown in. He noticed the size of the craft. It wasn't one of the huge vessels like Korr had commandeered. This was a small one, a starfighter.

Beyond the starfighter was a stack of storage containers. Some were already emptied, others were still being emptied, and the rest were being re-filled with bulkier-looking equipment than was being taken out. Off to the side of the main group was a solitary container, and something inside was thrashing about.

The Imperial officer and a squad of Zar-Mecks stood by the container, where the final piece of the puzzle was waiting.

From a corridor over by the starfighter, another Officer rushed out. "Officer Mantek, we've been summoned by Amari."

"The generators?" The first officer, Mantek, asked, noticeably irritated. "If central is demanding any more of our equipment-"

"He didn't say what. Just demanded we all assemble in the briefing room."

Mantek threw up a hand in the Zar-Meck's squad's direction. "Get this one out of here," He ordered, then stepped off to join the other officer.

Dex snapped one last photo of the group, and wasted no time getting back to Lacy, listening to the directions she sent him.

The closest safe place he could get out was a well-disguised vent grille that led to the exterior of the mountain. As soon as he was out, he sent a mental message to Lacy, telling him to meet him there. Based on her reading, they weren't far away.

Lacy was quick to pull him in and prod him for explanations. "Why the hell did you go off like that?! You could have gotten caught!"

"We came all this way for evidence, right? Couldn't see enough from up here." Dex tried to maintain control of his volume. His heart was racing and at the time, he thought what he was doing was the best option. Only now that he saw the fear in Lacy's eyes did he realize how reckless he'd been. "I'm safe, Lacy. I'm safe."

She had no more words of condemnation. Lacy threw her arms around Dex, thankful he was back.

"I get it now. I think I understand what's happened here, everywhere."

She dropped her arms from around his neck and instead took his hands. "So that's it then, right?" She asked. A twinge in her voice told him no answer would be good enough for her. The moral answer and the ethical answer would never sync up, and it wasn't something Lacy wanted to face, nor what Dex wanted to see weighing on her heart.

"We got what we came for Lacy. This is what the Empire's been doing across the universe. Those monsters aren't from this world. They ship them in! The Emperor has given these people, planets everywhere, something to fear. He uses that to build up his own myth and destroy everyone else's. Look at our friends! They have no history of their own! The Empire…the Emperor's destroyed that and made himself their god. He set himself up to be this great savior and he's enslaved all who try to help themselves. One day he'll walk in on a red carpet and no one will be able to deny him because they will literally not know anything else. They'll sacrifice themselves on his altar because there never has been any other truth." He held up the camera. "This will save countless people when it gets back to Earth."

She nodded, unsure what the next right step was.

"That's why you have to make it back," Dex said, slipping the camera into her rucksack.

"Me? *Me?* Dex what are you talking about?"

"Do you remember that cargo ship we were on? They were carrying generators and back-ups. Remember?"

Lacy searched her memory, then nodded, but still confused.

"This is where they said they were going! Taranok! I didn't remember it earlier when the boys said it," he gestured to Toork and Gurg. "That's the ship that came in the other night, the falling star we saw! Everything's a mess right now since the Emperor's moving his forces around to look for Earth. This planet gets the back-ups while the top-tier equipment is readied for war. Things are a mess in there right now. The officers are still trying to figure everything out. I can go back in and-"

"Stop! Just stop, Dex!" Tears welled in her eyes, but what the emotion behind them was, Dex couldn't tell.

He took a breath, a pause to collect his thoughts. "Lacy… I have to do this."

"I know. But you're not doing it without me."

Dex fell back a half-step. "Darling, I can't let you get hurt."

She tightened her hands around his. "You can't always be the one to save me. You just have to trust me. All of us."

Toork, Gurg and Robbie waited patiently off to the side.

From the way they stood, none of them would have left the mountainside without a fight.

And none of them did.

31. The Emperor's Wrath

A lone Mok Tau warrior entered the mouth of Torro-Kaal. He carried nothing but a spear and the spirit of holy retribution. Deep in the depths of the mountain, he heard the cries of his brother. It fueled him. Pushed him harder than fear could hold him back. And he was afraid. Afraid for his people if he were to fail to defeat the monster under the mountain. For his own life, though, he was ready to die with a smile on his face, just as long as he didn't go down alone.

Once the daylight was far behind him, the warrior was swiftly descended upon by the shadows.

Blue sparks of lightning struck him from all angles. The warrior swung his spear as he fell to the ground, praying he could hit something.

Every muscle in his body ached. He could barely move his legs, though he forced himself back up, and lunged his spear ahead. In the darkness, he had no target, just a prayer, and the prayer wasn't heard. He fell forward, and the lightning struck him again.

The warrior hit his face on the cold metallic ground. As he turned over, willing himself to get back up, he saw four bright purple lines hovering above him. Then he was being carried. Where his spear was, he had no idea.

They moved into the light, down a long corridor and he saw his captors. Shadows indeed.

Further they went into the belly of Torro-Kaal, until he was thrown into a crowd of faces his people had long forgotten. They helped him to his feet and checked him for wounds before the shadow men threatened to beat them again.

The warrior was chained to the rest of the captives, given a sharp tool, and told to "DIG!" with the rest of them. He moved with the line to the far wall of the room and did as he was told.

When the shadow men had moved on to abuse someone else, the warrior told the captive next to him, "I come with message." Then, in the native tongue of the planet word was passed down the line, *the gods have come to defeat Torro-Kaal.*

* * *

Dex and Lacy crawled through the ventilation of the Empire base. Robbie walked in the hall just on the other side of the wall from them. He didn't know the place any better than they did, but an assembly line robot blended in better than two intergalactic fugitives in loincloths.

"Don't walk like that, Robbie," Dex whispered through the grille as they came up on a clear section of the hall.

The robot stiffened and Lacy called him out. "Too rigid. You look suspicious."

Robbie sulked his arms. "How do I walk?"

"Just be casual. But not too casual." Dex.

"I think I will casually walk out of here," Robbie teased to the surprise of both of them. When they didn't respond he carried on.

Their primary objective was to catch an officer wandering alone. If they could get Lacy back into one of the Imperial uniforms, sneaking around would be easier by tenfold. They just had to get that outfit and then find a terminal.

Soon they came back to the hangar. The officer Dex had seen standing by the kron-kaal cage was gone, along with most of the traffic in the hanger.

Lacy pointed out the starfighter. "I thought that was a transport that came in."

"Let's count ourselves lucky it wasn't."

"But just one?" She was right to question it, Dex thought.

From what they'd seen, Zar-Meck starfighters flew in squads. It probably wasn't far out of the question for one fighter to break off, but none others had come or gone. This one had flown in on its own, lowering its chances of it being one of the Zar-Meck.

"Officer maybe," Dex guessed. "What do you think?"

Lacy agreed. "Could be. Or a messenger that missed that cargo ship."

Either way, Dex didn't like it. What could be so important that the Empire would send a lone starfighter all the way to the furthest planet from civilization? Although, while they didn't want to admit it, their unspoken guesses weren't far from the truth.

"Let's move. No officers here," Dex crawled deeper into the ventilation.

"But where is everyone?" Lacy asked, not moving.

"I don't know, darling. They're around here somewhere. Robbie! Let's go!"

They were moving again. The deeper they crawled into the mountain, the more Zar-Meck soldiers and robots identical to Robbie they saw. They all ignored the little robot. He was just one of dozens wandering around the outpost.

The officer though, was a different story.

He'd come out of nowhere, and his voice nearly made Lacy gasp and give away their hiding spot.

"You, there. Service bot. What is your designation?" the officer asked.

Robbie froze.

"By the Emperor, what happened to you?"

Lacy saw the officer kneel down in front of Robbie and inspect the dents and scratches on his body.

"Bad circuits," Robbie answered weakly. Though Dex and Lacy knew it was out of fear, they hoped the officer would chalk his tone up to damage.

The officer stood back up. "Shame. Report to maintenance. If they can't fix you promptly, tell them to recycle your battery. Off with you now." He stepped off, leaving Robbie standing in the middle of the hall. When it was clear Robbie wasn't doing as he was told, he stopped, turned, and clarified. "Take the next left. Two levels down."

It was a strange feeling for Robbie, an officer giving him a command and not having to immediately obey.

"You're more broken than you look," the officer sighed, then to himself he mumbled, "Why do we have to get all the malfunctions?" He approached Robbie again and gave him a quick kick in the rear. "This way, I'll take you down."

Lacy squeezed Dex's leg. *We're going to lose him!*

Thinking she spoke out loud, Dex shushed her and whispered, "We're not losing anybody today." He crawled in the direction that Robbie and the officer went until coming to a shaft they could ride to the lower levels.

Dex began to lower himself when Lacy jerked.

"I feel it again…" she whispered.

He held himself on the edge of the shaft. "What? Feel what?"

She turned to look back the way they came. A darkness stronger than just the Imperial presence was in the mountain with them, and it was growing. It felt so strong she thought Dex should have been able to recognize it too. "I have to check something."

"Now's not the time." Dex lowered himself down slowly, pressing with his feet and back on opposite sides of the thin shaft. "You want to save Robbie or what?"

The darkness pulled at her, like the Emperor's throne room, terrifying and unavoidable.

Robbie needs us, Lacy.

His words snapped her out of the trance.

Yes, Robbie, she remembered and waited until it was safe to descend the shaft with Dex.

They knew they were close when they heard Robbie's voice. He was no longer frozen with fear. Now, he couldn't stop talking.

"I think I am much better now. Yes. I should go back to my post. I am stationed in the mess hall. Thank you for your trouble, I can bring you a drink. I'll be very fast."

Dex peered through the grille in the ceiling. He was looking into a wide room littered with broken-down machines and racks upon racks of spare parts. The officer was the only organic being in the room. All of the workers were robots that moved on rails attached to the floor.

The officer kicked Robbie away from his leg and addressed one of the robot workers. "This robot needs to be decommissioned. Completely fried out in the jungle somehow. Recycle whatever parts you can." He tried to leave the room but Robbie clung to him for dear life.

"I feel better I promise. I just went for a walk, I will not do it again. All my parts are good. I do not need to be recycled."

Up above, Dex ordered Lacy, "I'll subdue the officer, you take out the robot. Ready?" He handed her the blaster.

She nodded.

"Get off me you broken scrap pile!" The officer kicked again and the ceiling crashed open above him. He only had a moment to look up before a spear pierced his chest and he fell backward into the hallway.

Lacy jumped down behind Dex and took aim at the maintenance bot. The first blaster bolt missed, flying past its thin head and knocking some tools off the back wall.

The robot shot down its rail to sound an alarm. How fast could they blunder this mission?

She took another shot at the robot as Dex dragged the squirming officer back into the room so no passerby would see. The second shot was aimed for center mass of the maintenance bot, but the bolt cleaned its head off of its body. The robot went limp but kept speeding down the rail until it crashed into a workbench.

The sound of crashing metals was enough to "wake the neighborhood!" as Dex admonished.

Lacy was already on her knees, checking on Robbie. "I don't think he was really gonna' listen to nice words."

Dex smirked. "Well, nice shootin' anyway, Tex."

Lacy grinned back at him until a new problem arose. "I don't think this uniform's going to work." She pulled the spear from the man's chest. Blood leaked out and spread across the fabric. "Now what?"

Dex looked around the maintenance bay. "Looks like we've got the room to ourselves."

"Now is *definitely* not the time, Dex."

"Not what I had in mind, but I like where your head's at." He stood slowly, making sure they really were alone. "There's gotta be a terminal in here. Help me look." Dex was off, searching the room for a terminal, hoping he would recognize it when he saw it.

Lacy stayed behind a moment longer with Robbie. "You okay?

That was pretty scary, huh?"

"He's fine, Lacy. Get him over here, I don't know what I'm looking for." Dex brushed aside the tools, scraps, and defective weapons lying on the maintenance bot's worktable and scoured the room for a terminal. "You'd think a robot would keep a tidier workspace."

Robbie hurriedly waddled over to the work area, with Lacy close behind him. "This looks like one." He pointed to an alcove on the back wall, that shared the dimensions of their data tablet.

Lacy unhooked the data tablet from her belt and pushed it into the hole in the wall. To her and Dex, the tablet screen briefly displayed the name of its owner, Officer Jaskek Dreed, before bringing up a command panel.

From there, Lacy carried out her part of the mission, and Dex stood by the door, listening for Imperials. From what sounded like far down the hall, the faintest echo of footsteps reached his ear. Dex glanced down at the corpse of the officer he'd slain. Blood pooled around him and ran across the floor to the door. There was no denying a few drops had by then seeped through the cracks.

"Make it quick, darling."

"I'm working on it!"

* * *

Gurg heaved his pickaxe at the mountain wall. Another chunk fell off and rolled to the floor to be picked up by someone else and dropped in a cart. The *Clink! Clink! Clink!* of the workers, after long enough time in the pit, was almost enough to block out the screams of pain.

Behind his row, the synthetic voice of their overseers boomed, "THESE TWO ROWS. GET THEM ON THE GENERATORS. MOVE!"

Gurg's shackles tugged at his ankles, and he was pulled away from the wall. His chain of prisoners was led over to the horrible machine that hummed like a maniacal spirit. The "generators," their overseers had called them.

"LIFT THIS. FOLLOW."

Even with thirty men, three times as many as their chain had, the generator would have been too much to carry. Except now, there was something in the air. Whispers that their salvation was nearby. Gurg whispered his encouragement to the others. "Gruuk brup pa." *This is the god's command.*

They carried the generator out of the pit and through the grey halls of Torro-Kaal.

* * *

The footsteps were nearly on top of them.

"Lacy, what's going on?!"

"I'm there! I'm done!" She pulled the data tablet off of the wall port and hopped over to the other side of the work table.

Dex held his arms out to help her back into the vent. Step one complete.

With his help, Lacy pulled herself up into the vent.

The footsteps grew louder on the other side of the wall, then stopped suddenly. "Do you- what is that?" It was a real voice, not the synthetic tone of the Zar-Mecks. More officers.

The blood had pooled too much on the floor. Things were about to start ramping up in the outpost, whether or not they were ready for it.

Dex grabbed the dead officer's blaster off of the corpse's belt and tossed it up to Lacy, then rushed over to the workbench for cover.

The door opened and a pair of officers drew their blasters at the sight of the body. "What in god's name happened here?" One said.

"I'm alerting security," said the other, taking out his data tablet.

"The two Amari is looking for?"

Before the second officer could acknowledge, Dex was up from his cover and opened fire on the officers.

The bolt seared through the data tablet, knocking it out of the officer's hand. They both drew back into the hall and drew their weapons.

"It's them! Must be!" One of them said and sprayed a round

of blaster fire into the room.

Dex fell back as the worktable was pounded by their assault. Blaster fire ripped through the air, pinning him down.

Lacy edged forward in the vent to get a shot in, but her angle stopped her. The officer's position behind the wall cut her off completely.

"You! Service robot!" The first officer commanded Robbie, "out of the way!"

On top of the officer's commands, Dex fired blindly and shouted back, "Robbie! Give me cover!"

Robbie felt pinned. With blaster fire going every which way, one step in the wrong direction would have him caught in the crossfire, looking just like the maintenance bot.

He opened up his left claw and sprayed the doorway with his extinguisher. The room filled with his gasses, illuminated by the onslaught of blaster fire.

Down the hall, more trampling of footsteps rushed their way.

"WHAT IS GOING ON? DO YOU NEED ASSISTANCE?"

Zar-Mecks, Dex knew by the sound of their voice. *Damn.*

Using the data tablet, Lacy shut the door to the maintenance room and locked it.

"They're in there! Amari's targets! Go in there and get them!"

There was no point in whispering anymore. Lacy shouted at Dex, "Get up here! Hurry!"

Dex glanced her way, then back at the worktable, grabbed a handful of glowing devices scattered on the floor, threw them into a small bin, and then rushed over to the vent. He helped Robbie up first, nearly throwing him as the Imperials on the other side of the door tried to break it down.

He took one of the devices out of the bin, and then handed Robbie the rest.

"What are you doing?" Lacy asked, but Dex ignored her as he pulled himself up to join them in the vent.

"Robbie, take these back to Toork. Hurry!"

The little robot raced through the vent and was quickly out of sight.

"Are those—"

"Yeah. Now come on, Lacy we've still got a job to do!"

Down below, the Imperials blasted the door open. They swarmed into the room, guns blazing, and lit up anything that wasn't already destroyed.

"Any sign of them?" The officer coughed through the haze of Robbie's extinguisher.

"NOTHING SIR. NO SIGNS OF LIFE."

"There should be two of them..." Their voices faded as Dex and Lacy escaped through the vent. But it wouldn't take long for them to track them through the vents.

Dex and Lacy climbed back up to reach the work pits, using the map of the facility she'd downloaded onto the data pad. Traversing through the vents now was far more difficult. With the number of Zar-Mecks running around below them, each step they took in the vents threatened to be loud enough to alert the whole outpost. They both knew it'd be a miracle if Robbie made it out without going off. God willing, he'd have enough sense to walk out in the open where it'd be less suspicious.

The dark energy came over Lacy again.

I have to check this out. She shot the thought at him.

Now's not the time! Come on!

Lacy was already turning around. *I need to know what's going on. I can't describe it. I'll be right back, you'll be okay! Trust me.*

She twisted his heart with the words. He did trust her, but that wasn't the concern when getting out alive was still up in the air.

Do what you have to and be ready to run.

She smiled at him one more time before disappearing down another tunnel of the vents.

* * *

"Officer Amari, if what you say is true, I believe it's time we sent a message to the Heart of the Void. The Emperor will want to know they've been found and dealt with."

Fires roared behind Romek Amari's eyes. The cracked iris shone a deep scarlet seeped deep into the whites of his eyes, one of the marks left by the Emperor's blessing. He was the only Imperial in the room not dressed in the customary officer uniform. Instead, Zar-Meck armor shimmered under his midnight black robes with scarlet trim, and a saber hung at his side. A shadow surrounded him, devouring light like a black hole. The officers at the table receded as he paced by them.

"You will pull your fighters away from them," Romek commanded them with calm iciness in his voice.

Lacy watched and listened from above, peering through the grille of the vents.

"But sir," one of the officers protested, "This mess is all but cleaned. The Zar-Mecks-"

"It was not the Zar-Mecks the Emperor entrusted with this. And by the build of your outposts here, the competency of your spies, you give me no reason to believe you are capable of handling these two. It would seem all this time away from civilization has dulled your men's senses."

Romek paused, letting the six officers at the table wallow in their shame.

"I searched every planet between their previous escape and here, within all of their possible trajectories. Now that they have been found, I will be the one to bring them in. The Emperor blessed me with this mission. To bring them back to him and *clean up the mess* people like you have made along the way." Romek put a hand on the shoulder of the last officer who spoke.

The officer twitched and dropped his hands on the table like they were glued to it. The rest of the officers recoiled as their comrade's eyes rolled back in their sockets. His skin illuminated briefly, a reaction to deep emotions until that was snuffed out of him with the rest of his energy. The man's skin sunk in on itself, turning a horrible green-grey color. It pulled taut on his bones and muscles. His heart weakly beat through his chest at a spitfire rate until that, too, shriveled and died.

The darkness around Romek grew, and his skin brightened the slightest shade of red. His Zar-Meck armor tightened on his skin, showing faint ridges of his muscles underneath.

The shriveled corpse hit the floor with an unnatural thump.

Its sunken dead eyes looked back up at Lacy.

"Your inactions may have compromised this entire planet," Romek told the room. "When this is over, you will all face the Emperor. Whether in his arms or to Maoul is your choice. Exterminate the locals. Every village within a thousand-mile radius."

A terrified voice spoke up, "But sir... that will take-"

"An orbital strike from the moon outpost. The primitives will think nothing of it but an act of god."

From off to the side a door opened and a young officer entered the room. "There's an error with the new generators."

Romek whipped around. The flames burned brighter in his eyes. Death lurked over the young officer's head. With fast, long strides, Romek crossed the room and towered over the young officer. His darkness surrounded them both. "What error is this?"

"Th- they've been moved. T- to the command center. The prisoners... they just keep bringing them faster than we can remove them."

That was Lacy's cue. She slid away from the briefing room and took out the data tablet again.

Romek reached out for the young officer's throat but paused as something played over the facility's speakers.

A strange melody filled the halls, halting everyone from prisoners to officers. A woman's voice came in singing something about the time's having changed.

Lacy crawled away, humming to herself *Anything Goes*, and agreed, the times were surely about to.

"Stifle that!" Romek ordered, pointing to one of the officers.

The remaining five all stood and fumbled about, unsure where the music was coming from. Before they could respond, Romek was out the door. They hadn't even realized the young officer's throat was cut by Romek's blade, and her body half drained.

* * *

The prisoners halted their work, confused by the melodies drifting through the halls and work pits. Was this the sign that everyone had been speaking of? Who had started the rumors, they asked themselves. Some inquisitive eyes turned to Gurg, who held back a smile.

"Ro nahh," *not yet*, he told them. "Ro nahh."

Whether or not they listened at that point was not up to Gurg. He'd started spreading whispers as best he could. What the gods looked like, what they wore, how they spoke, and what their sign was. But as the end drew near, they couldn't contain themselves. Hope had latched onto them too tightly.

The Zar-Mecks in the work pits displayed their stun batons with steel ferocity. Though the natives were taller, the Zar-Mecks had always commanded fear, until now.

Chains rattled on the ground. Tools banged against the walls, now in antagonism, not work. They were riling themselves up, and the more noise they made, the more they believed this truly was the moment the gods would save them. Hope was so high they didn't even question the plural. If any stopped to think, two gods would be a sign that the rumors were wrong. None of their teachings ever said two, and they hadn't seen the falling star that was the *Silent Horizon*, nor the scarlet gown Dex and Lacy had worn. Now though, doctrine didn't matter. Salvation was salvation in whatever form it came, and if it was divine, all the better.

"STOP NOW!" One of the Zar-Mecks commanded. In the blink of an eye, they swapped their stun baton for a blaster. The others followed suit, but it only encouraged the prisoners more.

What began as two fronts, Zar-Mecks on one side and prisoners on the other, quickly became a circle, with the Zar-Mecks in the center. It should have been an easy fight. With their armor and weaponry, the Zar-Mecks could have wiped out half a dozen work pits full of the primates.

What swayed the tide came from the heavens.

A Zar-Meck body slammed into the ground between the circle of prisoners and the squad, with a spear decorated with leaves thrust through its chest.

There was a moment of silence then. Even the music seemed to dip as everyone looked up to where the body had fallen from. Up on the rafters where the now dead Zar-Meck had once watched them from, a man in a loincloth stood, and thunder boomed.

The mountain shook.

Their salvation had arrived.

That was the moment all hell broke loose. The Zar-Mecks opened fire on the prisoners. Blaster fire shot out in every direction. Even as the bolts tore through the prisoners' bodies, they fought on bashing the Zar-Mecks with rocks and hammers.

Gurg swung his pickaxe upwards, driving it into the skull of the Imperial. Dull blood sprayed onto their faces.

Within seconds that felt like hours to the prisoners who'd prayed for this moment and reveled in it, the Zar-Mecks were destroyed, and their blasters stolen by the natives that could once again call themselves Warriors.

Amidst their victory cries, Gurg settled them and called their attention back to Dex. "He is come!" He shouted. "We follow you to freedom for Taranok!" Gurg punctuated the planet's name with a beat of his chest.

The Warrior next to him did the same, then the next, and the next, until the entire room was beating their chest, and cheering for the man who'd come from the stars.

Dex raced down to the pit. The glory was great, but there was more to be done. A chained-up army would do no good outside of the pit, and that room was far from the only one.

* * *

Lacy rushed through the vents to the command center, as fast as she could through a high crawl. The faster she trudged, the tighter the vents seemed to get, and the sight of Romek in the briefing room had done nothing to calm her nerves. Being in his presence was like being back in the Emperor's throne room. The dark energy, the dread and emptiness she felt on the Heart of the Void had found them again on this planet. 'Every planet on their possible trajectory,' he'd said. How many was that? How many worlds had this darkness searched for them? And to 'clean up the mess?' He couldn't have…

No, don't even think about it. Just focus.

She knew she was approaching the command center by the sound of heavy machinery and screaming officers.

"I don't care what orders you have, they're wrong! Get these out of- HEY! Get out! Move!"

Prisoners were delivering generators by the dozens and totally ignored the officers who yelled at them to re-deliver them back to where they came from.

Lacy held the glowing yellow battery in her hand, waiting for the moment to strike. If she acted too soon, she'd be taking all the natives with her to an early grave. If she waited too long, that Imperial killing machine would arrive and ruin everything, and he was already on his way.

There was no time to lose. Sooner or later, she'd have to show herself and this was as good a time as any.

Lacy kicked the grill open and rolled out of the vent in the wall, ducking behind one of the generators. A time bomb would have been optimal, but they worked with what they had.

Just as she fell, Romek turned the corner and stomped toward the command center. Feeling his presence, she cursed herself for her poor timing and pressed up against the machine.

The shadow around him seemed deeper now, a terrible energy that pushed away anyone in his path.

"What is going on here?" he demanded of the nearest Imperial officer.

"Officer Amari, sir," the officer's voice shook. "They just keep dropping these in the command room. We can barely walk in there!"

"And you have not been able to fix this problem? Is this not the command room? Do you not have the capacity to command these primates to remove these generators?" Romek Amari towered over the terrified officer.

"We've been trying! These animals won't listen! A-and- and- and it's on orders to deliver them here! We didn't know if it came from high-"

The man's head was removed with an almost imperceptible swish of Romek's blade. As the body fell to the floor Romek stepped into the command room.

"Remove these," Romek demanded of the prisoners, then to the Imperials in the room, he said, "What lunacy would send two dozen backup generators to the command room? You are all a disgrace to the Emperor." At the condemnation, they all shriveled at their desks. "I was sent here to find two fugitives, but I think in my report, I will let the Emperor know that you and all your families have failed him."

The officers let out an outcry of pleading and bargaining.

"It was a terrible mistake that will soon be remedied!" one cried.

"A small error!" cried another.

Lacy listened and spied the fleeing prisoners. Once gone, she readied the battery. 'Extremely volatile,' Robbie had described it during their planning. With the way Romek berated and threatened them, she felt a twinge of guilt sending them to their deaths. On the other hand, as soon as she made herself known, they would never feel the same about her. And in her defense, she was sending them to meet their god face-to-face… in hell.

She backed up to the nearest hallway intersection for cover. The battery felt hot in her hands. Even if she didn't throw it, it felt ready to explode.

Romek's voice carried from the command room. "Fix the order. Get these generators back where they belong."

Another voice, "Sir! There's a problem in zone nineteen. The prisoners are becoming hostile with the Zar-Mecks."

"Send another squad down there to assist." Romek shot his gaze from the security officer to the generators. Realization dawned on him that they were more than a distraction as he looked up and saw a pair of eyes the Emperor had shown him time and again in his dreams. He didn't even flinch as the glowing battery pack Lacy threw cracked open against the generator next to him, and flames engulfed the room.

Lacy ducked behind the wall, cupped her ears, and opened her mouth to regulate the ungodly pressure from the explosion. Heat tore across her exposed skin. The mountain shook, and with any luck, she thought, Dex would have made it to the work pits to rally the troops. She wished she could have been down there with him, searching for his thoughts, she saw it was a glorious moment.

Instead, she heard the screams of pain coming from the command room and caught the scent of burning flesh.

She raised her hand to her nose to block the smell, but a hand reached out and grabbed her by the throat and lifted her into the air.

Death blazed in Romek's eyes. His skin was alight with shadowed flames and Lacy felt herself emptying into him. His robes went up in flames that were absorbed back into him. The armor tightened further and pronounced his muscles more in sharp angular lines as if fused into one with him.

"I will earn the Emperor's glory," Romek whispered.

Lacy thrashed, throwing her arms and legs violently at him to free herself of his tight grip on her neck. She could already feel blood vessels popping and her head going light. Most terrifying of all though, she knew this would not be her death. This man wanted to bring her in alive, for an eternity of pain.

In all the eons of the Emperor's rule, he had conquered planet after planet, molded one civilization after the next, and maintained complete control over all that found themselves in his path. They had gone willingly into his arms. To the Emperor, Earth and all its people were just another life form that would sustain him. To the Emperor, there was only himself, those that would eventually belong to him. A single being. He believed in souls, that was what he craved.

What he did not see, what he, nor his followers did not comprehend, was the idea of spirit.

Lacy had spirit. Lacy had a will to live.

Energy flowed from Romek to Lacy, and back to Romek. As much as she pulled from him, he pulled back twice as much. She felt herself being drained and in the back of her mind, saw herself at the foot of the Emperor once again before the image changed to one of their ship. One of her and Dex together, lying in their bunk on the *Silent Horizon*, the room illuminated by the stars shining in on them.

She refocused and pulled energy from the flames. Strength flowed into her. Her mind became clear. She had tools, options. She had a blaster. Lacy grabbed the blaster that hung at her side and unloaded like a cowgirl into the horror in front of her.

It wasn't enough to disable him, but just enough for him to loosen his grip. Once she felt the littlest bit of freedom, Lacy kicked off again and freed herself from Romek's grip.

She fell to the floor and threw herself backward, crawling as fast as she could away from him, but unable to stand. Air rushed into her lungs too fast for her to steady her breath. She was hyperaware of everything, yet her body couldn't keep up.

Romek drew his blade and swung at her.

The sharp metal shone brightly as it passed in front of her eyes. A calculated swing meant to blind her.

Lacy dropped down another inch, barely missing the blow. She turned over, and threw herself forward, away from him and back onto her feet.

Romek didn't have to run to stay on her tail. He took long strides, almost gliding across the flame-engulfed hallway.

The grey walls quickly turned black with ash as the fire spread.

Lacy ran and fired another round of blaster fire blindly behind her. Some of the bolts were deflected by Romek's blade, while others hit but did nothing to slow him.

From the next intersection in the hallway, Zar-Meck forces intercepted them.

Lacy held up her hands as if that would block their blaster fire, and felt a cold smile spread across an evil face behind her.

One final thought crossed her mind before the Zar-Meck's fingers reached the trigger wells of their guns.

Dex, help me!

Dex did not arrive to save her. Instead, a group of Warriors from the Mok Tau tribe and others around the planet descended on the Zar-Meck squad.

Lacy froze for only a moment in surprise, then rushed through the crowd. "Him! On him!" Lacy ordered the warriors, pointing to Romek.

The warriors outnumbered the Zar-Mecks ten to one, and quickly finished them off, then turned their focus to Romek. They gave Lacy the small buffer she needed to escape Romek's grasp.

But he wasn't far behind. And none of the Warriors returned home that day.

* * *

Work pits four through twenty had emptied out. Its workers had abandoned them and picked up arms against the Zar-Mecks. Dull blood caked the walls of the Taranok outpost. For every fallen Zar-Meck, six of the Warriors fell.

When the Zar-Mecks fell, another took their place.

When one of the Warriors fell, the passion of the rest grew stronger. There was no stopping the craving for freedom that had been building up for generations under the mountain.

And at the front lines were Dex and Gurg, leading the charge against the planet's galactic overlords.

They pushed their way to the mouth of Torro-Kaal, destroying everything in their way. Every computer, every robot, every generator, beaten to scraps. It was animalistic how the Zar-Mecks were ripped apart. They covered the lone starfighter in the hanger like termites and destroyed it piece by piece.

At the mouth of the mountain, the army was met by a formation of Zar-Meck soldiers.

"HALT!" The Zar-Mecks demanded of them.

From their ranks, an Imperial officer stepped forward. "Return to your zones, and no further harm will come."

The Warriors bared their teeth and brandished their weapons.

"This not the end, is it Cap-tain?"

"Not by a long shot, private. When this is over, you've got a promotion headed your way." Dex nudged his friend.

The officer repeated, "Fall back now or we will open fire."

Facing the Zar-Mecks in the tight corridors of the facility was one thing. They could easily overwhelm them. Out in the open was a different story. Four long rows of Zar-Meck soldiers had their weapons at the ready, and it would only take seconds to exterminate the uprising.

"If you have more miracle, please show now," Gurg insisted.

The ground shook below them. In the jungle just outside the mountain, the trees rattled. A dark shape pushed through them.

"Definitely not a miracle. But it might work."

In a small display of something more than cold programming under the Zar-Meck armor, their gaze drifted to the jungle.

Falling back no longer seemed like a bad idea to Dex and his army.

The kron-kaal pushed through the trees. Its roar shook the mountain's guts.

Instinct kicked in for the Warriors. Those with commandeered blasters opened fire on the distracted Zar-Mecks. The Imperial forces became divided. The front half returned fire on Dex and his Warriors, while the others fired on the kron-kaal.

"Fall back!" Dex yelled. "Everyone fall back!"

In the midst of combat, almost no one could hear him. Blaster fire and stones flew overhead.

Before too many of the Warriors could fall to the Zar-Meck attack, the kron-kaal had pushed through. With one fell swoop, the rear squad was wiped out, and the rest turned their attention back to the beast.

Through it all, a familiar voice carried over the armies.

"Dex! I'm here!"

He whipped his head around and saw the most beautiful face in all the universe beaming at him. Dex took one more shot at the Zar-Mecks, missing but searing the officer in the face, and rushed through the crowd to his girl.

Dex slipped her a quick kiss then took her hand. "Ready to leave?"

"More than you know." She kissed him once more on the cheek and they pushed through the crowd.

The Warriors rallied behind them, and they all rushed the Zar-Mecks.

Light poured onto their faces, the first natural light they'd felt in a lifetime. It was a feeling they thought would never die... until half their ranks were swept away by the arm of the kron-kaal. Just like that, the Warriors scattered.

Once free from Torro-Kaal every one of them shot off in the direction of their home, while Dex, Lacy, Gurg, and a handful of Mok Tau ran straight down the road toward the Great Break.

Another roar rocked the planet. Lacy glanced back and was shaken to her core. Her hand tightened around Dex. He turned with her and they saw two of the monsters; their stalker from the jungle, and the one the Empire had just delivered. They knelt at the mouth of the outpost, and Romek stomped between them.

He held out his arms wide, and the two kron-kaal charged each other, crashed, and fused into a single monster twice the size. Romek stabbed into the side of the monster with his saber, and pulled himself up onto it, riding the beast.

"Into the jungle, *NOW!*" Dex pushed Lacy and Gurg forward.

They shot across the road, into the thick brush of the jungle, Behind them, but not far and coming closer, was the horrible offbeat THUMP-THUTHUMPTHUMP-THUM-PPTHUMPUMP of the monster.

Dex held back a wall of brush for Lacy to pass through when a blaster bolt grazed his arm. He screamed, recoiling in pain, and glanced at the man on the kron-kaal.

Romek aimed his saber forward. A trail of smoke rose from the hilt.

Dex gritted his teeth through the pain and dove through the brush.

"Gurg! Get her to safety! Now!"

Lacy opened her mouth to protest. This was a fight they were in together, one they *needed* to fight together.

Dex cut her off before she could speak. "It's an order! Lacy," He put her hands on her cheeks, "I trust you. You did amazing. Now trust me." Dex pulled her forehead to his lips, then Gurg pulled her away and rushed her off before she could argue.

The kron-kaal roared again.

Mok Tau warriors rushed past Dex.

He only had a moment to think of a plan. Last time he had the Zar-Meck armor and grenades. With those he could slow down the beast, let Lacy escape, and give Toork more time. All he had now were his surroundings. In every direction, he was surrounded by jungle creatures that were ready to tear him apart.

And maybe that was the answer.

The kron-kaal crashed into the jungle. As if knowing where he was, Romek already had his eyes locked on Dex.

Cutting off to the right, Dex rushed through the jungle, using its density to slow down the kron-kaal. But no matter how thick it got, the monster pushed through, tearing down trees, and sending splinters flying. And atop it, Romek fired blaster bolts from his sword. He then switched up tactics and deployed a grenade from his fused Zar-Meck armor.

Dex dove, dodging the grenade's blast.

Ivory shrapnel blew in across him, tracing ravines of blood in his chest and neck. Darkness clouded his mind, and a moment later when it cleared, Dex realized which clearing he'd jumped into…

A trio of hyper-raptors stared him down. They bared their many rows of teeth at him, threatening him for entering their nest.

Dex reached for his blaster. If he was lucky, he'd get a shot off to antagonize them before the kron-kaal made the mistake of following him. There'd be no getting back to the ship, but Lacy would make it across the Great Break and home safely with all the information Earth would need about the Empire. More than that though, the Mok Tau Warriors were returning home.

This is a good death, Dex told himself with a smile as he raised his blaster.

The hyper-raptors growled at him and prepared to lunge.

Another grenade detonated just outside the nest and captured the attention of the raptors.

Maybe today isn't the day… Dex was on his feet. Dirt kicked up behind him and filled the raptor nest like a tornado blew through it. He sprinted through and passed the distracted hyper-raptors as they attacked their new enemy.

All that was left to do was keep up enough energy to make it back to the Great Break. Without his pack, the littlest bit of remaining low gravity, and a head start on the kron-kaal, he might have a chance.

* * *

Lacy, Gurg, and the Mok Tau Warriors reached the Great Break. Without hesitation, the Warriors threw themselves off the ledge and clung to the nearest vines to swing onto a path.

Lacy held back, searching for a way to climb down safely.

"There is no time! You must jump!" Gurg tugged on her arm.

Sweat dripped from his brow in exhaustion, pain, and fear.

The ground quaked at the approach of the kron-kaal, sending blade-winged birds from their perches out across the great break.

"We must go!" Gurg insisted once more, then leapt off the edge.

Another shake.

I can do this, I can do this, Icandothis!

Unoccupied vines swung below her. She could make it, maybe, if her timing was perfect and God was merciful.

"Shit!" She backed up from the ledge. Adrenaline could only take her so far.

The birds flew past her, just overhead, and the ground quaked again.

Dex would do it. Dex would jump! He wouldn't even think he would just-!

"Jump!" Dex ran out of the jungle, with the kron-kaal and Romek Amari tearing up the trees behind him.

She jumped for her life. With her arms outstretched, she threw herself as far outward as she could, and grabbed onto the legs of a blade-winged bird. The bird screeched and glided through the air with Lacy in tow. She kept her eyes shut tight, blocking out the depth of the drop if she lost her grip on the bird.

Dex is fine, he'll be fine, he's fine!

Dex was not fine.

Romek fired his blade again as the kron-kaal swept its big claw at Dex.

Dex tripped forward, pushed by the wind of the kron-kaal's swipe, and fell off the edge of the Great Break.

Wind beat his face. He could barely keep his eyes open to see the vines. He reached out wildly for anything to grab onto, and as if by fate, Dex found himself clinging to the squishy ropes, and swinging across the Great Break.

A brief moment of victory was cut short by the roar of the kron-kaal and its leap into the break.

Romek steered the monster onto a large planetary root and gave chase to the swinging Earthling.

Blaster blots flew wildly by Dex's head. Just before leaping from one vine to another, a bolt cut the line.

Dex dropped thirty feet, landing on a root. The added gravity threatened to blow out his knees. He rolled out of the landing, biting back the pain, and threw himself for the next vine. There was no outrunning the monster anymore, just hoping he was fast enough and Toork was in position.

Just ahead of him, Dex could see Gurg and the Mok Tau Warriors. Above, Lacy was clinging to a bird for dear life. And behind, the kron-kaal leapt from one thinning root to another.

Clearer than anything else though, was the fire in Romek's eyes, the zealous look of holy determination that craved Dex and Lacy's capture.

Every jump Dex made gave him only seconds of safe distance before the kron-kaal closed in again. And with every leap, his arms were weaker. He had to get to the other side. The Warriors were there in front of them but what good would it do, sending them to their deaths so Dex could get a minute more of life?

The kron-kaal jumped forward, reaching out for Dex, bringing its claws on him like swatting a bug.

With no vines left ahead of him, Dex dropped again onto a root below the kron-kaal.

Taking only a moment to breathe, he saw the faint glow of yellow battery packs lodged in the flammable orange blobs. Toork and Robbie had done their job. Hope filled Dex once again. Through his aching bones, Dex pushed off, slipping once on the wet moss of the root, and sprinted for the dead zone.

* * *

Lacy passed over the dead zone and dropped from the bird, next to Toork and Robbie. The Warriors had gathered at Toork's signal and the ones with blasters stood ready.

"Push back!" She ordered them. "Toork, tell them to push back! Those packs will kill us all at this distance."

In the Mok Tau tongue, Toork relayed the command to his newfound brothers. They all did as commanded, hopping to higher vantage points and pushing back.

Dex swung into their view with the kron-kaal close behind. Lacy gasped in terror as he was nearly crushed, dropping into the depths of the Great Break.

Toork held her back from rushing to his aid. "He is okay. Look!" He pointed, and sure enough, Dex was back on his feet.

"Open fire now!" Lacy shouted, and the Warriors raised their blasters to rain hell on the kron-kaal.

The sudden onslaught of blaster fire halted the beast. It threw itself up in rage, where any other rider would have fallen off its back. Not Romek Amari, though. Romek stayed almost fused to the monster. After capturing the Earthlings, both he and the kron-kaal would feast on the souls of the Mok Tau.

Dex saw this lust in Romek's eyes. The dead zone was too far to reach on foot, and the kron-kaal was in its prime position now.

He drew his blaster again and fired at the primed battery packs.

The roots snapped. Every one of them within fifty meters, singed by the explosion and collapsed. Flames of the melting orange blobs rained down into the Great Break atop whatever was left of Romek and the kron-kaal.

The Warriors halted their fire.

As the smoke and flames cleared, there was no sign of the kron-kaal except its distant roar as it plunged to the depths of the planet.

There was no sign either, of Dex.

Lacy fell to her knees. Burning tears streamed down her face. No sound escaped her throat because there was nothing that could convey the emptiness in her soul.

Robbie came to her side and nuzzled up against her.

He felt cold against her skin. Dead. Like everything else in the world at that moment. There was no life left anywhere.

Just the roar of the slain beast. A soft echoing that… grew…

Lacy wiped the tears from her face and stood with shaking knees.

The beast roared again except, it wasn't a roar… it was a cry… a battle cry, coming from the side, not below!

Lacy and the rest of the Warriors turned to the south and saw a man swinging on the vine toward them, gripping the vine with his feet and thighs, beating his chest, and screaming a proud victory cry like an ape-man.

Hey there, Tarzan! The most beautiful voice in the world sang in Dex's head.

30. Earth

A heavy morning fog hung around the Mok Tau village. Sentries posted up in the trees were unable to see anything closer than twenty feet out.

The village elder had been rambling incoherently all morning. After the excitement of meeting the gods face-to-face, his health quickly declined. Ever since they left for Torro-Kaal, he'd been bed-ridden, rambling about the gods, and attended to by the priestesses. This morning in particular, Roak shouted about new visions, words none of them understood.

The Valley.

Up in their trees, the sentries heard Roak's ramblings. Everyone in the village did. Many of them had taken it as a sign that the gods wouldn't return from Torro-Kaal. It'd been two weeks, and Big Brother Moon was long gone.

Now they could only wait for another kron-kaal to attack. They'd fight bravely to the last man, knowing it'd be their final fight.

If not even the gods could save them, how could they save themselves?

Jurrnup scanned the jungle ahead of him. Nothing moved. Birds didn't fly, trees didn't sway. The grey fog was the jungle saying to him, "We've given up too."

When the distant *Thump…Thump…CRASH* came, Jurrnup gripped his spear tight with silent resolve.

The other sentries jumped through the trees to the east side of the village, joining Jurrnup in the final battle.

Thump… Thump… Thu-CRASH… Thump…

Roak's wailing grew louder one last time, then stopped.

An unspoken agreement passed over them that the old man had croaked.

Thump…Thump Thump… Thump Thump…

Not just one, they realized. As if one wasn't enough to destroy their small village. Maybe they are wrong to bring the gods in. Maybe they were false, and the true god's wrath was coming down on them.

Below them, the village gate opened.

Jurrnup looked down and saw Roak hobbling into the jungle.

Stupid old man, Jurrnup told himself.

Warm wet air hit Roak's face. It weighed him down the moment he stepped foot on the jungle ground. But a voice in his head, not Dex's or Lacy's, someone else entirely, told him to get on his feet.

He walked east, toward the sound of the approaching beasts, and as he turned, the sentries saw a bright smile on his old, wrinkled face. Roak's arms were held high in prayer.

"Bur torra mp-ta?" *Last rite for the village?* Jurrnup whispered to the man next to him.

ThumpThump-ThumpCRASH!- ThumpTHUMP!

The beasts were right on top of them. Any second now they would be close enough to see through the fog.

Roak kept walking until he saw a shadow take form in the distance.

"I knew… she told me… you… come back," Roak said into the fog.

"You throw too good of a party. Didn't want to miss the next one." Dex held out a hand to meet Roak. Lacy followed behind him, and behind her, Toork, Gurg, and Boritt road atop razorbacks. They were accompanied by a company of over fifty Mok Tau warriors.

The sentries alerted the villagers, and they all rushed out to witness the return of their lost brothers.

Roak spoke slowly, yet with joy in his heart. "What you do… bring back… our people. It is… wonderful."

Across the planet, families knew what peace felt like for the first time in over two hundred years.

* * *

After a shower, they changed into clothes and boots the Mok

Tau had made them. It was nothing as nice as they would have found in the Sears catalog, but it resembled civilized attire. Dex just missed seeing Lacy dressed for the jungle. At least they kept the old outfits as souvenirs.

Lacy dropped into her seat at the command console of the *Silent Horizon* with a hand on her stomach. A queasy feeling had persisted throughout the return journey.

Dex sat down next to her, taking his time through aching muscles.

"Looks like you've had your fill of adventure," she teased. "Or is that just the cake sitting heavy?"

Cuts marked up his face, and the laser burn still irritated his arm. He didn't want to tease back, though. The bruise on her neck from Romek's grip still shone a faint yellow. They'd both been through enough.

"Enough to last a lifetime. Cake and adventure." He turned on the ship's computer.

"Missing a step?" Something was off with Dex. She'd recognized it as soon as they left the village again to return to the ship. They'd been away two weeks, but she didn't think that'd be long enough for him to forget he had to start up the engine in order to fly.

Dex replied bluntly, "Nope." He flicked through the computer's space map and found Earth. The great big ball was just a few hours away. With the outpost destroyed, and the moon base making its way around the far side of the planet, they might have a shot at getting home.

"What are you doing?" Lacy couldn't tell if it was concern or intrigue in her own voice. She only knew, whatever decision Dex was making, she trusted him.

"I think I know why he wanted me to come out here. Couldn't help my dad back home, but we can do something for these people. This isn't the only world the Emperor's got a grip on. Besides, Earth can hold its own for a little while longer."

With a few button presses on the keyboard, Earth's coordinates were wiped from the *Silent Horizon*'s database. Even if the ship was captured, the Empire would never find it.

Robbie waddled up to them. "What are we going to do now?"

Dex and Lacy looked into each other's eyes.

"From one end of the universe to the next…"

"As long as I have you."

There was a whole universe out there that needed one little push, one small spark of hope, that their lives could be their own. It would be remembered that the fight against the Empire of the Void, began on Taranok. First a small infiltration of a ground facility, then, with a band of Mok Tau Warriors, a trip to the moon...

About the author

Andrew Valenza is an Author, veteran, and newspaper editor from upstate N.Y. He published his first novel, "Empire of the Void", in June of 2023 and soon after founded Valenza Publishing.

He is a major movie collector, much to the chagrin of his wallet. But hopefully his love of film and storytelling made this book more enjoyable for you. Thank you for reading!

Please leave a review on Amazon/Goodreads!

Follow us on social media!

@avcollecting on Instagram, Threads, and TikTok

@valenzapublishing on Instagram and Threads
@valenza_publishing on TikTok

Milton Keynes UK
Ingram Content Group UK Ltd.
UKHW020321070624
443692UK00016B/272/J

9 798989 136872